And Forever

Danielle Sibarium

And Forever

First printing, 2015

Book design by Danielle Sibarium

Published by: Platinum Crest Solutions, LLC

Printed in the United States of America

For
Patricia Genova Farrell and Amy Cohen Peretz
Without the both of you, there would be no Maria.

Chapter 1

The scent of death lingers nearby. Always. Only I don't attract it like I once thought. I repel it, like a deflector shield. This is my lot in life, my special gift, to extend the days of those I love. That theory comes from Jordan; the keeper of my heart, and the love of my life!

I sigh. I don't realize I made a sound until Jordan apologizes. Again.

"I'm sorry, Steph. I just don't want to be distracted."

"I know."

He misunderstands. It's a contented sigh. One that says I'm thrilled my boyfriend is driving me to school. It's a sign of how surreal sitting next to him and knowing that he loves me is. How I can't believe in a matter of hours he'll be leaving me alone on my college campus, and I intend to savor each minute with him, every possible second. The sigh is the only chance I have of communicating any of these sentiments because he doesn't want me to talk while he's driving. I know just being together in the car for this length of time is challenging for him.

Jordan still suffers the after effects of a terrible car accident that killed his ex-girlfriend. Ex as in he broke up with her minutes before it happened. When he served as my unexpected prom date, I pressed him to admit his feelings for me. That's what led to the break-up. Now he has to deal with the swamp of guilt-induced quick sand he's been left in. It hasn't been an easy road to get to where we are, but we worked through all that.

I hope.

"I'm doing the best I can, babe."

"I know." I don't bother saying anything further to reassure him that I'm not upset.

"Maybe you can find some music on the radio."

Maybe I would if I could hear what's on the radio. Every time I turn the volume up, he lowers it. The problem is he wants it down so low I can't hear the music. I glance at his hands on the steering wheel. He holds it in a death grip. His knuckles are white, and I think his fingers might snap in two at any moment.

"I'm fine. Just happy to be here with you."

"Liar."

"Am not."

A car swerves slightly towards our lane. He lays on the horn and goes back to stoic silence. I hate that this is so hard for him. I want him to find his way back to being the carefree, flirtatious boy I fell in love with. I doubt he'll ever go back to being that person, and it makes me sad. I don't want him to carry all this pain for the rest of his life. I wish I knew how to make it better, but the only thing I can do is stand beside him and hope in time he'll heal.

I turn to my window, watching the never-ending expanse of trees zoom by. I wish for a fleeting moment I'd gone in the other car with my mother and her new, at least new to me, boyfriend Eddie. I'd been clueless about Eddie, but after her health scare last week, she came clean.

"There's someone I want you to meet," she said when he showed up at our house to visit her.

At that point she had no choice. She'd been ordered to take a few days off of work, where they'd rendezvous during lunch. She'd been frightened when they first told her it looked like a heart attack and realized it was silly to keep him hidden away. I can't imagine the cheesy conversations taking place in the other car, but I'm happy for her. My father died a decade ago and as far as I know she never dated before, so it's about time she gives someone a chance.

"Sorry." I hear the tension in his voice.

"No worries. It's all good, as long as I'm here with you."

I mean it, because even with the deafening silence, and the tension he carries on his shoulders every time we're in a car together, there is nowhere else I'd rather be. From the first moment he spoke to me, he owned my heart. It's branded with his name. I'd tried for four years to move on, to forget him, but that wasn't an option for me. No one can hold a candle to him.

"Hey," He pulls my attention back to the here and now. "You know I love you right?"

I smile. I'm sure it's just the reaction he hoped for. It feels like that's all I've done over the last week since he found me crying on the beach. I'll never forget the wave of relief that washed over me when I found out he'd been spared from a terrible plane crash. He never made it on the plane because I called him at the last minute in an attempt to convince him to stay. Thank goodness he did.

I always believed myself to be the root cause of the bad things that happen to people around me. Jordan thinks I'm what keeps them hanging on. I don't believe him, at least not yet. But having him try to convince me otherwise promises to be an amazing adventure.

Chapter 2

"I think that just about does it," my mother says putting my last suitcase in my closet.

Check-in ended and still my roommate is a no show. My bags are unpacked, clothes put away, and my refrigerator stocked to capacity. With nothing left to do, my mother and I share a very emotional farewell.

"I expect you to call me every day."

She holds me tight, like she doesn't want to let go. Ever. I understand, because I know once the embrace ends, she'll be gone, and I'll be on my own. It's a scary moment for the both of us. It's the moment I take a giant step out of childhood and a small one right smack into semi-adulthood.

"I know, mom. I will."

"You better. Just so I know you're okay. That's all I'm asking."

"I understand."

I did. My mother isn't suffocating like other moms. Most of the time she might even be considered cool, for a mom that is. Together we lost so much; we understand communication is key. If she knows where I am and who I'm with, she doesn't give me a hard time, as long as I'm not riding on the back of a motorcycle.

With her gone, that leaves me alone with Jordan.

Just him and me.

"Alone at last," he teases.

My heart thrums.

Up until this morning he'd never seen my room. Before now it probably wouldn't have mattered. I'd just stare at him, racking my mind hopelessly, searching for something to say and sounding like a complete idiot when I did speak. Most of all I'd have high hopes of him making a move, and find myself falling hard and fast, crashing down to earth, when he didn't. That was the gist of our relationship before: before prom night, or the accident, and way before the plane crash.

I know now, this moment won't be like that.

"We're alone all right." I want to bang my head on the floor. Why can't I think of anything better to say?

I'm downright sick-to-my-stomach-terrified. Everything's changed between us and this is uncharted territory. I finally have what I want, and while exalted that I no longer have to pretend my body isn't aching to be in his arms every time he's near, I tremble with fear at the thought of being alone. The feeling is akin to what one feels when watching helplessly as an innocent person is about to be slaughtered in a bad horror movie. Guess who's staring in the role of the victim? This girl. Right here.

I glance at my handsome boyfriend. That's all it takes, that fleeting moment for me to get lost in his dark as night eyes and smoldering stare, and welcome the oncoming slaying.

"I wish I could spend all my days staring at you." The words slip out, and I'm mortified. I can't believe I just said that.

His eyebrow shoots up as he flashes me a yeah-right smile. A smile that warms me down to my toes. That's all it takes, just a simple look and he could have his way with me. What's worse is that he knows it. His lips draw up, and I'm nothing more than a lump of clay waiting for Jordan's hands to form and mold me. A fact he's never taken advantage of.

Instead, for years he gave my heart a serious thrashing by keeping his distance. But that's behind us. We're finally a couple. He's mine and I'm his, and since the day I laid eyes on him, it's all I ever wanted.

"That's what all the girls say."

"All the girls?"

"Yeah, you know, you, my mother."

I slap at his chest playfully.

"You're such a jerk!" I say as he grabs my wrists and pulls me against him.

"And you know what you are?"

"A dweeb?"

He looks at me like he can't believe what I just said and chuckles. "No, Steph. You're beautiful."

Beautiful. How long I waited for him to notice.

"Absolutely beautiful."

Between the deep, low rumbling of his voice as he speaks and the fact that I feel the heat of his body covering me like a blanket, my insides vibrate. Like freshly plucked guitar strings.

I remind myself I have nothing to be afraid of. He's Jordan. I'm safe with him. And I want to be alone with him. In the week that we've been together, that's the one thing we haven't had much of, alone time. Not with me packing for school, or my mother coming home from the hospital, not to mention his visits with friends and family that suffered hours of thinking he died in a plane crash.

I want it, but I can't deny that the mound of trepidation growing in my stomach comes from the thought of all this new-found alone time. I have no idea how it will go. Especially with him being him: sexy and confident, and me being me; young and insecure. The main problem is, I don't know what his expectations are, and I have no doubt I won't live up to them.

Not yet.

Maybe not ever.

I'm frightened to start this journey. Scared his hands might want to get acquainted with my body in ways they never have before. It won't take much time for them to find my flaws and imperfections.

"What's wrong?"

I shrug. Why is this next step so bittersweet?

The part that's keeping me on edge is knowing whatever happens now it's going to take place without a safety net. I don't have my mother roaming around the house, or Maria barging in from next door, and as it's becoming more apparent by the minute, I don't have a roommate to interrupt us. My stomach twirls and flips inside me at the thought.

I want this.

I waited for it.

I take a deep breath and will myself to relax. But the tension in my shoulders only winds itself tighter around my muscles. My heart pounds at marathon speed and I can't control the shaking of my hands.

His eyes lock on me and my breath catches in my throat. I'm sure I'm about to pass out from lack of oxygen, because I can't breathe. Watching me closely, the corner of his mouth turns up and he cups my cheek with his warm, strong hand.

"I love you, Stephanie."

The way he says it, his voice low and seductive, sends a thrill through every part of my body. I quiver as I take a step closer remembering once again that while in a dormitory full of people, we are totally and completely alone.

"What are you thinking?"

"Huh?" He catches me off guard. I can't tell him what's really on my mind. "I'm not thinking at all."

Jordan chuckles as he folds me into his arms, my favorite place in the whole world. The air around us changes. His head dips down and his mouth meets mine. Warm. Sweet. He continues using his lips to explore, leaving a trail of searing kisses along my jaw, all the way to the spot behind my ear. His lips, his breath, they make my skin tingle and leave me swooning in his arms, wondering if my knees are going to give out.

I close my eyes as my fingers grip his shirt, my hand is clutched closed around it, pulling, holding on for dear life. Jordan's lips part and his tongue laps against me, tasting me, caressing me.

My fingers open enough for me to adjust my grip so I'm holding onto him instead of his clothes. I dig my fingertips into the lean, defined muscles beneath them. I'm yearning for him so much I'm dizzy. Each touch, each brush of his lips and tongue are slow, purposeful.

"Mmm." The sound escapes my lips and intensifies his movements.

Jordan is kissing me. ME! And he's doing it with both tenderness and passion. Heat shoots through me and my brain speeds forward like a rocket about to break the sound barrier. It rushes to take his shirt off so I can touch his bare skin and explore the lines of muscle I found so enticing on prom night.

That can't happen now. No matter how much I want it to. There's still a chance my roommate might show up. Finding me groping my shirtless boyfriend doesn't exactly scream "good girl", or "serious student." "Slut" isn't the first impression I want to leave on her or her parents. But it's too easy to welcome Jordan's advances, to get swept up in the fantasy my mind is narrating for me. I'd waited so long for this, for him. Why shouldn't I enjoy it?

"Jordan," his name leaves my lips in a whimper. He moans in response.

Wanting more, needing more, I pull him to me, move my hands to his shoulders, and push him away. Jordan's mouth opens in surprise.

"Steph?" If I couldn't see the uncertainty in his eyes, I can hear it in the low quiver of his voice.

"Sorry."

"Are you alright? Did I do something?"

I shake my head. "No. I just . . . I've been waiting for this for so long, I can't believe it's actually happening."

His hands run down my arms and cup my elbows, his thumbs brush back and forth over my skin causing tiny tremors to shoot through my body. "That's a good thing, isn't it?"

I nod. "It's a great thing. But I'm so nervous, each time you touch me I think there can't be anything better than that. And then you kiss me or touch me somewhere else and I realize it is better, and I have no idea what I'm doing or how I should act and . . ." My teeth close on my bottom lip because I know I'm in the middle of an incoherent ramble and I need to shut myself up. His eyes fall to my mouth and then his lips. I feel it down to the ends of my toenails. He pulls back and leans his forehead against mine.

"You talk too much," he whispers.

Jordan's hands slip under the hem of my shirt, and across my back. Heat continues to surge beneath my skin. His warm breath tickles my ear, which does nothing to quell the overpowering desire I'm fighting.

"Jordan," I moan. "I'm scared to death!"

"Of me?" He asks looking both confused and amused at the same time.

"Of how good it feels every time you touch me. If you do what you just did again, I might not want you to stop. Ever."

I can't help notice how his chest heaves with each breath or how he pulls me closer.

"And that's a problem?" His lips curl up in amusement.

My eyes drop down. I mean to look at the ground, but that's not where they fall. I feel my cheeks get hot, red hot, when I realize where I'm looking. I don't want him to get the wrong idea. I know I'm not ready to get acquainted with that part of him. Even if my body might want to, my heart and brain know better.

"I'm sorry. I didn't mean . . ."

"Hey." He lifts my chin with a crooked finger. "Calm down. You have nothing to be sorry about. You think you're the only one that's nervous?"

"I guess."

"You're not. Not at all." He closes his eyes and draws in a long breath before speaking again. "I'm terrified, too."

"Of what?"

"Being with you. I'm afraid if I don't touch you enough, you'll think I don't want you. I'm afraid of touching you too much because of how you just reacted. I already told you, I'm afraid of everything changing between us. But worst of all, I'm afraid of losing my best friend."

"I didn't think you'd be nervous at all. I just expected . . ."

"That I'm older and more experienced so it comes naturally?"

"Sort of."

"Stephanie, there's no experience that can compare to being with you." His hand moves up to the back of my neck, his thumb strokes my cheek. "This is as new and frightening for me as it is for you."

I don't know how he can pull out the perfect words, the words I need to hear, with such ease. I don't think there is anyone in the world more perfect than Jordan. I meet his lips forcefully and grip his dark hair between my fingers.

"Besides," he pulls back breathless. "That's the great thing about you being here. We can lock the door and do nothing but this all day," his lips travel to the crook of my neck again. "And then all night." He backs off. "Or not. We can just stare into each other's eyes and talk. There's no rush. We have all the time in the world."

Such promises! I don't want to ruin the moment with the question on my mind, but before I can clamp my mouth closed, it falls right off my lips.

"What if I'm not enough for you?"

"Where is this coming from?" He smirks. "The girl that single handedly brought me back from the edge of oblivion is afraid she might not be enough?"

I nod.

"You're everything for me. You're my reason for living. Don't ever forget that."

I startle at the knock on the door and jump out of his arms as if we were caught naked on the beach. I hope my roommate is on the other side. I force myself away from Jordan and open the door. A pretty blonde girl with a big smile and no parents or suitcases stands in front of me.

"Hi, you are . . ." Her eyes dart to the left of the door where the name tags are hung in the hall.

"Stephanie."

"Hello, Stephanie, I'm your RA, Trina," she says, sounding way too bubbly. "My room is two doors over, and if you have any questions or concerns, I'm happy to help you."

"Thanks," I answer ready to close the door, not sure, and not caring about what exactly an RA is.

But I don't. I hesitate, waiting to see if she has anything else to say. Already I don't like Trina. She's encroaching on my quality Jordan time.

"And there's a hall meeting in my room later. This way, we can all get acquainted with one another and go over rules and expectations. I'll see you there!"

*

"Promise me something?"

Jordan's brows knit together, and there's not a hint of the playfulness we shared earlier. I can't imagine what has him looking so worried.

"Anything."

I mean it, too. Because there isn't anything I wouldn't do for him.

"Promise you won't drink?"

I hesitate. He takes that as a sign I don't want to agree. "If you want to drink, fine, just wait until I'm with you. This way I know you'll be safe."

"You don't trust me?"

"Of course I trust you. You just . . . " He smoothes my hair, "Let's just say you don't always make the best decisions when you drink, and I won't be a few blocks away. That makes me nervous." He pulls me close, and takes a long, deep breath.

I hug my arms around him, and rest my head against his chest. I'm so lost to the thumping of his heart, I almost don't hear what he says next.

"I want to know you're safe. That's all."

Perfect. He is absolutely perfect.

"Okay, I promise. No drinking unless I'm with you. But now I need you to promise something." I look up braving the intensity of his eyes.

He gives me a crooked smile, raises his eyebrow in a silent question, and my heart flutters just a little faster.

I look away. He's going to think I'm pathetic; like that isn't something he already knows about me. But he brought up the fact that we won't be a few blocks away from each other, and it terrifies me.

"What's wrong, Steph?"

"Promise you won't forget about me."

"How you could think for a minute I'd be able to forget you is beyond me. Even if I were across the country, across the world, I wouldn't be able to forget about you." He rests his hands at the base of my neck, forcing me to look up at him. "That's why I'm here, standing in front of you. That's why I'm alive, because I can't forget about you. Ever."

*

I look around the hall as I walk back to my room. Some families are still here carrying groceries, or furniture to their destinations, but most have gone. No one tries to speak as I pass them in the halls. No one even looks my way. Funny how I felt so much more comfortable a few minutes ago when Jordan was still here. It feels like he took part of me with him, the confident part that knows I'll make new friends and be all right. At the moment, I don't feel sure about either of those things.

I leave my door open hoping one of the girls on my floor might poke her head in and say "Hi." I'm not holding my breath. I sit on my bed and take a look around. There's nothing special about my room; it's boring, dull. Nothing but painted cinderblock, and no frills metal furniture. The desk being made of metal is one thing, but the dresser, too?

"Hi," I startle at the male voice. I turn to see who made the mistake of stumbling into my room.

I glance at the cute guy standing at my door then quickly look away. "Sorry, you must be looking for Angie. She hasn't gotten here yet."

"Yeah." He runs his hand through his hair not making eye contact. "There's always one that doesn't show. Maybe you'll be lucky and end up with your own room and not have to pay for it. Was that Jordan Brewer I saw leaving?"

Who the hell is this and what does he want?

"I'm sorry, who are you? And what are you doing here?"

"Oh Stephanie." His blue eyes are playful, as his hand covers his chest. "I'm crushed you don't remember me."

There's something familiar about him, but I can't make him out. "Help me. I really can't place you."

"Maybe it'll help if I put my glasses on and grab my briefcase?"

I look again at the big blue eyes and very defined arms of the hot guy now standing in my room. I take in his basketball shorts and polo bearing the school logo on the upper left corner. It doesn't help one bit. I hope he doesn't think I'm checking him out; that's the last thing I need. According to his description only one person I'd ever known, or rather known of, wore glasses and carried a briefcase. That was in high school and there was no way this could be him.

"Still nothing? I thought for sure the briefcase was a dead giveaway."

Could it be? "Jonah?"

"In the flesh." He smiles and spins around slowly so I can get a view of him from all angles.

Ohmigod.

He's gorgeous. There's no way the guy standing in front of me could possibly be Jonah! Maybe he has a twin, and this one hit the coolness jackpot in their DNA split.

"Wow. I thought I'd surprise you, but I didn't think I'd leave you speechless."

"Is that really you?"

He nods.

"You look so . . ." I struggle to find the right word. "Different."

"Different as in good, or bad."

His self-assured attitude tells me he know the answer to that.

"Good. Definitely, good. "

"It's amazing what contacts and hitting some weights can do for you."

"Yeah, but I mean everything about you is different."

"Not everything. Less than you think. The only difference is before you didn't think I was worth noticing."

"That's not true."

Wow. Jonah the nerd, is a hottie.

"Yes it is, and you know it." He smiles. "It's fine, though. Even I have to admit given the choice between me and a venomous rattlesnake, the snake had more appeal."

"Jonah."

"Can't believe you're still hanging around with Brewer. listen, I have to get back to my room, and make sure the guys are behaving themselves. I just stopped by to say hi." He turns for the door.

"Wait! Where's your room?"

"Oh, right." He slaps his forehead. A mannerism I recognize. "I'm the RA in the connecting hall. Any of those guys bother you, come get me."

"So you're on the same floor?"

"Yep. Which means you better behave yourself." He wags his pointer finger at me, "Because we'll be seeing a lot of each other."

I don't move for a few minutes, then I look down either side of my hall making sure he left. As soon as I'm certain he's out of eye and earshot, I close my door, pick up my phone, and call Maria.

"You are never going to guess who just came by my room to say hi."

As I suspect; clueless. But why wouldn't she be? We never spoke to him, and we had no desire to know what college he planned to go to.

"Jonah? Really? Lucky you."

"No. You don't understand. He's hot. I mean my mouth dropped. I couldn't believe it was him."

"It's not nice to make fun of people like that. Besides, what did the poor guy ever do to you?"

"Fine. Don't believe me. You'll see."

"If I didn't know better I'd think you have a crush."

"Oh please. You know I love Jordan. I just can't believe the change in Jonah. I'll have to point him out when you visit."

"Glad you remember you have a boyfriend seeing how you've pined away over Jordan for years, and now you finally have him. Don't mess this up, Stephanie. Don't give Jordan any reason to worry. Especially about someone like Jonah."

"I won't. Jordan's my everything. I'm not planning on losing him."

"Just keep that in mind the next time Jonah shows up to say hi."

I understand what Maria's saying, but what she doesn't understand is how lonely I felt in those first few minutes after Jordan left, and how comforting it is to know someone from home is right down the hall, even nerd-turned-hot-guy. And it doesn't matter how hot Jonah or anyone else is. Jordan is Jordan. I waited too long for him and we've been through too much for me to lose him now.

Chapter 3

With my clothes unpacked, my bed made, and not much to decorate with I don't know what to do with myself. There's nothing on television, I updated the feed on all my social media sites with pictures and comments fifteen times already, and Jordan hasn't called yet to tell me he's home. I don't bother calling him. He won't answer while driving. I tap the tips of my fingers together fighting the nervous jitters and the jiggling of my leg while waiting for him to call.

The knock on the door startles me. I hope my roommate decided to make an appearance. I expect the powers that be paired us together according to our interests and we'll become fast friends. Friends that will stay up at night talking and sharing secrets. We'll support each other through the freshman fifteen and have cram sessions before midterms and finals. We can't do any of that if she never shows up.

I realize as I head to the door it's most likely not my roommate. She would have been given a key to the room like I was. I turn the knob and pull the door open to find Trina on the other side. She still has her bubbly voice and big smile plastered on. And once again I think no one is that happy.

"Just wanted to remind you about the mandatory hall meeting in my room in five."

Great. I'll probably be the only one there completely alone, without a roommate, not knowing a soul. I send Jordan a text message, telling him where I'll be. I know he won't look at it until he gets home. I check the time. It's almost two hours since he left. What's taking him so long?

*

Eighteen of us sit in a circle on the floor in Trina's room. Yet again she introduces herself with the same annoyingly, happy tone she had when she stopped by my room earlier in the day. I know she wants to make us feel at ease, and like she really cares about each of us, but all that's coming across to me is phony, phony, phony.

I listen as she explains her job as RA, Resident Assistant. She's like the den mother of our dormitory wing, the enforcer, or depending on your point of view, the tattle tale. She explains the rules of dorm life. No lighting candles or hot plates in our rooms. Since we're all under the age of twenty-one, no drinking or smoking inside of the dorms. No drinking; that's a bummer, but it will help me keep my promise to Jordan. Next she talks about the enforcement of quiet hours, and guest protocol. The same guest can only spend the night three times a semester. If she's serious about adhering to that rule, it will put a serious crimp in my plans.

After explaining dorm etiquette and her open door policy, she passes around a roll of toilet paper. "Take what you need?" she explains.

"For?" asks a blonde girl whose name I can't remember.

"You'll see," Trina answers with a toothy grin.

Leery looks are given as the roll is passed around. Each girl stares at the toilet paper like it's about to attack in some sinister way. It reminds me of the game Hot Potato. Only now we each have to take a piece of it and wait for it to burn, or in this case perhaps explode, in our hands.

Uncomfortable with the idea of taking "what I need" when she won't tell me what I need it for, I rip off only one square. I hope I won't need more as I watch some of the other girls take about ten.

The role is returned to Trina, and she explains. "Since we're going to be living with each other over the next nine months, we shouldn't waste any time making friends. This is an ice breaker to help us all get to know each other a little better and make everyone comfortable with each other. For every square in your pile you need to tell the group one fact about yourself."

I smile, relieved I only have one square. Life tip: if you don't know what you're getting into, don't get yourself in too deep.

Eyes roll, teeth are sucked, and Trina continues to sit there smiling. Each girl before me uses her own name as a fact. I want to protest and complain that's cheating, but they all have more squares than me, so I bite my tongue. Carla, a chubby brunette, sits next to me and goes just before me. She has only five squares, but she doesn't look comfortable speaking at all. Her dark eyes fall to her lap, and I could barely hear what she's saying. I feel how uptight she is as the other girls start moving around, and look around the room.

Great. Way to set the table for me.

I don't want the group to dismiss me in the same obnoxious way they dismissed Carla. I need to grab their attention, but that isn't my strong suit. I look down at the flimsy paper in my lap. It's not going to intimidate or best me. I need one fact. I can pull out one kick ass, awesome fact about myself.

"It's your turn, Stephanie," Trina says. I think that's her lame attempt to rein the group back in.

I'm not sure what fact I should use. But decide to go with the one thing I feel confident about, the one thing that seems to warm people to up me. "I like to draw. I mean I draw. I sketch. Anything. Landscapes. Still lifes. Even pictures from memory."

Once I finish tripping over my tongue, I take a deep breath and force my shoulders down into a neutral position. After my mini confession, a wave of relief surges through my body. This is my first college challenge and while a small one, I consider it a win.

The meeting breaks up. Roommates walk in pairs back to their rooms talking and giggling. Everyone, but me. I leave solo. When I get back to my room I'm tempted to call Jordan. He has to be home by now. Insecurity floods my mind. What if he changed his mind about us after I pushed him away?

I don't even give that thought room to grow. I dismiss it, ditch it from my mind. I'm not about to blow us out of the water before we even start. Whatever reason he hasn't called yet, I'm certain it's a good one. With nothing better to do, I head for the student union building that houses the cafeteria.

*

The guys in front of me look like they know what they're doing, so I follow them over to the cashier, and swipe my ID card through the little credit card like machine the same way they do. I take a tray and silverware, and move to the end of the long line. I hope by the time I'm finished there will still be empty tables. I don't want to have to ask anyone I don't know if I can sit with them. How humiliating.

Looking at the selection of food behind the glass, I don't see anything appetizing. Sloppy Joe's and filet of flounder are our choices for entrees.

"Don't you have salad anywhere?" I ask. I can't believe the place that's responsible for our health and nutrition over the next four years doesn't have any healthy food. I guess the flounder is the healthy option, but I won't eat fish prepared in the cafeteria even in exchange for a semester of straight A's.

The server lifts her greasy spoon dripping with what passes for chopped meat and points it straight ahead. "Out there."

I look behind me to see a salad bar in the middle of the cafeteria.

"Thanks."

Seeing no one at the salad bar makes me nervous. How bad could salad be that everyone avoids it? I dish myself a generous helping and look around. I hate that already people seem to be making friends and here I stand playing the loner once again. I don't want to be alone, but I have no automatic buddy to navigate the first few days with.

"Stephanie."

I turn, wondering who called me. Feeling slightly overwhelmed by the crowd, and the noise, I can't make out the direction the voice came from.

"Come sit with us," Jonah stands in front of me. I look up and smile, relieved, and possibly even happy he's here. I follow him twenty feet over to a round table with a few other people: Trina and two guys. "Hey everyone, this is Stephanie."

"Hi." I place my tray on the table, give a small wave, and a force a smile on my face.

"I know you already know Trina, and these goofballs are Ian and Logan."

"Hey," one of the two guys says, sounding disinterested.

I pull my chair out a little and slip into it.

"So you two know each other?" Trina asks with a big smile on her face. OMG don't her cheeks cramp up from all that smiling?

"Stephanie and I went to high school together." Jonah clarifies.

"Oh. I guess that means when you get lonely for the hoodlums back home, Jonah will know how to make you feel better." Trina succeeds in humoring only herself.

My phone vibrates in my pocket. I check the caller ID, Jordan. Finally. "Excuse me a minute," I say before answering. "Hey, is everything alright?"

"Yeah, sorry. I stopped off at a friend's house." The place erupts as a group of rowdy guys enter, laughing and yelling out to the people around them. "What's all that noise?"

"I'm in the cafeteria, can I call you when I get back to my room?"

"Sure, no problem. I love you Stephanie."

"I love you, too."

"Aww, isn't that sweet?" One of the two guys sitting at the table sneers at me with a nasty gleam in his eyes. "How long you with him?"

"Huh?"

"Your boyfriend. That was your boyfriend wasn't it?" Logan asks.

I nod, looking him in the eye, noticing how much he reminds me of a rat. His brown eyes are beady and spread apart, his nose pointy. I could just see him gnawing his slightly bucked teeth into a cement brick.

"Since you're here alone I'm guessing he goes to a different school."

"He does."

"Then I'm hoping you don't have a lot of time invested in him, because these long distance relationships don't work. You'll both be cheating in no time."

I do not like Logan. Not at all. He doesn't know Jordan, or me. And he thinks he has the right to spew shit out about us? There's no way we're about to screw up this wondrous place that took forever to get to.

"Leave her alone." Jonah warns. "Besides, Stephanie and Jordan have been together forever. She won't cheat on him."

"Notice you didn't say he won't cheat on her."

I wait for Jonah to defend Jordan as he leans back in his chair and turns to look at the new wave of people coming into the cafeteria. I don't move while I stare at his lips, waiting for them to open again and for the words, "He'd never cheat on her," to leave them. But they never do. Realizing this part of the discussion is over, I stare at the salad in my dish and move it around with my fork. Classes haven't even started and already I hate my first day at college. So far nothing went according to my grand plan. Much like when I started high school. Only then I had the comfort of having Maria by my side. And then of course there was Jordan.

"So dude, you have to see the piece of ass that Ian hooked up with at orientation."

Ian doesn't say anything. I don't think he could as the color of his face turns a deep shade of purple.

"Logan! C'mon. There are girls at the table," Jonah warns.

Yep I definitely don't want to find myself anywhere near Logan for the rest of the year.

*

I high tail it back to my room and call Jordan as soon as I catch my breath.

"What's wrong, Steph? You sound upset."

He knows me so well he can read me by the sound of my voice. It isn't the hug I'm longing for, but I find it comforting.

"Nothing. I just wish my roommate showed up. Everyone knows someone and I ended up eating dinner with these obnoxious guys."

"Guys?" he sounds surprised.

"And Trina, my RA."

"Do I need to worry about these 'guys?' he teases.

"No." I laugh, "There's not one person on this planet you need worry about. I just . . . I hate to sound all pathetic and clingy, but I miss you."

"You're not pathetic or clingy. And if it makes you feel better, I miss you too."

"Do you really? I mean it's only been a few hours since we saw each other." I sound deflated, suspicious even. I don't mean to.

"You don't believe me?"

"I do. I'm sorry. This idiot just went on about how long distance relationships don't work, and it took you a long time to call me. I guess I let him get in my head."

"Stephanie. You might find this hard to believe, but you're not in this alone. I waited years to be with you, too." His voice is low, gravely, and is putting me under a spell. Part of me doesn't believe he waited for me, at least not in the same obsessed way I waited for him. Jordan continues sounding confident and in control. "I'm head over heels in love with you, and I'm not about to let some frat-boy-wanna-be steal you away. Understand?"

Every time I think I can't possibly fall deeper in love with him, he proves me wrong. "Got it."

"Good. Now, what are your plans for tonight?"

*

There's a freshman mixer taking place in the lower level of the dormitory. I want to check it out, but feel awkward going by myself. It's a place to meet other newbies like me. I know I really should go. I don't understand where these feelings of insecurity are coming from. I thought I was over that. But they've been flooding my brain all day, and at the moment I'm not certain they won't overflow and cause me to drown.

I already know Jonah, so I'm not completely on my own. I'm sort of on speaking terms with Trina, even though she's not my favorite person. And I forced the names of a few girls on the floor into memory. And there's no way I'd forget Logan and Ian. Although I hope they'll forget me.

I look in the mirror and check my make-up. I'll go. I have to. I stand staring at my reflection, trying to talk myself into it when I hear a knock at the door. Thinking my roommate might have finally arrived, I answer with a renewed sense of hope that I'll be spending the next few hours talking to her rather than getting swept up in all the craziness going on downstairs. Only it isn't my roommate on the other side of the door. It's Jonah. He's looking around the hall, one hand on the back of his neck. A trace of a smile forms at the corner of his lips as he starts speaking.

"I've been designated to go find the freshman hiding in their rooms and summon them down to the common area for tonight's getting to know you activities."

"I was just about to head down there."

"Uh huh, well then do you mind if I personally escort you? Besides this way you don't have to walk in alone."

"Not at all." I say as I step out into the hall, lock my door and pull it closed behind me. "Actually, I think that might be kind of nice."

Together we head down the hall and main stairwell, all the way down to the common area. Jonah points things out to me as we go, obvious things like the fire alarms and exits.

"This space is used for just about anything. Once in a while we show movies here, or some of the clubs will hold a meeting. Other times you might find someone studying or just tossing a ball around on a rainy night, even though that's not really encouraged."

I listen as we continue down the steps. For a minute my stomach tumbles. Where exactly is he taking me? I don't see or hear anyone else and we just went down flight after flight of steps.

"So, Trina told me you like to draw."

I nod. "I didn't know what else to say. It's just a silly hobby I picked up in high school."

"Why is it silly? If it's what you like to do you should be proud of it."

"I am."

We finally stop descending and now we walk straight down a long hall. Noise filters into the corridor we're in. Two girls appear at the other end, and just as quickly turn and disappear.

"I'd love to see your work some time."

"I don't really show anyone, like I said it's a silly hobby, and I'm not that good."

"We could always play show me yours and I'll show you mine."

I stop. An uncomfortable silence falls on us, and I'm not sure I want to take another step with him.

After a beat he continues. "What do you think I used to keep in that briefcase? You didn't think those were books and school work did you?" He starts walking again.

"I don't know. Honestly, I never gave it much thought."

He nods. "I get it. You cast me aside as just another nerd, like everyone else." He says it as a joke, but I can't help detect the bitter tone of his voice.

"I had a hard enough time trying to fit in high school and get those mean girls off my back. I didn't really think about what you had in your briefcase or anyone else for that matter."

Except for Jordan.

"I wasn't trying to make you uncomfortable or anything. Just stating a fact. I heard what people said about me. It's not like you could tune out a whole school for four years."

"Tell me about it."

Jonah says he understands, but that's not what I hear in his voice. I hear the bitterness his tone carries. It's the same sentiment I carried in my heart when high school started. If not for meeting Jordan and having him around as my protector and confidant that first year, my whole high school experience could've been just like Jonah's, ignored and ridiculed.

As we get to the end of the hall an eruption of noise pours out of the doors leading to the common area. There's a huge open space filled with people. I look around, wishing I chose to stay in my room.

"It's okay, they won't bite."

"You don't know that," I tease.

"You're right, I don't. But I'll be around to keep an eye on you. If I see anyone baring teeth, I'll come to your rescue, unless you say otherwise."

I give him a sideward glance.

"What? You might like it. Girls are kinky these days."

"Thanks, Jonah. I really needed to hear that right now."

He laughs. "Just go. Get a sheet, Trina has them."

The sheet Jonah's talking about is a scavenger hunt. Trina explains we're supposed to find someone to pair up with and complete both sides of the page. The first side has questions on it we're supposed to ask people about, like name someone with a July birthday, or name someone that likes riding horses. The questions go on like that down the entire sheet. Twenty getting to know you questions. Great we're being forced to talk to each other. The back of the paper has tasks we're supposed to complete so we get to know the campus, like what color placemats are in the cafeteria. What is written on the sign taped to the science building door?

I recognize a few girls from my hall and sort of stand near them, trying to find a way to include myself in their conversation. Finally I decide to take the bull by the horns and speak to them.

"Hi," I say.

"Hey," Emily replies.

The other girl Avery goes out of her way to look over me, around me, anywhere but at me.

"So do either of you have a birthday in July?"

The corner of Avery's mouth lifts into a sneer, while Emily answers, "The questions revolve around the RA's. I mean some of us might fit the bill, but they're sort of guaranteed to be answers. Avery thinks it's so we get comfortable with them since that's who we're supposed to go to if we have a problem."

"I guess that makes sense."

"It doesn't seem like she has a problem getting to know the RA's," Avery points her accusing eyes on me.

"Excuse me. Did I do something to you?"

"No. Not yet. But I'm not about to give you the chance to either, miss goody-two-shoes."

I make a mental note, steer clear of Avery. Unstable. Paranoid. Possibly psychotic.

I roll my eyes. "I have no idea what brought that on."

"Oh, ignore her," Emily says smiling. "She's just upset because she saw you . . ."

"C'mon," Avery pulls Emily by the hand, away from me.

Because she saw me what? I haven't been here long and there's nothing I can think of that I did to piss anyone off. What did she see me do that upset her? I watch in silence as they head out one of the exit doors.

How did I luck out to be the only one on the floor besides the RA without a roommate and with psychotic hall mates? I miss Maria. She'd know how to navigate through this. She'd be fast friends with all these people within an hour. I take a deep breath and think of what she'd do if she were here.

Feeling completely out of place, I look around and spot Jonah. I want to go stand by him so I don't feel so awkward, but he's talking to a cute freshman girl. So much for having a fallback friend. He writes something on her paper. I watch them, waiting to see if she's going to walk away or not. The hand holding the paper drops as she continues talking to him. She smiles a lot, no doubt flirting. Her empty hand comes up and touches his shoulder. Oh yeah, she's in flirt mode.

"Hey baby, you look like you could use a little company,"

I turn around to find Logan standing behind me. "Not yours, that's for sure."

"Ooh, so it's Jonah you're hot for?" He inches closer, making me want to run off screaming. "That's cool. I'll wait for you to come to your senses."

"I don't want Jonah, and there'll be an ice storm in hell before I ever want you."

I turn and head for the hall, hearing Logan call out behind me. "It's okay, I'm patient. You'll be begging for some of this before the year's up."

With my heart pounding harder than normal, I ignore him and head upstairs.

Chapter 4

Back in my room, I'm not sure who I should call, Jordan or Maria. I need a dose of Jordan, but Maria will know what I should do, especially about Logan. Bottom line, they're the two most important people in my life, and though I have not been gone for very long yet, I miss them both.

"You're not even gone twenty-four hours and already I'm hearing from you more than I did when you lived next door."

"Fine. I'll call someone else."

"So sensitive. Please tell me you're not calling to tell me about Jonah again. I think I'll have nightmares."

I smile. "You're so mean. Why did I never realize this before?"

"Because you love me. And while my meanness is one thing, going on about how good Jonah looks, is downright rip-your-heart-out cruel."

"Wait smart ass, one day you'll come visit me, and then you'll see for yourself. But until then, there's this other guy that's freaking me out. He's everywhere, and I can't tell if he has a thing for me, or he's just an obnoxious ass to everyone."

"Tell him you have a boyfriend; that'll put some distance between you."

"Already did. He went on to say how long distance relationships don't work."

"First of all, he's talking about long distance, like New Jersey and Minnesota. Second of all, Jordan's not your average guy. You two have been into each other since you started high school."

"Yeah, but . . ."

"But nothing. Jordan loves you Stephanie. And third of all, if this jerk doesn't keep his mouth shut, your boyfriend will have no problem shutting it for him."

"I guess."

"Don't guess. Know."

Part of me knows Maria's right. I have everything I want with Jordan. Although the romantic part of our relationship is new, the love isn't. I fell in love with him a long time ago, and I'd do anything for him. I know he feels the same way. He has to, or we wouldn't be together.

*

I lie down in bed with the TV on, hoping to fall asleep. I hear voices outside my door. Male and female voices. I get out of bed and check to make sure my door is locked. I look through the peep hole to see if I recognize whoever's out there.

People are kissing in front of my door. I recognize Avery's auburn hair, and think I hear Logan's voice. Relief washes through me. Good. Maybe she'll help keep his mind off me. I can't think of two people that deserve each other more.

*

Sirens blare. Loud, high shrilled screeching fills my ears. I yawn and stretch, not wanting to get out of bed. It's still dark outside. A quick look at my alarm clock and I realize it's only four in the morning.

Four in the morning!

The pounding at my door scares the living daylights out of me. My heart thumps as loud as the fist on the other side.

I don't have a chance to answer before Trina keys her way into my room.

"Come on, Stephanie. Get moving."

"What? Where?" I know she went over fire drills in the hall meeting, but right now I'm barely coherent and I can't remember what I'm supposed to do.

"Outside, now!"

"Give me a minute. Let me get dressed."

"No. Now."

Pushy this early in the morning? I definitely don't like her. That's when it hits me. This isn't a drill. That's why she's being so bitchy. It must be a real fire. Great, my first night here and the dark cloud I thought I outmaneuvered found me. I can't find my slippers, so I put on a pair of flip-flops instead.

I take a quick peek at my pajama tank and shorts. At least they match. I grab my keys and shut the door behind me. It sucks that she and all the other RAs have master keys to our rooms. I wonder if they're allowed to just let themselves in anytime they want, or how many people they've barged in on while they were changing, or worse, having sex.

Aside from Trina and me, I only notice a handful of people leaving their rooms and wonder why I'm so lucky to be personally escorted out. Until I see the crowd outside. Wow, talk about being dead to the world. How long did the alarm sound before I woke up?

"This is fucked up!" I hear some guy I don't recognize shout, "You need to let us back in! I just went to sleep!"

"Yeah, what are we waiting for?" a girl asks.

Trina, Jonah, and a few others stand in front of the doors, guarding them, keeping us out. I think if we charge at them like bulls in a run, we could trample them and get back to sleep.

"I love that I could see your nipples through that shirt." The warm breath is whispered in my ear, and I feel like I've just been slimed. "They're so hard and beautiful, it's like they're begging for me to suck them."

I cross my arms over my chest, spin around, and stare daggers into the ass that has the nerve to speak to me like that.

"Give it a rest," Ian pulls Logan away. "She doesn't like you."

"Oh, she likes me. Don't you, Stephanie?" His eyes pierce mine in a perverse way. "Come on, I see how you look at me. You know it's only a matter of time before you'll be on your knees su . . ."

Jonah inserts himself between us, shielding me. With Jonah acting as a barrier, and a little distance between Logan and me, I can breathe a little easier, but I still feel like spiders are crawling over my skin.

"Back the fuck off," Jonah warns.

Logan laughs as if he's in on a private joke.

"I'm serious. Don't make me write you up." That's RA speak for "Don't make me tell on you."

"You know I'm just teasing her." He leans into Jonah's ear closest to me, so that I can hear what he's saying. "But seriously dude, look at her tits, aren't they just calling out to you, begging to be sucked?"

I'm not sure if Jonah's eyes just went there, I can't look at him. I want to die. I don't need light, or a mirror, or anyone to tell me I'm blushing. I feel the heat coloring my face. Waiting to go back to my room switched from being annoying and unpleasant to painful.

A pair of safety officers walk out of the building and shout, "All clear." We're instructed to go back inside and back to bed.

Before I can make a clean getaway, someone grabs my arm. I spin around with my other hand balled up into a fist, ready to punch.

"I'm sorry."

It's Jonah. I meet his eyes, ignoring the flurry of activity going on around us. I want to lash out at someone, he seems like a good enough choice. "For what, having such an obnoxious pig for a friend?"

"I'm sorry he embarrassed you, but he's not my friend. He's my resident. It's my job to be nice to him."

"Yeah, well, I guess you have a shitty job."

"Just let me know if he bugs you. I'll take care of it."

I close my eyes, wondering how I'm going to make it through the semester with Logan, let alone the entire school year.

*

I open my eyes at eleven AM. I don't want to get out of bed. I'm too tired to move. Instead I close my eyes and try to force myself back to sleep. It only wakes me more. Feeling lazy, and having no reason to get up, I take my time stretching and yawning.

Stupid fire alarm.

I didn't fall back to sleep until seven in the morning. Logan creeped me out, and for some unexplainable reason, I thought he might find a way to key himself into my room while I slept. No one ever made me this nervous. Or paranoid. Not one of my obnoxious boyfriends ever made me feel so cheap and dirty. Not even control freak Chris or more recently I-want-in-your-pants Shawn.

My phone chimes. A text message. I don't want to look, my eyes burn and my head feels like mush. I can't get my eyes to focus on the message through my blurry vision. I need to wake myself up and get a move on. Time's running out to do nothing all day.

Standing at a sink in the bathroom, I wash my face with cold water, and look in the mirror. I look like shit; my eyes are puffy. I think about showering, but want to scrap that idea as I peek at the shower stalls. The sound of water hitting the tile echoes throughout the room. It sounds louder than it did a few seconds ago. I wonder who's behind the curtain. Do I even want to know? What if it's one of the guys from the other hall, how would I know? Eww. Even worse, what's if it's a girl and a guy from down the hall?

I want to throw up.

Do I really have to go there and get cleaned up where anyone and everyone else washes away their skanky germs? As if to accentuate my point, the water stops and a few seconds later, Avery struts out of the stall closest to me, swathed in nothing but two towels. One covers her head keeping her hair up and off her damp skin. The other barely reaches from her mid-breast to the top of her thigh. Even though her private parts are concealed, she's not leaving much to the imagination.

Way too confident in such a skimpy get up, she slinks past me casting a dirty look in my direction. What the hell is her problem? I want to scream, but instead I swallow down my anger and don't say a word. I can't help it, I feel exactly the way I did in middle school when Jennifer would torment me with her popular girl bullshit.

Trying not to show how insecure she makes me, I walk back to my room as calm and collected as I can. Once inside, I take a deep breath before returning Jordan's call.

"Hi beautiful. How was your first night?"

"Awful. I want to come home."

He sniggers. "I thought you'd make it a week before you'd think about coming home."

"I had the worst night."

"Why didn't you call me?"

"It was late, like middle of the night late, and I didn't want to bother you."

"You don't bother me, and you've taken your share of late night calls from me."

"I fell asleep, but then we were woken up in the middle of the night." I continue telling Jordan about the obnoxious fire alarm, how we were shepherded outside, and forced to stand in our pajamas and wait.

"I thought I'd give you space, so you could make friends, but maybe you could use a short visit."

Space? Why would he want to give me space? It's not like we were inseparable all summer long. Just over the last couple of days.

"I'd love a visit. And you can stay as long as want. In fact, I wouldn't mind if you moved in with me."

I hear the change in his breathing and picture the smile I know is on his face. "Go make friends, I'll text you when I'm leaving."

I swallow my pride, shove away the nasty thoughts and apprehension I have about the public showers, and clean myself up. I check my phone as soon as I get back to my room, then again once I'm dressed. No message.

The sound of my stomach growling reminds me that I'm hungry. I glance at the time. I missed breakfast in the cafeteria, but soon it'll be time for lunch. I don't like the prospect of going alone and possibly running into Avery or Logan. At least if someone's with me I won't feel like such a loser. I decide to go browse the bookstore, and get a jump start on the books I need. One last glance in the mirror to make sure I look presentable, and I'm on my way.

The bookstore's packed. I think a sardine can would have more room than these aisles. It's good to know I think like every other freshman on campus. My quick trip to the store turns into an hour and a half venture. The only good thing about it is I won't have to go through the painstaking ordeal of searching for my books with the campus at full capacity.

I walk back to my room to dump my stuff on my desk, when my phone chimes.

Just left. Thought you could use a surprise.

I smile. He wants to give me something to look forward to. He tries so hard to make me happy. At least for the last few days. In the weeks before that, it seemed like we went out of our way to hurt each other. I open a box of cereal stocked on my shelf and pour some into a cup. Nothing like dry cereal to start your day, but this one I happen to like better without the milk. Trying to keep busy until Jordan arrives I call my mother, and look through my crisp, new text books to get an idea of how much time I need to allot for each subject.

Finished, I check the time. It's well over an hour since Jordan texted me. What's keeping him? Traffic? I check my makeup in the mirror and brush my hair for the fifteenth time. Just as I'm about to lie down and mess up my over-brushed hair, the knock on my door sends my pulse racing.

He's here! FInally!

I jump up and open the door ready to leap into his arms.

"Surprise!"

I stop myself from letting the forward momentum send me flying into Maria. Before I can form my thoughts into coherent words, she pulls me into a hug.

"I thought since I can't bring you home, I could bring home to you." Jordan says as he steps around her."

"You can bring me home, you're just choosing not to," I snipe.

It's a nice surprise, but I'm irked. I hate that Jordan and Maria had the whole car ride here to talk. Over an hour this way and then another hour back. I don't say it out loud because aside from sounding jealous and petty, I also keep in mind that I drove here with Jordan yesterday, and can count on my fingers and toes the amount of words spoken in the car between us.

I know he doesn't have any romantic feelings for Maria, but the further I keep her from our relationship the less insecure I'll be, whether it's warranted or not. I guess I still resent the fact that he turned to her in his time of need instead of me. I know she was just being a friend and offering support, but still, that's when our friendship hit the skids. Both friendships, mine and Maria's, and mine and Jordan's.

I force a smile on. If either of them realize I'm not truly happy, neither is letting on. Maria steps away from us and looks around my room while Jordan pulls me against his chest, and holds me tight. My entire body tingles as I close my eyes and breath him in. Before I'm ready for it to end, he pulls away and interlaces our fingers, turning his attention back to Maria.

"So you like my new place?"

"We need to seriously redecorate. You need some pretty chairs, maybe a curtain of beads for when you walk in the room, and mood lighting," she wiggles her eyebrows up and down.

"You're so bad," I tease.

"Bad's the best way to be."

I nod in acknowledgement as she continues telling me what I need to turn my room into a love nest. Finally finished spouting off ideas to turn my simple dorm room into something out of the red light district, she turns and meets my stare. "So? Where is he?"

I open my eyes wide at her, willing her to shut up. You'd think after all the years of friendship she can pick up on my non-verbal cues, but she doesn't. Or she doesn't care to. I can't help but wonder if she wants to insert a thick wedge between Jordan and me. A reminder that she's still home, a few blocks away from him, and I'm all the way out here in the middle of nowhere.

"Who? The jerk that keeps giving her a hard time?" he asks.

Maria laughs, "No, the guy she wishes would give her a hard time."

My stomach speed crashes to the ground. Of all the stupid, thoughtless things she could say. I hold myself back from reaching my hands around her throat.

I steal a glance at Jordan. His face is blank, unreadable.

"I'm sorry. That was a bad joke." Maria bites her lip as her eyes dart back and forth between Jordan and me.

He turns to me, hands shoved in his pockets. "Who is she talking about?"

Before I can answer, she chimes in. "You didn't tell him?"

"What didn't you tell me?"

"I'm so sorry. How was I supposed to know you didn't say anything?"

My head follows them, back and forth, like I'm a spectator at a ping-pong match. I swallow hard trying to hydrate my over dry mouth so I can speak.

"Maria, could you shut up, please?! It's nothing. I told Maria that someone from high school was here and . . ."

As if on cue, there's a knock on my door. Maria makes herself at home and answers it. As she pulls the door open, I have no doubt on the other side, is Jonah.

"Hi, Steph, sorry, I didn't know you had company. I just came by to check on you and make sure Logan was staying out of your hair."

"Ohmigod!" Maria doesn't even try to hide her surprise. Way to go. "Jonah?"

"Hey." He waves still out in the hall, looking very uncomfortable. I don't care about making Jonah comfortable, it's the silence emanating from Jordan that makes my stomach churn. "I'm sorry, I'll come back later."

"Don't you dare," Maria grabs his hand and pulls him in the room. "Stephanie said I wouldn't recognize you, but I didn't think you looked like this."

Jordan's staring at me with a sarcastic smirk on his face. The eyebrow goes up, "Really?" he whispers as he steps next to me and heaves his arm around my shoulder pulling me close so only I can hear his commentary. "Jonah? You've got to be kidding me."

He's mocking me. I'm not just embarrassed, I feel like an idiot.

"Hey, Jordan. Haven't seen you in while." Jonah extends his hand.

"Hi," Jordan answers.

Maria leads Jonah over to my bed, and Jordan pulls me to the other side of the room, and turns me so that I'm looking at him and my back faces my guests. I'm nervous to meet his eyes. I don't know if he's upset or he just thinks I'm pathetic for telling Maria how good looking Jonah is.

"Hey, guys, Jonah's going to show me his room. I'll be back in a few," Maria shouts over her shoulder as she follows him out of the room.

I'm glad to be left alone.

"Jonah? Seriously?"

"What? It's not like I like him or anything."

"I didn't think so. I mean I know for a fact you have better taste than that." Jordan leans into me and smiles. "Because no matter what he might look like right now on the outside, he's still the same old Jonah. Still the same geek from back in high school."

I don't respond right away. Something about what he just said stings. A niggling voice in the back of my head asks myself if that's how Jordan sees me. Still the same old freak from high school.

"Hey, what's wrong?" He pulls back to look at me, but I don't want to meet his stare. I don't want him to know how his words just broke off a tiny piece of my budding confidence.

I shake my head. "Nothing."

"I know you're lying, Steph. Come on, don't tell me you really have a thing for him?"

"Of course not. But, what you just said. You know the same could be said for you."

He chuckles. "Trust me, I've never been called a geek in my life."

"No." My heart falls to the ground like a broken elevator. No one ever would. Jordan is too cool, too confident to ever be thought of as a geek. "But your girlfriend has. Not geek, but I've been called a lot worse."

"I'm sorry." He pulls me against his chest and holds me tight. "I didn't think that would upset you, because I never looked at you like that. I never thought of you as anything other than Stephanie, the sweet, beautiful, shy girl with the smile I'd do anything to see."

"So you're not mad at me?"

"Of course not. Not about Jonah anyway."

Good feelings gone.

"Then why would you be upset with me?"

He runs his thumb across my jaw line. "That you were afraid to tell me about him."

His eyes are locked on my mouth. His thumb strokes my lip, as he leans in and kisses me. Soft. Warm. Delicious. "Don't ever be afraid to tell me anything, Steph. I love you. Nothing is going to change that."

"So we're all good?"

"Of course we're all good. Now about this other guy."

"Logan?"

"Point me in his direction and I'll be more than happy to take care of him."

"That'll help me make friends. And what if he calls safety and gets you get kicked off campus? I wouldn't put it past him, and I mean he's not actually done anything wrong. It's just his stupid mouth. He says things and the way he looks at me, he makes me feel sleazy."

Jordan's arms slink around my waist as he holds me tight. "I still want you to point him out. No one messes with you. Got it?"

I nod.

Holding my hand, he spins me around under his arm and bends me backward into a dip. His lips meet mine for a quick kiss. A soft gasp escapes my lips as I stare up at him helplessly, trying to calm my heart.

"Why don't we go for a walk?" he asks helping me back into an upright position, leaving my nerve endings tingling in delight.

"Why don't we stay here and do more of that?"

He chuckles, "Because Maria's here and she might come back at any minute."

"So?"

"C'mon, Steph. We'll go see where your classes are so you know where you're going tomorrow."

I want to protest but don't. Instead I let out a long, drawn out sigh. "Fine."

"And why don't we swing by Jonah's room and see if he and Maria want to come with."

"Really?" I feel myself light up at his suggestion. "I think that would be great!"

Chapter 5

Just outside my door we pass Avery in nothing more than a pair of white boy-shorts underwear and a sports bra. Scarlet haired witch doesn't even try to hide the fact she's checking out my boyfriend. She eyes him up and down, soaks him in, and gives him some sort of silent invitation, as she licks her bottom lip.

Furious, I glance at Jordan and don't miss his eyes lingering on her. I smack his chest with the back of my hand, and he turns to me, one eyebrow raised, a smirk on his lips, knowing he's been caught.

"See something you like?"

"What? Of course not. I just didn't expect girls to prance around the halls in their underwear." He turns serious. "You don't do that do you?"

We're at the end of the hall, caught at a crossroads. Our only choices are the long boys hall to the right or following the exit sign over the door to the stairwell in front of us.

Although I'd never consider walking the halls topless, with or without Jordan there, I allow the green monster inside me to cut oxygen off to the rational part of my brain.

"Yeah, all the time." I reach for the bottom of my shirt and begin to lift. I only raise it two inches before Jordan's hand is on my arm dragging me from the hall through the stairwell door.

He turns around glaring at me, and backs me into the wall while pinning my hands to my sides. I struggle to release myself from the tight hold he has on me, but it's as useless as trying to dig through marble tile with a plastic spoon. It's just not working.

"What the hell do you think you're doing?"

"If that's the kind of girl you want then . . ."

He leans forward to speak, his jaw tensed, his body rigid. His face is inches from mine, fire burning hot and dangerous in his eyes.

"When did I ever say I wanted her?"

"Thirty seconds ago when you eye-fucked her."

His hands break their hold on me, and he brings his hand up to cover his mouth before speaking. "You're crazy, you know that?"

"I don't hear you denying it."

"Because it's ridiculous. When did I ever make you think I wanted anyone else? I mean even over the summer when we weren't together, did I ever give you reason to think it was because I was interested in another girl?"

My stomach flip-flops as I stare into his pained eyes. "No."

"Meanwhile you were off with that sleaze-bucket Shawn." He points animatedly to nothing on the side as he continues. "You were doing who knows what with him until you figured out all he wanted was sex. Meanwhile I sat at home, losing my mind every time I thought of it."

"I'm sorry."

"I don't want you to be sorry." He takes a calming breath before resting his forehead against mine. "I want you to know with every breath that I love you, and I will never be unfaithful to you. That's why I didn't kiss you at prom. I couldn't. Not because I didn't want to." He closes his eyes as his hands take hold of my shoulders, his touch gentle once again. "You'll never know how much I wanted you that night.

How hard it was not to kiss you. But I knew if we started like that, you'd never trust me."

"I do trust you."

"Good, or else we'll never make this work." He pauses and takes a moment to stare into my eyes and hypnotize me once again. "She caught me off guard. I never lived in dorms, or a frat house, or anything like that. I live at home with my mother, and trust me, she doesn't walk around like that. So, yes, I looked. More out of surprise than anything else. But not because I want her."

"It's just, you always seem to be drawn in by the girls that hate me the most. They go out of their way to make me feel like shit, and you seem to be so taken with them."

"I'm not taken with her."

"Are you sure?"

He nods. "I'm sure. But I have to admit I'm a little pissed that you're giving me such a hard time about a girl I could care less about, and I'm supposed to be okay with you fantasizing about Jonah who is right down the hall."

"I never fantasized about him. And for the record, he came to me, not the other way around." The eyebrow is raised as he folds his arms across his chest. "I didn't recognize him, and yes I was surprised that he looked as good as he does. C'mon, you have to admit he looks a lot different than he did in high school."

"He came to you?"

I nod.

Jordan's uncrosses his arms and reaches for my hand, his fingers finding the space between each of mine and entwining them together. "I always said he had a thing for you."

"When he came he said it was because he recognized you. I always said he had a thing for you."

He wraps his arms around my waist, pulls me against his chest, and chuckles. "I promise I won't look at any more scantily dressed girls as long as you promise to keep your clothes on."

"I see your promise and raise you one. I promise the only guy I'll fantasize about is you."

"Deal. Besides, it'll help me not feel like such a pervert, since I've been fantasizing about you for years."

*

I knock on Jonah's door, but not before I hear kissing noises coming from one of the rooms we passed. I don't have to look back to know who's doing it, I have no doubt it's Logan. I feel Jordan tense as he looks behind us.

"Is that your friend?"

"Probably. Does he look like a rat?"

Jordan smirks. "I guess."

"Then that's him."

"I'll be right back," he says removing his hand from mine. "I just need a minute with him, and the fucker will be pissing in his pants."

I shake my head and grab his arm. "I told you, I don't want to risk you not being able to come see me. I have plans for us, big plans."

"Oh yeah? Like what?"

The charge in the air around us kicks up a notch. I look up at him through my lashes, "Like acting out some of those fantasies you were just telling me about. And maybe one or two of my own."

He steps in closer to me and gives me the crooked smile I love so much, before leaning down and kissing my head. "Now that sounds like fun."

"Don't you two ever stop?" Maria teases. "If you can't keep your hands off each other maybe you should've stayed in Stephanie's room."

"Answering Jonah's door now? You really do make yourself at home wherever you go," I say moving past her into his room.

"What's up?" Jonah gives an awkward smile, turning his attention from his computer monitor to us.

"Steph, you have to see what he's done. He was just showing me a stop motion film he made, and some of his paintings. You have to see the one with the dolphins jumping over the boat; they look so real, like you can reach out and touch them."

Jonah, looking embarrassed, drops his eyes, and seems every bit as shy and geeky as he did in high school, yet adorable at the same time. Those are two images I never thought would go together.

"I wouldn't want to bore Jordan."

Jordan glances down at me, "It's fine. Besides, I'm sure Steph would like to see. She's an artist herself."

"So I hear. Trina mentioned it," Jonah adds, almost as if he wants to justify knowing something so personal about me.

Jordan nods. "I'd like to see the painting with the dolphins."

"Yeah, sure." Jonah stands, walks over to his bed, and picks the framed picture up for us to look at.

"No way you painted that yourself."

"It was my final project last year. Earned me an A+, and I've been commissioned to do a series."

"How did that happen?" My ears perk up.

"My art professor had us do a faux show for the final. He invited a few of his friends so it could feel as authentic as possible. This one guy spent a lot of time talking to me about technique and if I thought I could recreate the realistic impression. To my surprise he called me a few weeks ago and asked for a series of three paintings like this one for his beach house. He gave me a stipend up front, and then I'll get the rest of the money when I'm done."

"That is awesome!"

"I just got lucky, but who knows? Maybe it could lead to some cool things."

Reminding us that she was there, Maria chimes in. "We're not leaving yet are we?"

"Nah, just going to search out Steph's classes for tomorrow. We stopped by to see if you want to come."

"Yeah, sure." Jonah said grabbing the lanyard with his keys from the top of his desk.

I'm not sure if it's my imagination, or if Maria looks disappointed that we're taking away her private time with Jonah. I wonder how things are going with Rob. We haven't spoken much about him over the last week. Actually I haven't spoken to her much at all since Jordan and I found each other on the beach. I just had too much going on.

"Do you know where your classes are?" Jonah asks.

"It's here in my email." I open the app and hand him my phone.

He takes a look, nods, and then hands it back. "Most of your classes are in two buildings, but it's also good to know where the library is and the health center. I'll give you the grand tour."

*

We stop at a beautiful scenic spot. In front of us grass sprawls out as far as I can see. Behind us, a large fountain stands ready to spout water up into the air, only for it to fall right back down into the cement pool surrounding it.

"Sometimes in the nicer weather people will come out here for a picnic. At night you might want to be careful about coming this way, especially if you're alone."

"Why's that?" Jordan asks.

"It's sort of a popular place for people to hook up, so if you come with someone it's not too bad, but if anyone's here and you're alone, they tend to get a bit nasty."

"So how often do you come here?" Maria bumps Jonah with her hip.

"Umm," his face turns red. I don't know what opens wider, his mouth or his eyes.

Maria smiles, her eyes fixed on him. Uh oh. She's not just flirting, she's sending him an engraved invitation to come enjoy the rides at Maria Land. She winks at him. That's just like her to show up on my campus, act like the queen bee, and walk away. She's forgetting I still have to live here. I have to face him on a daily basis. What's worse, I can't say one word about it because she made Jordan think I'm into Jonah. And I feel Jordan's eyes glued to me, watching for my reaction.

"Why? Are you looking for someone to show you the ropes?" Jonah recovers.

Holding hands, Jordan gives a slight tug and with his head, motions over to the side. I can see something weary in his onyx eyes. He takes a step, leading the way.

We put enough distance between us to offer some privacy from Maria and Jonah. We can still see each other, but we can no longer hear their conversation. Thank goodness.

"Can we talk a minute?" Jordan's eyes aren't right. He looks off to the side and takes a deep breath. "Steph." He looks away. "I have something to tell you."

This isn't like Jordan. The more he hems and haws, the more nervous I am.

"I'm not going to like it am I?"

"Probably not." His eyes won't meet mine. "Fine. I'll just say it." He takes another deep breath. "I told you I stopped off at a friend's house when I left here yesterday right?"

I nod suddenly very curious about this "friend."

"These guys I know, they're in a band, Shred Em. And the drummer broke his wrist, so he can't play for a while."

"Okay."

"They asked me to fill in for him for like a month or two. They're finally getting noticed and it would really suck if they have to pull out things they've already committed to. It's not a permanent thing, but they have a bunch of gigs lined up."

"And?" I'm still not sure what the problem is.

He stops a moment and presses his lips into a thin line before recomposing himself and continuing. "Between school and practice, I don't know how often I can see you."

I exhale. As the breath wafts away from me, so, too, do the fear and anxiety that clamped their fingers around my throat. I wrap my arms around him, relieved. I thought he'd tell me it was too painful to be home and he needs to go somewhere far away. It's an irrational fear, but a real one nonetheless.

"If you don't want me to do it, I won't. But I sort of already agreed to play with them this weekend."

"Can you?"

He nods. "I've know them all a while and I've jammed with them a bunch of times at practices."

Jamming is one thing, but being counted on to play and play well, that's a whole different story.

"Do you want to do it?"

His eyes don't waver a bit. "The thing is, I do. You know as well as anyone how life can change on a dime. This is one of those things on my bucket list."

"Really?"

"Yes. Not playing seriously, but playing in front of people for fun." He shrugs. "If you have a problem with it . . . I mean you're more important than any stupid band." He reaches his hand out to me and strokes my cheek with his thumb.

"Then do it."

"Are you sure?"

"Yes. But what about your shoulder? Won't it hurt?"

"It'll be fine. I won't get crazy with the crash symbol, and if it gets too bad, I can take a pain killer."

I don't like that answer. I shift my eyes off to the side.

"I'll be okay. And I won't drink if I take anything. I promise."

I meet his eyes once again. "I know you said you jammed with them, but do you really know how to play?"

His lips draw up into the crooked smile that sends my heart racing. "You don't know that I played in high school?"

"What?"

"You seriously don't know?" The twinkle is back in his dark eyes. "Hey Jonah," he calls out.

Jonah pulls his eyes from Maria, "What's up?"

"You still play the trumpet?"

"God, no. I can't believe you remember that. Band was the worst year of my life. How 'bout you? Still beating on those drums?"

My mouth opens wide. "How does he know?" I whisper.

"We were in band together," Jordan answers as if that's the most ridiculous question ever. Jordan looks at Maria then Jonah, and shakes his head. "She claims to love me, and doesn't even know how I made my mark in high school."

"I know how you made your mark, you big flirt." I hit him playfully in the stomach.

"Oh, yeah," he grabs my arm and pulls me close as he starts to tickle me. I break away and run a few feet before he catches up, wraps his arms around my waist from behind and swings me around.

I laugh so hard, I can barely breathe. My chest is aching and my stomach hurts. Jordan places me on the ground and waits for me to get a firm foot-hold before letting go.

"What made you think of band?" Jonah asks as he and Maria, now holding hands, walk over to us.

Jordan fills them in on his news as we head back to the dorm. Maria looks just as surprised at both Jordan's news, and the fact that he knows how to play the drums. I feel better knowing he didn't tell her on the drive over.

"That's cool. Would you mind if I come watch?" Jonah asks.

"No, of course not. That would be great."

"Ooh, maybe you could pick me up on the way," Maria chimes in.

"I don't think that's a good idea. I'm going to have to pull major strings with the bouncer to get Stephanie in since she's under twenty-one, I don't know If I'll be able to get you both in."

"Where is it?" I ask.

"Bay Ridge."

"Oh." I know I sound deflated. I feel it.

"What's wrong?"

"Nothing, it's just if you, or my mother don't pick me up, I won't be able to go."

"I can drive you," Jonah shrugs. "I mean if I'm going there anyway, it's no big deal."

"Do you mind?" Jordan asks. "That would be a huge favor."

"Yeah, no, it's fine." Jonah tussles my hair. "I'll be her personal bodyguard. 'Till your done with the set," he adds looking up to meet Jordan's eyes.

"Are you okay with that, Steph?"

"Sure. As long as I get to go home with my rock star boyfriend."

"That's great for you guys; I guess I'm left out in the cold." Maria says.

Chapter 6

I wake to the sound of a ringing phone. That's worlds better than the fire alarm. I guess it's my mother making sure I'm awake. I yawn as I crawl over to my desk and pick it up.

"Hello," I mutter.

"I'm about to leave for school and I wanted to wish you luck on your first day." Not my mother. Jordan. I perk up at the sound of his voice.

"I hope I don't need luck yet."

"We could all use a dose of extra luck."

"I guess."

"I hope you have a great day."

"Thanks. You, too. And Jordan . . ."

"Yes?"

"I love you."

*

The hall is alive with activity. People are moving in and out of the bathroom to wash up. While brushing my teeth, I hear a few girls making plans to go to breakfast together. I work hard on summoning up the courage to ask if I can join them when Avery struts out of a shower stall, droplets of water rolling down her skin, and tells them to wait for her. Wonderful. There goes that plan.

I don't want to eat alone. I have too much nervous energy. I grab my notebook and lock my door behind me. I don't even realize I'm going there until I knock on Jonah's door.

"One minute." Jonah calls out.

The door opens and he stands in front of me in his boxers and a t-shirt, his hair a disheveled mess.

"Hey," Jonah smiles. "What a nice surprise."

"I'm sorry, I didn't mean to wake you."

"You didn't. I just haven't bothered getting dressed yet. What can I do for you?" He leans against the door jamb like it's the most natural thing in the world for him to be speaking to me in his underwear.

"Nothing. I just thought maybe we could go have breakfast together, but I can see you're not up to . . ."

"Says who? Give me a minute. Want to come in while I throw something on?" He asks opening the door wider.

I don't have to think, or hesitate with my answer. I don't want to send any confusing messages, and going into his room while he changes in it, would definitely confuse things. I shake my head, "No thanks. I'll wait for you out here."

"Okay, I'll be a minute."

*

I play with my phone while waiting for Jonah. Something about this feels wrong. I wonder after yesterday, if Jordan would mind me going to breakfast with Jonah. I'm fairly certain he'd mind me talking to him in his boxers. That crossed a line. I'd never even seen Jordan in his underwear.

"Ready?" Jonah comes out in shorts and the same t-shirt he had on when he opened the door, his hair still looking mussed, but purposely so.

"Yep."

We've only taken a few steps when I feel someone come up and put an arm around me. I cringe. No one would be presumptuous enough to greet me like that, no one but Logan.

"Hey, baby, miss me?" He leans over and kisses my cheek.

"Get off me you jerk," I push him away while at the same time shrugging his arm off my shoulder.

"Dude, it's too early in the morning to be starting shit."

"It's cool," Logan smirks. "Didn't want Stephanie to think I was jealous she spent yesterday with her boyfriend."

Jonah shakes his head. "Lay off. He already wants to kick your ass. You keep this up and next time I'll be the one leading him to your room."

Logan smirks, like he already knows Jonah's full of shit. The Jonah I went to high school with wouldn't even have attempted acting like a tough guy, but this "new and improved Jonah," I have no idea what to expect.

"Oh, I hope the kissing noises didn't upset Mr. Smoochy." Logan starts making those obnoxious sounds again.

Ignoring him I turn to Jonah, "I think I forgot something in my room. I'll catch you later."

Jonah grabs my hand before I make it safely out of his reach. "Don't. Logan will behave himself. Or he'll just have to find someone else to sit with."

"Why? You want to be alone?" I recognize the insinuation in his voice. "Won't the boyfriend get jealous?"

Ohmigod is he obnoxious! Why am I so lucky to be showered with his attention?

"I want to be anywhere, but with you."

Logan smiles. "Denial, I love it. As luck might have it, Stephie, I'm having breakfast with Avery. Maybe we can all share a table."

"Dude, back the fuck off. Don't make me tell you again."

"Don't you get paid to be nice to him?" I ask Jonah.

"Sort of."

"I wouldn't want you to risk losing your job on my account."

"Just forget him."

Forget him. That's exactly what I want to do. Walk away and forget the obnoxious pig Logan exists.

*

"Come on, I'll walk you to class. Since it's your first day."

I hesitate for about half a second before I agree. The great thing about Jonah, I don't have to worry that he has any romantic feelings for me. He knows I'm with Jordan, and after watching him flirt with Maria, I know we're tucked safely away in the friend zone. Best of all, he understands what it feels like to be a social outcast. As a former nerd, he's just trying to make me feel comfortable.

Jonah talks as we walk. He tells me about Professor Wilson, and how he'll assign some sort of writing assignment after every class.

"Even though it seems like a lot of work in the beginning, it's not too bad. The more out there and creative you can be, the better you'll do."

I nod because my mouth is too dry to speak.

In front of one of the buildings he led us to the day before, Jonah stops and looks around. I think he might be looking to make sure no one sees us together. Is he embarrassed to be walking with me? Before I can utter the words to tell him I'm not a pathetic loser in need of his company, and that it was his idea to walk me to class in the first place, he bends down at a flower bed lining the building, and plucks a couple of deep, red mums.

"Here." He shoves them at me, "You know, for luck on your first day."

"Thanks." I take them and look around to make sure no one is staring at me. "But I'd feel funny walking into class with these. And I wouldn't want everyone looking at me like

I'm some sort of city freak that's never seen real, live flowers grow, so I needed to pick some."

"Yeah. No. That's not . . ."

"I know." I try to save him. I don't want him to think I don't appreciate the gesture. "It's just, you know how it is when you feel like everyone is looking at you and laughing. I just don't want to hit the radar just yet. Or at least not for doing something wrong."

"Yeah, no. I get it. I'll just take them back to my dorm, or you know what?" He brings his hand back like he's going to toss them back into the flower-bed.

I reach for his hand mid-swing and stop him.

"Don't. They're beautiful. I'd love if you could take them back for me. I'll come get them later."

He nods. "Okay. And Stephanie? Just so you know, I doubt you're going to fly under the radar. But when they spot you. When you feel the eyes crawling over your skin and you want to rip it off, it's not because anyone will be laughing at you."

I can't help myself, or the smile that pulls my lips up at the corners. I fling my arms around him. "Thanks."

After I release him from the awkward embrace he doesn't bother to return, he turns and leaves.

*

I take a seat in the last row. I think sitting in the back will automatically win me "likable" points from my classmates. That just being further away from the professor will invite conversation to swirl around me, and eventually suck me up into it, making me one of the crowd; one of them. But it never happens. I struggle to think of something to say, something funny or even relevant, to somehow include myself in conversation. It doesn't happen. The people in front of me are talking about how much they drank the night before.

Already? Really?

Instead of winning hearts and minds with witty banter, I listen to the professor review the syllabus, discuss expectations, and explain grading.

"The key to passing this class is being here," he says. "You can't participate if you're not here and all of your assignments will stem from class discussions."

Sounds easy enough, but much like I felt at the start of each new semester in high school, I'm overwhelmed. I feel like I have a heavy weight around my ankle ready to drag me down into the deep end of the pool. I doubt it will be as easy to do well in college, that showing up and paying attention will carry as much weight as he claims.

My next two classes are no better. With a ten-minute break to get to class on the other end of the campus, I barely make it in time. Breathing hard, I take the first open seat I see, which just happens to be front and center. So much for making new friends on my first day.

After my final class, Introduction to Sociology, I head straight back to my room. I would like to go to lunch with someone, but I haven't made any real connections yet. I wonder if it's too late to transfer to Brooklyn College. At least there I know people, and even if no one speaks to me in my classes, I'd go home to Jordan and Maria.

I sigh. That isn't the answer. I need to stand up and do this on my own, even just to prove to myself that I can. I just have to suffer here until I find my way.

I stick the key in the lock of my door, turn the knob and push it open. I plan to drop my books on the desk and crash in bed. Before I have a chance, I stop mid-step. A plastic soda bottle filled with water sits on my desk holding the mums Jonah picked for me. Leaning against it an index card with a happy face reads, "Hope it went well."

It's a nice surprise and makes me smile. Maybe I don't have to do it completely on my own. I do have one friendly face here.

I jump at the knock on my door. I guess its Jonah coming to check if I found the flowers, like I could miss them. I don't even bother to look through the peephole, I just swing the door open.

"Hey, Jonah," My heart picks up speed, and races as my eyes meet the dark black orbs in front of me. I blink hard, making sure my overstressed and overactive mind didn't conjure his image. I don't try to hide the excitement rising up inside me as I am struck with the certainty; it is indeed my boyfriend standing in front of me.

"Jordan." I say with confidence, as if I meant to say his name all along.

He's leaning against the doorjamb, a sad smirk on his face, looking unsure of himself.

"Surprise!"

"Hi, handsome." I smile and hug him tight. I feel the deep breath he pulls in as I press my head against his chest and nuzzle against him. I listen for a moment to the strong, rapid beat of his heart. It's one of my three favorite sounds, followed by his voice and the sound of my name coming off his lips.

"What are you doing here? Aren't you supposed to be in class right now?"

He shrugs, "I skipped my last one. Today's not important." He lets go of me, walks into my room and sits at the edge of my bed. "Seeing you is important."

He looks around, and I'm so happy to see him, I don't even comment on how strange it is that he cut class on the first day. I sit on the bed next to him. The mattress sinks from our weight, pushing us even closer together. My body faces his with one leg bent under me, the other on the floor.

He brushes my hair back behind my ear and smiles. "How'd your first day go?"

"Okay. I didn't trip while walking in or out of any of my classes." I hope to make him laugh.

"I thought you only did that when I was around so I can catch you."

Not thinking of a retort quick enough I ignore his jab and continue. "I didn't stutter when I said my name, so all in all, I'd say it's a win."

He's smiling at me, and the tenderness in his eyes makes me feel adored.

"Stutter? Since when do you stutter?"

It's my turn to shrug it off. "I don't. But there's always a first, right? I worry I'll make the worst possible impression on pretty much everyone here."

He chuckles, and I love the sound of it. I love that I can curl his lips up and make his eyes shine.

"How about you? Happy to be back at school?"

His eyes dart around my room again, and even though we're not touching, I can feel how rigid his body is.

"Happy isn't exactly the word I'd use." His lips are still slightly curled up in the corners. It's not exactly a smile, definitely not the smirk I'm so fond of. He's trying to keep things light, and doing a terrible job of it.

"Why?" I inch closer to him and take his hand between both of mine.

He looks down at our hands and smiles before speaking. My eyes follow his and I notice little bits of broken skin on his knuckles.

"I thought about taking this year off, at least this semester. I can still withdraw." His eyes meet mine and I can see he's serious. "I think it might be a good idea."

"Did you punch something?"

He nods.

"What's going on?" I brush my thumbs over the back of his hand, back and forth over his skin, waiting with my breath caught in my throat for him to go on.

"Today was rough. I expected it to be, but I didn't think it would be this bad."

"What happened?"

"Nothing," he says as he turns away, and I know he's lying.

I want to push him, but I understand I'm walking on eggshells. He doesn't usually let me see this side of him, this cautious, insecure side. He's only ever let me see flashes of vulnerability. Moments that passed at lightning speed, but this, this is entirely different.

"Why was it so hard?"

"It's the first time . . . I mean I haven't seen too many people since the accident. I haven't had to face them."

Now I understand. Madison. She's the leading player in the live production of Jordan's private hell.

"You went to the same school?"

Of course they did. I shake my head annoyed with myself. I should have remembered but it was one of those facts I tried my hardest to forget. They met in art history. Art history! I always wanted to deny that, pretend it didn't happen in that way because it felt like the cruelest joke the universe could possibly play on me. Art was my release, my escape, and that's where Jordan met the girl that threatened to steal him away from me permanently. Even now I still found her clawing her way between us.

He nods, his eyes on the floor. "Do you know what it's like to have everyone stare at you like you're some kind of freak?" Did he forget who he was speaking to? "Most people avoided me. I'd like to think it's because they don't know what to say. Instead they just stared. And I know they were talking about me because I caught whispers as I passed, saw the guilty look in their eyes as they'd turn away and pretend I wasn't there."

I swallow hard. I know exactly how he feels, only I'm sure the stares he got are ones of sympathy, versus the ridiculing ones I suffered through middle school. He snaps my attention away from my memories and back to the present as he hammers his fist down on my bed.

"I mean if you have something to say, man up and say it to my face. And then the one asshole that had the guts to say something . . ."

I pull myself closer to Jordan so that my knees, both now tucked under me, are touching his thigh. I'm relieved that he makes no move to create space between us.

"I doubt anyone has anything bad to say. They probably don't know what the right thing to say is, so they're watching you to make sure you're okay before they say anything."

He looks at me through the corner of his eye. "That's a load of shit and you know it."

"No, really." I run my hand through his hair. "Listen, after my father died, even Maria would sometimes just stare at me without saying anything. One time I called her on it. She said she was searching for words that would make me hurt less."

He moves my hands away. "This is different."

"Maybe. Maybe not. I mean for years I thought she lied. I swore she did it because she knew he was dead because of me."

He reaches for my hand and squeezes it. "No one knew what happened the night before he died. There was no direct link between the two. I drove. There's no getting around it. I drove the damn car. And even if I could forget it, there are people that won't let me."

I close my eyes hating that I have a front row seat for this self-lashing. His logic makes sense. It's wrong. I know that, but I can understand his line of thinking, and all he seems to want to do is punish himself. Jordan never hid his guilt or the difficulty he has dealing with the accident and the after effects. Only now he's speaking about it, which is exactly what I want, what I've wanted all summer. He's finally giving me the chance to be the friend he needs, the one he leans on, and I feel like crap because I don't think I'm helping him at all. I have no magic words, no secret remedy for his pain. I acknowledge his feelings and hope knowing I will stand by him no matter what will eventually negate the guilt.

"I'm sorry. Is there anything I can do?"

"You already are. The whole ride over here all I kept thinking about is holding you close and smelling your hair." I listen as he takes a deep breath and slowly releases it.

"My hair?" I don't mean to giggle. I try to hold it in, but it only makes the urge to laugh stronger. He surprised me. No, shocked me. I didn't expect that to come out of his mouth.

"Yes. Your hair. I know it's insane, but every time I'm close to you and I get a whiff of apples . . . It drives me crazy. My head gets full of you," he pauses. "It's like I can shut down all the inner bullshit. You settle me and bring me back to my senses. And then I don't just feel like everything is going to be all right, I believe it."

"Okay," I say, still unable to hide the smile in my voice, tilting my head so that's it's right under his nose. "You can spend a full hour smelling my hair and I promise not to make fun of you."

"Wise ass." He sounds playful, much better than he did a moment ago. "Don't think you're getting off that easy." He reaches over and pulls me down so that I'm lying on the bed and he's lying beside me. "This is only the beginning."

"Of? Why don't you tell me exactly what you plan to do?" I challenge him with my eyes, staring up at him through my lashes. I hope between the come and get me look I'm trying to pull off, and the low, sultry tone of my voice, he knows the direction I want the conversation to go.

"If you insist." His voice changes, it's quieter, more serious.

With caution, I bring my hand up to his firm chest, and inch it up and down his center. I keep my eyes locked on his, watching his reaction, making sure I'm not overstepping any boundaries since a minute ago Madison was front and center on his mind. Unable to bare the intensity of his eyes, I look down. Jordan places his crooked finger beneath my chin and raises it so my eyes will meet his again.

"Exactly what I'm going to do?" he whispers.

I nod.

"I'm not much for narration, but I'll give it a shot. First, I'm going to take a long look into those beautiful eyes of yours, just like this."

I drop my hand and try to shift my gaze away from him because I'm suddenly feeling very self-conscious. He doesn't let me. If I move or turn my face to the side, he adjusts himself so that he's right in front of me.

"I'm going to hold your stare. I won't, no matter what, let you break it."

My lips part. I'm not sure if I'm inviting him to kiss me or if I need to take in some air because at some point in the last minute, breathing became very intense.

"I want your undivided attention," he admits.

That's easy, I don't have to do much there, just look at him.

"Once I know you're completely focused on me I'm going to lay here," his body is as close to mine as he could possibly be without actually touching; so close that I feel a veil of energy buzzing between us. "And watch you."

"Watch me? Stalker." I don't know why I attempt to say anything, let alone try to be funny. I'm barely able to speak.

He pulls his bottom lip between his teeth and the corners of his mouth rise up into a smile. "That's right. I want to watch you. I want to study you, memorize every curve, every look you flash in my direction. I want to see how you react to me."

Jordan's eyes trail down to my lips, where they stop and pause a moment before coming back up to meet mine. This begins a pattern. His eyes crawl down to my neck, and then climb back up. Each time they descend, they move lower than the time before, and linger longer. I see excitement building in him the longer this little game goes on. When his eyes drop to my breasts, he takes his time examining each one; his breaths are longer, deeper. I don't even realize at first that I'm arching my back in his direction, giving him easier access, showing him it's not only okay to touch me, but it's what I want. I close my eyes, breathing hard. I'm going to lose control if I keep my eyes on him.

"Stephanie," he whispers.

I open my eyes at the sound of my name. My mouth is so dry I don't think I could answer.

"Eyes open," he instructs. "If you cheat, I'll move away and we'll have to start all over again."

"No." I reach out and clutch his shirt tight between my fingers.

"Uh uh. No touching." He removes my hands and places them over my head. His eyes skim back down my face, and neck, lingering once again over my front and center breasts.

"What are you doing? Why don't you touch me already?"

He chuckles. "It's all about the buildup, the anticipation. If it comes too fast, too easy, it won't be as good. I'm enjoying watching you get frustrated waiting for me to kiss you."

"And that would be different from prom night and the last four years how exactly?"

He leans in close, still holding my arms over my head, his warm breath tickling my ear. "I wasn't going to kiss you at your prom. No matter what. Now you know I'm going to kiss you. And touch you. I want you to feel each kiss, each touch through your entire body."

My lips are pressed into a thin line as I try to hold back the overwhelming desire surging through me. Even though my internal temperature is climbing, my skin is covered with goose bumps. I don't think I can take much more, and I'll be damned if he thinks I'm going to beg.

"I want it all to mean something, every touch." His lips barely graze the skin on my neck as he dips down and places a very gentle kiss there. "Every kiss." I gasp, full of anticipation and trepidation, and the need to feel his hands on me. Maybe begging isn't such a bad idea? "And one more thing, Steph. Starting right this minute, I plan on making up for lost time."

My heart is on hyper drive hammering hard against my chest. A mixture of blood and adrenaline shoots through my veins with a strength that leaves my hands trembling, as if I just drank eight cups of coffee. I swallow hard as his mouth crushes mine and I can tell I'm not the only one overwhelmed by the mountain of need between us. His free hand smoothes itself up my neck, up the side of my face and into my hair before moving down and wrapping around my waist, holding me tight against him.

I'm lost.

Totally.

Completely.

My breathing is hard and labored. I feel lightheaded, buzzed, just from the power of his mouth. One leg is wrapped around him. I can't move the other one because it's pinned beneath him. This is the most intimate moment we've shared together and there's nothing I wouldn't agree to right now. Not one thing on this earth. It's like I'm not even here in my room anymore, but swept up in some swirling cloud of rainbows and fairy dust; it's the most exhilarating moment of my existence. I love him. With all that I am, with all I will ever be. He owns all of me. I'm so happy to be in his arms, I don't even care if he's using me just to forget about Madison.

Madison.

Her name bounces around in my brain and I can't think of anything but her. My lips are no longer seeking his. Instead I turn away.

"Stop," I whisper, not even aware the word has left my mouth.

Jordan pulls back. He releases my hands, and stares at me, his eyes intense once again. Something changed. I feel it immediately, only I don't know what. For a brief moment, I'm not sure why he stopped. And then it hits me, hard and ugly in the face. I just told him to stop! I didn't mean to. I know I thought it when Madison popped into my head, but I can't believe I'm allowing her to be the reason we aren't kissing.

"Are you okay, Stephanie?" He doesn't say that he's nervous, that he feels terrible, he doesn't have to. I see it in his eyes, in the way his eyebrows furrow together.

I nod, knowing it's my fault. All my fault. I told him to stop. Again. Slammed with guilt, not for what I did, but why I did it, I can't take his scrutiny any longer. I bury my face in his chest. He strokes my hair while I fight my failing brain to think of something to say, some excuse that might explain why I wanted him to stop. I just thank God I didn't say her name out loud.

"What happened? Did I do something wrong?"

I look up at his face. I can't find words. His eyes are full of worry. I hate that I just ruined a beautiful moment between us. I took a highlight of our relationship and scribbled over it with an ugly magic marker.

"I'm sorry, baby. I wasn't trying to rush you."

"I know."

"I mean it. No pressure."

Each time he speaks, I feel worse. I hate that he feels the need to reassure me, and deep down, I'm terrified this is going to give him a reason to pull away and use his old standby excuse about our age difference. I don't need to get him thinking that I'm too young to be in a relationship with him. Or too weak to handle his feelings for Madison. I consider telling him the truth and admitting what spooked me, but decide against it. Maybe it's better that he believes it has everything to do with me being the naive young thing he likes to make me out to be, and not the fact that I'm terrified while he touched and kissed me his mind drifted to his ex-girlfriend.

Is she really an ex? Just before she died he promised her he'd stay away from me. Does that mean they were back together? When someone dies, do they retain the title of girlfriend or boyfriend forever? Is that how he'll think of her? Will she always be his girlfriend in his heart? I know I'm obsessing over something I have no control over, but the questions run in a loop pattern through my mind. I focus on clearing my head and forcing my thoughts back to the here and now. Jordan and me. I'm his girlfriend. I waited for him. I fought for him. I'm not about to let Madison come between us. Again.

I hate her. I know this makes me a bitch. Superbitch. I'm going to go to hell for sure. The second I die my soul will be raptured in flames, and Madison will stand on the sideline laughing. Knowing this doesn't change my feelings towards her. Or him.

Jordan pushes himself up, extends his hand and pulls me into an upright position next to him.

"I should get going."

I want him to stay. I want him to lay in my bed beside me again, and hold me, or talk to me. But under the circumstances, as much as I want him near, I know it's best if he leaves. If he stays he'll want to know what spooked me, and I can't tell him. I don't try to stop him.

"Thank you," he says getting to his feet and pulling me up on mine.

"For what? For freaking out on you again?"

He laughs. "No, that's on me. I just get carried away when we're together, and now that I know I'm not going to get slapped . . ."

"I never would have slapped you."

He smirks, "You would if you had any idea of the things that ran through my head."

Chapter 7

The second day of school I decide to brave the cafeteria by myself for breakfast. I find an empty table and open the text book I need for my first class. So what if I look like a nerd? Nerds are cool thanks to that hit TV show. As I move my scrambled eggs around on my plate taking the occasional bite, someone approaches.

"Do you mind if I sit here?"

I look up and meet the frightened brown eyes of a girl from down my hall. "Of course not." I close my book and smile.

"You're Stephanie, right?" I don't miss how her eyes avoid mine. "We live on the same floor." I rack my brain for her name as she speaks. The shy girl that sat next to me at the hall meeting, Cara? No, Carla. A silent bell rings in my head indicating I came up with the correct name. I want to jump up and fist pump the air, but decide I'll look less like a crazy person that should be avoided if I remain in my seat. "I live on the other end of the hall."

"Carla, right?" She looks surprised that I remember her name. "Sit." I motion to a chair. "It would be nice to not have to eat alone or depend on Jonah to sit with me."

"Jonah." I notice the pinkish hue to her coloring when she says his name. "He's the RA in the boys hall, isn't he?"

I smile as I nod. I know that look. I've seen it on my own face over the years every time I heard the name Jordan Brewer. Someone has a crush.

"Is he . . . I mean are you and he . . ." She scrunches her eyes before finding the words. "Is he your boyfriend?"

"No. Just a friend."

"Are you sure? You seem . . . I've seen you together, and it doesn't matter either way. Besides, it's none of my business."

"It's fine, Carla. If we seem comfortable with each other it's because we went to the same high school."

"Oh. Not that it's any of my business."

"If you'd like, I can introduce you."

"No." She answers shaking her head, her eyes glued to the table. "Thank you, but I wouldn't know what to say to him anyway. I'm sort of shy."

I remember the days I'd been too intimidated by Jordan's mere presence to remember my name. I'm surprised I never actually stood with drool spilling out of my mouth when we'd stop by his locker in the morning. I'm so happy those days are behind me.

"If you change your mind, just let me know. He's a nice guy, and pretty easy to talk to."

"Yeah. Okay. I will, but, no. I won't change my mind."

Silence descends on us as if it were an invisible blanket. It feels like the longer it covers us, the less likely we are to throw it off.

"You're so lucky," she says stabbing her scrambled eggs. "That you don't have a roommate. I do, and we don't really talk. It's kind of hard to be in the room when she's around."

"Why?"

Carla looks at her plate and shrugs her shoulders. "She's got a lot of friends already. Anytime she's in the room people come looking for her and then they hang out there and totally ignore me. It's not even like I have anything to say to them, because I don't. But it almost feels like I'm invisible."

I wonder if this girl has any idea of how well I could relate to her. "If you ever feel like you need to escape, you know where my room is."

"Do you mean it? Maybe we could do homework together, or study. Especially for sociology, we're in the same class."

"I didn't realize, but, yeah. Sure."

She nods and silence falls upon us once again.

I pull my cell phone from my pocket to check the time. I still have twenty minutes until my first class of the day starts. I can leave for class, but I think that will be rude and I don't want to do that to Carla.

"Give me a minute," I say as I send a quick good morning text to Jordan.

"Where are you from?" I ask turning my attention back to Carla.

"New Jersey. I only live half an hour away. My parents thought living here would be fun." She shrugs. "I guess the good news is I can go home on the weekends."

I rack my brain looking for things to talk about. Luckily we only have a few more minutes together before it's time to leave. I smile as I toss my garbage and return the tray. Today is going to be a good day. I made a new friend, and I did it all on my own.

*

Jordan and I text each other through the days. That's our primary source of communication. I miss him most at night, when there's not much to do. If I were in the hunt to drink and party I'd be plenty busy, but since I'm not into that, I find I'm pretty lonely. He's so busy practicing with the band, he hardly has time to say goodnight. Usually I wake at some point to a missed text from him. It makes me smile to know

I'm on his mind, but I miss him and home more than I care to admit.

Tonight I get a treat. I get to party and have fun. Best of all, I get to do it with Jordan. Sort of. I can't wait to see him perform on stage. It's such a surreal thought. I still can't wrap my head around Jordan as a drummer. In a few hours my boyfriend will play live in a band for the first time. This thought doesn't gel in my head. I never knew this side of Jordan existed. And musicians aren't my thing. But here I am getting ready to go watch him play in a bar. I don't know if he's even good. Not that it matters. He has me under a spell, I can't imagine I'll even notice if he plays off beat.

My phone chimes.

Can't wait to see you.

Me either. Looking forward to watching you pounding those drums.

So you're into musicians now?

Only hot ones.

Should I be worried?

Only if you mess up. I'll pretend I don't know you.

*

In high school a few girls talked about spending weekends watching their boyfriends rehearse in someone's basement or studio. Even though I'd been invited to a few rehearsals, I never bothered to go. It just wasn't my thing. Now, I wish I did. At least once. I have no idea what to expect tonight. Will there even be a crowd? I mean, sure it's a Friday night, but do people go to bars to listen to music? I thought the whole idea of the bar scene is to find someone to hook up with.

This thought punches me in the gut. Just because I'm not into the band scene doesn't mean other girls aren't. Now I worry some band-whore might spend her night making googley-eyes at Jordan. I want to throw up. Adding the finishing touches to my make-up I do my best to make sure he only has eyes for me.

I hesitate outside Jonah's door and take a breath before knocking.

"What's u . . ." The door opens and Jonah stops dead when he sees me. His eyes crawl down the length of my body and back up again. "Wow, Stephanie. You look hot."

"Does she! What did you do? Paint those pants on? I can see every crease and crevice." I hear from behind me. I make a face at the sound of Logan's voice. "Can I soap you up and peel them off?"

"Why can't I go anywhere without seeing you?"

"You love it and you know it,." He says coming up behind me and snaking his hand around my waist, pulling me back against him. "Besides if I stopped paying so much attention, you'll miss me."

"Don't flatter yourself," I say as I pry his arm away, slipping out of his grip.

"So where are we going?" he asks Jonah.

"Stephanie and I are going out. You aren't coming."

"Ooh, won't the boyfriend get mad?"

"I'm taking her to go see her boyfriend."

"Cool. I can't wait to meet him." Logan rubs his hands together, like he's hatching an evil plan. "I'll be ready in twenty minutes."

"You're not coming. You're not old enough."

"And she is?"

"I'm different. I'm his girlfriend."

I hope I sound more confident than I feel. Jordan promised he worked things out with his bouncer friend, but still I worry I'll get turned away at the door. At least I'll be in Brooklyn if that happens.

"You guys suck." Logan takes off, shaking his head as he quickens his pace and walks away.

"Ready?" Jonah asks.

"Ready." I nod.

*

"You can put the radio on if you like," Jonah offers.

"Are you sure? What if you think the music I listen to is crappy?"

He smiles. "I have an eclectic taste in music. There's not much I consider crappy."

"Maybe I like listening to Irish bagpipes."

"In a parade, possibly. At a wedding, or even a funeral I could see it, but that's not usually something one finds on the radio."

"What if I find a little known station that specializes in obscure zombie music?"

"Do the zombies play it or listen to it?"

"Both. They listen to it in order to pump themselves up for a fun night of brain eating."

We continue discussing the unrealistic music options without actually listening to any. Talking to Jonah is easy. Once we've exhausted ridiculous music possibilities the conversation moves on to art, focusing on perspective and mediums. I don't feel embarrassed asking him what some of the terms he uses mean since I've never actually studied art. It's nice to speak to someone so knowledgeable about something I love.

Before I know it, we're in Bay Ridge scouring the area for a parking spot. We spend twenty minutes driving up and down Fourth Avenue and the surrounding blocks. It looks like we'll never make it in the bar before the set is over when we see a car pulling out of a crowded spot. Jonah pulls alongside the line of parked cars and leans on his horn to stop another car from pulling into it. As soon as we're in and he cuts the engine I almost trip over my feet trying to get out.

"Hey, slow down there. He's not going anywhere."

"Sorry. I'm just excited."

"I understand, but if you push through the door like I've got a contagious disease or something, your boyfriend might get the wrong idea. If it takes us an extra minute to walk in, he'll still be waiting."

Guilt surges through my veins. I don't want Jonah to think I'm not grateful he brought me. I am. Very. I'm grateful for everything he's done for me since I moved into the dorms; for just being there and keeping Logan away from me. I hook my arm around his and stop walking.

With a confused look on his face, Jonah's eyes meet mine.

"In case I haven't said it yet, thank you."

"No problem, it's not like I had anything better going on."

"I don't just mean about tonight. I mean for everything. For, you know, being a friend."

His eyes narrow as they drop to our intertwined arms.

"No problem, just doing my job." His eyes meet mine again. This time they're hard, serious. It feels like I bounced hard off of some invisible barrier he put up.

I nod and release him. Feeling completely awkward in a way I hadn't in years, I keep my eyes trained on the grey, cement squares of the sidewalk. These last few minutes alone take forever to pass. A heavy, never ending silence forms between us the size of military tank. It feels as explosive, too.

"Sorry, Stephanie. I didn't mean anything by that. It's just. It's better if you're not hanging all over me as we walk in the bar. I happen to know for a fact your boyfriend is the jealous type and he might get the wrong idea about us."

"Of course." I let it drop, but I recognize an excuse when I hear one. Jordan the jealous type? No way. And especially not with me. He never had to be. When he saw Shawn's motorcycle parked outside my house he left in a jealous fit, but it had more to do with Shawn's age than actually being jealous. And when he saw me leave the bar with my former gym teacher, Mr. Dwyer, he followed us out willing to fight because he thought my teacher had unsavory intentions. But again he worried about my safety. Jealously wasn't involved. Was it?

Either way, it doesn't matter now. We're together, he has nothing to be jealous of, and I'm not buying Jonah's bull.

Jonah stops walking two storefronts away from the bar, "Can you look at me a minute?"

I hesitate wondering if I should. The bar stands only feet away, and all I want to do is walk through the door and see Jordan. My chest aches knowing we're so close and yet so far. My body feels Jordan's proximity and keeps pulling, tugging me in his direction. We already missed the first set. I just want to see him, to be with the boy who owns my heart. But in a few hours, I'll be back at school, back to the place where Jonah acts as the buffer between me and jerks like Logan. I stop, but don't dare meet his eyes.

"Listen, I'm happy I could be here for you. And I don't just mean tonight. It's been fun reconnecting." I look up in time to catch him rolling his eyes, "I guess we would've had to have had some real connection other than just existing in the same place to reconnect, so it's been cool getting to know you."

I nod, still a little put off.

"And us, our friendship, it's not because I'm an RA. I mean it sort of is, but that isn't the only reason."

Once I realize Jonah is flip-flopping like a fish on land, I wonder if I should jump in and let him off the hook. Still the weird, standoffish demeanor he sported a minute ago has me put off.

"Feel free to say something, anything, at any time here."

"It's fine. You don't owe me anything. Certainly not any explanations."

He crosses his arms over his chest. "It's just that I . . . I . . . forget it." His arms fall to his sides as his shoulders drop.

I don't know what his problem is. Why is he acting so strange?

*

Music oozes out of the bar and onto the sidewalk where a beefy, blonde buzz-cut-marine-wanna-be greets us at the door.

"ID," he orders.

I swallow hard hoping he won't notice my trembling hands as I hand him my all too-real Identification admitting I'm only eighteen and shouldn't be permitted in. But Jordan told me he'd given my name and birthday to the bouncer, Ross, and that he is expecting me.

"So you're, Stephanie," he says taking in a deep breath and looking me over as if I'm a delicacy on the desert menu.

"Yes."

"Do me a favor." He leans close to me and speaks directly into my ear, "Don't cause any trouble or this will be the last time you come. And I'll owe Jordan a major ass kicking."

I nod, and step forward looking at the small black and white sign advertising the band on the door. "Shred Em, They'll tear you apart." With my heart pounding in time to the drums inside, I stand and wait for Jonah.

*

The loud music invades my body as we walked through the door. I recognize the song. It played on the radio non-stop a few years back. Even with the overpowering noise, one beat stands out and has me moving forward in a hypnotic trance. With every strike of the drum I advance, moving closer to Jordan. My heart thrums as loud and hard as the rhythm he's keeping. As always my heart beats in response to him.

It beats for him.

Once I squeeze my way past the front of the bar, he finds me. Our eyes lock. My mouth goes dry. How did he find me so quickly in this crowd? Is his heart just as hopelessly drawn to me, as mine is to him? Before I tear my eyes from his, Jordan flashes me his crooked smile. The smile that turns me into a pile of soft, sticky caramel; the smile I can't get enough of even if I woke to it every day for a thousand years.

Soaking him in, I realize the black tee shirts the band is wearing have long, diagonal slashes running from the shoulder down. A bear claw comes to mind as I stare with my mouth open. It looks as if a bear ran it's paw across Jordan's chest and ripped open his shirt. He's showing just enough skin to hint at how perfect his body is beneath. He looks hot.

Super-hot.

A pang of jealousy spreads through me. I don't want the other girls in here to want him. I waited forever for him to admit his feelings for me; he's finally mine. It's not fair that he's giving these girls, these women, so much to drool over. I'm afraid he will spark the same erotic thoughts in their minds that I have running through mine.

And then what?

I shake it off. I'm worried for nothing. I've always known that I meant more to him than he let on. I glance at the other band members, but my eyes can't stay off of Jordan. While showing more skin than the other guys, he leaves me and I'm sure every other girl in here wanting more.

I imagine jumping into his arms with my legs wrapped around his waist and ripping the shirt off him. My hands want to slide over his damp, glistening skin and up into his dark hair. I think about his mouth and how much I want it to devour me while he holds me like that, right there, in the middle of the bar. Instead of feeling shy and embarrassed by these thoughts, the way I normally do, I feel pulse waves shooting through my body.

"They're pretty good."

Until he speaks directly into my ear, I forget Jonah's standing beside me. Pulled from my trance, I nod in agreement.

I continue to gawk, transfixed as I watch and listen to the band play.

"Want a drink?" Jonah leans in so he can speak directly in my ear.

"I just want to watch for a while."

I don't know how long that "while" lasts, but I don't move until the music stops and the band leaves the stage. Jordan moves toward me. My excitement is over the top and out of control. Standing in place, I keep my hands wrapped together. My knees are jiggly and bouncy as I wait for him.

With his eyes glued on me, Jordan pushes his way through the crowd. Hands reach out to touch him, and pat him on the back, but he doesn't seem to register any of it. His eyes never leave mine. I don't know if he reaches me first, or if I dart for him, but as soon as we're close enough, I lunge into his chest. Jordan wraps me in his arms and squeezes tight, lifting me off the ground.

"You were amazing!"

He pulls back to look at me, mischief shining in his eyes. I haven't seen that look, that shine from deep within him, since . . . Since my prom.

"Really?"

"Yes!"

Still holding me tight, his lips cover mine, making my body tingle.

"Go sit at one of the tables we have reserved in the back, I'll get us drinks."

I don't move. I can't peel my eyes off of him. It feels like years since I've seen Jordan this happy, and it's the most amazing feeling to watch this transformation. I can't tell if he knows all the people he interacts with while making his way to the bar, but he seems pretty busy acknowledging each one with a nod, smile, or a quick word. The pride swelling in my chest threatens to explode and burst through.

I can't move my lips from the silly turned up position they're frozen in as I watch Jordan squeeze his way past people to the edge of the bar. He leans over, speaks to the bartender and nods his head. And then my stomach takes a nosedive, past the floor and straight down to the center of the earth.

A familiar ache spreads across my chest. It's my heart screaming out a loud and clear warning. Inhale. Exhale, I remind myself as "Danger," flashes before my eyes. I watch helplessly as a pretty blonde pulls Jordan into a long, intimate hug. His eyes are closed as she speaks directly into his ear. This warm, familiar interaction makes me uncomfortable. He doesn't look like he wants to get away from her, and while she wraps her arms around him, he holds her back.

There's something familiar about her. I do a mental scan of his ex-girlfriends and girls he liked. He's shown me pictures of them all, she doesn't register, but that doesn't mean they don't have some sort of history together. Clearly she means something more to him than almost everyone else here. I only wonder if she might mean more than me.

Jonah's hand is on my lower back, ushering me forward. I wonder if he saw the same thing I did, and if he has the same sinking feeling that things between Jordan and I suddenly took a turn for the worst. I can't force my eyes off my boyfriend and the woman in his arms. I feel like a sick voyeur passing a car so mangled and destroyed you know someone is critically injured, but still can't help looking to see the details of what happened.

"Why don't we go sit," Jonah, sort of yells in my ear.

I nod, and allow him to lead me to the back while I keep my eyes glued on Jordan. Both he and the blonde look over in our direction and smile as he gathers our drinks in his hands.

"Do you know her?" Jonah asks leaning in close to me.

I shake my head.

"You're much prettier."

Great. I'm not crazy. He noticed something going on with Jordan and that bimbo, too. Either that or my hopefully unfounded jealously is shooting out of my eyes, along with the invisible daggers I'm throwing her way.

Before I can muster anything to say, the lead singer from the band saunters over and pulls out a seat, a very busty brunette who has to have no smaller than size triple D boobs stuffed into a single D bra and an itty-bitty waist hangs off his side. I didn't realize it while he was up on stage, but he has the deepest, bluest eyes I'd ever seen. The dark ring around the iris almost makes them look violet.

After what I can only describe as an attempt to see how far he could get his tongue down the girl's throat, he turns his unnerving stare on me.

"You know this table is reserved for the band, don't you?"

"Hey, Blaze." Jordan says as he places the glasses down in front of us and slips into the chair next to me. "It's cool, they're with me. This is my girlfriend, Stephanie." His arm slides around my shoulder, and I scoot over closer to him. "And this," Jordan looks to the seat on my other side, "is our friend, Jonah."

Blaze raises his eyebrows with interest and licks his lips. "Friend, huh?"

"Hey baby," a voluptuous red head says as she slinks over, straddles Blaze, and kisses him on the mouth.

I stare, no gawk at them. I can't help it. He just played a game of tonsil tag with one girl, and right in front of her, only a minute later, she watches as he does the same with a second girl.

After what feels like an hour, red pulls away. Blaze leans across the table, his eyes glued on mine, and says, "Hey, Stephie, these are my friends, Lela and Coco."

Blaze, Lela and Coco. They sound like the cast of a low budget porno. I turn, trying to hide the hint of a smile that forms as I think it. Jordan's hand squeezes my shoulder, and I wonder if he knows what's running through my head.

"You did good, Jordan. You still need to learn our songs, but for your first night you did all right."

"Thanks."

"You need to be sure you're not too much of a distraction." Blaze's eyes pierce mine as he points to me. "Your boy needs to focus."

I didn't know what to say. Distraction? Me? What the hell were Lela and Coco? They were a hell of a lot more distracting than I could ever be.

"You almost ready to leave?" Blaze asks Jordan.

"Leave? No. Besides I haven't seen Stephanie in a few days." He squeezes his arm around me tight.

"We're done," Blaze says. "There's no need to stay."

"You can go. I'll just hang here. I'm in no rush."

"Like hell, tonight's your first night. We're going to celebrate."

"I'm only filling in. It's not like I'm really part of the band."

"Doesn't matter. It's tradition. Even if someone fills in for one night, we go to the Hustler Club and party afterwards."

"Count me out. I'm not into that."

"You're a guy aren't you?"

"Dude, stop."

Blaze turns his violet eyes on me. "Don't believe him. No matter how much he denies it, he likes it. We all do."

Jordan takes a long breath. I can tell he's not comfortable with the turn of the conversation, but I don't know if Blaze is making him uncomfortable or if I am.

"Blaze, c'mon."

"What, mommy won't approve?"

The way Blaze's eyes meet mine, with a shit-eating grin on his face, I know it's a direct challenge to me, and I don't like it. Or him.

I raise my glass, not sure what Jordan got me. I could see it has cola in it. I assume he ordered me a rum and coke. Great. I don't like rum. I tilt the glass to take a sip and almost spit the watered down cola out. I expect something different, something stronger.

"I got the same," Jordan says seeing my reaction. "I took a pain killer before the second set.

I got it, Jordan doesn't plan on drinking and he doesn't think I should either. Wonderful, just when I could deal with a dose of liquid courage. I tear my mind away from being annoyed at Jordan and focus on letting my anger and frustration out where they belong; on Blaze.

"Jordan doesn't take orders from me, the same way I doubt you take orders from Coco and Lela."

"No, more like he tells us what he wants, and we make it happen." Lela chimes in with a sly smile.

Gross. Now I have X-rated images of him setting up a scene between the three of them. Yuck.

"If you'll excuse me, I'll be back in a few," Jonah says before getting up and leaving the table.

"Great job up there." A new guy joins us. Even if he wasn't wearing the ripped up black tee and jeans, I would recognize him. When he had his solo, I couldn't peel my eyes off of him. The instrument came alive in his hands. The way he stroked it and revered the inanimate object, I knew he treasured it. He reaches for Jonah's chair, turns it around and straddles it.

"Stephanie, this is Chaz. He's the lead guitarist."

Chaz winks at me. "Nice to meet you, pretty lady." He turns to Jordan, "So she's the vixen that stole your heart?"

"I guess you can say that." Jordan chuckles.

"Well if you're not sure, that leaves an opening for me," Chaz says leaning towards me. "What do you say? Have I got a shot with you?"

I glance at Jordan enjoying the grin on his face, smile at Chaz and shake my head. "Sorry, my heart was made to love Jordan. He's my always and forever guy. I've always loved him and I'll love him until the end of forever."

"I like that, until the end of forever." Chaz's eyes light up as he pulls a phone from his pocket and starts tapping away at the screen. "You don't mind if I steal that do you?" Chaz looks up at me, excitement shining through his soft brown eyes.

"Chaz also writes the songs," Jordan explains.

"Not all of them, only the good ones. Blaze is responsible for the rest."

Ignoring Blaze and his newly discovered talent, I keep the conversation with Chaz going. "You think that would make a good song?"

"It just gave me great inspiration. C'mon guys. Let's go back to my place and work."

"Fuck that," Blaze chimes, in. "Let's go party," he says with his hand wrapped around Lela.

"Just a few hours. This way we could teach it to Jordan while we finish it, and be ready to perform it."

"It can wait until tomorrow."

"Blaze, stop being a dick. We have a good thing going right now, but if we don't capitalize the gigs will stop and we'll be back to where we were a few months ago, groveling just to play in front of a live crowd. We work now, party later.

"Fine." Blaze shoots an angry look at me. "But she's not coming. If we're going to work I want his head in the game."

"Agreed." Chaz says looking at me. "Sorry, beautiful. But he does have a point. No girls. Just us."

"What? I didn't say no girls!" Blaze argues.

"You made a good point. I'm agreeing with you, bro. And if Stephanie can't come, it's only right that the rest of us don't have our girls hanging on us. It's new music, and they'll only get our heads focused on other things, not to mention, Jordan, who would be absolutely right to be pissed that Stephanie isn't with us."

"You suck," Blaze yells at Jordan, who just glares at the lead singer.

"Sorry. I had no idea." Jordan turns his attention back to me.

"It's all good," I lie hoping he won't pick up on my disappointment. "I got to be here to watch you."

"Do we have to leave right now?" Jordan asks.

"Ten minutes," Chaz answers.

"No. Two minutes," Blaze argues. "I'm not spending my entire night with you losers. I want to get this over and done with."

"You have ten minutes, Jordan." Chaz shoots Blaze a warning look.

At that moment I realize the band belongs to Chaz. Even if he doesn't get top billing, he's the thinker, the planner, the organizer. Without a doubt Chaz is the leader.

Blaze stands, and heads for the back with Lela and Coco attached to him on either side.

"I'll give you two a few minutes to yourselves," Chaz says. "But we leave in ten. Got it?"

Jordan nods as he pulls me from my chair onto his lap. His hands find a spot to rest on my thighs. I like the way they feel there, and the warmth they're creating inside me.

"I'm so disappointed I won't be taking you home tonight." He leans his forehead against mine.

I force a smile. "Oh, yeah?"

"It's what's gotten me through the week. It's all I could think about since I left you. Now I'm going to have to wait until tomorrow night."

"Take advantage of the moment. I'm here in your arms right now."

"I know, but I don't want you just for a few minutes. That's like not having you at all. I've been waiting to spend the night with you, to feel your body up against mine all night long."

His hands run up my sides, leaving a tingly trail in their wake, all the way up to my hair. He holds the back of my neck, pulls me forward until his lips touch the corner of my mouth and then the other one.

I think I'm about to attack him, right here in front of everyone.

"You don't want to kiss me?"

"I am kissing you," he whispers in my ear before bringing his mouth to the skin just below it. "I just have to be very careful about the way I do it. If I kiss you the way I want right now, I might not stop. And I won't really care."

"Neither will I."

"That won't be good, because I have to leave in a few minutes, and that's not nearly long enough to get my fill of you." His thumbs massage the base of my neck as his dark, hooded eyes take hold of mine and look right into my soul. "Stephanie, you're the air I breathe. I'm afraid if I take in too much all at once, I'll suffocate when we're apart."

Did he really say that? My hand reaches for my chest to make sure my heart didn't leap right out of it. Whew, the rapid beating beneath my palm means it's still there, pounding hard. He's never said anything like that before, and his words leave me intoxicated.

He continues to brush his lips on me, leaving feather light kisses in their wake. My skin singes beneath his mouth, beneath his fingers. Aside from breathing hard, every other function in my body has come to a stop, to a complete halt.

I'm thrown off Jordan's lap as he shoots up out of the seat. My feet search for a hold on the ground, as I lean on the table and struggle to steady myself. I look up at him confused. I never heard him use as much profanity in all the time I've known him as he's shouting in anger right now. I don't know what caused the sudden outburst, until I see Blaze snickering behind him.

"Sorry, but we're about to leave and you looked like you could use a little cooling off."

"Jackass." Jordan shoves his chest. "You pull another stunt like that and I'll . . ."

"You'll what?" Blaze pushes him back before coming around the chair and getting in Jordan's face. I feel the tension between them and have no idea what's about to happen.

"Break it up." Chaz pulls Blaze a step or two back, "He's doing us a favor. I don't care what history you two have, it ends now."

Blaze shakes his head. "No worries, your boy here isn't going anywhere."

"And how do you know that?" I know I shouldn't get involved. It isn't any of my business, but I can't help myself.

"Because Jordan made a promise. And he'll go out of his way, even if that means dealing with me, not to break it. Isn't that right?" Blaze is goading Jordan, and Jordan doesn't meet the challenge. He just ignores it. I'm surprised he doesn't punch Blaze in his nose. What surprises me even more is that Jordan doesn't respond. At all.

Everything about this exchange is off. Way off. Blaze has something on Jordan. He has to, because Jordan would never let anyone talk like this to him. I imagine whatever it is, it's bad. That's the only way to make sense of this scene and it only makes me dislike Blaze more.

"My apologies for Blaze," Chaz slings his arm around my shoulder and leads me to the side, a few feet away from the table. "I promise we'll all remember our manners next time we meet."

I can't help but offer Chaz a sad smile. "You're so sure there'll be a next time?"

"We need Jordan right now, so I'll do what I have to in order to keep him. And you see the way he looks at you?" He jerks his head toward Jordan. "It tells a story. The story of a love that will, as you said, last after forever ends. Even if he wasn't wearing his heart on his sleeve every time he looks at you, he wouldn't have gone out of his way to make sure you could be here if he didn't feel the same about you. He's not about to let you go. So yes, I'm sure you'll be back."

"I didn't think you'd do anything," Blaze says as he turns from Jordan and walks by us, making sure to run his blue/violet eyes up and down my body as he moves.

"I didn't hurt you did I?" Jordan asks wrapping me in his arms.

"No. I just didn't realize what was happening."

"Jackass poured ice water down my back."

"Hey, Jordan. She shouldn't be involved in this." Chaz's tone holds a warning as his eyes lock on Jordan's.

"I know."

"So keep her out of it. Meanwhile, you and Blaze need to work shit out."

Jordan nods. "Maybe it would be better if you find someone else until Pete's feeling better."

Chaz shakes his head. "It would take too long, we'd have to back out of gigs, and you've already clocked enough time with us in practice that we sounded pretty good tonight."

"I just don't want any problems."

"I'll deal with Blaze, you say goodnight to your girl." Chaz looks at me, "Goodnight, Stephanie."

"What's going on?" I ask. "Why doesn't Blaze like you?"

"It's nothing you need to worry about. I'll take care of him, but if I do it now, it might cause problems for Ross, and for the rest of the band. I'm sorry he was such a dick to you."

I shrug. "It's fine. I hate that you're going to be spending so much time with him though."

"You know I'm nothing like him. Never was. Never will be."

I nod. I only have another minute with him. While I have more questions about Blaze and the blonde from earlier, I want to spend our time wisely. After what just happened, and us not being able to spend the night together like we planned, I chicken out of asking about either of them. Besides, Blaze is gone, and Jordan hasn't looked in that woman's direction since he brought the drinks back to the table. Still, not knowing her, not understanding the way they interacted eats away at me. I want to know why they looked so comfortable in that embrace, so familiar, like they'd held each other before.

"If you want, I'll pay for a cab to take you back to your mom's, and then I can drive you back to the dorm on Sunday. Tomorrow's going to be a late night, and I can't get you in, so I'll have to pick you up from your mom's house first. I don't think she'd like me coming by so late."

"It's fine. I'll ask Jonah to drive me back to school, and maybe if you're up to it you can come over tomorrow night when you're done."

Jordan scans the crowd. "I don't know. I don't want you getting in the car with him if he's been drinking.

"I won't. I promise."

"Come on," Jordan leads me by the hand through the sea of people and over to Jonah, who's talking to a pretty red head. Jordan gives Jonah the third degree about his drinking, along with his driving habits (a little late for that if you ask me). Once he's satisfied with the answers, we walk out together, and say goodbye.

"Text me as soon as you get back to campus. I'll answer if I can, but at least I'll know you're safe."

"Okay. And Jordan, please don't forget that I love you."

The corner of his mouth rises into the crooked smile I love. "Never. Never, ever."

Chapter 8

"Sorry you're stuck going home with me."

"Don't be. I like the company."

"Are you seriously going to try and tell me you'd rather be going home with me than Jordan?"

I can't tell if he's serious or just messing with me. And by "going home with" I hope he understands he's just driving me. My expression must give me away.

"Don't worry, I know my place, I'm the chauffeur helping the princess rendezvous with the humble servant." Jonah's tone turns light and playful. That paired with the smile on his face assures me he's teasing.

"Oh stop." I push his arm playfully. "You're just upset I ruined things with that red head you were talking to."

"You think I had a shot with her?"

"Are you kidding? She was so pissed at me. I thought she was going to spit bullets out of her mouth when she saw us leaving together. I'm surprised she didn't reach over the bar and hit me over the head with a glass bottle."

He looks at me and smirks. "Exaggerate much?"

"What? I'm serious. She was into you."

Jonah doesn't say anything more, and I feel awkward. An uncomfortable silence falls between us.

"Hey, if you want to go back, you can drop me off at home and Jordan will drive me back on Sunday."

Jonah shakes his head. "It's fine. Besides, who wants to spend time with a smokin' hot red head I'll never see again, when I could have the pleasure of driving back with you."

I smile in the hopes he meant it to be funny. I really don't know him well enough yet, and at times he comes across so awkward I can't tell if he's joking or if he's just plain rude from his years of being king of the nerds.

"Jonah?" He said something earlier that keeps niggling at my mind. I don't understand it. I hope I could get him to explain. "You said something about Jordan being the jealous type. What did you mean?"

Jonah smirks at me. "It's pretty straight forward, not really any shades of grey to confuse you."

"What I mean is, I never noticed him jealous with his other girlfriends." As I say it, a memory races back to my mind. The night Jordan found me crying on the curb; the night he offered to take me to my senior prom, he mentioned he didn't want Madison to go away without him. Why?

"That's because he wasn't like that with other girls." The sound of Jonah's voice pulls me back to the present. "At least not that I noticed. But I didn't pay much attention. As far as I know, he's only ever been like that with you."

"Just me? Now I'm really confused. Did he say something to you at the dorm?"

"No." He takes one hand off the steering wheel and runs it through his hair. "You really don't know what I'm talking about?"

I shake my head lost, confused. "Not a clue."

"Your freshman year of high school, you went out with that slacker."

He doesn't need to give any further descriptions. There's only one guy I dated freshman year.

"Chris?"

Jonah nods. "Yeah, I'm pretty sure that was his name. I guess something happened between you two, and he started talking shit about you in the boy's locker room."

"Like what?"

Jonah shrugs. "Honestly, I don't know. I was more focused on using my peripheral vision to make sure the guys on either side of me weren't about to give me a wedgie or run off with my clothes."

Again I don't know what to say. If high school was uncomfortable for me, it must have been pure torture for Jonah.

"Anyhow, I'm not sure how it started, but before I knew it, I heard yelling and noticed Jordan in Chris' face. Chris said something to the effect that you put up a good front with your "good girl" act, but really you were so eager to get laid you were willing to do them both at the same time."

"What?" I feel heat rush to my face, and I'm glad Jonah's eyes are on the road. I think of his surprise visit the day I moved into the dorm, and how nice he's been to me. Is he expecting something in return? Is this all because he has ulterior motives?

"Don't worry. I didn't believe him. I doubt anyone else did either. Chris had a reputation of being full of shit. But I'm pretty sure that's when Jordan shoved him hard into a locker. The back of Chris' head hit the piece that sticks out. You know where you put the lock through? That set Chris off. They were going at each other pretty fiercely. That's why I remember it so well, because by this time all of us in there were watching."

I can't help but try to picture the scene as Jonah describes it. I don't know what to say. How did I never hear about this before? He had to be exaggerating. He just had to be.

"And no one tried to break it up?"

"No one really liked Chris, and Jordan didn't need any help. He shoved Chris' face into a locker and held his arm up behind his back. I don't know what kind of freaky hold Jordan had on him, but he must have been a hair away from breaking the arm, because he brought Chris down to his knees and made him apologize for what he said about you."

"Did he?"

Jonah nods. "Between whimpers of pain. Then Jordan looked around and told everyone to take a good look at Chris because if we so much as thought about touching you he would do the same to us."

An empty numbness runs through my chest. I don't know how to feel about what I just heard. Part of me feels vindicated that even back then, Jordan's feelings for me were strong enough for him to threaten a locker room full of boys. He did have a front row view of Chris twisting my wrist. That bothered him. Years later he made comments about Chris hurting me. And he did promise Chris wouldn't look my way again. Was that just Jordan keeping his promise?

I know it happened so long ago, but still, instead of feeling all "that's my boyfriend," it bothers me in a way I don't understand and can't articulate. I can't help but wonder if that's the reason none of the guys from school ever really spoke to me. What if one of those guys liked me? What if I liked them? Did he defend me or make sure if he couldn't have me no one else could either?

It only makes what happened at the bar with Blaze bother me more. If the fight in the boys locker room happened the way Jonah said it did, wouldn't Jordan have stood up to Blaze for the way he spoke to me and goaded us? I mean really stood up to him? And what about the comment from Chaz, that I shouldn't be "involved in this." He also warned Jordan to settle the "shit" between him and Blaze. Something more is going on that Jordan's not telling me. I suspected it before, but putting it all together with what Jonah just told me, solidifies it in my head.

"You know, Chris saw Jordan and I talking at a party," I feel the need to explain. "He got the wrong idea. Chris acted like a jerk and I wouldn't leave with him. We were over and he knew it, so he tried to bully me into going with him by twisting my wrist. Jordan witnessed it, and I thought they were going to go at it then and there, so I'm sure Jordan just wanted to make sure Chris didn't touch me again. I mean physically touch me. Jordan has a thing about guys beating up on girls. I'm sure that's all that happened. And I'm sort of disappointed I missed it."

"I didn't say Jordan was wrong, or that Chris didn't deserve it, but there was more to it than that. He made it clear to every guy in there you were off limits."

"So tonight you worried if Jordan saw us walk in the bar arm and arm he'd go after you?"

"He didn't look too happy to see me at school when he came to visit you, and I flashed back to that day in the locker room. One on one I might be able to hold my own. But if it's me against a group, like if the entire band took me out back to get a point across, I wouldn't have a shot."

"First of all, he wouldn't do that. Second of all, don't you know I'd stand up for you? I'd never let him hurt you."

"Let's work on not getting to that point to begin with."

"Deal."

*

Jonah and I make it back to campus after 2 AM. While the dorm looks the same as it did when we left, it doesn't feel the same. I'm not used to the silence filling the halls. The only other time I'd walked them at such a late hour was when the fire alarm went off. I don't hear anything. No voices. No music. Nothing but the sound of our shoes on the stairs as we walk on them. Before we reach Jonah's room I clear my throat and speak.

"Are you tired?" I ask surprised to hear my voice echo in the empty corridor.

He shrugs, "I'm still sort of wired."

"Want to come hang out? Maybe we could watch TV or something."

"I'd love that. Just give me a minute to change."

"Great. Come to my room in five."

As I walk away, regret swims in my head. I shouldn't have invited him to my room. Not at this time of night, or morning depending on how you look at it. I like hanging out with Jonah. Having him within an arm's length keeps me from missing home so much. It helps that we have a shared background and social experiences. Conversations flow naturally. We don't struggle to find things to talk about. If the silence feels funny we return to our safe subject, art. Best of all Jonah knows all about Jordan, maybe even more than I do. But still I shouldn't have invited him to hang out alone in my room.

Once in my room I send Jordan the text I promised, letting him know we arrived safe and sound. Next, I strip out of my clothes, crumple them into a ball, and toss them on the bed. I glance down at the pretty lace bra and panties I'd worn, pushing aside my disappointment. When I picked them out earlier, I didn't plan on undressing myself. The light wrapping at the door pulls me back into the moment and the fact that Jonah's waiting on the other side.

"One minute."

"Hurry!"

I reach on the bed for the yoga pants and black shirt I'd worn earlier. I open the door surprised to find Jonah in his boxers and tee shirt. I gasp. What happened to the rest of his clothes? I'm so surprised with his attire, I don't even notice the towel folded between his arm and side. His eyes dart around the hall nervously.

"Let me in," he says in a stern tone.

I move out of the doorway making room for him to pass.

"Close the door."

Yet again, Jonah acts strange with his harsh tone, and I have no idea where it came from. Now I really regret having him alone in my room. Once the door closed, Jonah turns to me. He holds the rolled towel in between us so it looks like its standing straight, and then with his free hand, pulls the towel up revealing a bottle of beer. Jonah smiles as my eyes take it in.

"I thought you might like to share a beer since you didn't drink earlier."

"Thank you, but no. I'm fine."

"It's okay, Stephanie. I won't tell him."

"Who? Jordan? This has nothing to do with him." Did he know Jordan asked me not to drink? But, how? A nervous feeling swarms in my stomach. Not the light fluttery one Jordan causes. I could only liken this feeling to that of being chased by a swarm of bees.

"Like hell it doesn't." Jonah sits at the edge of my bed and works the top off the bottle. "He's doing the same thing to you now that he did in high school."

"Really?" My muscles tighten and grow rigid. "And what's that?"

"He gives the orders, and you follow with a smile."

Where the hell does he come off? "He doesn't order me around."

Jonah shakes his head. "Of course not. I'm wrong. Sorry. I shouldn't have said anything."

His flippant attitude upsets me even more. He's lying and I know it. Worst of all, he knows I know it. "He doesn't," I say as I moved toward him and take the bottle from his hand. He lets it go without any resistance.

"I believe you."

"No, you don't."

"Yes, I do. Besides, what does it matter?"

I look down at the bottle in my hand and think about my promise to Jordan. Jonah isn't about to have something like that to hold over my head, even if I could use that same thing to cause trouble for him. I don't know how bad he needs the RA position, but I know what Jordan means to me, and neither Jonah nor the beer are worth that kind of risk.

Come here," Jonah reaches for my hand and pulls me toward the bed.

"Maybe your being here right now isn't such a great idea." I hand him back the beer and glance at the door hoping he gets the hint.

"I said I'm sorry. I guess I just don't understand, and it upsets me."

"Understand what?" I ask defensively with my arms crossed over my chest.

"Can you sit, please? I'm not going to try anything. But it's late and you look tired, I don't want to feel like I'm not only keeping you up, but making you uncomfortable in your own room."

"Maybe you should've thought of that before you insinuated I was a dumb bimbo taking orders from my overbearing boyfriend."

"I never said that."

"That's what insinuate means, you don't come out and say it. You hint at it."

"Ok, last time I'm going to say this. I'm sorry." He holds up the bottle before taking a long swig. After wiping his mouth with the back of his hand, his blue eyes meet mine again.

"I didn't like Blaze."

Blaze seems a safe enough subject. I take a seat on the bed. "Me, either."

"I didn't like the way he spoke to you, let alone what he said, and knowing how Jordan is, it surprised me that he didn't do more to shut him up."

It did seem strange that the same boy that threatened an entire locker room of guys when we weren't dating in high school didn't put up much of a fuss against one guy tonight when we are dating.

"I'm sure he had his reasons."

"Yeah." Jonah nods. "Me, too. And I guess that's the part the bothers me the most."

I don't bother to ask him what he means by that. The image of Jordan hugging that blonde flashes in my mind. I know Jonah saw them, too. I won't, I can't let him lead me down that road. Instead I sit next to him on the bed, saying nothing. Maybe if I don't agree with Jonah's assessment of both Blaze and Jordan's strange behavior it wouldn't be so uncomfortable? But, I do. And before I know it, that feeling of camaraderie is gone with the wind. Instead, we're knee deep in awkward silence.

Why can't Jonah pick up on how uncomfortable he's making me and leave? I assume it has to do with the social deficiencies that come with being shunned by an entire Brooklyn high school. I don't know how to make what I want more obvious and less subtle, because while more accepted than Jonah, I wasn't the poster girl for popularity.

"Have you met Carla yet?" I ask, breaking the tension. "She lives down at the end of the hall. I think you should meet her."

He shrugs with a smirk. "Why's that?"

"She mentioned you at breakfast the other day." I stretch and yawn, suddenly a thousand times more tired than I'd been five minutes ago. "At least I think she did. I'm not really sure right now."

"Lay down." Jonah stands and pulls my desk chair over, next to the bed.

"No. It's fine." I answer, my eyes begging for me to close them.

"How about this. I'll sit here and put the TV on, and you lie on the bed and watch."

I know I should argue. I should tell Jonah to leave, but I don't have the strength to argue. I don't have the desire to stay up a minute longer. Besides, he has the key to my room. If he wants to key himself in while I sleep, he can and I wouldn't know any better unless I woke up. Once the television is on, I hand him the remote control and close my eyes. I vaguely hear him telling me something about an art show and the opportunity it promises.

An annoying chirp startles me. It takes a few seconds after I open my eyes for me realize it's after eleven in the morning and I have a text message. In zombie mode I reach across the bed for the crumpled pile of clothes I wore the night before, and retrieve my phone from my pants pocket. I anticipate Jordan sent the message and wants to talk about what happened after we left each other the night before. Instead the message is from Jonah.

Still snoring sleeping beauty?

My mouth twists into a sarcastic grin. Sleeping beauty!

I don't snore!

Yes you do, and it's not very becoming. Does Jordan know?

I decide to ignore the last text. I throw on a shirt, a pair of shorts, and sweep my hair into a ponytail. My stomach growls, reminding me I haven't eaten since dinner the previous night. There's still time to make it to brunch, and I'm hungry. After I brush my teeth I head for Jonah's room to see if he wants to join me.

His door stands slightly ajar. He's talking to someone. I don't know why I stop and listen. I know I shouldn't, but I almost can't help myself. "So then he scares the shit out of everyone as he kicks the window out and jumps off the bus. I mean can you say loser?"

My stomach turns and flips, like it has two feet and is tripping over itself. Is he talking about Jordan? My Jordan!

I push the door open before thinking of what I want to say. I can't believe he'd trash talk Jordan like this. I thought we're friends. Before I can find words appropriate to express my outrage, my eyes meet Logan's. The dumb smirk on his lips alerts Jonah to my presence.

"Stephanie." Jonah stands and takes a few steps toward me with a smile, "I was just telling Logan and Ian about the day Jordan jumped off the bus."

I can't believe he's acting like I didn't just walk in and hear him call my boyfriend a loser.

"You remember that don't you?"

I don't answer. Instead I narrow my eyes and glare, ready to lace into him.

He shrugs. "Let's just say it was one of the most memorable bus rides I ever took. "Anyhow," he turns back to the guys sitting on his bed, "He stands on the sidewalk with his arms crossed over his chest waiting for the rest of us to get off, like nothing happened. I only wish I could think on my feet like that. I mean even if I did, I would've been too nervous to act on it. So like I said, Capital L pasted on my forehead." He uses his pointer finger and thumb to illustrate his point.

So he called himself a loser?

"What's wrong, Steph? You look confused. C'mon, you have to remember."

I'm leery. I don't trust him.

"I do, but . . . When I walked in, it sounded like you called Jordan a loser."

"What?" Jonah laughs. "Please, we all know the roles we played in high school."

I'm not sure I believe Jonah, but I don't have any reason not to. I can't ask Logan or Ian if he's lying, especially not right here in front of him. Out of the three of them, I currently have more trust and faith in Jonah than the other two boys put together. Ian might be okay, but he hangs out with Logan, and Logan makes my skin crawl.

"I'm sorry, I got all caught up telling the guys about that day, I don't even know why you're here. Is everything okay?"

I start to think maybe it's in my best interest to steer clear of Jonah. I don't really know anything about him besides the fact that he looked and acted like the king of the nerds in high school and seemed to go through some sort of whole body transformation here at college. And he keeps Logan in line. That's huge. I like having a friend around, so I decide to take his word for it. I chose to believe him until he gives me a reason not to.

"I was on my way to grab something to eat, and I wanted to thank you for last night."

"Oh, really?" Logan chimes in. "How do I get a piece of the action?"

"Shut up, dude." Jonah picks a pair of rolled up socks off of the floor, and tosses them at Logan before turning back to me, his blue eyes twinkling. "Anytime."

I leave Jonah's room feeling confused. I plan to avoid him for the rest of the weekend. I can keep myself busy today with school work. And then Jordan will be here, and I plan to spend the whole day Sunday with him.

Chapter 9

The ringing of my phone wakes me. Finally, Jordan is here. I stretch and yawn as I shuffle my feet into a pair of slippers, grab my key and close the door behind me. I have to meet him at the front door to let him in. It's almost two in the morning, and while I'm excited to see him, I'm also exhausted. And unnerved. I hope he doesn't want to fool around too much tonight, because I want to remember every detail of our first time, and at this moment I can barely keep my eyes open.

"Hi," I say opening the door to let him in the building. I smile as our eyes meet, feeling a nervous rumbling in my belly. It hits me that we're about to spend the night together. In my bed! I feel my face get hot. I know I'm blushing.

"Hi?" Jordan says, stepping toward me, his eyes piercing mine as his lips draw up into a mischievous smile. "I drive all this way, this late at night, and that's all I get?"

"You're really here," it comes out in an awed whisper.

"Wasn't that the plan?" Another step forward. Another breath trapped in my lungs.

"Yes, of course, but I mean, it's you." Why do I still manage to say the lamest things to him?

"Were you expecting someone else?" His eyebrow is raised as he takes a step closer to me. My body trembles.

"Of course not, I . . . "

"Just shut up and kiss me." With his arms around my waist, he pulls me hard against him.

I can't speak, can't think. I suck in a deep breath, so I have enough oxygen traveling to my brain in case I forget to let it out. I don't answer him, not with words. Instead I do as I'm told and bring my lips to his.

Jordan's fingers get lost in my hair as our mouths open, allowing our tongues to meet, twirl and dance. He fills my head, my lungs. Every part of me that needs something vital to live is filled by Jordan, and he satisfies every life sustaining need, every necessity I have.

"That's more like it."

He leans back enough so he could look down at me, but not enough that he lets me go. I stare up at his dark eyes, hypnotized, gasping for air. He pulls my head against his chest and holds it there, stroking my hair.

"I'm so glad you're here."

He kisses the top of my head, and reaches down for my hand, entwining our fingers. I look at our joined hands, still afraid to believe we're real.

"Then why don't you take me back to your room?"

I can't believe those words actually left his mouth. Heat surges through me, from each hair follicle on my head, down to the tips of my toes. Every moment with him since he found me on the beach has me thinking I've been sucked through a wormhole and transferred into a surreal alternate universe. But hearing that he wants to go back to my room where we'll be alone all night long, has my stomach back flipping in a free-fall.

I take a moment to center myself enough to walk, instead of dragging him along as I sprint down the hall at full speed. Focus, I think while taking the lead and moving along as if this is just some ordinary night, some ordinary walk, instead of what promises to be the highlight of my life so far.

*

The door to my room barely closes before his hands are on my neck pulling me to him. Standing a heartbeat away, he cups my face in his hands, his thumbs gently swipe my cheeks. His dark eyes lock on mine as his lips inch toward me. All I can do is stand frozen in place looking up at him, feeling my heart race as I anticipate his next move. I'm stuck in some sort of pleasure paralysis.

My blood shoots through my veins in a fierce but steady rhythm. With every beat the warm liquid races to my heart, squishes through, and then sails away. His touch has my skin in hyper drive. I feel every brush of his lips against mine, every warm breath from his mouth, not just at the surface of my skin, but deep into my heart and soul as well. Jordan pulls back a moment to skim his eyes over my body in my pajama shorts and a cami. I feel like they reach out and caress me the same way his hands do. I'm no longer worried about being tired and forgetting any details of being with him. I'll remember every moment of this night for the rest of my days.

"God, you're sexy." He strokes my cheek with his thumb.

That voice, his voice, comes out low and husky. It holds a longing, a desire, I never heard before. Not from him. Not for me.

"Looks who's talking. I don't think there was one girl in the bar last night that didn't want you. I'm sure tonight was no different."

He chuckles and pulls back just enough to allow rational thoughts to once again enter my mind. "It was different all right. I was distracted because you weren't there. I played staring at the clock the whole night, waiting to get to you." He kisses me on the nose.

"I'm sure Blaze loved that."

"Don't take anything he says to heart. He's an idiot."

"Then why are you helping him out?"

"I'm not so much helping him as I am Chaz and Pete, the drummer. I don't want him to lose his spot."

"Still, I don't like Blaze."

"Can you stop talking about him?" Jordan inches in closer to me, so that not only are we standing chest to chest, but the front of his body, his thighs, his hips, his abdomen are touching those same parts of my body. I feel his heart drum against me. Any thoughts of Blaze or anyone else are tossed out the window.

"Last night, the minute you walked in, I felt it. I looked up and there you were, watching me. I couldn't take my eyes off of you. I worried I'd forget the song we were playing. I couldn't wait to get you in my arms and show everyone that you're my girl."

"Worried someone was going to try and sweet talk me away?"

"Nah, I've just been waiting to show you off," he teases folding me into his arms, squeezing tight. "I love you."

"I love you, more."

Again his thumb moves over my face. This time it runs across the line of my jaw causing tiny little bumps to rise to the surface of my skin. After another long, deep kiss that has me floating above the ground, Jordan leads me by the hand to the bed. My stomach flip-flops with excitement. Breathe I remind myself over and over. Just breathe.

He sits in front of me and wraps his arms around my waist. I think this is it, the moment I'll die because my heart is pounding so furiously it's about to burst through my skin and race in circles around the room. Jordan smiles and pulls me down to the spot next to him. My eyes never leave his as I move. I sit so we are shoulder to shoulder, our thighs touching. I interlace my fingers behind his neck and bring my mouth to his again.

"If I'm dreaming, I never want to wake up."

He brushes a lock of hair behind my ear before speaking softly into it, "If I do my job right it won't matter, because I'm working on making your dreams come true."

Before I know what happened, Jordan maneuvers us into a laying position. I lean my head against his chest, and listen to the pounding of his heart. It beats hard. A giant smile covers my face as I breathe him in.

"It's not fair, you know. Not fair at all."

"What?"

"That now you're here at school, and it's too far to drop by if I can't sleep, or just to sneak in one last goodnight kiss. I missed you this week. This is all I thought about."

"Just this?"

"Actually I thought about this for years, and not just this. Holding you close, knowing you're mine is just the tip of the iceberg. I've imagined so much more."

"Good. You had me worried."

"But this is all we're going to do tonight. Cuddle, kiss, and sleep."

"What? Why?" I can't mask the disappointment in my voice.

"Because it's what we need. We've never done just this."

"We've never done a lot of things."

"C'mon, Steph."

What does he mean? I don't speak. I don't know what to say.

"I know it took us a long time to get here. Too long. And the attraction between us has been strong for years. So strong there were times my body ached when I left you. But that's not all we're about. There's always been more. More than two people that want each other. More than a simple friendship. It's important to build that part of our relationship, too. I'm not saying we fight it anymore, I'm just saying we shouldn't rush it." He yawns. "And while you might think you want to take this further right now. Tonight, that would be wrong, for both of us. I know this is the right thing to do. I've been thinking about it ever since you pushed me away. The second time."

"Great, it's my fault."

"No." He smoothes my hair and smiles. "Not at all. You didn't do anything wrong. I'm not pointing fingers or assigning blame. I want you to be absolutely sure, one hundred percent comfortable with everything that happens between us. Let's just let things evolve naturally, Okay? No pressure."

"What if I naturally want to do this?" I say pulling up on the hem of his shirt.

He raises one eyebrow, "That's all you want to do?"

I shake my head and bring my hands to his firm chest. I look him over, amazed at how well chiseled his upper body is. "I want to touch you here." I run my pointer finger over the lines of muscle etched into his stomach, then from just beneath his belly button down the waistband of his jeans. "And kiss you here," I say bringing my mouth to the crook of his neck.

A pleasant moan leaves his lips as one hand grazes my neck and reaches up into my hair, holding it tight.

"Do you feel yourself trembling?"

I shake my head, afraid to speak.

"Touch me all you want, Stephanie." His voice is low, sultry, his black eyes on fire. "Touch me. Kiss me. I'm yours, and you're mine. But make me earn everything you're willing to give me. Your love. Your heart." His breath changes, his eyes trail over me again, "Your body."

"You already have." My eyes leave his and drop down to the button on his jeans, and then back again, betraying my thoughts.

"No." He pulls me close and presses my head against his chest. His voice rumbles as he speaks. "The way I treated you the last few months, I'm lucky you're still giving me the time of day."

"You earned my love a long time ago. When I told you I caused bad things to happen and you didn't turn and run."

"I didn't do anything that day. Just showed you what friendship is. And if I remember correctly, the only reason you told me that is because I hurt your feelings."

I position my body so that I'm lying on top of him. I hope to use this as a way to change his mind. Instead, he flips me onto my back, causing my breath to catch in my throat. His eyes lock on mine and don't waver a centimeter, as he pins my hands on the sides of my head letting his weight rest on top of me. His demanding lips explore my mouth and neck, my heart races, and jumps with joy. I never felt this kind of wild abandon before.

We do just as he promises. We kiss and touch for hours. I don't worry that he isn't attracted to me, I know better. And it doesn't hurt that I can feel his excitement pressing and grinding against me, begging me, urging me to hold him closer, to hold him tighter and never let him go.

I don't want to admit it, but I've been worrying that sex will be super important to Jordan. Especially since without even meeting Shawn or hearing me speak about him, Jordan knew he only wanted to sleep with me. That's part of why I pushed Jordan away. Some small part of me worries that once the sexual mystery is solved between us, he'll lose interest and move on. I know it's ridiculous. If I want this relationship to work, I have to let go of my insecurities and trust in what Jordan and I have, because it's beyond special, beyond an attraction. What we have is a once in a lifetime love.

Chapter 10

I open my eyes happy to find Jordan still asleep. Good. That means I can watch him, stare at him without feeling weird. My eyes take in the rise and fall of his bare chest.

Up, down. Up, down.

I amuse myself finding a rhythm in his breathing and matching my own to it. This feels like a dream. Like I'll wake up at any moment and the image of him will evaporate, shimmer from the place beside me on the bed. I prop myself up on my elbow to get a better view. He looks so peaceful I can't help myself, I reach out and stroke my hand down the side of his face.

Jordan's hand shoots up and snatches my wrist in a vice-like grip. I swallow and blink. Before I gain my bearings, he pins me flat on my back, straddling me, his knees digging into my hips, his forearm crushing my throat. I try to push him off, but I can't, he's too strong, and I don't think he even realizes it's me beneath him. His eyes are wild, frightened. His free hand is balled into a fist, and cocked back ready to pound something.

Oh shit!

The something he's about to pound is my face!

I'm in a panic, thrashing beneath him, but he's too strong and too heavy. I can't shake him off, I can't speak. Not with his arm squeezing against my vocal chords. With the speed and surprise of his movements, I have no time to get words out. Instead, I force something close to a whimper out of my mouth. I have one arm free. All I can do is lift it to shield myself.

It's in this moment everything slows down. Just as fast as the scene starts, it ends. He loosens his grip and pulls back. I brave a glance at his face. I look in the eyes I didn't even recognize a moment ago. They seem clear of the angry fog clouding them as he went wild. Instead a look of horror seeps out and spreads across his face.

"Stephanie! Oh, God, Steph. I can't believe I almost hit you." He chokes back the words and scoops my limp body up into his arms. "I'm so sorry." He alternates between kissing the top of my head and stroking my hair. "Are you okay? Please tell me I didn't hurt you."

Once I think I'm able to speak, I clear my throat. My voice is low "What the hell was that?"

I know whatever happened a minute ago is over, and he acted out of character. Far, far out of character. A voice in my head tells me to make sure he's okay, but no. He almost bashed my face in, and I couldn't do anything to stop it. Not one thing.

The only words Jordan seems able to say he keeps repeating over and over, "I'm sorry. I'm so, so sorry."

Feeling betrayed, I pull my trembling body from his embrace, and push against his chest not only to break his hold on me, but create distance between us. This only seems to encourage him to tighten his grasp.

"Don't be afraid. You know I'd never hurt you."

"What just happened?" I'm not quite yelling, but my voice is louder than usual.

"I'm not sure."

"Bullshit! Jordan, it was like you didn't see me, like you didn't recognize me. What the hell happened?"

He sits up and lets me go. His lips are pressed together in a thin line, and his eyes are glassed over with tears. Shaking his head, Jordan turns his back to me. His feet hit the floor and he runs a hand through his hair, then holds his head. When he speaks, his voice sounds strange.

"I don't know!" He insists. "I guess I was dreaming. I felt something, and I . . . I . . . just reacted."

"Is that how you usually react when you wake up?"

"No. I'm not used to being touched when I sleep. I usually wake to my alarm."

I close my eyes a moment collecting myself.

"Did that ever happen with Madison?"

He shakes his head. "We never spent the night together."

"Was it her? That you were dreaming about?"

"No." He hesitates so long I'm not sure he's going to say anything more. When he speaks, his voice is low, as if he doesn't want to say it, or doesn't want me to hear it. "It was my father."

My stomach sinks like an elevator in free fall. Jordan's confession of being beaten and locked in the attic by his father as a young boy jumps to mind. Shit. I didn't realize those memories were still so fresh, so raw. I should have though. Only a couple of weeks earlier he wanted to go see his father so he could tell him off face to face.

I move around the bed and get to my knees in front of him. He turns away so he doesn't have to look at me, but I need to look at him. I need to see that his calm demeanor is there, and he needs to see that I'm okay. I reach up and place my hand on the side of his face.

"I'm sorry. I shouldn't have touched you."

His eyes meet mine. They're sad, haunted. "Please don't. I already feel like garbage. You didn't do anything you should be apologizing for."

"Yes, I did. I didn't think."

"Stop, Stephanie."

"Look at me. I'm fine. I swear."

He nods. "I know, but I could've . . ."

"No buts. Nothing happened." I wrap my arms around his waist hoping my actions will back-up my words and convince him. "I won't ever touch you like that again. Not while you're asleep."

"Just stop." He peels my arms off, stands and reaches for his pants lying on the floor beside the bed.

I can't let him go. Not like this. He'll shut down and pull away. I can't, I won't let that happen. Not when it took so much time and effort to get here.

"I'm much more frightened this instant, that you're going to walk out the door and push me away. You didn't hurt me, but if you leave right now, like this, you will. You'll break my heart."

He doesn't move. I see the conflicting emotions clouding his face. "I have to Stephanie. This isn't something you should forgive so easily. It's not something you should forgive at all."

"Maybe I wouldn't if it was someone else, but it's not. It's you. I know you didn't mean it. And you didn't hurt me, you wouldn't."

"Don't be so sure."

"I am. I know it the way I know my name."

He takes a step forward, just one tiny step. I think it's a sign I'm making progress. I believe if I could get him to keep taking those baby steps towards me, we can work it out.

"This is one of the reasons I worried about us being together. I don't want you to put up with things you don't deserve."

"I'm not."

He takes hold of my shoulders and looks deep into my eyes, but doesn't move to pull me to him or come any closer. I do my best to beat down the fear that he's going to turn around and walk away. It's not working.

"You shouldn't be with anyone that could smash your face in."

I try to look away, not liking where this is going, but he won't let me.

"That's what I almost did, Stephanie. The problem is, you've dated so many jerks and losers, you don't have a clue how you should be treated. You should be demanding that I leave and never come back. But you're not because you don't understand what it's like to be treated right."

"That's not true. I'm not an idiot you know. And Charlie treated me right."

"Until he called you by the wrong name."

"You don't understand."

"I understand that I found you crying your eyes out on the curb, and it was his fault."

I close my eyes and let out a long breath. "Jordan," the words are like lead weights in my mouth. "I have something I need to tell you."

"I know a few months passed, and looking back now it doesn't seem like such a big deal because you're over him, but don't try to downplay what he did."

There's a twisting in my stomach. Right now nothing feels right between us. I don't know how to fix it, and I have no idea how he will react. It's in the past, and until this morning I thought we were in a good place. I tell myself I have no reason to worry. But my pounding heart says otherwise.

"Charlie was a good guy. It was me. The break-up was my fault."

"You're defending him the same way you're trying to defend me." He takes another tiny step in my direction. "But I was there remember?"

I nod. "He did break-up with me. But I deserved it."

His breathing pattern changes. His breaths are longer, deeper, louder; he's annoyed. I want to believe telling him is better than holding on to the lie. If he knows the truth, maybe he'll understand that it doesn't matter how any of my previous boyfriends treated me. They weren't him, and he's the only person I want. Only he wove his way into my heart. And my love for him is so deep and real, I could forgive just about anything, especially in this case where nothing really happened.

"We were alone at his house, and he set up this really beautiful dinner."

"I remember what happened after the dinner." One more step closer to me. "So it doesn't matter what he did before that. The bottom line is that you were left hurt and he caused it."

"Jordan. Please, stop. You're not making this easy."

This time I move forward. Almost no space exists between our bodies. I want to reach out for him, but I'm afraid of his reaction. Not physically afraid, emotionally afraid. He looks like he wants me to drop it, and part of me thinks that would be best, but I can't. What if it somehow comes out later? Or worse, what if Maria tells him thinking he already knows? Clearly they still speak, and she still lives only a few blocks away from him. It could happen. Jordan deserves to know. And I need to be the one to tell him.

"Charlie was very sweet and we were in his room."

"Call me crazy, but I really don't want to hear the details of how you almost had sex with another guy."

"I think you do." I let my eyes drop for a moment before summoning the strength to continue. "Because while he spent the night doing everything he could to make me happy, my heart was somewhere else, with someone else." Breathe I remind myself. I hear my voice crack and wonder if I have the strength to go on. "He told me he loved me. Me. Not anyone else. No other girl's name came out at the end. But when I responded, when I told him I loved him . . ."

Jordan steps back, creating a small distance between us again. I can still reach out and place my hand on his hip or against his chest. I don't. The reality of my confession weighs too heavily on me, and I can see the change in his eyes, feel the tension radiating off him.

"What did you do, Stephanie?"

"When I said 'I love you,'" my heart hammers against my chest, little beads of sweat form at the base of my neck. "It was your name that slipped out. I said Jordan instead of Charlie."

He closes his eyes and tilts his head up. His hands rake through his hair then scrub over his face. "I don't believe this. You lied to me? It was all a lie?"

"This was the only thing I ever lied to you about. I swear."

I see anger in the strong set of his jaw. I feel it swell up between us, like a floor to ceiling barrier. I need to touch him, to break through, but I can't move my trembling hands. Seized by fear, I worry he will walk away and never look back.

"Do you realize what happened after that? Do you have any idea how my life changed because of it? The hell I've gone through?"

My heartbeat sounds in my ears. I feel it in my throat, pounding like a hammer through every part of my body. I nod and choke out, "I'm so sorry."

"Sorry? Of all the selfish things you've done . . ."

"Now we're back to that?" He reopens a deep gash he slashed into my heart a month and a half ago.

"Don't."

"What do you want me to do? I said I'm sorry."

"Sorry doesn't cut it."

"Jordan!" I plead. "Calm down."

He ignores me as he grabs his sweatshirt and pulls it on over his head.

"Please, don't leave."

He continues not looking at me, not answering while he puts his sneakers on and heads toward the door. Panic takes hold of me. I jump in front of him, blocking his way.

"Please, you can't drive like this, you're too upset."

"Get out of the way, Stephanie." There's nothing light or loving in his tone. He's serious, and worst of all, he won't even look at me.

"Jordan," I reach out to touch his face, but he won't let me. He takes hold of my wrist and throws my hand down, away from him.

"I need to get out of here and away from you."

Amazing. No matter how much he claims to love me, time and time again he slices my heart into pieces. There isn't one person alive that has the power to hurt me the way he does, and I've never felt lower than I do at this moment. I step out of the way, using all my strength to hold back my tears until after he walks out.

*

Confessing my love for Jordan, and hearing him proclaim he loved me too, should have been one of the most amazing experiences of my life. Instead it started an ugly trend of him turning his back on me and leaving me alone with nothing but tears for comfort. Our relationship was much less complicated before prom, before I pressed him to admit his feelings, when I loved him from afar.

I know where we are now; right back at the impasse we reached when I found out he blamed me for the accident and Madison's death. When I think of the impossibilities of making this relationship work, the answer seems simple. Forget him and move on. The problem is I've tried and failed, failed miserably time after time. It just doesn't work. I'll torture myself cyber-stalking him. I won't be able to pay attention in my classes, and I'll imagine what he's doing at every moment of the day, and who he's doing it with.

I have to find a way to deal with these issues head on. I look around my room, and feel the walls closing in on me. I need to get out of here. After changing, I go splash cold water on my face, and brush my teeth. There's still no sign of him. Alone in my room I sit on my bed, and wait. I wait for anything; a knock at the door, a call on the phone, I don't know what.

"Arrgh!" I moan. This is crazy. I don't know what to do. All I know is I need to hold it together until I can talk to him. I. Will. Not. Cry.

Those days are over.

I won't call him. Not for a while. He won't take my call anyway and I don't want to distract him anymore than he already is while he's driving. I decide on a walk to clear my head hoping the fresh air will give me a different perspective.

Once I'm out of my building, I don't know which way to go. I don't want to run into anyone, especially Logan, so I head in the direction opposite the student union. I don't bother to look where I'm going, it doesn't matter, I see a brown bunny hopping along. I follow it, jealous of its carefree nature. Wish I could just bounce through life. Frustrated I squeeze my eyes closed and center myself.

I open my eyes and find myself in front of the visitor parking lot. How did I not realize this is where I headed? I think my subconscious just wants to see with my own eyes that Jordan's car isn't here, that he could turn and leave me so easily, that nothing really changed between us.

Instead I'm feet away from his car. My Heart leaps into my throat. He didn't leave. I force myself to keep it together as I try to force my eyes away from Jordan sitting at the wheel.

The lump in the back of my throat is thick and makes swallowing hard. I stand frozen, wondering if I should turn back and wait for him in my room, or continue forward. Like he senses me the same way I sense him, Jordan turns to me, and our eyes lock. His eyes, those dark, piercing eyes reach under my skin, through my chest, and grip my heart. He uses them to coax me forward, toward him. It's a gravitational pull I can neither fight nor deny. I can't ignore him, can't pretend I'm not standing before him desperate to make things right.

With a mind of their own my feet move, first one, and then the other. A million thoughts race around my head. I'm not sure what I'm doing, or what I'll say, but I need to do something. I need to be next to him. I pull on the passenger door handle to see if it's unlocked. It is. I suck in one more breath of air before I get in. Jordan doesn't move. He doesn't acknowledge me at all. Not through words or a glance. He just sits there, focused on the section of the steering wheel he's tracing over with his pointer and middle fingers.

I'm not sure how long we continue the ignoring game; not speaking, not looking at each other, but it feels like hours. When the silence threatens to drive me into the land of the insane, I can't hold my tongue any longer.

"I'm not the only one with secrets you know."

"Don't try and shift the blame."

I can tell by the vitriol in his voice he's still seething. His eyes burn through me, and not in the way that turns me on and makes me gooey. His eyes don't smolder, as he trains them on me, instead they freeze over. I hug my arms around myself because I need to hold on to something, and I think it might help ease the chill between us.

"I'm not shifting blame, I'm stating a fact."

"Fact, you lied to me, and it changed everything between us. It changed my whole damn life, and I want to know why. Why didn't you tell me the truth?"

"Are you kidding?" His eyes narrow and he looks even more annoyed if that's possible. "Let's be honest. If I told you Charlie and I broke up because we were in his bed about to have sex and I said your name instead of his, what do you think would've happened?"

He squeezes his eyes shut and turns away. "I don't know."

"Well, I do. You would've backed away from me. Our occasional conversations would've become non-existent. You would've gone out of your way to make sure we didn't have the opportunity to spend time alone." He doesn't argue. I hope that means he's being objective. "I'm betting, it would've pushed our friendship past the breaking point."

He scrubs his hands over his face before turning back to me.

"You should've told me. If not then, you had plenty of opportunity to after the fact."

"I did tell you. Now. I didn't have to. I doubt you would've found out," I lie. "But I told you and look at how you're acting."

"Not now. At prom."

"Right. When you were throwing excuse after excuse out at me about how we shouldn't be together. When you tried every way you could to convince me you were turning me down for my own good."

"I was."

"No. You weren't. You've always had an issue with me or my age, it doesn't much matter because in the end . . ."

"In the end I've always been there for you. I've always been just a phone call away."

"Really?"

"Yes. Really."

I shake my head, annoyed, frustrated.

"It didn't feel that way this summer when you avoided me." Low blow. I shouldn't have said that. I wait for him to lash back at me, but he doesn't. He goes back to killing me with silence. "You knew how I felt about you. I never lied about it, and Lord knows, I was never good at hiding it. If you were too dense to know I loved you, then my telling you wouldn't have helped."

"Yes, I knew you liked me and I never, never turned my back on you. So why do you think it would've changed if you told me the truth?"

"Because look at us right now." I point between us. "You can barely look at me."

He shakes his head.

"Now you know the truth and you're ready to walk away."

"No, I'm not." He reaches for my hand and squeezes it, making my skin tingle. "I'm so mad at you right now. I am. But I'm not about to let you go."

His words just about undo me. "If you're not going to break up with me, why did you walk out? Why were you sitting here by yourself when you could've been with me trying to sort through this?"

"Because I needed to sort through it myself first. You want to know what would've been different? If I would've known the truth, maybe I would've broken up with Madison before your prom. Maybe the accident . . ."

"Don't. Go. There." I hate that everything always rounds back to the accident. It destroys me to have this front row view of him torturing himself. "You have to stop." I reach across him, place my hand on his cheek, and turn his face so he'll look at me. "You wouldn't have broken up with her."

"You don't know that."

I nod. "I do. You were upset and confused. You weren't sure what you wanted from her, but it didn't sound like you were ready to walk away. I was just a complication."

"You were never a complication."

"You weren't looking for the prom to be the beginning of a great romance between us, but the truth is I was. And if I told you and it made you change your mind, I don't think I would've taken it too well."

"At the time I knew you had a crush on me, but I thought that's all it was, just a little crush."

"That had been going on for years?"

"Yes. Because I'd been dealing with that, too. The night I found you, you were drunk. If I knew the circumstances, I would've realized it was much more than a simple crush."

"Exactly. That's why I couldn't tell you. And you volunteered to take me to prom. To. Prom! That was huge for me! I was afraid if you knew you'd change your mind and start avoiding me instead. I couldn't tell you."

He shakes his head. "I couldn't keep away from you. Even when you were younger. I tried my hardest to do the right thing and stay away, but I wanted you more. And I wanted you to have your special night."

"Then what's the problem?"

"I just wonder if everything would have been different if I knew and I went there with no strings, no attachments."

"Maybe you would've used her as an excuse not to go to the after party, not to spend any time alone with me that night. Either way it doesn't matter. We can't change the past. If we had any way to go back and avoid the accident, I would. I swear. Even if means we stop speaking, and you run off to marry Madison and live happily ever after. I hate seeing you so torn and hurt."

"I'm not the only one. I'm hurting you again."

"I'm a big girl, I'll deal."

He reaches his arm across my shoulders and pulls me close. "I don't want you to deal. I don't want to hurt you. I want to make you happy. I want to be the reason you smile."

"You are. You're just too dense to realize it."

Chapter 11

"Where are we going?" I ask as he pulls out of the parking lot.

"On a date. We haven't had a real date yet."

"What do you call prom night? That wasn't just a date. That was the ultimate date. And even though you didn't kiss me, I had the time of my life."

He pulls the car over to the side of the road, puts it in park and leans over, brushing a lock of hair behind my ear. His dark eyes mesmerize me, put me under a spell.

"We've done this all backwards. We've exchanged I love yous as we said goodbye. Our first kiss came months after we went to the prom together." He hesitates, and shakes his head. "We both came into this with baggage. I get it. I can't change my past any more than you could change yours. But maybe for today we can just go back to the beginning? Maybe we can go on a simple date?"

I nod and smile. "That sounds nice."

"Okay. Good. Do you think you can handle a long car ride with me?"

"Long? How long?"

"I don't know, forty minutes, an hour?"

"Where are we going?"

"To have some fun."

"Are you sure you're okay to drive?"

He takes my hand and squeezes it. "I can do anything as long as I know I have you by my side."

"Okay. Let me run back to my room and get my earbuds so I don't bug you too much."

"No." His eyes pierce mine. "We'll talk or listen to the radio. You control the music, and the volume."

My eyes opened wide. "Do you mean it?"

He pulls my head against his chest a moment and cradles it. "I may never be truly comfortable in the car, but I can't let fear control me. I can't let my life spiral out of control anymore."

I lift his hand to my lips. "Just know if it does, I'm here to pull you out of the free fall."

He shakes his head. "No, Steph. I'm not about to put that burden on you. Besides, I'm more frightened that if I don't get my act together, I'll drag you down with me. If I do, that's the one thing I won't ever be able to come back from."

"You're not burdening me, I'm volunteering. And I don't care where I go, as long as we go together."

*

Even though Jordan insists we can talk and listen to music, I know these things bother him, so I keep both to a minimum. I don't once reach for his hand and make a point not to speak unless the car stops. When we cross the border into upstate New York, I can't hold back any longer.

"You're really not going to tell me where we're going?"

He turns to me with a raised brow, his lips drawn into a mischievous grin, "If you wait long enough, good things will happen."

"Trying to put a positive spin on making me wait for you all these years?"

"You weren't the only one waiting," he says pulling into a mall parking lot.

"You're kidding, right? Please don't tell me you drove all this way so we could go to a mall. There's one ten minutes away from school."

"But that mall doesn't have what we came here for."

"And what's that?"

He ignores my question, parks the car, and cuts the engine. "I hope you're hungry."

I don't realize until he mentions it, but we didn't eat anything all day. My growling stomach answers for me. I'm not hungry; I'm starved. We get out of the car, and he leads the way into the mall. With my hand tucked in his, Jordan turns to the left. We ride a series of three short escalators up to our destination. As we climb each level, I look over at the large Ferris wheel to our right. I never saw one of those in a mall before. Maybe he plans on going for a ride after we eat.

We walk into the restaurant, and I still can't tell why he chose this place. I see nothing special about it. It's loud, and looks like every other restaurant/sports bar around, lots of television screens hang from the wall behind the bar tuned into Sunday football games. To the right of the bar are pool tables and what look like miniature shuffleboard tables set up in a lower level. He catches me looking, and follows my gaze.

"We'll eat first, then go play."

"Play pool?"

He answers with a smug smile, then points beyond the bar and restaurant to what I think is its end. A small archway leading into another room stands in the spot I would have expected the bathrooms to be.

"It's a really cool arcade."

"Okay, tough guy. Can't believe you brought me all this way to take me to an arcade." I admonish playfully.

A server greets us, leads us to a table and takes our drink order. I glance at my menu. It has the same options I can find at any other sports bar: wings, nachos, burgers. I place it on the table and look up into the eyes I love.

"So, this is our first official date, right?"

"Yes." He places his hand over mine, brushing his fingers over the back of my hand, his eyes caressing me.

"So I get to ask you questions that might be asked on a first date?"

His brows pull together. "What's wrong?"

I look away. I don't want to ruin our reconciliation, or our first official date, but I've been driving myself crazy ever since I saw them together at the bar.

"The other night, at the bar, there was a blonde girl. Who was she?"

"There were lots of girls there. And honestly, I didn't even notice most of them because you were the only girl on my mind, so I have no idea who you're talking about."

I fold my hands in front of my mouth trying my hardest to keep it shut. Drop it. Just drop it. I try to listen to the voice inside my head and end the uncomfortable conversation, but I can't let it go. Deep down, I know pursuing it might open a can of slimy, disgusting worms, but I need to do this. After a deep breath I continue.

"She was over by the bar when you went to get us drinks and the thing is, you were hugging each other. And it wasn't just a quick hug or someone there for the band infatuated by the way you played. I could tell you knew each other."

Jordan doesn't answer immediately. He hesitates, staring at me with a blank look on his face. I can't read him. Not at all.

"She was there for the band. And for me."

I look away, trying to hide the fear and panic in my eyes. I know they're there lurking, because my brain is flooded with them. But, I won't relinquish control. I won't let them take over.

Jordan takes my hand between both of his and strokes my thumb, sending soothing messages to my uptight and confused brain. She was there for him, I remind myself, and he didn't push her away or blow her off. She was there for him, and he's going to try and justify it to me.

"Look at me."

I don't want to. I want to bolt from my seat. Instead I do as he said because I can't resist him.

"She's Pete's girlfriend."

I release my breath. I hate being so afraid of losing him. I don't need a boyfriend to feel whole, I'm not one of those girls. But I do need Jordan. I need him in my life like water needs hydrogen. Without it, it's just oxygen, good and nourishing, but not at all what it's meant to be.

"Pete, the drummer?"

He nods, his flirtatious smile back in place. "She came to thank me and make sure I didn't screw up so badly they'd never be asked to play there again."

I smile. Crisis averted! Take that fear and panic; that will show you who's in control.

"Well, what did she think?"

"She thought we did well. And then I pointed you out to her. She thought you were pretty."

I know I should be happy and satisfied that she isn't anyone special. She has a drum beating boyfriend of her own, so there's no reason to think she has her sights set on mine, but then why would she care if I was pretty or not? She shouldn't. She shouldn't care that Jordan has a girlfriend at all.

*

We finish eating, and Jordan leads me through the doorway, into another world. The crowded room is a sensory buffet. Brightly colored lights flash and spin, loud music pumps through the air. The atmosphere is jubilant. It feels alive, like a throbbing piece of happiness.

Jordan brings us to a stop in front of a racing game, and settles himself into the seat.

"Come on." He pats the open spot next to him.

We each start building our own virtual custom kart choosing which exclusive features we prefer. He glances over at me, with a devilish grin as we whip our way around the laps of a virtual racetrack.

"Can't catch up?" He teases.

I pool together my internal resources to pretend I'm angry and shoot him a menacing look. I press the gas pedal down as far as it will go, shift the kart into overdrive and crash into a wall, flipping my vehicle over. Jordan turns to me with his confident, cocky smirk. As I get caught up losing myself in his eyes, he extends his lead.

"What's the matter? Can't catch me?" He teases.

I know he's going to win, but it's not like me to give up. Not where he's concerned.

"Beat you," he exclaims as he crosses the finish line.

"Rematch." I don't care if he beats me a thousand times. It will be worth it to keep him in this lighthearted mood.

He wins again, and again, all three times we race. I'm glad, because the entire time I pretend to focus on out maneuvering him, I steal peeks at him and catch the smile drawn up on his lips. That smile lights my world and makes me believe anything is possible. Just one glance at him and all the problems we had earlier in the day are long forgotten. Instead we're back to the playful banter that's defined our relationship for years.

"Okay, it's no fun beating you if you can't compete," he says getting out of his seat.

"I can beat you, I just haven't yet," I answer following him past the bar in the center of the room to another section of the arcade.

There stand new, spruced up, super-sized versions of old school games. We sit in front of a jumbo screen of a popular eighties game. Instead of taking turns, we play at the same time, on the same screen, trying to gobble up all the bright dots in the maze without getting eaten by a monster, or each other. We each win one game and decide to move on to a life size electronic version of an old board game.

"Ha. Take that loser," I taunt.

He doesn't want to spend much time here. I don't think he likes how little time it takes for me to outwit him and connect four of my pieces in a row to win.

The next challenge comes at a soccer game. The task: kick the soccer ball past the circling figure of the cartoon character to score goals. Jordan goes first and puts up an impressive number.

"Ten? That's all you're good for?" I ask determined to beat him.

"Go ahead hot shot, let's see what you could do."

Happy to accept his challenge, I step up to start line, kick the ball and score a goal. Easy as pie. I know I can take him!

My next attempt is blocked.

"That's it? That's the best you can do?" He goads.

The ball rolls back to me, and I bring my foot back as far as I can to kick it again. This time as I move my leg forward to make contact with the ball, my shoe gets stuck and flies off onto the four foot turf of the game. I lose my footing and feel myself falling backwards. My hands flail out on either side of me to help regain my balance, but it isn't working. Before I land on my backside, or make a complete fool of myself, strong arms circle around my waist and steady me. I allow myself to lean onto his solid chest as he guides me back to my feet.

Warmth spreads in places I don't expect as I breathe him in.

"I've got you," he whispers.

Hearing his soft voice I go limp in his arms. I turn my head and look up right into the welcoming darkness of

Jordan's eyes. The onyx diamonds sparkle and shine as they lock with mine. The world stops spinning. The people, the noise, they're gone. Vanished into thin air. In this moment we're all that exists. Just Jordan, me, and the violent thumping of my heart.

Thump. Thump. Thump.

He holds me tight against his chest and kisses the top of my head, making my heart skip and leap. This is everything I've ever wanted. I want to stay here, in his embrace and never leave. The timer on the game buzzes bringing me back to the noise and bright lights of the arcade. I look at the soccer game, ready to give it another go, but my turn ended. I only scored the one goal.

Jordan's arms release me. "Game over. I won."

"What?" My mouth opens wide, as I turn to face him. "You distracted me so I would lose?"

"Pretty much." He smirks. "If I wanted to win, I had to use any means necessary."

"Cheater!"

He laughs as he entwines our fingers. "Don't look so upset, it looked like you had the time of your life letting me win."

"Don't get used to it. I don't like to lose."

"In that case, we better get going while I still have bragging rights."

I don't argue. I let him lead me back through the archway and into the restaurant. Even though his arms are no longer around me, my heart hasn't stopped its wild sprint. I don't know what he plans to do next, but I hope it involves getting lost in his eyes once again.

"Ready?"

I nod. I am ready. Ready to follow him anywhere, to do anything he asks.

Chapter 12

Days pass. I can't say they fly by because as I sit and stare at my computer screen, the minutes drag. I've fallen into a routine. I try to get the bulk of my homework and reading done between Monday and Tuesday. These are the longest days because they are the furthest from the weekend. Jordan's been coming for an hour or two on Wednesday the last few weeks. It helps break up the monotony. It's not nearly enough time with him, but it's better than nothing.

I'm getting along better with my floor mates. Avery still hates me, and no one will talk to me when she's around. Luckily she's not here much. She spends most of her free time at the sorority house. I don't know which one. I just know the bitchiest girls are in it.

She's in tight with them. When she's not there, they spill into the dorm and overrun our hall. The other girls on the floor continue to treat her like queen shit when she's around, and she loves it. She flaunts her nasty-ass attitude just as often as she flaunts her body. But when she's not here, life is good. The other girls look to hang out with me, and I even get invited to sit with them at meals.

I'm bored. I call Maria, I'm not even sure why. She never has time for me anymore. She's Always with Rob. Or going to meet Rob, or obsessing that she can't find Rob. The few times we've actually connected over the last month, she's been in a rotten mood.

"What?"

"Way to make me feel good."

"Sorry, Steph. Can I call you back? I'm supposed to meet Rob."

Same old, same old. "Sure."

I don't hold my breath. She rarely ever calls back, and when she does, I often wish she didn't. These days we communicate more using funny faces and symbols through text messages than actual words. I pick up on her grumpiness even through those.

The only time that speeds by are the moments filled by Jordan. We have our quickie Wednesday visits, and all day Sundays. No many how many hours we spend with each other, it's never enough to satisfy me.

I shiver and decide to close my window. I love the fresh air, but it turned crisp almost overnight, and the leaves on the trees turned from their lush green color to hues of red, orange and yellow. Growing up in Brooklyn, I didn't have the privilege of witnessing the evolution of natural beauty like this. The ground isn't yet carpeted with leaves, but I see it happening in the near future. I watch a leaf wind surf on the cool, blustery breeze. It reminds me of a magic carpet. I wish I could I could band a bunch of them together and ride the wind.

A knock on my door startles me, pulls me away from the window and the leaves. Not expecting anyone, I look through the peephole to make sure it's not Logan. Breathing a sigh of relief I open the door to let Carla in just in time to hear the voice I dread.

"Is lover boy coming tonight?"

I turn to shut the door without answering Logan, but before I can close it, his hand is pushing it open.

"I never pegged you as a groupie."

I just stare at him.

"Seriously, you're totally head over heels for this guy and you're never with him. Don't you wonder what he does with all the girls throwing their panties at him?"

"You're an ass."

"Bet he has quite a collection." He smirks. "Any time you want to even the score, just call my name and I'll be happy to offer up my services."

"Get out of here."

"Truth hurt? Don't tell me you don't think about it when you're alone in bed at night. When no is there to touch you, that you don't imagine him fucking the girls showing him their tits."

"Maybe you're the insensitive jerk that would get off on that, but Jordan's not, and I trust him."

"How sure are you that he's Mr. Loyal?" Logan leans in. "Willing to bet on it? How about this, If you find out he's fucking someone else, you agree to a night with me."

"Get the hell out of here."

He smiles. "No problem. Avery's waiting for me anyway. But keep my offer in mind. It doesn't expire."

I slam the door just as my phone rings. Jordan. I close my eyes and answer. I need to hear his voice right now.

"How's the most beautiful girl in the world?"

Thump. Thump. Thump. I feel my heart pound against my chest.

"Better now."

"Liar. You sound pissed. I'm probably interrupting something."

"No. I really need to hear your voice."

"Oh, please. You don't even think of me anymore."

"Are you kidding?" I turn my back to Carla and lower my voice. "Can you come when you're done tonight? Please. I really need to see you." I know I sound pathetic. I don't care.

I just feel like I need to be with him, like we need to be with each other. "Sunday is two whole days away."

"I know, but since it's already Friday night, it's more like a day and a half."

"Come on, Jordan."

"Do you want me to come back later?" Carla interrupts.

"You have company?" Jordan asks at the same time.

I hold up my extended pointer finger to Carla for her to wait a minute, while I answer. I'm becoming good at this, whether it's Carla or Jonah, someone always seems to be around when he calls.

"Yes. Carla."

"Go have fun."

"No. Don't hang up yet." Something explodes like a firework inside my chest. Sadness? Disappointment? "Will I see you later?"

"No, baby. I'm sorry. It's not a good idea."

"Jordan!" I want to order him to come, but then I'll be acting like a baby, like a spoiled brat, and I refuse to give him any sort of age ammunition to hold against me.

"I have to go, Steph. I love you."

The call ends. I have no reason to be upset, but I am. Right now I just want to go home.

"Are you okay?" Carla asks.

With my eyes on the ground I nod.

"Ignore Logan. He just does it because he knows it bothers you. It looks like you could use a little fun. Come on." She takes my hand and drags me out of my room.

*

My phone vibrates in my pocket. I perk up, it's Jordan. I know it is. No one else calls this late. I hate to admit it, but I've been waiting for him to call back since we hung up. I hope he changed his mind and is on his way here right now. The excitement inside me is bubbling against my chest at the sound of the ring tone. I pull the phone out, but before I have a chance to answer Jonah snatches it from my hand, holding it high above my head.

"Nope. Can't answer in the middle of the game or else you forfeit."

"Stop. Give me the phone."

"Not until you say it."

"No, Stephanie! We'll never hear the end of it," Carla yells.

"I'm not going to say it."

"Come on, Steph. It won't hurt, I promise." His eyes twinkle. "They're only words. Repeat after me, Jonah is my god and my king."

"My phone."

He turns serious as he starts to lower his hand, then hesitates and stares at me. I can only imagine he's deciding whether or not to give in.

"Don't give it to her," Ian yells. "Make her beg."

I shoot him a warning look. I'd expect that from Logan, but Ian? I thought Ian was a decent, likable guy. I guess since Logan's off with Avery Ian has decided to take his place.

"Jonah!" I order, hoping he'll understand I'm not about to beg. If he doesn't hand it over right now, I'm going to kick him in the shin. Hard.

"Don't worry. He'll wait for you." Jonah's mouth twists into a funny expression I don't recognize. "Anyone with half a brain would."

He knows it's Jordan, too. The fact that Jonah knows who's on the other end and still hasn't handed over the phone frustrates me. I ball up my fists, hoping he could see things between us are escalating.

"It's not funny anymore."

That had been the point to this crazy challenge. Carla and her roommate Eve invited Jonah, Ian and a few other guys from the adjoining hall to hang out. Everyone's gone now, but Jonah, Ian, and me. The game had been Carla's idea. Boys vs. girls. One side had to do their best to get all the members of the other team to laugh in under a minute. The idea wasn't original, but it did keep us amused on a Friday night. Nothing like a bit of nerd humor to pass the time.

Jonah, shakes his head and hands it over. "Whatever."

With the phone in hand I step out of Carla's room and close the door behind me. I don't bother listening to my voice mail. Instead, I call him right back. I smile when I hear his voice, and suddenly the world feels like a much friendlier place.

Jordan answers on the first ring. "I didn't wake you did I?"

"No. We were hanging out in Carla's room."

"Oh, good. I hope you girls had fun."

The squeal is sudden, loud, and piercing. The real surprise is that the ridiculous sound is coming from my mouth. Without warning, my feet are off the ground, and my heart is racing.

"Jonah, put me down!" I scream as he flings me over his shoulder.

"Not yet. The games not over, we're just taking a break."

"I said put me down!"

Once we're back in Carla's room my feet hit the ground again, and I put the phone back up to my ear.

". . . going on?"

He sounds annoyed. I can't say I blame him. I'm annoyed too. I take a deep breath before I answer.

"Sorry," I say, attitude heavy in my words. "I'm back."

"Are you okay?"

"Fine. We were just in the middle of a game when you called."

"I thought you were with Carla?"

I clear my throat. "We're in Carla's room, but there's a bunch of us."

"Mm hmm. No problem. I'll talk to you tomorrow."

"What? No. Please don't be mad."

"I'm not, babe. Like I said when you started screaming, I only have a minute to talk. Hold on," I can't tell if he's lying or not. Someone's speaking to him, but the voice is muffled, so I can't hear what's being said. What I can hear is that the voice is female. "Yeah, I'll be there in a minute." I can't help it. I hear Logan's voice in my head. My heart twangs a bit. I don't say anything and wait for him to return his attention to me. "Steph?"

"Be right where? What's going on?"

"Nothing." His voice is lighter than it was a moment ago. "I'll let you get back to your friends."

"What if I don't want to?"

He chuckles. "Go have fun, Stephanie. I promise, everything is fine. I'm just grabbing a bite to eat with the guys."

I know it's not just the guys. I look at Jonah and Ian. This is innocent fun. I shouldn't assume he's up to no good.

"Is Blaze there?"

He pauses, and I have that sinking feeling in my stomach. I know I have no reason not to trust Jordan. I do trust him. With my life. But Blaze makes my skin crawl, him and his porn-star-wanna-be girlfriends.

"Yeah, it's all of us, including Pete."

A soon as I hear Pete's name my mind races to his girlfriend. The girl I hate because I can't erase the image of her in my boyfriend's arms.

"Are the girlfriends there, too?"

He takes a long breath, before answering. When he does I hear a touch of melancholy. "Yes. I'm the only one without my better half."

I should feel flattered that he just paid me a compliment, that he sounds sad, like he misses me. Instead I can't get my mind off of her. She shouldn't bother me, but there's more to Jordan's relationship with her that he's not telling me.

"Steph," his voice is serious again. "Maria and Rob didn't break up, did they?"

"No, why?"

"He's here with someone, and she's definitely not Maria."

That sinking feeling I have grows and spreads like a virus.

"Maybe she's just a friend?"

I try to give him the benefit of the doubt. Rob wouldn't cheat on Maria. They're perfect together, always laughing, always all over each other.

"Trust me. This girl is a lot more than a friend."

I think about how crazy Maria's been acting lately. Is this why? Does she suspect he's cheating on her? If so, why hasn't she told me?

"C'mon, Stephanie. We need to finish." Eve calls. "We can't end the game in a tie."

I place my hand over the phone's microphone. "Play without me."

"Shit. He just saw me."

"And?"

"Nothing. He moved away from her, and now he's watching me, like that makes a difference. Listen, why don't you go back to your friends and have some fun. Besides, I have a feeling Maria is going to be looking for you tomorrow."

"Jordan, you're not going to tell her are you?" My throat is constricting and for all the wrong reasons.

"You don't think she should know?"

"I do, but . . ." I think back to when Jordan warned me about Chris. I wanted to crawl into his arms, nuzzle my face into his chest and stay there forever. I didn't of course, but Maria, she just might. I squeeze my eyes and swallow hard pushing back my insecurity. I know I'm strong, so why do I feel so damn weak? Why does being in a relationship with Jordan leave me more high strung than not being in one with him at all?

"I don't know. Just don't do anything yet. Sleep on it before you decide."

I won't influence his decision. It's the wrong thing to do. I always regret the stupid decisions I make bred out of insecurity. We're friends first and foremost, the three of us. And I know without a doubt he and Maria are the two people I trust the most.

After we hang up, I can't shake the feeling of doom swirling around inside me. I tell myself it's about Maria. When she finds out Rob is cheating on her, it will break her heart. So why do I want to cry? The more I think about it, the more I internalize the feeling and I know I'm not just upset for her. Still, I repeat over and over inside my head that all is good in my world. I'm just sad for my friend. I keep saying it in the hopes that I'll grow to believe it. In the meantime, I close my eyes and pray Maria is the only one that will end up broken hearted.

Chapter 13

The ringing of my phone startles me. I shake my head, knowing it's not a happy ring. I don't know how I know, but I do. I close the book I'm reading, wishing I didn't have to take this call, but I won't be able to live with myself if I don't.

"I need you. When am I going to see you?" Yep this is the call I dreaded.

"Um, I'm not sure. I'm stuck until I can get a lift home, but if you can get here I'd love for you to visit."

Silence.

The sniffling starts and I'm sure the tears will follow in a moment. I'm right, she's all out crying now. And I can tell by the sadness in her voice, and how quick she went from sniffles to snot and tears, it's been going on for a while.

"I can't believe he broke up with me. We've been together over six months, I thought he was the one."

"I'm sorry." I consider reminding her by the way she flirted with Jonah, there's been trouble in paradise for a while. That's not what she needs now. Instead I listen and agree with her. I hold my tongue. I very nearly bite it off trying to be the friends she needs.

"What am I going to do?" Sniffle. "I have to see him and his new slut at school every day." Sobs. Long, loud sobs. "I knew something was up. The way she'd always come and talk to him when she'd see us together. And the way he'd look at her, like he wanted to fuck her, right there in front of me."

I want to ask Maria how she thinks Rob would've felt about the way she hung all over Jonah. But that's not what I'm supposed to do. Right now it's my job, my duty to tell her what a jerk Rob is. How he's making the worst mistake of his life, and when he eventually figures it out it will be too late.

"My mother will freak if I drive all the way to New Jersey. Especially since I can't stop crying. Maybe I can catch a ride with Jordan. Can he pick me up tonight?"

Great. Just as I thought, she's going to look to lean on him. I need to get the green-eyed monster inside of me under control.

"No. He's not coming."

"But it's Saturday."

I don't want to get into this. The last thing I want to do is explain to Maria that for the last month Jordan refuses to spend the night with me since he woke and almost single handedly rearranged my face. I don't want to hear her criticize Jordan, and even worse, I don't want to give her an excuse to call him and involve herself where she's not needed.

"They have a gig and it's going to end late, so we decided it would be better if he doesn't come tonight. He'll be here tomorrow."

"Oh." Her voice is low, defeated.

"But, we can talk all night."

"You probably think I'm an idiot, huh?"

"No. Why?"

"I was just thinking, I don't think I remember you ever crying over a break-up."

Of course not, the only time I ever cried over a break-up Jordan showed up to save the day, and the moment I saw him, Charlie was all but forgotten. The others just didn't matter. I do, however, remember crying my eyes out this summer over Jordan. Only I didn't reach out to talk, I waited until I was alone in my room. I'd lie on my bed, ball myself up, and pull the covers over my head. I cried because I faked living through the day and it caught up to me at night. I cried because I ached for him so bad, I thought if I allowed the tears to escape, the pain and pressure in my chest might ease. I cried because I couldn't help myself. Alone, in the dark I tried to rid myself of all the pain, all the hurt. The problem was, just like my love for him, there was no end to it.

"Listen, Maria. I know you love Rob. And I know you gave him everything you possibly could. Everything. And for that he was incredibly lucky. But now you can see him for what he really is. A giant ass. He's a big, old, stinky one, too. And who wants to hang around with a smelly ass, let alone kiss one?"

I hear a snicker and know I'm on the right path.

"And if this girl he left you for likes the smell and taste of shit, then let her have him. He'll only turn around and do the same thing to her. Unless she does it first. Oh wait," I conjure up as much excitement as I can. "Maybe what she does is weed out the shit-heads that don't know how good they have it, lures them away, and then brings them to a giant dump that stinks so bad, no one will ever go near them again."

I hear a short, but quick breath on her end. The crying stopped. One point for me.

"I hope so."

"Don't waste your tears on him. Because if he could want to be with some disgusting skank when he had someone as terrific as you, he doesn't deserve you. And why's that? Cause he's a shit-head, and you're too smart to be with such an idiot."

I hear the hint of a giggle.

"You're sure Jordan's not coming tonight?"

"I'm sure."

"Good, then I won't be interrupting. Let me go make a few calls, but don't make plans, I'm spending the night."

*

Twenty minutes after I hang up with Maria there's a knock on my door. It can't be her, unless she tele-ported herself. It's otherwise impossible for her to make it here in such a short time. I open the door and find Jonah on the other side.

"Are you ready yet?"

"For?"

"To go get Maria?"

What?

"We're going to get her so she can hang out with us."

With us? Why don't I like the sound of that? Now instead of being supportive of my best friend, I'm a little pissed. She should have given me the heads up that she called Jonah and asked him to pick her up. I wonder if he said yes right away or if she had to bribe him. And what did she put on the auctioning block?

"I don't know. If she called you, maybe you should go without me." Whatever her scheme is, I don't want to be part of it, and I don't want to be part of an "us" with Jonah.

"Nuh uh, you're coming, that's the deal. This way you can give me directions."

"You can put her address into GPS."

"Yes, but I want company for the ride there."

"Can't you drag Logan?"

"I can, but don't you think it'll come out that you live right next door to her? Do you really want him to know where you live?"

I can't argue. The last thing I need when go home for break or over the summer is to find Logan standing on the other side of my door. Been there, done that.

"Fine. I grab my sweatshirt and phone before closing the door behind me.

Once we're in the car, I text Jordan and tell him what's going on.

If you're leaving now, you should be in Brooklyn before we go on. Maybe you can swing by and sneak in a little kiss?

I feel giddy inside. The thought of seeing Jordan brings a smile to my face.

Ok, I'll ask.

Now I want to go. I'm jumping up and down inside.

*

The ride home reminds me a lot of the first time Jonah drove me back to Brooklyn. It's full of talk about art mediums and perspective. He tells me about a show coming up that he was invited to participate in. I nod my head and honestly try to listen, but instead of focusing on what Jonah is saying, I'm thinking of the best way to ask him if he can drive by the club the band is playing at tonight.

And then it hits me; all the air in my sails disappears. I can't possibly go get Maria without stopping at home to see my mother. She didn't visit today because Eddie surprised her with tickets to a Matinee showing of her favorite Broadway play. I miss her, but my body is craving Jordan. Besides, Mom and I just had a nice day shopping together last Saturday. Still there's no way I can choose Jordan over my mother, she'll never let me live that one down.

The car is stopped at a red light. We're about ten minutes away from home, and I feel Jonah's eyes on me. "Everything all right?"

"Yep." I decide to lay it out for him. "I was going to ask if we could pass by the club Jordan's playing at so I could say hi, but I just realized I'm going to have to spend some time at home with my mother."

"Is there a reason why we can't do both?"

"Do you mean it?" I feel my body rising up, inflating itself once again.

He shrugs. "Why not?"

I throw my arms around him and kiss his cheek.

Maria's on the porch with a bag slung over her shoulder when we pull up. She heads down the steps the second the car comes to a standstill. I'm surprised she's actually wearing make-up. The way she cried earlier, I thought she'd be bare faced for at least a week before she found enough control to fight back the bouts of tears.

I don't say anything, just throw my arms around her once we're out of the car, and pull her into a long embrace. She melts into me as we rock back and forth, and then she sets her sights on Jonah. If I didn't know better, I'd think she's completely over Rob. My little pep talk didn't just work, it pulled out a miracle.

"Where are you going?" Maria asks as I head up the stairs to my front door.

"I have to see my mother."

"Oh."

I ring the bell and try to come up with an excuse to cut my visit short. Before I think of anything good, Mom answers the door. She's wearing a fuzzy, blue robe and a deep shade of crimson colors her cheeks.

Surprise, surprise.

She didn't expect me. And I didn't expect to find her having her own Saturday night fun. Good thing I left my house keys in my desk drawer. Mom pulls the door open for me to come in. I step inside the hall, but don't dare take a step any further. There's nothing in there that I need to see. In fact, seeing anything more can only scar me for life.

"My friend Jonah and I came to pick Maria up," I explain. "And I couldn't be here without saying 'hi'."

"Oh. Do you want to invite your friend in?" She clears her throat and looks down as she tightens the tie on her robe. "I can go change."

"No, Mom." We're both too embarrassed to look each other in the eye. "Besides, Jordan's expecting me to stop by for a minute, so I should get going."

I give my mother another hug and kiss, keeping the visit short and sweet. I scurry down the porch steps, hoping I can find some way to erase the image of her post sex, or mid sex, or whatever the hell that look was.

*

On my way

I text Jordan as the car pulls away from my house.

"Thank you so much Jonah." Maria leans forward in her seat.

"No problem. So any idea about what you want to do when get back to school?" He looks at her through the rearview mirror as he speaks, and I wonder why she's in the back and I'm sitting next to him.

"You're the big man on campus. Are we going to party tonight?"

"He's an RA, he doesn't help us party, he's supposed to stop us from having fun and make sure we spend our nights bored and sober."

"What?" Jonah shoots me a look like I just insulted him. "That's not fair. When have I stopped you from having fun?"

"You haven't yet . . ."

"Yet?" Maria asks, "Do you guys hang out a lot?"

"Depends on what you qualify as a lot. I save her nightly from wandering the halls like a lost puppy."

"You're such a liar! I never wander the halls! And who are you calling a lost puppy?"

"First of all, never use absolutes. When you use words like always and never, the statement is bound to be untrue. Second, you have nothing to be embarrassed, of. Maria's your friend." I want to slap the sarcastic grin on his face right off.

"So what you hang out every day?"

I hear an undercurrent of something in her voice. Judgement? Jealousy? Whatever it is, I don't like it. What I do at school and who I do it with is none of her business. In fact she's one of the reasons I couldn't wait to break away. Her and the shadow she always casts over me.

"We have breakfast and dinner together almost every day," Jonah explains.

"Really?"

And there it is again, that hint of something saying she doesn't approve. Well if she doesn't like the idea of Jonah, she shouldn't have called and asked him for a ride. At least I have an excuse to be friends with him. She has nothing. And now that I think of it, I'm seriously pissed she had the nerve to call him. I know I should be sympathetic, but she's making it incredibly difficult.

"I'm her security blanket." Jonah says using the mirror to meet her eyes again. "In other words, Stephanie just uses me when she has nothing better to do."

That catches my attention. "That's not true!"

"Yes, it is. You use me for company in the cafeteria, or when you need a ride to see your boyfriend, like right now. And most of all you use me to keep your sanity when Logan's on the prowl."

"Now that I know you think I use you, I'll try not to bother you so much."

"Who said you bother me? Facts are facts and these can't be disputed. Is it not a fact that I'm driving you to see Jordan as we speak?"

"Yes."

"Is it also a fact that you come ask me to eat with you so you don't have to eat alone?"

"I guess."

"Yes or no?"

I don't realize that Maria is completely out of the conversation at this point and Jonah's focus is now one hundred percent on me.

"And who keeps Logan in line for you?"

I hate that he just proved his point.

"You do."

"And who's your hero right now? Right this minute?" He asks as he pulls his car to a stop. I look out the window to see where we are. Jordan's parked car is right next to us in front of the bar. "That's fine, you don't have to answer," he says before I can respond. "Just let lover boy know you're here."

I send Jordan a message and get out of Jonah's car.

The door to the bar opens. My heart races and leaps, skipping at least one beat along the way. The crooked smile I long for spreads across Jordan's face when his dark eyes meet mine. He stalks toward me with a steady confidence, like a sleek, dangerous cat. Before I can think clearly, he's in front of me, against me, heating me up in the cool October air. His hands are on the back of my neck, pulling me in to meet his lips. Time stops. People disappear. We're no longer the nobodies cast in the low budget B film I once imagined us to be. No, this is now an epic romance that will stand the test of time. We are prime time. A-list actors only.

He pulls his lips a centimeter away from mine, and I let out a breath, the breath I've been holding since I saw him. His eyes crawl over me, from top to bottom, as he shakes his head and bites his lip backing me into the cool metal of his car.

"You look hot," His words are soft, low.

"So do you."

He uses his arms to cage me in. "You need to come home more often."

I don't answer. Instead I enjoy the feel of him leaning against me, his lips trailing feather-light kisses along my neck line.

I'm not sure if I'm hot or cold as my skin tingles beneath his lips causing heat to surge on the inside and goose bumps to form on the outside. Whatever I feel, whatever he's causing, I don't want it to stop. I lean forward a little and bring my lips to the dip between his neck and shoulder. Without thinking, I open my mouth and nibble at him gently as my tongue swirls on his skin, tasting him, drinking him in.

He lets out a throaty groan. "Don't," he whispers, his voice deep. "You can't get me crazy like this and just leave. Especially when my night hasn't even started."

I offer him a sad smile, realizing our time together is about to come to an end, and hating that I can't stay. "Sorry."

He shakes his head, "There's nothing to be sorry about. I'm glad I got to see you for a minute. It's like getting a fix to help me through the night."

We spend another minute wrapped up in each other, hands, mouths, and bodies mixing, clashing, clutching, trying to get their fill before Jordan says goodbye and pulls away. I want to reach out and pull him back as he turns and takes a step toward the bar. Instead I know I have to leave and head in the opposite direction.

That's when I spot it. It should be inconsequential, but it's not. Cars have flyers stuck under the windshield wipers all the time in Brooklyn. But I feel it in my gut that this isn't what I'm seeing. I don't understand how I know, but I do, this is bad.

One time when I went to the store for my mother, I came back to my car and found a folded note on the windshield, just like the one I see on his. Some guy saw me and left his number along with a message to call him.

I assume that's what this is. Some girl probably saw Jordan when he arrived, left her number for him on the paper, and tucked it neatly under the wiper. What if this isn't the first time? I don't know why, but I peek into the car before I say anything. I see a bunch of crumpled up papers on the floor. My heart sinks. I wonder how many girls that is, and why he hasn't thrown them away.

"You don't mind if I get rid of this for you?" I call out as I pull the paper from under the windshield wiper. Jordan turns, and a look of horror crosses his face.

"No, Steph." He lunges back and before I could open and read it, he rips it out of my hand.

"What the hell?"

"It's nothing. Just garbage."

I narrow my eyes at him. He wouldn't react that way over nothing. "Is it from a girl? A number or a love letter?"

"Love letter? What? No." He forces an uncomfortable laugh as he crumples it without even looking.

"Then why'd you race back before I could see what it said? What didn't you want me to see?"

"Nothing. Why are you getting so riled up over something that means absolutely nothing to me?"

My stomach is queasy. He's lying. I know despite his protests and denials, that paper is a big, huge deal.

"Because you're acting strange. Maybe even suspicious."

"Listen, I don't care who wrote it or what it says," he smiles and pulls me into his arms. "If you wrote it I'd care. But since you're acting all crazy, I'm guessing it's not from you. Am I right?"

I nod.

"Then just forget it. I love you, Stephanie." His thumb brushes my cheek. "Only you. Until the end of forever, right?"

"Right." I say, but suddenly I'm not sure I believe it.

"Now please, get going so I can go back inside and concentrate."

I don't say anything. I don't dare move. I just stare at him.

"The sooner we get through tonight, the sooner tomorrow will be here, and we'll be together again."

He steps up and engages me in one more deep, hard kiss on the lips, and then he and the mysterious paper are gone. I watch him walk backwards into the bar, his eyes holding mine until he gets to the door. A million and one questions run through my mind. The most pressing one, what was on that paper?

I climb back into the car, feeling sick and sluggish with the weight of the world on my shoulders. He lied to me. He lied to my face without hesitation, and I can feel nausea working it's way up from my stomach into my throat. I hug my arms tight around my belly as if that will somehow make things better.

*

I'm numb. It's a feeling I'm all too familiar with. Every time I feel this empty feeling, like I'm about to fall off the edge of the planet, it has something to do with Jordan. Maria moved into the front seat with Jonah before I got back in the car. I'm glad. Maybe they'll forget me for a while.

"Everything okay, Steph?" She turns back to ask.

"Yeah, fine." I hope she'll leave it at that. "Thanks again, Jonah."

"No problem."

I look out the window as the conversation picks back up between them. It's one I'd have no interest in joining even if I weren't feeling dead inside. They're disagreeing about the old-time playwrights such as Shakespeare and Chekhov.

"Are you kidding, these plays have no place in the world today. People can't relate to the characters."

"Of course they do! Why else would people flock to see the Royal Shakespeare Company perform, or better yet have you ever heard of Shakespeare in the Park?" Maria asks.

"Shakespeare is the most overrated playwright ever. The ideas for his plays aren't even original. That's why the plays in the park are free. People go because they have nothing better to do."

I tune them out. I could care less about work written hundreds of years ago. I'm solely focused on another piece of writing. The writing on the paper I found stuck on Jordan's windshield, and on the crumpled papers on the floor of his car. I close my eyes and try to devise a plan that will give me an opportunity to sneak one of them out without Jordan realizing it. No matter what I come up with, I can't find a reason to be in his car without him. Even if we go somewhere and I leave my pocket book back in my room, there's no reason for Jordan to go back and get it without me. Not unless I couldn't go back for some reason, like if we're going somewhere and just as we get to the car I twist my ankle.

As we leave Brooklyn in the dust, I work out the details in my head.

Chapter 14

I'm dancing with a giraffe. First, I drove through a safari, and then I pulled this huge, long, green leaf out of my pocketbook to feed it, and now, he's standing on his hind legs with his front paws on my shoulders. This should make him taller, but for some reason he's not, he's shorter, and we're dancing.

"Answer the phone already."

The music is getting louder. I'm sucked through a black hole. Everything is dark around me and someone is shaking my arm. I still hear the music, but the giraffe is gone.

"Stephanie!"

I open my eyes, confused, and look around at the mess. Wow! That's the last time I hit the hard stuff. Once we got back to school, Jonah sent Maria and me to wait for him in my room. When he came back, he did so with two six packs of beer and a bottle of OR~G hidden in his backpack, and Logan by his side. I almost slammed the door in his face when I saw Logan, but Jonah promised Logan would behave himself, and Logan swore he wouldn't get out of line. Still I didn't like the prospect of having him in my room let alone drinking with him, but Maria seized the opportunity to have yet one more option available for project forget Rob.

I warned her that Logan was not only an idiot, but a taken idiot. Whatever they call the status of their relationship, Logan and Avery are together.

"Answer the phone so I can go back to sleep."

I listen for a moment to hear where the music is coming from so I can locate my phone. It's on the bed next to me. I grab it, hoping to answer before it goes to voicemail. It's already after eleven in the afternoon.

"Hey cutie."

My stomach swirls at the sound of Jordan's voice with a combination of excitement and guilt.

"Hi."

"Did you girls have fun last night?"

"Um," I look around my room at the empty beer bottles. I need to get rid of those before he gets here. "Yes."

"Is that why you didn't answer my texts?"

I hear the vulnerability in his voice. Shit, Shit, shit!

"No. I just didn't hear them. Sorry."

"Didn't hear them, what were you doing? Having a pillow fight?"

"You wish." I hesitate saying anything more. I can't give him an honest answer to that question. I can, but I don't want to. Not yet. "Not much." Just getting drunk in my room, and then trying to stop Maria from stripping down and skinny dipping in the fountain. I didn't do anything wrong, so why do I have this uncomfortable feeling gnawing my gut like an infestation of termites in a wood framed house?

I messed up. I let Maria talk me into having a drink. If only I stopped at one. That part is on me. I don't want Jordan to know I broke my promise to him. And how understanding do I expect him to be if I explain we drank so much, I forgot to take my phone and my shoes with me when we chased after Maria?

"Steph, are you still mad? I hated leaving things like that last night."

"I'm not mad."

"Are you sure?"

"Yes. With Maria here, things just got a little out of hand."

"Not so out of hand that you're not up to seeing me I hope."

"Of course not."

"Good. Because I'm here."

"Here?" I shriek looking around the room. He usually comes around noon.

"Come open the door and let me in."

I'm not sure if he means the door to the dorm or the door to my room. Either way I'm hoping for a miracle. "Sure, give me a minute." Without waiting for an answer, or letting on how panicked I am, I end the call.

I give Maria a shove. "Jordan's here and I have no time to clean up," I whisper as loud as I can in case he's standing outside my room. She groans, and I shove her harder.

"Get up!"

"No." She rolls over.

"Come on, Maria. You have to help me. Clean up while I stall him."

Another groan leaves her mouth as I peek in the mirror. I'm not about to win any beauty contests with my hair looking disheveled. I reach over onto my desk for a hair tie and sweep it into a ponytail. That will have to do for the moment. And it serves as an excuse for taking so long.

I open my door and freeze before pulling it closed behind me. Jordan is standing on the other side holding a small vase with half a dozen red carnations, and a panty dropping smile.

Thump, thump, thump.

I hear my heart in my ears, feel it up in my throat. I lose myself, my thoughts, in his eyes and forget that I'm trying to stall. I forget how much he upset me last night. I bury the fact that he's hiding something from me and take a deep breath as I stare at him feeling the butterflies in my belly wake and flutter. This feeling, this internal mania he brings out with a simple look or touch is addicting. It's more addicting than drugs or an athlete's endorphin release. He is my personal supply of life sustaining oxygen, of my all-consuming happy.

"I love these skimpy getups you wear." His smoldering eyes take their time skimming over my body, making me even more aware of my erratic heartbeat. His free hand rests on my hip making my skin below it tingle as he bends slightly to kiss me on the lips. "How's she doing?" He motions towards my door with his head.

"She's okay. She didn't talk about him, didn't cry, it was like she erased all memories and thoughts of him."

"You know it was all an act. No way she's over him already."

I nod. "I guess."

"She didn't say anything about him?"

"Not one word. She was ugly crying on the phone so I expected a long night of tears and hugs, and maybe even an ice cream run. But she was fine."

"Ice cream run? Does that mean Jonah stayed with you?" Jordan asks knowing I have no other access to a car.

I shrug like it's no big deal since in reality, it isn't any big deal. "She asked him to. And it wouldn't be right to ditch him after he went to get her, and brought me to see you."

His eyes dart to the side. "Guess he's an all-around great guy."

Sarcasm. Heavy, biting sarcasm. I choose to ignore it. Instead I take the flowers and bring them to my nose before offering a smile, hoping I've stalled long enough for the beer bottles to magically disappear. "Thanks for these. I love them."

"Sorry they're not long stem roses."

"It doesn't matter. Besides, flowers all die."

I can tell by the strange look he's giving me I need to explain.

"They're a nice gift, but no matter how much you love them or how hard you try to keep them looking fresh and perky, they all die eventually."

His eyes narrow. "Are you always this negative?"

"Death magnet, remember?"

He chuckles. "Yeah, but you're my death magnet. I thought that should count for something.

"Of course it does. I just mean why waste the money on roses when carnations are just as good?"

He reaches for my arms, and pulls me by the elbows close to him. "Because it's not a waste if it makes you happy. Nothing is ever a waste when I buy it for you. It's a privilege. Now, are you going to let me in, or are we going to spend the day here in the hall?"

"Sorry. I just wanted to give her a minute to get dressed."

"Dressed?" The eyebrow is raised, and the smirk is on his lips. "Don't let me interrupt. Please, go back to what you were doing. I'll just sit quietly and watch."

"Sleeping. That's what we were doing." I shove his chest. "That's all we were doing."

I Spin around and open the door. Maria is sitting at the edge of the bed looking a little green. A quick glance around my room tells me I have nothing to worry about. She got rid of all the incriminating evidence, except for how awful she looks. That could easily be blamed on her crying, if only I hadn't just admitted she didn't cry at all. She sees us and shakes her head.

"Do you have to be such a morning person?" She asks. Her eyes are red, and the bags beneath them could hold enough luggage for a family of five.

"It's not that early," Jordan answers.

She lays back down, "Too early for company. I'm going back to sleep."

"You have half an hour. Then we leave."

"You're going home?" I'm deflated. Suddenly the flowers aren't as pretty, and they don't smell as nice. "Why?"

"Of course not." He wraps his arm around my waist and pulls me close. "You're not getting rid of me that easy. We're going out."

"Out? Where?"

"You'll have to wait and see."

*

We trudge to Jordan's car. Actually he and I walk, Maria trudges. She's still tired and ornery. He hasn't said anything about it yet, but the angry glances shot my way every now and again tell me he knows she didn't drink alone. I wish he'd just come out and confront me. I have no problem admitting it to him, I just didn't want him to see so many empty bottles before we had a chance to discuss it. Besides, I'm not nasty and hung over like Maria. I'm sure he can see that.

I try to push these thoughts from my mind. I don't want to think about last night, or have to explain anything to Jordan. I just want to come up with a plan to manipulate the situation so I can be alone in his car. None of us speak as we climb in. My eyes drop to the floor where I saw those crumpled pieces of paper. They're gone. Great.

"Do you have an extra pair of sunglasses in here?"

The dirty look comes my way even though Maria asked the question.

"Maybe next time you shouldn't drink so much." He looks at her through the rear view mirror. Ah there it is, the elephant in the room, or in our case, the car.

"Seriously? Since when did you become such a control freak? You tell her when to breathe, too?"

"Shut up, Maria. You know I'm not a control freak, but whatever understanding Stephanie and I have between us, you should stay out of it."

"Understanding? The way I see it you're the one out at bars and clubs every weekend doing whatever and whoever you want. Whatever understanding you have is bullshit, so back the fuck off."

I hear the sharp intake of breath next to me, and place my hand on his thigh to get his attention. I know she's upset and hurt right now, and Jordan is a convenient outlet for both of those things, especially because he's a guy.

"For you to be this hung over, you didn't just have a beer or two. You had to have a hell of a lot more than that."

"So what? I let off some steam."

He shakes his head in disapproval. "Next time you look to let off steam leave Stephanie out of it."

"Hello, I'm here, remember?" I can't keep my mouth shut any longer. "Stop talking like I don't have a mind, or mouth to speak for myself."

They both stop and look away, as if they each retreated back to their corners in a boxing ring. I know they're not really arguing over me. I know what's behind Maria's foul mood, but I'm not sure the real reason behind Jordan's.

I turn my body around to the back seat. "Did you take anything before we left?"

"You mean like a shot of something strong enough to bring back my buzz? Nah, not yet."

"No. I mean something to help your head stop pounding."

"No."

"Would you mind stopping off somewhere so she could get some ibuprofen?"

He sighs, letting me know he's annoyed, but agrees. Jordan pulls into a strip mall and parks the car in front of a large pharmacy. Maria opens her door and curses as she stumbles out.

"Wait here." Jordan squeezes my hand. "I should apologize."

"Sure. Go ahead."

Great I found a way to be alone in his car, but now I no longer need to be. I make a face as they walk into the store. I can't believe he cleaned it out before coming. That makes me even more suspicious. I don't know what possesses me to do it, but I push my seat back as far as it can go and reach my hand underneath. I'm about to give up when the tip of my pointer finger brushes against something that feels a lot like paper. I stretch a little further, and shifting my weight forward I'm able to grasp it. I pinch my thumb and forefinger closed and pull the crumpled ball out from beneath the seat.

Bingo!

I glance up and peek out the front windshield. People are in line at the cashier, I can see them through the store window, but Maria and Jordan aren't there yet. I'm nervous, scared of getting caught, as if I'm about to sit in the living room and thumb through a pile of porn while my mother cooks in the next room. I've never done that, but I imagine this is what it would feel like.

There's no sign of them. I have to make it quick. I should have enough time to read what it says, and then I can toss it in Jordan's face. My pulse races as I straighten the paper and smooth it out. My nerves twist in my stomach, and my hands are unsteady with the trepidation of getting caught. I throw another quick glance in the direction of the store, they're on line. Damn it! I just need to do it. I have to just suck up the courage and see what it says.

My eyes drop to the paper on my lap. It's open but I see no phone number. No scandalous message. There is only one word written on the paper. Just one miserable, heart-wrenching word.

Murderer.

I feel like I've been sucker-punched. I take a deep breath and cover my mouth with both hands. I'm paralyzed staring at the stupid word. I try to deny it, tell myself my eyes are tricking me, like that will make any difference at all. It doesn't. My cheeks are hot, burning, and I'm certain they're red, too. Pull yourself together. My heart pounds hard, too hard. I'm not sure if it's fear of getting caught or the fact that someone is being so brutally mean to Jordan.

I don't understand who would do this. Anger boils up and replaces most of the shock of what I've seen. I'm angry at myself for ever doubting him, at the message, and most of all at the unidentified author of it. I re-crumple the paper and shove it back under the seat so he won't suspect I saw it.

Maria smiles at Jordan as they walk out of the store. I look at him and wonder what's going through his mind. I don't have a clue right now, and I can't peel my eyes off of him. I watch them, trying to force my heart back to its normal speed as he hands her a bottle of water. She gives him a quick hug, and I see that annoyingly cute smirk cross his face. The smirk that sets me on fire. The one I'd cross oceans in a raft to see. I want to run out of the car, throw my arms around him and never let go. I hold back. I can't act off of irrational emotions. I need to stay right where I am and wait for him to come to me.

I steady my breath as Maria twists the top back on the water bottle and hands it to Jordan. It's hard to swallow with the giant lump that formed in the back of my throat. My chest aches as I stare at him trying to act like everything's okay. I only ever wanted the opportunity to make him happy, to be his rock. I can't be doing a good job at either if he's not telling me about these twisted letters, and going out of his way to hide them from me. They're hurting him, keeping his pain and guilt simmering on low heat so that they're always close to boiling over. I'm afraid, just like a pressure cooker with no release, he's getting ready to explode.

This isn't what I want for him. I know there's no such thing as happily ever after, but this is too much. I wish I could wrap him up in my love, like a protective layer of bubble wrap, and insulate him from the harshness of the world. But, I can't, and that's the part I'm struggling with the most.

Once he's in the car and turns the key in the ignition I unbuckle my seatbelt, and pull him into a long embrace.

"What's this for?" he asks as he kisses the top of my head.

"I needed a hug." I hope he doesn't hear the sadness in my voice. If he does, he doesn't call me on it.

"A hug or are you trying to squeeze my insides out?" he teases.

"I'm on the verge of throwing my guts up back here. I don't need you two to add to it."

"That was the shortest lived truce in the history of the world."

"Jordan, you know, I love you, right? I mean no matter what."

His eyes narrow as his lips curl up in the corners.

"I mean you know nothing is ever going to change that? Until the end of forever."

"Steph, you're acting strange." I feel the tension in his arms and chest.

I know he's right. I have to pull myself together. I don't want him to know I saw the note. He'll think I don't trust him. I can't blame him. My behavior last night and five minutes ago doesn't exactly scream an infinite amount of faith in him.

"Sorry. I just . . ." I need to think of something to say, some reason for me to be acting like a basket case. "I just miss you so much when we're apart, even when it's just for a few minutes."

I don't know if he believes me. I hope he does, because while it might not be the root cause of my strange behavior right now, it's true.

Chapter 15

"Pumpkin Picking? That's your big surprise?"

"Come on, Maria. When's the last time you went to a farm to pick a pumpkin?"

"Never. This is stupid. You could buy one at the grocery store, or at a fruit stand."

"Would you stop being so Brooklyn and try getting into the spirit of things?"

Her hand snaps up, with one finger in the air, "First of all, I'm all Brooklyn, and there's nothing wrong with that. Second of all, if you're serious I'll wait in the car."

"Then you'll be waiting a long time. The hayride alone is about half an hour without stopping for the pumpkins."

"Hayride? Do you not get that I have a splitting headache?"

"Then the cool air might make you feel better."

She grumbles, but doesn't argue any further. Instead she gets out, leans against the car and crosses her arms over her chest. Without looking back to see what she's doing, Jordan takes me by the hand and leads me to the cashier to buy tickets.

Once we're paid for, we join a group of people behind a roped area, waiting for the tractor to return. Maria still hasn't joined us.

"I should go get her." I start to break away, but he doesn't let me go. Jordan's arms wrap around my waist as he pulls me against his chest. I close my eyes and take a moment to breathe him in and enjoy how good, how right, this feels.

"Anything you want to tell me?"

I hope this is about last night and not about me searching his car for what I suspected were girls' phone numbers. Part of me wishes they were numbers and that he trashed or burned all of them. Unfortunately, that's not the case.

"I drank, too. I'm sorry, but I thought since I wasn't alone it wasn't such a big deal."

"Steph," he sighs. "I'm not worried about you drinking when you're alone. I'm worried about you drinking when you're around people that could hurt you."

He doesn't seem angry, and I'm relieved. Still feeling guilty, I offer up an excuse, a reason why I thought it would be okay.

"Jonah swore he'd keep Logan in line."

"Logan?" His arms drop from my waist like lead weights. One hand runs through his hair, then down over his face. I'm too nervous to say anything. Instead I wait for him to speak, and it feels like forever before he does. "The guy that you complain about daily? You were drinking with him?" He's angry, disappointed. I hear it in his voice. I take a small step back and create distance.

My eyes fall to the ground. "I know it was stupid. But I didn't drink a lot. I thought since I had Maria there and Jonah . . ."

He doesn't let me finish, instead his lips press together in a thin line and he nods before speaking.

"First of all, I wasn't even talking about you drinking. I just wanted to know if you told Maria I saw Rob with another girl so I know what to say to her. Second, depending on Maria to look out for you in the condition she was in before she drank is like counting on the fox to guard the hen house. You should've been looking out for her. Third of all, Jonah?" He looks away and pauses. I wish he would say something. Anything. Until he continues. "What is it you think Jonah could've done if Logan got aggressive? Huh? Jonah would've run off with his tail between his legs."

"He wouldn't let Logan hurt me. He's been the only thing keeping Logan away."

"That's your fault. I told you I'll take care of Logan. Give me two minutes with him and he won't bother you anymore. I'm not saying Jonah wouldn't try, but come on, he's not the type of guy that could protect you."

"Are you jealous?"

"Of Jonah?" He laughs, but it's fake, forced. "You're kidding, right?" He pauses and shakes his head. "I never thought I had a reason to be jealous of anyone, least of all that dork, Jonah."

It's the way Jordan said his name, with distain, like it's beneath him, that bothers me.

"Can you please stop calling him names?"

"You like him." A look of disbelief crosses his face. "You have a thing for the geek."

"No, I don't. He's just a friend."

"Wow. I didn't see it coming. You've replaced me with Jonah."

"I can never replace you. I love you."

"I know." He nods, "But whether you want to admit it or not, things have changed. You don't talk to me the way you used to. Not about all the little stupid things."

"Like what?" I want to prove him wrong.

"I don't know, like the cute guys in your classes."

"Cute guys? That's what you want to hear about?" I don't wait for him to answer. I decide not to pussyfoot around the subject any longer. He's deflecting. "You're right. Things have changed. But you're the one that changed. You're quiet, moody, and half the time when we're together I feel like you're somewhere else. It's like there's this giant fence you keep between us, and no matter what you won't let me through, and you won't fully come over to my side. There's something going on that you're not telling me." I hope this will give him an opening to release some of the steam rising up inside him.

"Really, you want to go there, Steph? Fine. I miss you. That's it. That's all there is. I miss seeing you, hoping if I wait outside long enough you'll pass by. I wait all day to talk to you, to hear your voice. But when I call, you're with someone. You're always busy."

"What am I supposed to do? Hide in my room and wait for you?"

He shakes his head. "Lately it just feels like we're leading very separate lives."

"That's because we are."

"I can deal with that, but you breaking your promise . . . You know that was important to me. The only thing I asked was for you not to drink if we weren't together."

"But we're never together. Are you really going to stand there and tell me you never drink when you're playing?"

He looks away, shakes his head and lets out a long sigh. "I'm allowed to drink."

"Because you're a guy and I'm a girl?"

"Because I'm legal and you're not."

There it is a dig at my age. I wondered when that would come up. It's been a while since he threw that at me. I bite on the inside of my bottom lip trying to maintain my composure.

"The part that's really eating away at me is finding out who you were drinking with. You hate Logan. You tell me how he gives you the creeps and you were drinking with him?"

What I hate most of all is the legitimacy to his argument. At least the part about Logan. "Jonah promised . . ."

"Don't get me started on Jonah."

I'm completely blindsided by his issue with Jonah. This is so out of character for Jordan.

"What about Jonah? I don't like him, not like that."

"But he likes you 'like that.' He's just waiting for an opportunity.'" He's not quite yelling, at least not yet, but his tone is cold, and angry. "Anything you need, he's more than happy to help with."

"Because he's there. He lives on the same floor as me."

"I've been there, Stephanie. I know there's more to it than that. I've played the part of the best friend for years. Remember?" He pauses. I wait for him to speak again, because I'm not sure if I can speak, or if I do, what will come out of my mouth. "Steph," he says somewhat calmer while shoving his hands in his pockets. "What scares me is that you don't even see this coming."

"What coming?"

"We're spending less and less time together. You made it perfectly clear last night that you don't trust me, even though I've given you no reason to feel that way. And to top it all off," he looks back in Maria's direction, then meets my eyes with a look I've never seen from him before, a look that not only holds me prisoner, it paralyzes me. "You went partying with guys that you know are trying to get in your pants." His inner turmoil seems to have risen up and spilled into his eyes. "You're drifting away."

I shake my head, denying what he just said. It's not true. End of story. "I'm not. Not at all. I'm exactly the same as I've always been. You're the one that's changed. You're the one that's too busy for me. You joined this stupid band. You're the one that won't spend the night. You could've come last night when you were done, but you chose not to."

"I didn't join the band. They knew I could play and they needed help. And you know why I don't want to spend the night. Do you think I could live with myself if I hurt you?"

The cracking of his voice causes a sharp twisting in my stomach, like a knife is slicing through it. No. I don't. He already thinks he hurt one girlfriend, and I see the toll it's having on him. I know what he's gone through, how he's changed since Madison's death. The image of the crumpled paper under the seat comes to mind. I know it's playing a part in his irrational fear of hurting me, but I don't know how to make it better. I take a few breaths before speaking.

"You wanted me to make friends didn't you?"

He nods.

"And you want me to make the most of college?"

"You know I do."

I pull one of his hands out of his pocket and interlock our fingers together hoping he has as clear a view into my heart as I have into his.

"I'm just starting to get comfortable there, and yes, part of that is because of Jonah. Maybe I depend on him too much, but for some reason I don't understand, Avery hates me. She has from the first day, and it carried over to most of the other girls. I think it's starting to wear off some because I'm finally making friends."

"I know, and I'm happy about that, but Logan? You drank with him, you left yourself vulnerable, and he could've hurt you."

"This isn't about Logan. Or Jonah. This is about us, and I'm scared to death right now because this isn't like you."

I can see by the rise and fall of his chest how deep his breaths are. He isn't trying to pull away or let go of me, so I take his other hand and place each of my fingers between each of his, and fold them over so I have a good grip on him.

"I love when you come visit me, and I'd love for you to be part of everything that goes on in my life, but you're so busy. I feel like you barely squeeze me in. I love the days we spend together and talking to you, but the truth is, I want more."

"That's what I'm afraid of."

With my heart trying to punch its way out of my chest to seek shelter somewhere safe, I step in closer to him and place his hands back on my waist. "I want more of you. Just you. Always you."

"You have all of me. I'm giving you all that I can. I'm trying to do the right thing. I swear I am, but no matter what I do, it doesn't seem like enough." He loses me. "I always seem to let someone down. I hate when that someone is you."

His words confuse me. I'm scared. I have that terrible feeling in my stomach like I'm about to fall off a cliff because whatever is bothering him is so much more than the fact that I drank last night. It's about him, and I'm afraid in the end I'm going to lose him, who he is, who he's always been to me.

I squeeze his hands. I want him to feel me, to feel that I'm right here, in this moment, and I'm not going anywhere.

"What can I do? How do I make this better?"

"I don't know."

"I hear the tractor coming, do you think I have enough time to go buy myself a ticket?" Maria's voice sounds from right behind me.

"Here," Jordan pulls the tickets from his pocket and hands her one.

"Thanks." Maria looks between us. "Do you want me to go back to the car?"

"Of course not," Jordan says before I can answer.

"Yeah, no."

"Well then lighten up. The tension here is thicker than a boatload of whale blubber."

Jordan climbs up on the wagon, reaches down, and takes turns giving both Maria and I a hand as we get on. He sits between us careful not to touch me, or put his arm around me. I understand he doesn't want Maria to feel uncomfortable, but I want to snuggle against him. I need to touch him.

"How's that headache?" he asks Maria.

"A little better."

"Glad to hear it."

We don't speak for the rest of the ride. Instead we exchange glances and bounce around as we are driven out to the pumpkin patch. I have a lot of time to replay our conversation over in my head. I'm not sure what I'm feeling. I'm a little angry, and a lot annoyed. I walk away from Jordan as I search for a pumpkin. What I really feel like is finding one to kick hard.

"I'm sorry."

He's standing behind me, and I close my eyes because I don't want to do this here. Not in the middle of the pumpkin patch, not in the middle of a crowd. He turns me around to face him so that I have no choice but to look up at him.

"I'm sorry. You're right. This is stupid. All of it. I should've been with you last night. I should be with you every night. I'm going to fix this, Stephanie."

Funny, up until a few minutes ago I didn't think there was anything to fix. I don't say anything. I'm not sure what he's even looking for.

"You can start by telling me what's really going on."

"Nothing." He rakes his hand through his hair. "Maybe I overacted because of what just went down with Rob and Maria. Maybe it's the fact that you don't trust me and I don't know why. And then knowing you were pissed when you left me, you went back and got drunk with two guys that I know are looking for more than friendship with you."

"But I'm not looking for anything more from them. That should be enough for you."

He reaches out and brushes my hair behind my ear, his eyes locked on mine. "Friday is Halloween, and I want you there. With me. I'll pick you up right after your classes end and we'll spend the day together. Is that okay?"

"Don't you guys have a gig?"

"Yes. At the bar we first played in, so you can come."

"How are you picking me up if you have school?"

"I'll skip my last class."

I shake my head. "No."

I see a hint of a smile and the quiet confidence I've come to expect from him peeks through his eyes, "Are you really saying no to me? I didn't think you could resist."

I know he's teasing, and I give his chest a playful shove. "You wish."

He closes in, stepping toe to toe with me. I have to tilt my head up to meet his stare. He's serious. Dead serious. "Right now I'm wishing you'd say yes."

"Then you need to sell it better than that."

He laughs. "Okay. You want more, and so do I. When the show is over, I'll drive you back to school, and we'll spend the night together." He leans in and whispers in my ear, before pulling on my earlobe with his teeth. "In your bed."

I think he's alluding to more than sleep. It excites me and terrifies me at the same time. I feel my belly fluttering. My nerve cells are alive and awake as the wind brushes over my skin. I only wish it were his fingertips. "Do you mean it?"

He's serious, as he nods. I know he's telling the truth. If I don't look away, my heart is going to burst with excitement. "Yes. I mean it."

Chapter 16

"I hope you don't mind," Jordan says on the ride to Brooklyn, "But I sort of bought a costume for you to wear."

"You didn't tell me I have to get dressed up."

"I'm telling you now. If I have to, so do you."

"How are you going to play in costume?"

He huffs. "I never said it was a great costume. I'm going as the devil. You know red cape, horns and tail. Nothing bulky or crazy."

"So if you're the devil, what am I?"

"What else would you be? My angel?"

He pulls up in front of his house.

"Is your mother home?"

"Yes."

My heart patters just a little faster.

"Maybe we should go somewhere else?"

"Don't worry, she wants to see you." Jordan assures me as he uses his key to unlock the side door of his house.

I don't want to go inside. I've only ever been in there one time, and I haven't seen his mother in months. I don't know what to say to her.

"I don't think she really likes me," I confess. Maybe because Maria weaseled her way into every conversation I ever had with the woman.

"You're crazy. Hey, Mom." Jordan calls out as we walk in the door." He takes my hand and leads me to the right, up the steps that lead into the kitchen and the main living area of the house.

"Hi, Stephanie."

Breathe. I remind myself, scared out of my mind that she's going to yell at me. It's bad enough that he skipped class to come get me, but to then bring me to his mother, so she knows what he did, I'm mortified.

"Hi." I squeak out, hating my voice.

"Jordan, you're lawyer called. He needs to talk to you about depositions."

Jordan nods, and I feel the change in his mood. The light carefree boy is once again gone.

"I need to return his call. Can you give me a few minutes?"

I nod. "Of course." I hope he can't tell I'm in the throes of an internal panic attack.

"Would you like something to drink?" His mother offers as he slips out of the room.

I shake my head, waiting for her to lace into me about what a terrible influence I am on her son. Deep down I'm afraid she might blame me for Madison and the accident as well. I haven't seen her since it happened and I'm not sure how much she knows about Jordan and I and what led to his break-up with Madison. Did he even tell her he broke up with Madison? Does it even count as a break up?

"Sit down." She motions to a chair at the kitchen table. I do as I'm told and wait for her next move. "I don't need to tell you how difficult things have been for him."

"No." I wonder where she's going with this.

"He seems worse since he's gone back to school. Moody and depressed."

I nod in agreement.

"He doesn't talk about it, and that's what has me worried. I assume it's hard for him to face their friends. But he's different when he's with you. He's happy. I don't know if you can see it behind all the mood swings, but I thought you should know."

I exhale, finally able to breathe. "Thank you. Thank you so much. I was so nervous that you were upset with me."

"Not at all. You're keeping him going right now."

Jordan's hands are on his head when he comes back in the room. His eyes have a pained, faraway look, and I know he's upset.

"They have a date."

"That's good." She approaches and rests a hand on his shoulder. "That means you can put it behind you sooner rather than later."

"Valentine's Day."

I catch the sarcastic look on her face. Now I know where Jordan gets it.

"I thought these things take years."

"Normally they do. This part is easy. At the scene the driver admitted to the cops that he fell asleep and caused the accident. He didn't try to blame you, honey. That's part of what takes so long, gathering up evidence and eye witnesses. All the stories were the same, he barreled through the light. It's a big company, too. I bet they're going to try to settle out of court rather than have a long drawn out trial."

He nods. I watch the interaction, and the lost, helpless look on Jordan's face tells me that she's found a way to wrangle herself right back to the spot I so often find Madison's ghost. Right in between us.

Her presence in his mind is so strong, so all consuming I can't help but wonder if he's aware that I'm sitting there in his kitchen. As if he heard my thoughts, his eyes turn to me. I recognize the torn, pained look on his face. It's the telltale sign that he's thinking of her. It makes my chest ache, for him. For the both of us.

What am I supposed to do? How am I supposed to act? Do I press him to talk? Or pretend everything is okay? I'm in need of a lifeline, and there's not one to be had. I wish I could find a user's manual for how to deal with a traumatized boyfriend that's haunted by his dead ex-girlfriend. This is her revenge. Every time things are going well between Jordan and me, Madison finds a way to slither into his mind and infiltrate his thoughts. I should probably leave before I say what's on my mind and upset him.

"Maybe I should go home for a little while." I offer with a shrug.

"No. I want to spend time with you."

"I know. Today's been great. And we still have tonight." Now that I know he's thinking of her I'm not looking as forward to tonight as I was an hour ago.

"Don't leave. Come on."

He takes my hand and leads me back down the steps to his room. It looks exactly the way I remember it. The heavy bag, the books. I do notice one thing that wasn't here the first time I came. On his desk, in a frame, is a picture of Jordan and me outside my house on prom night. My heart picks up speed. I don't think I've seen it before. It's not one of mine. It doesn't even look familiar. I wonder where he got it.

I walk over to his desk to take a closer look at the picture. In it, Jordan's standing behind me with his hands on my waist. He's looking down at me, like I'm all he can see, all that matters in the world. His lips are drawn up in a smile as I look back at him over my shoulder, laughing. It isn't a staged pose. He said something funny and I reacted. It's natural. Real.

I don't know which surprises me more, the fact that he has the picture or that he has it displayed on his desk. For months I haven't allowed myself to look through the digital images from that night. There's too much pain associated with what came after prom. I pick the frame up not expecting my eyes to fill with tears. It's just a picture. But it's everything that night means to me, and everything that happened since that has me choked up.

"It was Maria's. You look so happy." His voice is thick, heavy.

"I was." I looked back on that night all through the summer. Until he told me if he had it to do over he would, and that it was the biggest mistake of his life. Those words, no matter how he tries to sugar coat them, still cast an ugly stain on the most perfect night of my life.

His chest presses against my arm making my skin tingle, it's the only part of him that's touching me, but I'm feeling closer to him at this moment than ever before. "I needed you." His voice is little more than a whisper, and the raw emotion in it has a tight grip on my heart. "When I wouldn't allow myself to be with you, this picture was my lifeline. I'd think of you at night and stare at it for hours, until I gave up the struggle and called you. When you kicked me out of your life, I had to fight myself to respect your wishes and stay away. This was all I had left. Memories and this one picture."

I do my best to blink back the tears in my eyes.

"You look so beautiful. I don't remember you ever looking happier." He strokes my hair, "That's why I took it. I want to remember you looking just like that. And knowing I had some part in it, it's gotten me through some really dark days. I hope you don't mind." He takes the frame from me and places it back on his desk.

I turn to face him and lose myself in his dark, soulful eyes. It takes me a moment longer than it should to find my voice.

"Mind? Are you kidding?" I wrap my arms around him and press my cheek against his chest. Thump. Thump. Thump. "Maria never told me. I thought you just wanted to forget . . ."

He tilts my head up and brushes his thumbs across my cheeks. His eyes are locked on mine. His stare is so intense it's almost painful. I feel it inside me, in my chest, in my heart. We are connected on every level. This is intimacy. This is what I couldn't find with anyone else, this emotional connection. I never needed to look for it with Jordan; it's always just been there.

"It's a night I never want to forget. Ever."

He sounds sad, and distant. Far away, as if he's back there in that picture instead of here with me now. I want to reach in and pull him out of the past. I want him to know there is no better moment for me than right now, this moment. Fighting the tears is useless. Instead, I let them fall and swipe at them with my fingertips. This does the trick, because when he speaks, his voice although close, is strong.

"Steph, I know I've said a lot of things that hurt you, but you have to know, I'm crazy in love with you. I don't regret anything that happened between us. Not then. Not now. Nothing."

Too emotional to speak, I nod.

"Don't get me wrong, I wish things worked out different with Madison. But not if it means I'd lose you instead. I know it's selfish, but all I want is you."

"You don't have to explain." I sniffle.

"Yes, I do. I've been . . . I don't even know what I've been. Some days I'm fine, others I feel like everything is spiraling out of control. The only good thing, the only constant in my life is you, and I don't want any of this other stuff to tarnish what we have."

He rests his forearms on my shoulders and clasps his hands behind my neck. His mouth is a breath away from mine. It's hard to swallow, let alone speak, but I force the words out of my mouth. "I just want to help you. I want to make you happy."

"You do, baby." He kisses the top of my head. "Believe me, you do."

I hold him, cling to him with every breath. He does the same. I know if something crazy were to happen, like an asteroid came crashing through his roof, and I was to die right now in his arms, I'd die happy.

*

"Don't leave," he whispers, with his arms around my waist, his lips trailing along my neck.

It's dinnertime and I have to force myself to say goodbye. We'll only be apart for a few hours, but neither of us separates willingly. Each time I take a step away, Jordan pulls me back and picks up where we just left off.

"Too late. I already called my mother." I reach my hand under his shirt and lay it flat against his hard chest, feeling his heart beneath my palm.

He looks at where my hand is and presses one hand over mine. "Are you sure I can't convince you to stay longer?" The fingertips of his other hand slide beneath the waistband of my jeans at the small of my back, moving in small measures, brushing against my skin. "I think you'll agree I can be convincing."

He could convince me to ride an elephant through Manhattan naked on Sunday by promising it would make him happy, and he knows it. There isn't much he needs to do to convince me to stay in his arms, so I'm glad he isn't trying hard. But his mother is upstairs, and if I stay . . . I know I need to leave. Right now.

"I think a few hours apart will be good for us."

"Then you better go, because if you wait one more minute I'm going to lock you in my room, and neither of us are going anywhere."

I nod and give him one last, lustful kiss goodbye before he hands me the bag with the costume, walks me to the door and watches me walk away. I feel his eyes on me, like a warm blanket until I round the corner. I stop for a moment, and take a deep breath collecting myself. I bring my hands up to my face. I can feel the heat of the deep blush shading my cheeks. Once I continue walking, I rub my sore lips, swollen from the hot and heavy kissing we've been doing on his bed for the last hour. I can still taste him. My skin tingles in the places his hands touched and explored.

While nothing changed between us, everything is different. I can see not just desire, but all out passion in his eyes when he looks at me. We've made some sort of breakthrough. My stomach roils with excitement as I replay the last hour in my mind. It's a perfect day, and this time neither of us allowed Madison to wedge herself between us.

I dial my mother's phone number and press send one last time before I go any further.

"Hi, honey, I can't wait to see you."

"Are you sure it's okay?" I know my mother spends Friday nights with Eddie. I'm betting she spends all her nights with him, but I don't want to interrupt if they have special plans. I would've surprised her, if I wasn't the one who got surprised last week. I can't handle the idea of walking in on her again.

"Are you kidding, we can't wait to see you."

We. It's hard for me to wrap my head around the concept that my mother is part of a we. She hasn't brought him to school when she's visited me. I'm sort of happy about that. It's not that I don't like him. I just don't want him rammed down my throat. Coming home for a visit, I'm back on her turf, and that means he's part of it.

"Me, too."

"Great I picked up steak on the way home from work. I'll see you soon."

There's no better place for me to crash for a few hours than in my own bedroom. No matter how long I'm away at school, I can't imagine this not feeling like home.

I think about stopping off at the cemetery, since I haven't visited my father in months, but it's too late. The gates are already locked. The strange thing is, I'm not disappointed. I would've been before I left for school. The cemetery had been my sanctuary. Now I don't want to be surrounded by the cold, hard slabs of granite. I long for the living, to feel skin and warmth, and the pounding of my heart.

It's only taken me forever to get here, and I wonder where Jordan is on his journey. He's still inundated with guilt, trying to hide his feelings by avoiding certain subjects. I didn't miss today that instead of talking about Madison and how he feels about having to give depositions on Valentine's Day, he turned the spotlight on us and his feelings for me. Maybe it's for the best. Why dwell on things you can't change? Isn't that a point he tried to get through to me, even if not in those words?

He taught me that I matter. Jordan convinced me that I deserve to be loved and to lead a good life. I can do the same for him and now he's actually letting me. Today surpassed all hopes and expectations. I only hope tonight we'll pick up where we left off.

I have to admit, I'm a little nervous about meeting him later. I should be shaking in my boots over what's going to happen back at school, but I'm not. I'm ready for it. It's the bar scene that's making me nauseous. I don't know how I'm going to make it through watching him tonight. I know he talks to other girls, when he's there. He has to. Interacting with the fans is part of what keeps them coming back, and while they're trying to build a fan base they need to bank on the personal interaction. I don't know if I can handle watching silently in the background as other girls flirt with him.

I look down at the bag in my hand and smile. He bought me an angel costume. I'll just have to make sure I accessorize it enough so that when I walk in there, he'll think he died and went to Heaven.

Chapter 17

It's nice to have a home cooked meal. Mom never went all out on a dinner unless company came. I guess my college student status puts me in a special category. She lays out a spread of soup, steak, mashed potatoes, and spinach salad. She even bought pie for desert, but I'm too full, and too excited to eat anything else.

Through dinner I watch the interaction between Eddie and my mom. The little glances, the way she lights up when he reaches over and touches her hand for a moment. I can relate, but I have to admit I'm surprised by what a softie she is. She's always had such a hard exterior, I'm not sure I know who this woman is.

"Have you gotten involved in any school clubs?" Eddie asks.

"No. I'm just sort of trying to blend in."

"It's a great way to meet people. And even better when they are people with similar interests."

Eddie continues to offer suggestions and advice on making the most of my time away at school, but my head is elsewhere. It's with Jordan. After dinner I help clear the table then run upstairs to get ready.

Showered and clean I look at the clock. It's later than I expected. Time to get ready. I decide to give my costume a closer look. I should've checked it out a long time ago, but better late than never. I considered trying it on at Jordan's, but he didn't mention it, and every time the thought crossed my mind, something would pop up and make me forget, like his hands gliding over the skin beneath my shirt. I close my eyes and clear my head. The costume. I need to try on the costume.

Knowing Jordan, I expect to pull out a white billowy sort of thing that falls just above the ankle. My mouth drops when my eyes take in the image on the cardboard insert. I open the snaps on the plastic covering and pull out the lace-up corset with the ruffled bottom, which ends at the very top of the thigh, nowhere near the ankle. I reach for my phone.

Are you sure you want me to wear this tonight?

Now I'm worried it might not fit. It looks small. I'll be mortified if it doesn't fit. I do my best at stuffing myself into the super-sexy costume I'd never have the guts to pick out myself. Before looking in the mirror, I slip the wings on, and place the halo on my head. I want to get a good sense of what it's like as a whole before I tell him there's no way in hell I can leave my house in this. My phone buzzes and I grab it, making yet another excuse not to rush to the mirror.

Absolutely. The only thing I can think of that'll be more fun than seeing you in it, will be taking it off.

As I read, I feel the words embed themselves in my heart, but that's not the body part that's reacting strongest to what he just suggested. I feel something unfamiliar down below.

I walk over to the full-length mirror on the back of my door, and swallow hard. I have my eyes fixed on my bare legs. I always liked my legs. I continue looking upwards, and I'm struck by how good the rest of my body looks. My curves don't look frumpy or out of place. They look sexy, and perfect. Suddenly my legs feel like a weakness rather than a strength. And what am I going to wear on my feet?

I call Maria. Luckily she's home. I don't move a muscle as I wait for her to rush over with every pair of white boots, shoes, and sandals she owns. I don't say anything as she opens the door and assesses me.

"The boy has taste, that's for sure."

"You think it looks good?"

"I think you're having sex tonight. Actually, I know you're having sex tonight."

"Thanks. I'm so glad I called you." I hope she catches the sarcastic tone in my voice.

"What's wrong? Don't you want to knock boots?"

"Ohmigod! You're not helping."

Maria steps closer to me and fans my hair out behind me. "You look amazing. Every guy in there will have his eyes glued on you. But, there's no way you're going to make it to tomorrow with your virginity intact, so give it a proper farewell and prepare to cross over to the dark side."

"Can you stop. Please!" I implore. She's silent, and I know I need to strike now before she continues. "Shoes. I don't have shoes. What am I going to wear on my feet?"

Her eyes fall down to the extremely low cut neckline of the bodice that is pushing up and enhancing my breasts.

"Trust me. No one's going to be looking at your feet."

*

I look in the mirror at the finished product. Sort of finished. Maria suggested I wear a long white goddess gown she used for her costume last year to cover how skimpy this outfit is, so my mother doesn't freak when I leave.

"It hides the boots." Maria's referring to the white, thigh high boots she's lending me. Why she has them and where she wears them is beyond me, but right now I'm very grateful because they are the perfect accessory.

"It hides the outfit."

"Throw a jacket on over it, or else your mom might notice there's something underneath.

I do as I'm told and reach in my closet for something to throw on. "You really think I can pull this off?" I motion to myself.

"Absolutely. But you need to walk in there with confidence. You look great. Know it. Own it."

I nod, still not convinced. And I'm not sure how I'm going to react if Maria's right and everyone does ogle me. I've never been one for that kind of attention, but then again if I captured the eyes of a crowd it's been so they could laugh at me, not because I wowed them.

"Walk me to the door. I want to introduce you to Ross."

Maria rolls her eyes. "Isn't it enough that I'm sneaking you out incognito, saved your ass with my boots and driving you? Do you have to insult me by trying to match me up with some dork."

I smile at her feigned annoyance. In the last week since leaving me on Sunday with Jordan, she's spent all her free time at home. I know it's just a passing phase, but I think she's embarrassed because everyone knows her as part of a twosome with Rob.

"Ross is no dork. Bedsides, I've seen how you act with Jonah. Seems like you're the one with the interest in dorks."

"Watching Jonah that close, huh?"

"I'm not watching him."

She gives me a look that tells me she doesn't believe me, but leaves it at that.

*

Surprised to find a parking spot, Maria takes advantage of the rare occurrence and backs her car into the small space.

"Leave the gown here. You don't want to be pulling off clothes outside a bar, no matter what day of the year it is."

"Okay." I hesitate and stare at her a minute.

"Don't worry. I'll walk you to the door." She says getting out. "I get it, it's one thing to look like prostitute, but to actually be out walking the streets . . ."

"You think I look like a hooker?" I ask looking at her over the hood of the car.

"I'm teasing you, Steph. Geez, lighten up."

"So then why are you walking me?"

She shakes her head, "I can go back if you'd like."

"No, no, no."

"Fine, I'm escorting you to the door to make sure no one bothers you."

"Sweet, are you going to protect me if someone gets out of hand?" I tease.

"Protect you? No. I'm thinking you might cause an accident, and this way, if there are any cute guys in the cars I can go administer CPR or first aid, or whatever the hell they might need."

"You're terrible." I giggle.

Half a block into our walk, still a block away from the bar, I spot Jordan's car. My eyes automatically sweep over the windshield. Stuck under the wiper on the driver's side is half a sheet of white, lined, loose-leaf paper with something written on it. My heart sinks fast and deep, like a steel anchor. Remembering how the floor of his car was littered with balled up papers and what I found scribbled on the one stuck under the seat, I almost wish it's a girl's number I'm about to find. I walk around to the driver's side and snag it.

How do you live with yourself knowing you're a killer?

With a tight chest and a mountain of anger, I crumple and tear the paper to shreds. "Stupid jerk!" I mutter.

"Hey, what's wrong?" Maria's voice reminds me that I'm not alone. I close my eyes and take a deep breath before I look at her and try to pull some bullshit explanation out of my ass. But I can't think fast enough so I don't say anything.

I shake my head as I walk back onto the sidewalk towards the nearest trash container. I take a moment to look around. If I wrote something vile like this, I'd want to see the person's reaction, wouldn't I? Cars whiz by. People walk. I don't see anyone looking at his car, or me. Damn coward.

"What was that about?"

I shake my head. "I don't want to talk about it."

I can't.

I know she means well, but I can't trust her to keep her mouth shut. Jordan doesn't know I found one of these notes in his car. I don't want him to know I snooped around. It will reinforce his belief that I don't trust him. Today went so well. No arguments. No misunderstandings. Today was just us, falling a little deeper in love. I can't say one word to her about what I just read.

"Stephanie." She reaches for my arm to stop me.

"You can't say anything about this to Jordan. Promise me."

She stares at me like I just grew a third eye. "I'm fine. Really." At least it's not a lie. I am fine, and I know that I saved Jordan from seeing one more disgusting message. It's one less time whoever is doing this can rub salt in his wide open, gaping wound. "Just please, forget it."

"If I need to tell Jordan to get his head out of his ass . . ."

I grab her arm. "NO! You don't mention this to Jordan at all. Promise."

"Then tell me what . . ."

"No. It's nothing. If our friendship means anything to you, promise you won't say anything to him."

She's breathing heavy. I know I upset her, but she'll just have to get over it.

"Fine."

We walk the last block in silence. I'm so angry, I don't even think about how uncomfortable walking is in the ridiculous high heeled boots I'm wearing. I won't admit it, but

I'm glad Maria's walking me to the door. She's keeping my mind occupied and forcing me to put my game face on before I get there, before I face Jordan. Then again, if he does suspect something's wrong, I could always blame it on Maria.

"Hi, Ross."

"Stephanie," he says in a deep, official sounding voice to go along with his costume.

The second Maria spots him standing outside with his biceps bulging out of the short sleeved, blue shirt, fully accessorized with the policeman's hat and badge, I'm all but forgotten. After introducing them, I walk into the bar, nervous, scared, and feeling like an idiot.

First, I look around to make sure I'm not the only one dressed in a costume. Not like I can do anything even if I am. I'm inside, so it's too late to cut and run. It looks like most people are dressed in plain clothes, with a smattering of costume wearing patrons. That is until I take a closer look. The bar tenders are decked out in white shirts, vests, and arm garters making them look like they've come to tend bar in an old western movie. Among the crowd, I spot a bunch of male vampires, a few female witches, some sexy cats and French maids. I even spot Batman in the back, making out with Cat Women.

Without hesitating any further, I wedge my way through the ocean of people, closer to the stage. Blaze is clearly doing his best Hugh Hefner impression, wearing silk pajama pants shirtless with a matching silk robe, giving the crowd a good look at his six pack abs. I bet he's been waiting for tonight, looking forward to the opportunity to get on stage like this for months.

Chaz is dressed as a Vampire with his usual shredded black tee and jeans under a black cape. If not for his slicked back hair and fake blood dripping from his mouth to his chin, I wouldn't realize he's wearing anything out of the ordinary.

Wayne is covered in dark wily hair. It's peeking out of every cuff from his ankles to his wrists, with a long sleeve plaid shirt and his usual ripped up jeans.

And then there's Jordan.

Thump. Thump. Thump.

My heartbeat is erratic once my eyes fall on him.

Jordan is wearing a ripped up red tee instead of his usual black shirt. I almost don't notice the red horns and cape. He looks just as amazing under the poor lighting as I remember when I first saw him play. I catch my breath as our eyes meet. Even from ten feet away, his mere presence is causing my pulse to race.

He soaks me in and raises his eyebrow playfully. I feel heat rush to my cheeks, shading them with what I'm sure, from past experience, is a bright pink hue. It doesn't help that he's looking at me with a hunger in his eyes I've never seen before. I want to spin around to give him the full three hundred and sixty degree view, but there isn't room. It doesn't matter; the way his eyes drink me in leaves me with little doubt we'll be picking up right where we left off in his room a few hours ago.

I avert my eyes to the table right up against the stage. Two Playboy bunnies (no doubt Coco and Lela) are dancing. Maybe dancing is too kind a description. Each girl has her hands on the other, sliding them up and down the other girl's body, garnishing the attention of all the guys in the bar.

I can't help but wonder if Jordan's watching them, if he finds their display to be a turn on the way Blaze does. Instead of catching him stealing glimpses at the girls, his stare is singularly focused. On me. His eyes are stuck to me like glue. My heart thuds heavier in my chest. The giddy, jittery feeling in my stomach, grows stronger along with the pulsing desire that's been building inside me all day.

I'm jostled and almost lose my footing.

"Are you my eternal guide?" Is shouted into my ear as my nose is assaulted with the nasty beer smelling breath of the guy that bumped into me.

I ignore the jerk that's so busy laughing at his own lame joke he doesn't realize I didn't find it funny. He reaches out and touches a tendril of hair falling at my neck.

"Did I die and go to Heaven?"

Again he's laughing. I don't know if he thinks responding to his own lines like they're actually humorous will add appeal to them or if he's just too drunk to realize I'm not interested. I don't respond at all. Instead I move out of the way, closer to the stage. I feel hands brushing up against my thighs and my ass. I'm not sure if this just a way for perverts to get off, or if it's so crowded this close to the stage that people can't help but touch me as they're standing. Or moving. Or breathing.

Finally the set is over. Jordan wastes no time in stepping down from the platform and pushing his way to me. Before I have a chance to say anything, his mouth crushes mine, making me dizzy. I can feel the eyes around us staring. I bet we're putting on a side show of our own as Jordan's hands on my bottom, just beneath the frilly ruffle, squeeze my flesh and hold me tight against him. I'm not used to him being so aggressive, especially not in public, but I don't mind. Quite the contrary. I love it. I press myself further into him as his tongue massages mine.

Pulling back just enough that our lips are no longer touching, Jordan reaches up and loosens his cape.

"What are you doing?"

He flashes his crooked smile at me while bringing the cape around and fastening it over my shoulders.

"Marking my territory," he says with a wink.

His territory.

I do my best not to laugh. Not because it's funny. I know there's a part of him that's serious, but I like being the recipient of his jealous shows of affection. It's just further proof to me that I'm much deeper in his heart than he'd like to admit. That no matter what he's said in the past, I've made my way far enough into the fabric of his soul that he wants the world to know I'm his and to keep it that way.

"Still think having me wear this was a good idea?" I tease.

His eyes take their time crawling over me, from head to toe.

He dots a trail of kisses across my jaw, behind my neck, and up to my ear before answering. "I think this is the best damn decision I've made in months."

*

We only stay for about thirty minutes after Shred Em leaves the stage. Jordan holds me close as he introduces me to the girlfriends. I already know Coco and Lela, although I'm not sure if they actually qualify as girlfriends since Blaze seems to have his sights set on yet another girl that he has cornered in the back. Not that she minds, if her groping hands are any indication.

Jordan leads me by the hand over to the table Coco and Lela had been dancing on. I use the term dancing lightly since it looked like more like a girl on girl exhibition. Wayne and Chaz stand a few feet away. Before speaking to any of them, Jordan leans over and whispers in my ear, his breath tickling me and sending a surge of heat all the way down to my toes.

"Just so you know, you're absolutely the hottest girl in here."

Accentuating his point, his hand slides from my shoulder down to the top of my thigh under the ruffle. His thumb slides up, ever so slightly under the elastic trim of the costume and I suck in a deep breath. I look up, wondering where he plans on moving his hand and fingers next, trying to act like I'm okay and not about to explode with excitement. What surprises me most is the fact that his hand is cupping my ass cheek and he's acting as if this is normal, like he holds me there all the time. He looks so comfortable, so natural, he doesn't even glance down to gauge my reaction.

"Hi, Wendy," he says to a very pretty girl dressed in plain clothes with fake blood running down her neck before leaning over and talking in my ear. "This is Chaz's girlfriend."

Her arms reach around my shoulders and pull me close. "Thank you so much for helping get into that thick head of his."

"You're welcome."

I smile, not sure to what she's talking about, but I figure either Jordan will whisper it to me, or I'll figure it out if I play along like I know exactly what she's talking about.

"He was killing himself trying to find something catchy and quirky enough to make the song work."

"I didn't do anything." I glance up at Jordan. "Just told him how I felt."

"Good thing you're so happy and in love. What do you think of it?"

I shrug, "I haven't heard it yet."

"Jordan! Are you kidding me?" She admonishes him before turning back to me. "Lucky you, I have the privilege of hearing it at least three times a day as he tries to make it better." She laughs and rolls her eyes before stepping away from us and returning to Chaz.

Another girl dressed as a witch saunters over.

"Hi, Jordan." She blinks her eyes at him. "I like the horns." She lowers her eyes and reaches for the red tail behind him. "I wonder what else you're hiding in those pants. I can't believe she said that in front of me. It makes me worry about what she says when I'm not around. I want to kick her hard in the shin and splinter her bone so she can't walk. That'll teach her to flirt with a guy in front of his girlfriend. I don't know if he picks up on my irritation or not, but he pulls me closer, holds me just a bit tighter.

"Steph, this is Fiona, Wayne's girlfriend."

Funny, if you ask me, next to Jordan she doesn't know Wayne exists. There's no warmth, no friendly welcome from Fiona, just a coy smile that tells me she wouldn't mind swapping boyfriends for a while.

Fiona pulls up her phone, "Let me take a picture."

Jordan positions me in front of him, and brings his head next to mine. Once she snaps her picture, she's gone, back in the sea of people.

"She's pleasant."

He chuckles, and leads me by the hand toward the door. "Come on, let's get out of here."

I nod like an insipid school girl.

"I knew you'd look amazing in this." He says outside with his eyes raking over me, "But I had no idea how impatient I'd be about taking it off."

"I'm looking forward to it."

My voice cracks. I'm sure he thinks it's fear or nerves of what's to come that has me shaking in my boots. I'd rather he believe that than know I'm terrified, as his car comes into view, that we're going to find another note on the windshield. Seeing that there isn't one, I take a breath and allow myself to relax.

He stops and turns so he's facing me. "Stephanie, nothing has to happen tonight."

"Yes, it does." I step in closer to him and weave my fingers through his hair. "I want it to. Jordan, you have no idea how much I want it to happen."

"Are you sure? You seem nervous."

I smirk. "I am nervous. I've built you up for years in my head, and I'm just not sure you could live up to the hype."

Both eyebrows are raised as he stands to his full height and looks down at me. "Are you saying I don't know what I'm doing?"

"No." I smile.

"Because I can assure you, I know what I'm doing."

I can't help the smirk that's covering my face. "I guess you'll have to prove it."

"Challenge accepted."

Chapter 18

A battle rages inside me as I watch Jordan drive. Moonlight streams into the car, illuminating his features. Just looking at him sends the butterflies in my belly tumbling. I'll never get tired of looking at him. As I stare, I'm swept away with the gravity of the situation. My heart throbs against my chest. He's my everything. My wants and desires. My disappointments and the promise of the future. He is the sum of believing in myself enough to go after what I want and wishing on a star all wrapped up in one.

I want to reach out and touch him, but I don't dare. Not while he's driving. This part he needs to get over on his own. I know better than to push it. A heavy electric charge crackles in the air between us. I know he's struggling with the urge to touch me, too. I see it in the way his eyes drift down to my legs every once in a while, until his hand reaches over and rests at the top of my thigh. It's awkward and rigid at first, but my heart is doing backflips. There is nothing better, nothing more exciting than knowing he's letting go, just a little bit, just enough to be with me in the moment and feel alive. He's taking one more step in the right direction. It's one more sign of progress.

Once the car is parked, and we're out, Jordan backs me up against it. His fingers thread through my hair as he leans against me, pressing my body into the hard metal. His mouth meets mine, with a deep, hungry kiss. A kiss that leaves every cell of my body screaming for surrender, encouraging me to drop down to my knees and succumb to him in the moonlight.

Instead I do my best to ignore the tightness in my belly and the heat in my veins. I try to further ignite the kindling of desire between us and send it shooting into flames, with my own smoldering kiss. A greedy kiss meant to be equally demanding and scorching to his skin, to his nervous system, as his was to mine.

My fingers are clenched tight in his hair. With a deep breath, I release him and allow my hands to skim down, roaming over his arms and chest as his gyrating hips have me pinned against the car. I clutch his shoulders, hold him tight, as my body pulses and throbs against his. I feel it all building inside me, carrying me up, higher and higher, a ball of tension and need, twenty thousand feet in the air, waiting for release, to parachute back down to earth.

"We need to go inside," he whispers. His warm breath tickles me, adding one more blow to my senses, and causing me to shiver.

I don't want to move, I want to finish this off and explode right here in the parking lot, but my dry mouth won't utter the words. Unable to do anything else, I nod and allow him to lead me back to my room.

We walk at a hurried pace down the path, and up the steps. I can't lock the door behind us fast enough. Even though his hands haven't been on me for as long as it takes to get back up to my room, my skin still feels the tingling after effect of his touch. Before we connect again, I slip my wings off and unclasp the back of my costume. My chest is heaving. I've never felt this way before, this physical craving, this all out need to be touched, to be part of another human being. It's hard to breathe. Each breath is like a burdening weight that will only lighten once I get out of my costume.

He steps up and crushes his chest against mine as his lips brush along my neck, and shoulder. It's his turn to let his hands wander. They move across every inch of my body, cupping and fondling my curves along the way. Once he's satisfied with his exploration, he gently tugs at the white garment and pulls until it falls at my feet.

His eyes rake over my body, studying me as if I'm a rare treasure, something exotic and beautiful that he's never seen before. I roll my shoulders back making sure to stand with good posture, wanting to exude confidence while he appraises every bit of me. Normally I'd be trying to cover myself up with something, but between the heat bouncing off his body, and the crimson flame of my blush, I think the temperature of the room has climbed twenty degrees.

He continues to soak me in. I watch in silence enjoying the look of pleasure and approval on his face, getting more aroused as the seconds pass.

"Stephanie," he struggles to say my name. "You're even more beautiful . . ." He swallows hard and brushes his thumb over my lips, and then against my cheek. "You're absolutely perfect."

Jordan takes my hands in his and brings them to rest at the hem of his shirt. Aware of how very vulnerable I am at this moment, I stand frozen, unsure of what he wants me to do. I ask the silent question with my eyes, feeling my hands tremble against his body. He nods in response.

This is happening. It's really happening.

Once I lift the shirt off him, he places my shaking hands on his chest, his piercing gaze doesn't waver an inch.

"Touch me," he whispers.

Tentatively, I move my hands up to the base of his neck, across his shoulders, and over the muscles defining his arms. When I get to his wrists, he gives my hands a squeeze before bringing them up to his mouth, bestowing a warm kiss on each palm, and placing them back on his chest.

I close my eyes for a moment and suck in a deep breath. I'm on sensory overload. I've touched him before, but not like this, with such expectation hanging between us. I don't want it to stop. But I'm nervous, and can't feign confidence any longer. My eyes drop.

I'm as scared of what's coming as I am thrilled by the anticipation of it. Jordan pulls me over to the bed. He sits on the edge and wraps his arms around my waist. His warm lips skim over my belly before he sits me down next to him. I'm all-out-terrified, still unable to meet his smoldering stare. Jordan's crooked finger lifts my chin so I'll meet his eyes. I swallow hard as I do and I'm rewarded with another delicious kiss that starts at my lips and touches every part of my body. Before breaking away, he pulls my bottom lip between his teeth and suckles on it, using his tongue to caress it.

"I want you to know what tonight means to me." He leans in and rests his forehead against mine. His eyes are tender, and full of emotion. "I don't just plan on being your first. I want to be your only." He pauses, adding another layer to the already thick tension in the air. "And even though you're not my first, you're going to be my last."

Tears of joy sting my eyes. I'm so lost in the moment, I can't speak, I can only hold on and follow his lead.

*

My life is perfect. I'm not sure how I magically switched tracks and ventured from the land of destroying everything I touch into Utopia, but I did. Perhaps that's what my earlier years were about, understanding loss and pain so that when sunshine broke through the thick, steel barriers, I would recognize and appreciate it.

"Mmm." Jordan's arms tighten around me, and I nuzzle my head against his chest. "I love you so much." He kisses the top of my head, and I've never felt closer to anyone in my life as I do to him, at this moment.

I'm at a loss for words. What can I say that can express how I feel? How content and complete I am? How I can't think of one thing to add to it to make it better? I can't. The only words that I hope convey a portion of the depth of my feelings slip from my lips. "I love you, too."

I hope they're enough.

His bare leg drapes over mine. "Go to sleep," he whispers as he smoothes my hair.

"No. I don't want you to leave." I hold him tighter.

"I'm not going anywhere. I'm done running. I'm giving you everything I can, even the broken, jagged pieces of me that you may not want." I scoot up so I could look in his eyes. "I'm not holding back anymore, Stephanie. I can't and besides, it didn't help, it only hurt you."

Seeing him bared to me, not just in the flesh, but holding his heart in his hand and offering it to me, I don't think it's possible to love him anymore than I already do. I think my heart would burst from being too full, from loving beyond its capacity.

The chiming sound of his cell phone not only breaks the sentiment of the moment, but alerts him that he has a new message. Jordan stretches for the phone sitting on the desk next to my bed.

"Who's texting you?" I ask checking the time. My heart sinks. It's late, super late. Later than I ever text him. It's two in the morning.

"Wendy. It's the picture she took of us." He smiles as he turns the phone for me to see it.

I look closely at the picture, and message she sent along with it." She said she posted it to the band's page. How come you never told me they have a Facebook page?"

He shrugs. "I don't know, I guess I never thought it was a big deal."

Jordan deleted his account after the accident. He told me he couldn't deal with all the drama it brought. Strangers that heard about the accident sent him friend requests and messages on a daily basis. Some were sympathetic, but others were mean spirited and meant only to hurt him. As if he needed reminders of what happened or what he lost. For a while, every time he closed his eyes he relived those last moments with Madison.

I lean across him, reach for my phone, and search for the band's page. Once I find it, I scroll down and look through the pictures. I don't know why I feel such a bitter sting of betrayal not knowing about it. I would've been checking it out regularly if I did. Maybe it would've been a way to feel like I was with him on the nights I couldn't be.

I don't expect it to be chock full of pictures of Jordan, and I'm right, it's not. There are a bunch of pictures from earlier in the night, before I got to the bar: pictures of all the band couples, a picture of the band in costume. One of the girlfriends, minus me. And then I spot her. I wasn't even looking for her, but there she is, and Jordan has his arm around the blonde's shoulder. Aside from that, there's nothing romantic about the pic. They aren't even looking in the same direction. But I can't ignore it.

"Isn't that Pete's girlfriend?" I ask.

"Huh?" He glances at the picture. "Yep. That's her."

"Why do you have your arm around her?"

"I love that you're so jealous," he teases.

"You're not answering the question."

"She just happened to be standing there and Fiona told us to stand close together so she could take the picture."

"You're not even looking at the camera, either of you."

He sits up in bed, the look on his face changed, he's not playing anymore. "We just had amazing, mind-blowing sex, and you don't trust me?"

"Of course I trust you. But it's not like you have your arm around some random girl, some fan that you just met."

"Because that wouldn't bother you?"

"I'm not saying that. I don't like her. I feel like there's something you're not telling me."

He takes the phone out of my hands and scrolls back up to the picture of us. "Look at this picture. It's obvious that we're together." He takes a moment to get back to the other picture. "Do you see a difference here?"

I do. Their bodies aren't up against each other, they don't look connected, but still, why is she there? I look down further at older pictures, looking for her, looking for trouble between Jordan and me. There's a large group shot of all of them, but it's not at a bar, more like a restaurant. I check the date. It's a week old. This must be when they went to the diner. And there she is, right behind my boyfriend. I study the picture. Pete has his arm around her, but she's touching Jordan's shoulder. I think I know why he never mentioned this page. There were things on it I was never meant to see. I toss the phone down on the bed, wishing I could rewind my life and forget the last five minutes ever happened.

I glance over at him before rolling onto my side, opposite him.

"Don't," he whispers as he gathers me into his arms and pulls me against his chest. "Don't let anything ruin tonight. I swear to you, there's no one else. Just you. I just wish I could understand why you don't trust me."

I keep my back to him, if I'm going to be honest, I can't look at him. Not right now.

"I trust you. I just hate that I'm so afraid of losing you. You pushed me away for so long, I feel like it's only a matter of time before you realize you'd rather be with someone else. Someone older."

"Stephanie," His arms tighten around me, and I hear the sadness in his voice. I know it's my fault. I didn't want to be the cause of his sadness ever again. "I never pushed you away. I waited for you to grow up."

"Same thing."

"No. It's not. If we got together when you were younger . . . You weren't ready for this, and it wouldn't have been fair to either of us."

"I've been ready for you since the day I met you."

He brushes the hair back behind my ear. "Baby, don't you know I don't ever want to live without you?"

"Yeah, but you would've been just as happy if we stayed friends. That's what you wanted. I pushed the issue. I wanted more."

"No. That's what I'm trying to get through to you. Yes, I held back. Yes, I fought my feelings, but that was never the answer. This, you and me, this is exactly the right thing for both of us."

I don't answer. I allow him to kiss my head while he holds me close. My eyes are heavy and burning. I shut my lids and allow the sweet seduction of slumber to lead me on its path. Maybe I am overreacting. Maybe a goodnight's sleep in Jordan's arms will make it all go away in the morning.

*

I wake in the same position, wrapped up in Jordan's arms. I'm one part surprised he didn't sneak out on me in the middle of the night, and three parts thrilled that he's holding me just as close, just as tight as he did when I fell asleep. I've learned my lesson from the last time and don't attempt to run my fingers over his arms. I don't touch him at all. In fact, I do my best to not even breathe.

Little more than a minute passes before his hand runs down my arm. "Good morning beautiful."

I roll over and face him. It's a new day. The first I've ever started being held by him. Last night is all but forgotten. He doesn't mention it, and I have no intention of bringing it up. I over reacted plain and simple. There's no reason to beat a dead horse.

"Are you okay?" I ask as Jordan props himself up on his elbow.

He smiles, his pointer finger running down my nose, over my lips and neck, and in between my breasts. "Never better."

I believe him, and just like that I'm able to put last night and the blonde behind me.

Chapter 19

I love that as I lie in bed the faint scent of Jordan's cologne still lingers. I wrap myself tight in the warmth of the blanket, pretending it's the warmth of his body instead. Father Time has stepped on the accelerator and is racing at full speed now that Jordan spends some nights with me. I no longer have to deal with the anxiety and withdrawal symptoms I used to feel when he would leave so soon after he got here.

I think the actual sleeping part was the most difficult for Jordan that first night. We woke in the morning in exactly the same position, and I wondered if he slept at all. Now he's much more relaxed, and while he still wakes up before I do, I know he sleeps. I've woken up a few times in the middle of the night and been serenaded back to sleep by the soft rhythm of his deep breathing.

Life is once again perfect. Jordan and I are great. I finished my first semester with straight A's. Probably because I didn't see him too often for the first few months, so I focused my energy on schoolwork. It's not much harder than high school, and I find that as long as I'm in class and participating I don't have to study much.

I've won over most of the girls on my floor. It started at dinner before we left for winter break. I noticed a few of them sitting together one night, as my spaghetti slop was being spooned into my dish. I decided to take a page out of Maria's book and saunter on over as if I belonged there, just one of the girls. Before I approached the table Avery leaned in close, glanced my way and said something that caused all the girls to break out in laughter.

Something came over me. If they wanted something to laugh at, I'd gladly give them something. I waited until I stood just behind her. I pretended to trip over my own foot as I tilted my tray, spilling all of its contents over Avery's head.

"I'm so sorry." I said as she jumped to her feet and cursed at me.

"I can't believe you did that you dumb bitch! You're so stupid and clumsy."

"Yeah, but you're the one that has spaghetti hair. I mean literally. It's just all hanging there like a bunch of wet noodles."

"Stephanie, why don't you come sit next to me," her roommate Emma called. I gave Avery a wink and a smile before she ran off in a huff.

I looked over my shoulder for days, waiting for the retaliation that never came. I found it impossible to believe she'd just let it go. I know she wanted to lash out, I saw it in her eyes, but other than continuing with the cold shoulder and calling me names in the hall, she didn't do anything.

At the start of the new semester, Avery moved to the sorority house. Life has been good ever since. I still get shot wicked glances when our paths cross. I can deal with that, but her influence over the other girls has waned significantly, and I'm a full-fledged member of their group.

My only complaint about the New Year is that Jordan is still playing with Shred Em. It was supposed to a month or two at the most. Now, it's going on five months. I hate it, because that stupid band is still the one thing that keeps us from seeing each other, since they've been branching out further lately. Last weekend they had a gig in Pennsylvania, and last night they were up Connecticut. I resent not being able to be there for all their shows, especially when Pete's girlfriend can, and according to the Facebook page, is. I don't tell Jordan, but I check the page often. First I looked back at pictures from when Jordan first started. It looks like she was at a bunch of shows, some with Pete, some without. And she always seems to be standing next to, or staring at Jordan. In the back of my head, I know she's a threat, but I don't bring her up. I'm not going to give him an excuse to bail on me.

Either way, I just have to get through tonight. Because this is the night it all comes to an end. Pete's been practicing with the guys, and Jordan promised, one way or another, this is his last performance.

*

"Does this mean you don't need me anymore?"

"What?"

"I mean after tonight, Jordan will be around more and you won't need me to drive you anywhere."

"Jonah, I hope you don't think I'm using you for your car." The excitement I felt a moment ago at the prospect of seeing Jordan has all but seeped out of my body.

He's gripping the wheel tight, his eyes glued on the road ahead of us.

"I know."

"I didn't even know Jordan asked you drive me tonight."

"He wanted to surprise you. Can't say I blame him." His lips draw up into a tight smile.

"I hope this didn't stop you from doing something else."

He shakes his head. "I just wanted to ask you. I mean I know it's not the best day for it, but I was hoping . . . Aww forget it."

"No. Tell me."

Jonah sucks in a long, audible breath. "Okay, here goes. I told you my work is being featured in an art show." He glances at me. I nod, with a vague recollection. "Well, it's going to be on Valentine's Day. And it's in a really small gallery, a hole in the wall in Manhattan, but still, it's sort of a big deal. Well to me it's a huge deal and I'm nervous. Like I want to throw my balls up nervous, so I was wondering if you'd maybe come as my guest. Mainly to make sure I don't pass out or say something stupid, or just to keep me company." He releases a breath, similar to the one he took before his mini rant. "And then when it's over, I could drop you off at Jordan's, or he could meet us back at school. If he doesn't mind that is."

Valentine's Day. That's a tough one. Not only because of what it represents, but I know Jordan has depositions. Come to think of it, I'm not even sure he'll want to be with me after that. It might be hard enough for him to have to think about Madison and talk about her all day, without then having to look at me and feel guilty about it.

"Do you mind if I get back to you on that one? I have to think about it, and I want to talk to Jordan first."

Jonah nods. "Sorry, I shouldn't have asked."

"I'm glad you did. I think it would be a lot of fun. I just don't want to commit to anything without discussing it with him first."

"Sure. I understand."

We continue driving in silence until Jonah pulls up in front of the bar. "Have fun tonight," he says without looking at me.

I nod, uncertain why things feel so strange between us. "Are we okay? I mean are you upset that I didn't give you an answer?"

Jonah shakes his head. "I kind of expected you to say no, so . . ."

"I didn't say no. I said maybe."

"Okay. And Stephanie," He looks at me, "You look beautiful."

"Thank you." I lean over and kiss his cheek before getting out of the car, glad this is the last time he'll be driving me here. Whatever just went down between us didn't feel right. I think I need to put a little distance between Jonah and me.

I turn and wave as Jonah pulls away. Ross is outside talking to a group of three girls. His eyes leave them for a minute and meet mine. Recognizing me, he smiles. "Go on in."

"Thanks."

I'm excited to be here for Jordan's last night with the band. I'm more excited that it's the final call. After tonight, I get my boyfriend all to myself. Finally. It will be the first time since we found each other on the beach that I'll have his full attention. I want to hold up a flashing "applaud now" sign every time I think of it.

I look around the bar. The crowd more than tripled since the first time I came. It's even packed compared to Halloween. Jordan said the crowd's been growing consistently, that each time they play more people cram into the confined space to see them. It certainly looks that way tonight. I search the sea of people looking for her; the one person I dread seeing. Unfortunately, I know if I look long enough, search hard enough I'll find her. She always shows up when they play here. I've seen her in pictures at other venues too. Still, no matter what Jordan says, I hate her. I push my way through the crowd so I'm close enough that he can see me, and count the minutes until the end of the set.

"And for our last number we have a special song going out from our drummer to his very beautiful girlfriend, Stephanie." Blaze searches for me in the crowd. When he finds me he winks and smiles. I turn my attention to Jordan, who looks surprised. Instead of locking his eyes on mine and giving me his warm, playful smile, his eyes drop to his drums. He doesn't look up, doesn't search for me among the crowd. I know it's crazy, but I feel like he's purposely avoiding my eyes.

The bad feeling spreads inside me when Chaz turns back and speaks. Jordan's only response is to shake his head. Something's not right. I see it all over Chaz's face. After another brief exchange between the two, Jordan hits his sticks against each other and the music starts. From the introduction Blaze gave, I know the song he referred to. The one they worked on the first night I saw them play. I'm not sure if they played it before I arrived on Halloween, but I haven't heard it yet. Knowing Chaz said I helped inspire some of lyrics, I pay extra attention and listen carefully.

Our eyes met
I lost my heart
You stole it
Ripped me apart
Flames bubbled from my stream of blood
Burned bright, fed with your pure love
You're the air that gave life to the fire
You're the drug that keeps me climbing higher

You're the only one for me
Don't turn your back
Never set me free
Know I'd rather die
Than watch you walk away and say goodbye
I loved you from the very beginning
The beginning of always
And I'm yours until forever ends

Like a stalker I watched your every move
Was afraid to tell you, afraid you'd disapprove
I need to keep you in my arms
Until the end of days and all beyond

Your absence suffocates me
Chokes me of air
Feels like I'm going to lose my mind
It's too much to bear
I don't want to live if it means we're apart
Because from now until forever you own my heart

You're the only one for me
Don't turn your back
Never set me free
Know I'd rather die
Than watch you walk away and say goodbye
I loved you from the very beginning
The beginning of always
And I'm yours until forever ends

Don't ever forget these words they're just a few
Inscribed in my heart, belonging just to you
I loved you from the beginning of always
And I'm yours for the test of time
Just say the words I want to hear
Tell me that you're mine

I loved you from the very beginning
The beginning of always
And I'm yours until forever ends

Tears fill my eyes. The sounds coming off the instruments and the words spilling from Blaze's mouth create magic. It's almost impossible to keep in mind what a jerk Blaze really is when he's reaching inside my chest and touching my heart. I swallow hard, trying to push the emotion back. I move forward, towards the platform serving as a stage and notice Jordan staring daggers at Blaze. Why? Did he want to be the one to introduce it?

Fear starts creeping its way into my conscious. Jordan hasn't looked at me since Blaze made the announcement. Not once. Not at all. Did he lose me in the crowd? He never acts like this. I have to get to him. Now. Before I can make a move, someone grabs my shoulders and kisses my cheek.

"So glad you could be here, Stephanie," Chaz says. "I hope you liked the song."

"I loved it!" I wrap my arms around his neck and give him a quick hug. "It's my new favorite."

"Good. I'm just sorry I have to go. Wendy's home waiting for me. She's been away all week, and I promised I'd leave as soon as we got off the stage."

Once Chaz walks away, insecurity strikes. In the middle of a wall-to-wall crowd, I feel completely alone. Jordan still hasn't made his way over to me. He should have been at my side by now. I search the cramped room and find him off to the side of the stage. He looks upset, maybe even angry. I can't be sure from the distance.

With him are the blonde I've come to hate, and Blaze. I keep my eyes on the threesome as I push my way to Jordan. I'm close when I run into a bottleneck of people and stop making forward progress. Not close enough to hear them, or for him to realize I'm only a few feet away. He's still not looking for me. He's too preoccupied with her. She speaks animatedly as she pokes her finger into Jordan's chest. He shakes his head and holds his hands up, palms facing her. I can't tell what he's saying or what's going on, but neither of them looks happy. If I have to guess I'd say he's pleading his case before he turns his dark, angry stare onto Blaze. Blaze doesn't participate in the conversation. He just stands beside them with a dumb, satisfied smirk on his face.

I'm almost there, just three feet and about fifteen seconds stand between where I am and approaching Jordan to demand answers from him. Before this moment, I wanted to deny the connection he had with this girl. I wanted to believe the one person I trust most in the world when he said she doesn't mean anything. But I can't any longer. There's more to them than he's willing to admit, and while I feel I need to give him the benefit of the doubt, I need the truth. I can't keep lying to myself, and that's what I've been doing. Feeding myself a diet of bullshit.

It's loud, and he doesn't hear me call out to him when the blonde slaps him. How dare her! I start to move again, ready to tell her off, but watch dumbfounded instead as she turns, and pushes through the crowd in the direction opposite me with Jordan on her heels. I watch, unable to stop him as he follows her out the front door. An unfamiliar pain rips through my chest. What the hell just happened? I stare at the front door, waiting for him to turn back, throw his arms around me, and apologize. It doesn't happen. There's no sign of him.

None.

The door to the bar opens and closes with regularity. A steady stream of people come and go. None of them are Jordan. I don't know what to do. Do I go out the door and hope he's out front? What if he isn't? Will Ross let me back in? What if Jordan just left me here? I decide to give him a minute before I do anything. I keep my eyes trained on the door the whole time, except for when I look down to see if the minute has passed. Not only has it come and gone, but three more minutes passed as well. Blaze is over by the bar having a drink.

Still holding my phone in my hand, I change directions and push through the crowd toward him. I know he's involved in whatever is going on. Feeling a small vibration in my pocket I look at my phone and check the new message.

Sorry, Steph. I have to take care of something. I'll be back in a few, as soon as I'm done.

He didn't really just send this did he? Does he think I don't know the something he needs to take care of is another girl? With Jordan gone, that only leaves one person to give me answers, and I hate that I'm considering giving him the time of day, but Jordan left me no choice.

Blaze stands at the bar ordering a drink when I tap him on the shoulder. He turns to me. "Stephanie, can I get you something?"

"No."

"Suit yourself." He turns back to the barmaid, finishes his order, and ignores me.

I move around to his other side as I'm being pushed out of the way by some rowdy girls.

"Can we talk?" I yell over the loud music.

"Come," Blaze reaches his hand around my shoulder. I want to slink away from him, but I don't. I decide to play nice in order to get the deets I'm looking for.

Blaze moves us to a spot in the corner, where the bar and wall meet. It a little quieter here as the speaker mounted on the wall over us is projecting the music into the open space, and not down below it where we're standing.

"What's wrong? You look upset."

"She's more to him than Pete's girlfriend isn't she?" As the words leave my mouth, I feel my stomach twist like a drill bit, down to the center of the earth. It's weighed down and heavy by the truth of what I just said. I'm holding my breath feeling my airways constrict as I wait for Blaze to answer, to confirm what I already know.

Blaze nods. "Pete broke up with her."

I feel the color drain from my face. If I didn't know better, I'd think someone just dumped a bucket of ice water over my head.

Blaze shakes his head, "Jordan hasn't told you about Missy?"

I wrap my arms around my stomach, afraid I'm going to be sick. "No."

"Then I guess the best thing I can say right now is that he's a dumb ass."

The server is back with his drink. Blaze nods at the waitress, and I assume he's ordering another.

"A toast then. To the dumb ass." He holds the cup out for a moment, as if I had something to clink against it.

"Where are your girlfriends?" I ask.

He smiles and blinks his lashes at me, "Should I be flattered you're asking?"

"No." I snap. "I've just never seen you without them."

He looks away before meeting my eyes again. "Lover's quarrel."

"What, they finally grew a pair and said no to you, so now you're pissed?"

"You really don't like me do you?" I don't answer, I don't need to. He already knows the answer to that. I just look long and hard into his beautiful eyes. "Maybe you haven't noticed, but they're much more into each other than either of them is into me."

I smirk. He could tell from my face I think he's full of shit.

"Seriously, I'm sort of their plaything. A hot, warm blooded dildo for all intents and purposes."

I squeeze my eyes shut. "Stop. Please." I want this conversation to end. I need it to end because instead of keeping my mind off Jordan and the fact that he jilted me for that blonde bitch, it has me wondering if he picked up Blaze's perspective on things like love and dating. I wonder if that's the part Jordan's playing for Missy right now a hot, warm blooded dildo.

Blaze's violet/blue eyes are bright and shining as he watches me. They soften up his gruff exterior. He smiles, and rests his hand at the bottom of my neck. It's a shame I can't get his jerk image out of my head because he really is amazing to look at. And he's the perfect distraction for my broken heart. I know that's all anyone will ever be, just a distraction because Jordan is weaved so deep in the fabric of my soul, I'll never be over him. And as much as my heart is aching right now, it still belongs to him.

"Missy's the reason he's been playing with us. She poured on the water works and laid some guilt trip on him. Made him promise to stay until Pete was ready to come back. Only, until two weeks ago Pete wasn't sure he even wanted to come back. But a promise is a promise and Jordan wouldn't leave until Pete made his decision."

"You don't like her much do you?"

He shrugs. "She's not my problem."

"But she's Jordan's?"

He doesn't answer. He just stares at me.

I take a deep breath before asking the next question. "She was pissed because the song was dedicated to me, wasn't she?"

"Yeah." He looks toward the door and then back at me. "That's why she was pissed."

"Can you do me a favor? If he bothers to come back, tell him I said to go to hell."

"Will do." Blaze wears a triumphant smile. "And Stephanie," he leans his elbow on the bar. "If you ever want to have some fun you know where to find me."

Chapter 20

I'm not sure where I'm going, but since I'm walking around Brooklyn, late at night, I think I'm going home. I can't believe Jordan ditched me without so much as a second thought, in a bar full of sleazy guys looking to hook up. He'd be the first one to tell me to dump the loser if a guy ever did this to me. Maybe that's his plan, get me to break up with him.

A car slows at the side of the street, and the driver rolls down his window. "Want a ride?"

Not in the mood to deal with any bullshit, I flip him the bird.

"Bitch!" He rolls his window up and speeds away.

It's too late to walk by myself. I call Maria. She can't come get me, her parents are out and they have the car.

I refuse to call Jonah. Not now, not for this. I think his feelings for me are already muddled. And again it's not something I want to deal with at the moment. With no other choice, I call my mother. Besides, it might be good for me to spend a night at home.

"We'll be there in a few minutes, sweetheart."

We. Great, Eddie's with her.

"It's okay, Mom. Stay where you are, I can get a ride from someone else. I'll go back to school."

"Absolutely not. Just give us a few minutes. We're getting into the car right now."

I hate that I resorted to calling my mother. How many times did she tell me to forget him? I bet there's a part of her that's thrilled. I just set myself up to be bamboozled with I-told-you-so's for the next twelve hours.

My phone vibrates.

I'm looking for you all over. Where are you?

He finally remembered I exist. I look at his first message. He sent it forty minutes ago. Forty Minutes! Now he's worried?

As far away as I can get from you.

I'm sorry. Did you go home or to school? We need to talk.

Fuck You.

Stephanie, please let me explain.

Explain what? How you left me alone? How you bailed on me for her? How dare you? And how dare you think you can talk to me now and smooth things over. You wanted her, now you have her.

Ten minutes pass between the time I spoke to my mother and the moment Eddie pulls up to corner we agreed to meet at. My phone continues to buzz but I'm struggling not to look at the texts, or answer his calls. Part of me wants to see the messages telling me how sorry he is, how if he had to do it over, he would never leave me like that again. Another part of me thinks he might be hurting at least a little bit. That's the vindictive part that wants to snipe back at him with nasty comments and rub salt in the wound. I know better than to act on those feelings, I'd regret it almost immediately, and that's when bad things tend to happen to the people I love. There is yet still another part of me, the numb part that's protecting my brain from feeling the sharp, all-consuming pain I felt watching him chase after Missy.

Each time I tell myself it's time to forget him, to move on, my mind starts rationalizing that maybe I misunderstood what happened. That's when I hit it gently against the glass window, hoping to knock some sense into myself.

"You all right back there?" Eddie asks looking at me through the rearview mirror.

Yeah. Wonderful, idiot. I get that he's trying to make small talk, trying to break the awkward tension, but I don't want any part of him.

Maria's watching for me from her window. Once I'm home, she climbs over the wrought iron banister and comes over. We go straight up to my room while my mother and Eddie say goodbye. I tried to convince them I don't mind if he stays over, but they agreed he wouldn't spend the night when I'm home. It was a relief to not worry about bumping into him in the middle of the night during winter break, but tonight, it's late and I'm the one intruding.

I lie in bed telling Maria about the heart-wrenching scene. Heart-wrenching for me, and how I've suspected something between Jordan and Missy all along. She understands how betrayed I feel since she just went through the same thing a few months ago. To my relief she plays with my hair and listens instead of going on about what an idiot I've been wasting years waiting for him.

I don't sleep, but somewhere between three and four in the morning Maria conks out. My phone's been quiet. I guess he realizes he's not getting anywhere. I can't help myself, without Maria's supervision, or conscious company, I grab my phone and listen to the voicemails. He sounds scared.

"Please, baby. Let me explain."

"I've been everywhere looking for you. No one's heard from you. Please just let me know you're okay."

"Steph, I went to your dorm, no one's seen you. Jonah checked your room, said there's no sign of you. Please call and let me know where you are."

I break.

You can rest easy, I'm alive.

My phone chimes immediately. I take some comfort knowing he's not getting any more sleep than I am.

Where are you? We need to talk.

Nothing to talk about. I know all about Missy.

I figure seeing her name in black and white will send him a message. But just in case he has any difficulty translating my words, I add on for good measure.

Goodbye Jordan.

*

Maria drives me back to school the next day. She wanted me to stay home, but I can't. It hurts too much because everything I see, everywhere I go, it all reminds me of Jordan. Not that being at school is much better, but at least I don't worry that I'll break down and go see him. Even if I wanted to, I have no car, no means to get to him.

"He called me," she says when we are about ten minutes away from the campus.

"I don't care."

"Yes, you do. I didn't speak to him though. I haven't answered his text messages either."

"Can you do something for me? Can you stay out of it?"

"Is that what you really want?"

"Yes."

"I think you need to talk to him, see what happened."

"I thought you were on my side."

"I'm always on your side, but anyone with eyes can see he's in love with you, maybe . . ."

"If he loved me so much we would've been together a long time ago. If he truly loved me, he wouldn't hurt me over and over again."

"Okay." She nods. "I won't call him back, but what do I do if he comes to my house?"

"Do whatever you want, as long as you leave me out of it. Don't mention me. Don't talk about me. Most of all, don't tell me."

Chapter 21

Maria spends the day with me trying to keep me occupied and my mind off Jordan. She knows that's about as useful as shoveling snow in Antarctica. Once she leaves I put on a pair of sweats and an old tee shirt. The shirt had been my father's. There are still two drawers full of his clothes at home. Tee and sweatshirts. At least they were still there before I left for school. HIs scent is completely erased from the material since he died over ten years ago, but still wearing it makes me feel a little better, like maybe in some small way he's with me.

I'm glad I snuck the shirt out while I packed for school. Seeing how close my mother and Eddie are I wonder if she replaced my father's things with Eddie's. I don't have anything against Eddie, and I have no doubt how much my mother loved my father, I just wish my father were around. Not that he could do anything if he were, but just knowing I could go home to him if I wanted to would be nice. Or that I could call him and cry about the boy who broke my heart without having to worry about hearing "I told you it would never work." I believe my father would let me cry doing nothing more than stroking my hair and telling me how much he loved me.

Maybe if he were still alive I wouldn't have fallen so hard for Jordan to begin with. And once I got him, I wouldn't have been so afraid of losing him because I'd be ignorant to the how deep losing someone you love slices through your heart. Maybe if I were less afraid and more confident I would've been able to keep Jordan's attention. Maybe it wouldn't have made the slightest bit of difference, but I'd trade anything for a real live hug from my father right now.

I'm not asleep when I hear the light wrapping on my door. I don't know if I'll ever sleep again. I've been in a sort of trance like state since last night. I can't imagine things getting any better tonight.

The knock comes again, this time with a voice. "Open up, Steph."

I swallow hard. He came. I don't understand the jumble of mixed up feelings running through me. I get up and stare at the door, my body making small adjustments that keep me moving forward, towards it. Towards him. I ache to open the door and see him, hear him out. I yearn to open the door and punch him in the face. Most of all I want him to wrap me in his arms and never let me go.

"Open the door, Stephanie. I'm not going to leave."

I reach out for the knob, and wrap my fingers around it. I can do this. I'm strong enough. I lost so much and yet here I am still standing. A cold chill runs over my skin. I feel like it's a sign from my father that he's with me, that he'll lend me strength.

I know the only way I can keep strong is to keep away from the poison slowly killing me. I need to keep away from Jordan. I lean my back against the door and slide down so that I'm sitting on the floor.

"I thought you said you knew about Missy?" His voice isn't loud, it's not angry. Instead it mirrors the things I'm feeling right now. He sounds sad, defeated.

How am I supposed to answer? Knowing doesn't make knowing they're together any easier.

"Go away, Jordan. You made your choice."

"Steph, you're my choice. Always. I need you to take a leap of faith and listen to me."

I know what to do. I get up, grab my phone and sit at the edge of my bed. I pull up my music app and turn the volume up as high as it can go. If I could drown out the sound of his voice I won't be tempted to open the door and fall into his arms, arms that have held me like I'm the only one that mattered. Arms no longer meant for me.

I lie in bed, my phone next to my ear, a pillow over my head. I stay like this for a while. I'm not sure how long, but I'm almost done listening to my playlist, that's at least an hour. I've heard my phone buzz a couple of times alerting me to text messages. I don't doubt they're from Jordan, but I don't bother to look. Not yet.

I yawn, feeling like I can't move a muscle. Breathing feels like a chore. My eyes are closed, and I feel myself start to drift. I hope sleep will act like a protective shelter. That it will serve as a cocoon and transform me into a new and improved version of myself so I could put Jordan Brewer behind me once and for all.

*

I growl when I hear my alarm alert me that it's time wake up. I haven't slept in days. Not the good, REM kind of sleep that keeps you from losing your mind. Instead I've suffered through a mind numbing drifting in and out of consciousness for an hour at a time. It doesn't help time pass or avert my mind from what's missing from my life. It only makes it worse. I understand now why Jordan had such a hard time with the silence night offers. I hate that my mind keeps falling back to him. But I can't stop it. He didn't just hurt me, he destroyed me.

Still I miss him like crazy.

I barely leave my room the first week. I even skip classes, which isn't my smartest idea because the semester just started, and I might need those days if I get sick. I don't do much more than lay in bed and hide from the world waiting for my phone to ring. When it does, my heart sinks because it's my mother, or Maria, or someone that's not Jordan. I don't answer, but send them text messages that I'm okay so they won't worry, but most of all so they'll leave me alone because if by some miracle I did forget my broken heart for all of thirty seconds, they're right there to remind me.

By the end of the week, I'm showering and attending classes. I can't focus on my schoolwork, but I hope being there will be enough to eventually snap me out of the quicksand of depression I'm sinking in.

Carla comes by my room a few times, looking to go to dinner or hang out, but I don't answer the door. All my hard work in making friends the first semester is flushed down the toilet bowl. Jonah gives me space, too. At least physical space. He, too, is driving me crazy with the non-stop texting. I don't answer his texts the first few days.

By Monday night Jordan gave up trying to get in touch with me.

I'm giving you time because I think that's what you need. I'm not giving up on you or us. So don't even think it. When you're ready to talk, call me.

That was it, the last that I heard from him. Not a phone call or text message after that. Not even an impersonal email. I know he says he's leaving it up to me, but when he chased after Missy without a glance in my direction, he made his choice. I'm choosing not to fall back under his spell. So much for until the end of forever. That came and went in a matter of months.

Music is ruined for me. I can't listen to the radio, or my iPod. Any time I do, I'm turned off because it's a love song that reminds me of how broken my heart is, how much I miss him, or how deep my love for him is. For the few songs that aren't all sweet and mushy, as soon as I hear a drum beat it sends my mind on a one-way trip to Jordanville.

I shouldn't be surprised that he gave up so easily. He'd been stringing me along with his friendship and flirtatious smile for years, only to two-time me for the duration of our entire relationship. And the fact that he left me standing like an idiot while he went after her is a clear indicator that she means more to him than I do. And that kills me.

I reach for my phone and pull up a picture of him. "I hate you!" I yell before chucking it on my bed.

Valentine's Day is tomorrow. Jonah keeps texting to see if I'm going to the stupid art show with him. You'd think he'd get the hint already. If I wanted to go I would've said yes when he asked, or the first time he sent me a reminder.

It will be good for you to get out.

I'm not good company.

I'm not surprised by the knock on my door. I've rarely seen him over the last week. I haven't been going to eat in the cafeteria and have decided to become a hermit.

"I know you're in there, Steph."

I know I can't keep hiding. It's not doing me any good anyway. I need to get back into the swing of things. Jump back into the land of the living. I answer the door in an attempt to take that first step.

Jonah stares at me. "You feel okay?"

"Yeah, wonderful. My life is perfect. Things have never been better. Why?"

"You're just not looking so good."

"You're such a jerk." I turn and flop onto my bed.

"I'm not going to act like there's even the slightest chance that you forgot the significance of tomorrow. But I think it might be good to not be alone, and spend every minute thinking about him. The art show might distract you."

I shrug my shoulders. "Whatever. It doesn't matter."

"Have you heard from him?"

I don't attempt to speak because if I do and my voice cracks, I won't be able to deny that I don't care about Jordan any longer. I shake my head, annoyed that Jonah has the nerve to ask.

"He wasn't here yesterday?"

"I think I'd know if he was. Everyone on the floor would probably know."

Jonah nods. "Why don't you call and talk to him? It might not be too late to work things out."

"Work what out? He cheated on me."

"Look." His eyes dart off to the side, and he looks annoyed. "It kills me to stand here and defend him because I think you can do so much better, but you're miserable. So here goes. Did you ever think you might be wrong about what happened?"

I play that night at the bar over and over in my head. Blaze dedicated the song to me from Jordan. It upset Jordan. It upset Missy. He didn't even look in my direction while he tried to smooth things over with her. And then he just left me there, all by myself.

"I don't think so. Besides, Blaze confirmed everything. And the kicker, Pete broke up with her earlier that night.

"For what it's worth, if you didn't actually see anything physical between Jordan and Missy, you might have misunderstood. I'd love for you to come with me. If you don't want to I understand, but I'll be driving through Brooklyn on my way to Manhattan."

"What are you saying?"

"I'm saying you should talk to him. If you can't work things out, maybe you'll have closure and you'll be able to leave your room and start living again."

I call Maria when Jonah leaves. "I feel myself caving."

"It's about time."

I don't want to. He always meant more to me than I did to him. I don't want to give him the upper hand again.

"All I'm going to say is this. Is it possible they were friends before you started dating him?"

"I guess."

"If her boyfriend dumped her ass, she was probably more sensitive. Maybe she thought the song was something between her and her boyfriend."

"I don't think so."

"But do you agree that it's possible?"

I think about it and I suddenly feel like an idiot.

"And even if she wants him, doesn't it say something that after all was said and done he went back to you? Just because she likes him doesn't mean the feeling's mutual."

"You really think I should call him?"

"I think you don't have anything to lose."

*

Hi.

I hit send and tap my foot while I wait. It's a stupid idea. I shouldn't have texted him, but I was too much of a coward to call him straight away.

My phone vibrates almost immediately.

Hi.

Now what? A million thoughts are running through my head. What do I say?

I start to type, but before I finish, a new message comes from Jordan.

I miss you.

My heart pounds hard against my chest as my eyes water with tears.

I miss you too. Can we talk?

I'm so nervous. Texting is so much easier than speaking. There's no tone, no emotion in the typed words. The spoken words are much more telling.

Yes. But not now.

Oh.

Sorry. I need to get through tomorrow.

Depositions. I forgot. An image of how distraught he looked after getting off the phone with his lawyer rushes to mind. I know tomorrow is going to be tough. He should have support. I want to be there for him, I'm just not sure he wants me there.

Tomorrow or some other day?

Tomorrow night.

Are you sure? It's fine if you're not up to it.

I don't know if I'm hoping he'll agree or push it off. This is where hearing his voice would clue me in.

I'll be fine. But I want to talk in person.

Okay.

My decision is made, I'm going to go with Jonah and have him drop me off.

Will you be in court?

I hope he doesn't ask why I want to know.

No, at my attorney's office downtown.

Awesome. I remember his attorney's name, and now that I know the office is downtown, I have something to go on.

Do you know what time you'll be finished?

Not sure. I have to be there at three.

Okay. If you need me, just call.

I always need you. I'll talk to you tomorrow.

Chapter 22

I wake from the best night's sleep I've had since Jordan and I broke up. I keep looking back over our brief exchange, and each time I come to the words, 'I'll always need you,' I break out in smiles. He doesn't hate me. If he did, he'd never write that. Even if it were true, he wouldn't admit it. I've calmed down enough to hear him out with an open mind. I don't know if I can forgive him and go back to the way things were between us, but I'm feeling better knowing we're communicating again.

*

I catch Jonah glancing over at me again. I get a swishing feeling in my stomach, like ocean waves are rocking back and forth inside it, a sign that I'm nervous.

"What?" I ask.

He shakes his head. "Nothing."

"You sure?"

He loosens his tie and nods.

"By the way, you look amazing." He's dressed in black pants, a dark purple button down shirt and a thin grey tie. "I don't know if girls go to art shows, but if they do, I'm sure they'll be quite taken with you."

His lips curl up into a warm smile as he pulls up in front of the building. "Thanks."

I pull my phone out and look back over the text Jordan sent me half an hour ago.

Had to come early. Finished up sooner than expected. Going for coffee in the restaurant across the street. I'll let you know when I leave.

"I can wait a while if you'd like." Jonah offers. "I mean that way, if anything you can come with me and then you don't have to worry about a ride back."

I pull down the visor and look in the mirror one last time to make sure my make-up isn't smeared. Regardless of what happens, I want him to feel it in his pants when he sees me.

"Thanks. But I'll be fine. Besides, I'll cramp your style. Go have fun. Live it up."

"Stephanie." He reaches for my hand and swallows hard. I have that weird feeling in my stomach, like he's about to say or do something that's going to make me feel uncomfortable and change our relationship. I have to stop him because I can't handle any more drama right now.

"I'm in Brooklyn. If I need to, I can hop on a bus and go home. Now don't worry about me, go have fun."

He nods again. "I was just going to say, you look really beautiful." I hear the emotion in his voice. I see it in his eyes. I can deal with this later. Right now, I just want to get to Jordan. I pull my hand from his loose grip, and smile back at him before opening my door and getting to my feet.

"Thanks. And good luck."

"You, too."

I straighten out the bottom of my black dress. It's one of two dresses I'd taken to school with me, just in case Jordan wanted to go somewhere nice. Little did I know he'd join a band and I'd hardly see him the first semester. My heart's racing knowing I'm going to see him in a few minutes. I close my eyes and take in a deep breath, full of all the pollutants Brooklyn air has to offer.

"Here goes nothing." I say to myself as I look around. There are two coffee shops, and a nicer, at least from the outside looking in, restaurant. He said he was going for coffee. I decide to look in the coffee shops first. The first one is half full, but there's no sign of Jordan. The second only has one table being used. It's not Jordan.

I look at the restaurant. It looks too nice for him to go to for coffee, unless he's not alone. Maybe his mother came along to offer the moral support I should've given him. I close my eyes and shake my head, silently scolding myself.

The hostess looks up and comes out from behind the counter where the register sits, with a menu in her hand. "Table for one?"

"Oh, I'm meeting someone. He's already here."

"Really?" Her eyebrows furrow together as she looks back into the dining room. "No one mentioned they were waiting for other guests to arrive."

"It's sort of a surprise." I whisper, although I'm not sure why. "He doesn't know I'm coming."

"Oh." She smiles. "Go right in. I'll send a waiter over in a minute."

"Thank you."

I take a deep breath and step forward. Now all I have to do is find him. I glance around the room. Everyone is dressed nice, the men in suits, the women mostly in dresses or skirt suits. I never thought about what Jordan would be wearing to meet with his lawyers, but I assume he must be dressed up as well. And then I see him. I can't take my eyes off him in his white button down shirt and tie. He looks mature, handsome, professional. My heart wakes up and races to a frantic rhythm. I soak him in, take in the whole scene before I approach him. He looks calm, confident the way he sits with his dark grey jacket draped over the back of his chair, leaning forward, smiling at the woman sitting across from him.

My hand automatically rises to my mouth. My body tenses. I'm so rigid if a strong breeze blows through the restaurant I think I'll snap in half. I want to scream, but I can't. I can't make a sound. Not with the elephant sitting dab, smack on the middle of my chest.

Chapter 23

I just dumped a glass of water over my boyfriend's head. Correction. My ex-boyfriend. That lying, cheating, slime of slug that I've been in love with since my freshman year of high school. The boy that up until two minutes ago I believed I couldn't live without.

I blink back the tears from my eyes as I power walk down the block. Stupid tears better not fall. I refuse to let them. Not now, not where he could see me. If he cares at all he'll come chasing after me. I look behind me. He's not there. I don't see him. I don't hear him calling my name.

I. Hate. Him.

And now I want to poke my eyeballs out, force them right out of their sockets. Maybe that will erase the image of him all sweet and cute with Missy, from my brain. I've never been more blindsided than I am at this moment. And I shouldn't be. I know better, but once again I allowed myself to hope, to believe maybe we could work through this.

I stood frozen in the spot I stood for at least a minute when I spotted him. I didn't expect him to be alone, but I knew immediately she wasn't his mother. With her blonde hair draped over the side of her face, she looked different. I took a tiny step closer, trying desperately to convince myself not to jump to conclusions, not to listen the twisting of my stomach and the nagging voice in the back of my head. There had to be a logical explanation.

Of course there was. I just didn't want to believe it.

I cleared my throat trying to find my voice, but I wasn't close enough for them to hear, not close enough to interrupt what turned into the worst moment of my entire life, and the Lord knows I've had plenty of bad moments. I watched silently in horror as Jordan, handed her the little, black, box covered in velvet. Their eyes met and locked. That's when the tears stung and I knew I had no choice but to face the truth, no matter how ugly it was.

I looked on in silence, like I was invisible as she pulled her hair back behind her ear. He nodded to her. I wanted to run over and hit the box out of her hands, but I couldn't move. I needed to see what was on the inside. When she opened it, when I saw it, I felt like I'd been punched in the chest and had the wind knocked out of me. It happened so fast. Both our eyes took in the diamond engagement ring at the same time. We both covered our mouths. She threw her arms around Jordan's neck. My knees buckled and I fell to the floor.

"Are you all right miss? Can I help you up?"

If I was anything it wasn't all right. I couldn't speak, I shook my head, but it didn't stop the waiter from grasping my arms and pulling me up. I felt eyes on me, people stared, but not him, thankfully. He was too focused on Missy, that blonde bitch.

"Jordan, it's beautiful!" Her eyes watered.

"I'm good. Thank you," I snapped at the stranger who still had his hands on me.

"I'm so happy. I can't believe it!" She gushed.

I glared at Jordan. I never thought he would treat me like this. I thought he loved me. Real, true, I-want-to-spend-the-rest-of-my-life-with-you, loved me. I think back to his text the previous night, 'I always need you," and my heart aches even more. He offered me a seed of hope that in a matter of hours grew into a towering stalk leading into the clouds. And in a heartbeat he destroyed it, chopped it down at its base. With small, narrowed eyes, I approached the table and did the first thing I thought of. I reached for a glass of water.

"Stephanie!" His eyes opened wide.

Surprise, baby!

"I'd wish you a happy life together, but I hope you both rot in hell." That's when I dumped the water over his head.

"Jordan!" the witch shrieked. "Do something."

"No need." I said staring at him gaping open mouthed, "I'm out of here."

*

Luckily I have money on me. Being a college student, that's not always the case. But I knew the possibility existed that I might miss him and need to take the bus back home. I'll need to transfer busses to get there, but I'm not even sure home is where I want to go. I don't want to call Jonah. Things were weird enough when I got out of the car. That's a situation I need to avoid at all costs. I need to get the hell out of here, just in case Jordan grows a pair and comes after me, either to tell me off, or make sure I'm okay.

I jump on the first bus I see pulling up. I'm not familiar with this part of Brooklyn, or these bus lines. I'm not even sure where it's headed, all I know is it promises to take me away from here, away from Jordan.

I wait a while before I ask the driver where the bus is going. It turns out I have to take three buses in total to get home. All said and done, it will be about two hours before I get there. I consider calling Maria and asking her to meet me, but I rather be alone. I think about how fast she seemed to get over Rob, and decide to call her after all. She is my best friend, and maybe she could clue me in on how I can get rid of the sharp pain ripping through my chest with every breath.

"What the hell happened? I thought you were going to talk to him?"

"I guess I don't need to anymore. He cheated on me the whole time. And I just caught him . . . " I don't think I could say it, but I have to. If I say it, it will become more real in my mind, and at this point I have to move out of my castle in the sky and take residence in a dirty, dingy apartment right in the middle of realityville. "Maria, he didn't just cheat. He proposed to her."

"No way. I know he loves you."

"Sometimes love isn't enough."

"Didn't he at least call to tell you . . ." She clamps her mouth shut, and now I know she's holding out on me. Now I'm pissed at her.

"Tell. Me. What? I swear, Maria. If you don't tell me right now, this instant I will never forgive you. I'll hang up and you will never hear from me again."

"I'm sorry. I just found out a couple of days ago, and it's not like he told me."

"What? Did you know he planned on asking her to marry him?"

"Of course not. I avoided him because I promised you I would, but the other day I passed his house and his mother was outside, so I stopped to talk to her."

"And?" I can't believe she's dragging this out. Is she trying to torture me? What in the world could possibly be worse, or as bad as him proposing to Missy?

"He moved, Steph."

"Moved? His mother sold the house?"

"No. She didn't move, he did. She said he left Brooklyn, and asked her not to tell anyone where he is. She promised he'll get in touch when he's ready."

I run my hand back and forth across my forehead. "He must have moved in with her. I can't believe he'd do this to me."

"Are you okay?"

I nod. "I'm wonderful. Peachy-freaking-keen."

"Do you want to come with me to Jonah's art show?"

"Nah." I don't mention that he weirded me out earlier.

"I don't have to go, I can drive you back to campus, and we can hang out."

"Nah, I'm good."

"You're not even crying."

"You didn't cry for long."

"Yes, but Jordan isn't some random guy you casually dated."

"You're right. He's an asshole."

"An asshole you've been in love with since you were fourteen."

"Still . . ."

"I know you're hurt. If you can't let it out with me, then who?"

The answer to that is simple. The one person I lost forever. Jordan.

*

I have an idea, and while I'm on the bus, I look at Shred Em's Facebook page. They aren't performing tonight. Funny up until last week, they never seemed to have a weekend night off. Maybe the girlfriends forced their hand since it's Valentine's Day.

From there it's easy to find Blaze's personal page. Of course it's covered with pictures of him with random, barely dressed girls. I stare at the pictures of him. Too bad he's such a jerk. But I'm not looking to replace Jordan. I'm looking to hurt him. I can't think of anyone that would stick it to him more than Blaze. I tap away at the keys and send him a private message.

Knowing that I have a plan in action helps me keep a calm, cool exterior. Once I transfer buses, I check my phone. My hands shake, my heart races when I see Blaze responded to my message. I nibble on my bottom lip, knowing the action I'm about to take will probably leave me feeling worse in the morning, but right now I don't care. I just need to get home. Then I can let myself start to feel, start to rip apart at the seams.

When I get to my house, it's empty. My mother and Eddie are at dinner. Perfect since I'm not up to talking. The adrenaline buzzing through my body has me bouncing off the walls. I shower, pile on make-up hoping I could hide my pain and humiliation beneath it. I manage to piece together an outfit. I find a pair of old jeans I can barely squeeze myself into and an equally small shirt that hugs my breasts tight. Perfect bar attire. I know I look good and I'm certain Blaze will agree. He's the key player in project forget Jordan.

Once I'm done dressing, I check the time. I'm supposed to meet Blaze at the Tortoise Shell in less than an hour. I'm not worried about getting in. I've done it before. Getting Jordan to know I'm there might be a challenge, but I have a feeling I'll be able to convince Blaze to help me rub it in his face.

I call a car to drive me to the bar. I've spent enough time on buses today. I pay the driver and take note that I'm almost out of cash. I haven't thought about where I'm going when I leave, home or to school, or how I'm going to get to either one. I can figure it out later. Right now, I focus my energy on perfect posture. I stand straight up, boobs front and center looking perky, and flounce my way into the bar. Just as I suspected, no one bothered to ask for ID, although the bouncer did take his time soaking me in and undressing me with his eyes.

I look around for Blaze, but I don't see him. I'm second-guessing my impulsive behavior. Why did I think this was a good idea? It wasn't a good idea over the summer before Jordan and I got together, how is it better now? I can't do this to myself, but I can't think of any other way to erase Jordan from my life. I remember the pool tables in the back and push my way through the crowd. If Blaze stood me up, I'm certain I could find some other good looking guy to spend some time with.

I spot him, and my mouth goes dry. Blaze is engaged in a game. He's leaning over the table, lining up a shot, pulling the long stick in his hands back slightly. He hits the cue ball and sinks three balls on the single shot when he looks up and our eyes meet. A fire burns in his eyes as they inch over my body.

"Hi." I shout over the noise.

Blaze looks behind him, hands some guy I've never seen the pool stick, and comes around the table to where I'm standing, waiting for him.

"So you want to have some fun?" He asks skeptically repeating the question I asked him in our brief exchange earlier.

"If you don't have anything better to do."

"Let's just say yours was an offer I can't pass up." He places his hand on the small of my back, and nudges me toward the front. "Let's go get a drink."

Blaze leads me to the front and maneuvers us into a corner. Once we've taken ownership of the area, he reaches for his phone.

"Mind if I take a picture of you? You know, something to post on the page."

Getting this out to Jordan might be easier than I thought. "Go right ahead."

I can see the way his eyebrow rises he's surprised by my answer. I give him my sexiest look, hand on my hip, lips puckered. I wait as he does something with his phone. I'm guessing he's posting the picture. I'm sure once Chaz, or the other girlfriends spot it, they'll alert Jordan.

"You're seriously done with Brewer?"

"I am."

The corners of Blaze's mouth draw up into a smile. "That's just what I hoped to hear. Let's get this party started."

Even though there is a throng of people waiting either to order or to receive their drinks, once Blaze motions for her, the female bartender comes straight over.

"Anything special you'd like?" He asks.

"Do they have OR~G?" I didn't like it when Jonah gave it to me. I thought it was too strong, but right now the stronger the better.

"OR~G huh?" I see the humor playing in his eyes. "I like the way you're thinking. Make that two," he says to bartender. "Double shots." After she heads in the other direction and Blaze has taken a good long look at her ass, he turns back to me. "You gonna tell me what's really going on?"

I shrug. "Nothing to tell. I'm home, and my friends are all busy tonight, I took a chance on you because I figured even if you were with Coco and Lela, you probably had room for one more.

He steps in closer to me as the bartender returns with our drinks. He takes them from her and orders a second round.

"Here you go," Blaze hands me the cup. "To being single." He winks at me before bringing the cup to his lips, throwing his head back and downing the liquid all at once.

I follow suit. I throw my head back and chug. I can't empty it in one shot. I wipe my mouth with the back of my hand in between gulps. It's strong just the way I remember. While I'm not loving it, it isn't terrible either. Right now I'm looking for something to numb the pain, and this promises to lead me in the right direction.

"You okay there, Stephanie?"

I nod.

"Maybe you should slow down a little?"

"Hell, no."

"In that case, another?"

"Yes, please."

It sounds like a good idea. The alcohol should be able to silence my conscious. Not just because I know what I'm doing is wrong, but because I want so desperately to forget the look on their faces when Jordan gave Missy the engagement ring. I want to forget the hurt and betrayal and just be in the moment with the gorgeous guy eye-fucking me right now.

My head already feels a little funny. I'm not sure if I'm already feeling the drink, or if it's the stress of the last few days combined with a lack of sleep getting to me. Before Blaze has a chance to order, the waitress is back with two more double shots.

He leans in close to me, bringing his mouth to my ear. I didn't realize it before now, but I'm standing with my back against the wall, and Blaze is incredibly close. Close enough that I can feel him, feel the heat bouncing off his body and onto mine.

"Are you sure you're up for another drink?"

I nod as I reach for the refill. I hold it between us, because I feel like I need some sort of barrier to maintain the little bit of air between our bodies. I look down at it for a second, not even sure why I'm playing this game with Blaze. I know I should apologize for wasting his time and walk away. This is a game I don't need to win. I can afford to forfeit and go back to school with egg on my face, but I don't.

I don't want to. I don't want to feel anything for Jordan anymore, and if I can do this, it's a first step.

"Great. You're turn to toast."

"To blue eyes," I say with a smirk.

I see the humor playing on his lips, and peeking through his eyes.

"To blue eyes."

He clinks my cup and I'm surprised that he's pressed against me. My immediate reaction is to want to push him away. I don't. I entertain the idea of getting physical with Blaze. While I don't find it appealing, I'm not getting myself sick from the thought either.

Two girls break through the crowd and reach out to him. He turns so that he's facing them, and somehow, I'm not sure how it happens, but his arm is around my shoulder, pulling me close. I can't tell if he knows these girls or not, I don't really care. I'm just relieved that there's a little distance between us, because I liked feeling him against me much more than I should have. After the girls finish gushing about seeing him perform at some other bar, Blaze says goodbye and turns back to me.

"How are you feeling?" Blaze asks.

"Like I shouldn't have had the second drink."

The walls of the room are moving in wave patterns. The noise and people are almost unbearable. And I hate the fact that I'm upset that Blaze just moved away from me.

"You shouldn't drink without eating something. I have something in the car. Let me go grab some cookies or something." He steps always.

"Wait . . ."

He's gone. I watch him walk out the front door. I'm not sure where he went or if he really intends to come back. I press my back against the wall for support. I want to close my eyes, but my lids are so heavy I don't dare. I think if I shut them for even thirty seconds I'll fall asleep standing up.

Blaze is back before I know it.

"Miss me?" he asks pulling the corner of his bottom lip between his teeth before flashing a dazzling smile my way.

"You wish."

"Here." He holds up a brownie wrapped in aluminum foil. "I have more in the car if you want. I hope you like chocolate."

"Thanks." I nibble on the rectangular shaped cake. It's a little bitter. I suspect along with the chocolate, sugar and flour there's one other potent ingredient. I know I shouldn't eat it, but tonight I'm not about what I should do, I'm about doing what feels good, what feels right at the moment, and what will wipe Jordan Brewer out of my head. "Did you make this?"

He grins. "It'll take the edge off. You should feel better soon."

"That's what I thought."

While I eat, three more girls come talk to Blaze. I don't blame them. If I didn't know him and I could drum up the courage, I'd try to talk to him, too. Actually, I do know him and that gives me the edge over these girls. I pop the last bite of the brownie in my mouth and then suck hard on the tip of each finger to remove the remnants of chocolate from them for a moment. A move that's caught Blaze's attention. The girls are gone, and he's staring hard at me. His gaze is so intense, my chest tightens because somewhere in my fucked-up, foggy brain I understand how wrong this is.

All of it.

I close my eyes, knowing I shouldn't be having these thoughts of Blaze. I shouldn't want or like his attention, but seeing how Jordan doesn't care about me in the least, I yearn for more of it. Like having Blaze look at me the way he is right now, like an animal in heat, will somehow prove to Jordan that I'm important. That I matter a lot, if I matter at all, to someone like Blaze.

I close my eyes again trying to clear my mind, and think rationally. The room is swaying. The floor is moving, tilting up and down. It's like I'm in the spinning tunnel of a fun house. I can't stand on my own. I reach out and grab Blaze's shoulder.

"It's okay. I've got you." He pulls me in against his chest and holds me tight. I run my hand over his chest. It's hard and warm under my fingers. My hand feels like it's melting into him.

Blaze turns me around so that his chest is against my back, his arm holding me securely against him. I feel feather-light kisses at the back of my neck. Each time he kisses me there I feel it travel down my arms and back. I'm not sure if he realizes it or not, but his hand is squeezing my left breast. I think about pulling it off, but I'm fairly certain I'll drop and melt into the floor if I do.

"Is this what you had in mind when you asked if I wanted to have some fun?" He whispers, his breath tickling my ear.

"Mmm." I moan and lean back, using Blaze's body to steady myself and keep me upright.

"Good. Come on." Blaze helps maneuver me through the maze the crowd creates, into the back of the bar.

"Where are we going?" My head is tilted up just at the base of his neck. Blaze smells amazing. He smells just like Jordan.

"There's a small room in the back, this way we can have a little privacy."

Privacy? Why would we need privacy? I want to stay out in the open so everyone can see and word can get back to Jordan.

We get to the back, and I realize we're outside the bathrooms.

"You want me to go to the bathroom first?"

Blaze leans me against the wall, and brings his mouth close to mine. It's so close I feel warmth against my lips when he speaks, and smell the fruity scent of the drinks on his breath. I can't pull my eyes away from his lips. I wonder what kissing him is like. I want to kiss him. I can almost taste the warm welcome of his mouth.

"Can you stand a minute? I need to get something."

I nod.

There's a little alcove three feet away, next to the back door. All I can see from the angle I'm at is a bucket on wheels and a mop sticking out of it. Cleaning supplies? What could he possibly want with those? Blaze returns with an "Out of Order" sign in his hand. It's magnetic, and he has no problem affixing it to the door.

"What are you doing?"

"Making sure no one walks in on us." He twists the knob to the bathroom door open. "Come on, it's empty," He says pulling me inside after he's peeked in. I don't put up a fuss and find the whole thing funny. I'm in the boy's bathroom. I never even snuck a peek into the boy's bathroom before. I've always been too afraid I'd catch someone with his pants down and be more embarrassed than the guy. I burst out in a fit of giggles that I can't stop or control.

Until the room goes dark.

"Blaze!" I shriek.

"Shh. It's okay, I've got you." I feel his arms around me, and my heart thumps loud. Hard. I'm relieved. I'm excited. I'm scared to death.

"Why'd you do that?"

"So no one comes in. If they see the light on under the door, they'll think the sign is bullshit."

"It is bullshite."

Again the laughing begins. This time it's aimed at myself for my mispronunciation. I can't see anything in here, except the bit of dim light peeking in through the bottom of the door. I close my eyes and take a deep breath, Jordan's image, his large black eyes are all my mind is allowing me to think of.

"I'm so fucking mad at Jordan."

"Shh."

"I hate him. Hate. Him."

"That's why you're here with me." Blaze's arms wrap around my waist. He leads me backward to the wall behind me. "Trust me. I'll make you forget all about him."

"No one has ever been able to make me forget him."

Blaze's tongue runs down my neck where his lips caress me once again. It feels so good when he kisses me like this.

It's easy to use the dark to fool myself. Without looking at Blaze, I can pretend he's Jordan.

"I promise, once we get started you won't be thinking of him. You're not the first girl that came running to me when he wasn't enough for her."

Blaze crushes his mouth against mine. I kiss him back, at the same time thinking I should push him away. Instead he morphs. He turns into Jordan, and I welcome more, winding my fingers through his hair, I pull him closer to me.

Grabbing handfuls of hair, he holds my head in place and continues to probe his tongue around my mouth, with urgency, circling, twisting, and twirling around with mine. He's forceful, and I realize he's not Jordan. I push against his chest, trying to break away from him, but he doesn't budge. I give up fighting against him. It's useless. He's like a brick wall.

His words are bouncing around in my head. I'm not the first girl. How many girls? One? Many? I'm just another to add to his list. I can't go through with this. Besides, I never planned on more than some intense kissing out in front of everyone, and being holed up in this dark room with Blaze isn't part of my plan.

"Stop."

"Shh," is all he responds with. One hand runs up my neck and holds my chin, while the other slips under my shirt. He pulls my bra cup down beneath my breast and flicks his thumb back and forth over my nipple before pinching it. His lips are moving from behind my ear down my neck, and I feel myself getting lost in the moment, because it feels so good. If I could see him, I could forget what I'm feeling.

"Put the lights on."

"No. I don't want you over-thinking this."

"We should go back out there," I manage to say as he nibbles on my neck eliciting a whimper from me.

His body presses mine into the wall. "You want an audience? Do you like when people watch you?"

"I want Jordan . . ."

"Trust me, once I'm inside of you, you won't even remember him. It's just us here. Just you and me."

My heartbeat hammers in my ears. Fear has a solid grip on me. This isn't why I came. I want to fight him off, but I'm weak, and my mind is functioning in slow motion. His hands drop and grab my ass tight. He's grinding his hips against me. Pressing himself hard into me.

"Stop."

I push at his chest and again.

"Come on baby, stop fighting." His voice is gentle, not at all as hard and demanding as his hands and body. "You know you want me. That's why you're here."

"Get off me. I love Jordan."

"You can love him and fuck me. The two aren't connected you know."

"They are for me."

I'm trembling in his arms. I feel a little slack in his hold on me and I think I convinced him to forget this. He backs off just enough for our bodies not to touch anymore, and I take a step away. I plan to move around him, but he latches on to my waistband and pulls me back against the wall.

"Just a few minutes. That's all we need. And I can show you how amazing this could be."

"Blaze."

"That's right. Say my name. Keep saying it. In a few minutes, I'll make you feel so good you'll be screaming it."

I want to panic, but I can't. I'm not even sure what's going on. "I can't." I whisper. Nothing can happen with Blaze because even though I hate him at this very moment, I'm still very much in love with Jordan.

"Of course you can. And I'll make it good. I'll make sure you come." I feel his thigh between my legs, rubbing against me.

Before I could say another word there's slack in my waistband and his hands are on my hips, pushing at my pants.

"This isn't . . ." My lips are having a hard time getting the words out. "Jordan." Is all I can say.

"Trust me."

My pants are down, and I feel him against me. OHMIGOD! I feel him against me! NO! I want this all to stop. Right now!

"Jordan!" I squeal.

The lights come on and I'm blinded by the sudden sea of light.

"Stephanie!" I hear my name, but I'm not sure who's saying it. I squint at the figure standing in the doorway, waiting for my eyes to adjust to the brightness of the room.

"She's here." Whoever flicked the light switch on calls to someone else.

"Steph!" I'd know that voice even if I went decades without hearing it. My heart thuds. It hammers and races at the sound of his voice. I hate my stupid, heart for leaping toward him, for rejoicing that he got here in time to save the day.

"Fuck!" comes from the other voice.

"Sorry babe," Blaze reaches up and strokes my cheek as he plants a last kiss on my lips. I want to stick a stake through my heart and die because I know Jordan is watching. He's watching and there's no coming back from this. "Maybe next time, Steph." Blaze smirks at me as he rushes to close his pants back up. Not wanting Jordan and who ever he's with to see me with my pants down, I reach down and fumble with my clothes.

Blaze's body moves from right in front of me, but not like he stepped away. It's an unnatural motion, as if he's been shoved or thrown. With my eyes adjusted to the light of the room, I see Jordan standing in front of me, his back to me. He shoved Blaze away, and now he's looking at me over his shoulder, his eyes dark. Dangerous.

"Get dressed," he orders.

My cheeks, my face, hell my whole body is on fire. It's not just embarrassment coloring my face, it's the heaviness of a full, thick layer of shame spreading through my bloodstream as well. While Jordan's eyes are glued on me, Blaze jerks forward and knocks him into one of the sinks. His head hits the mirror above it, cracking and splintering the reflective glass.

I cover my mouth, it only barely muffles the volume of my ear splitting scream.

"Jordan!"

Blaze throws a dirty look my way. "Come on, Brewer. I've been waiting a long time for this."

Jordan's eyes flicker from Blaze to me, and back to Blaze. His face is contorted. Not in pain, I've seen him in pain before. No, this is pure, unadulterated rage.

"Get her out of here." Jordan instructs the person standing frozen at the door through clenched teeth.

"What's wrong? You don't want her to see your true colors? Or are you trying to get rid of the witnesses so you could mangle me the way you did Madison?"

I gasp and cover my mouth. "You wrote those letters."

"I said get her out of here."

I understand that Jordan wants me to leave, wants whoever is standing there to lead me out of the bathroom, and possibly out of the bar. Even if I could move my feet, I don't want to. I know they're going to fight, and I'm afraid. For both of them. I know Blaze is goading Jordan, and I'm worried Jordan might lose control.

"Now." Jordan's voice booms and reverberates through the small tiled room, making me jump and hurting my ears.

Fingers wrap around my arm and pull me away from my spot, towards the door. I yank myself free and dart between Blaze and Jordan. I'm shot an angry look from Jordan as Blaze shoves me out of the way toward the door.

"Don't you ever touch her again!" Jordan's voice is menacing.

Those are the last words I hear before a pair of arms close around my waist, pick me up, and carry me to the front of the bar. Once my feet hit the ground, I want to run back, but I can't. My captor has a vise like hold around my waist. I stop struggling, and Jonah allows me to face him.

"Come on," he instructs. "I'm taking you back school."

"Damn coward! He doesn't even have the courage to break up with me in person."

"What are you talking about? He's been a lunatic since Blaze sent him the text that you were here. And then you wouldn't return our calls."

"He never called me!"

"Yes, he did. So did I."

I reach in my purse and pull my phone out. Of course I never heard my phone chime with the noise in here, and it doesn't help that I turned the volume off earlier so I could ignore the messages coming in from Jordan.

Now guilt is mixing in with that layer of shame. The screen is lit, alerting me to the seven missed calls and fifteen text messages. I raise my hand up to cover my mouth. I fucked up.

Royally.

I think I'm going to be sick.

*

"How?" I ask expecting him to know what I mean. He doesn't answer, so I try to find the words to express myself.

"You were at your show. How did you end up together?" I ask as Jonah steadies me while walking to his car.

"He called Maria looking for you. Guess you mentioned it to him at some point or Maria told him. I don't know. She sounded panicked when he forwarded her the text." He says before opening the passenger door and helping me in. "Are you sure you're okay?"

"Yes." I say covering my mouth with my hand, not sure that I'll be able to hold every bit of alcohol I drank down.

"You'd better be. If you throw up in here, you're cleaning it."

I nod. "I'm good. Just as long as I don't have to walk a straight line."

"We got here at the same time. I gave him shit for cheating on you when I saw him." Jonah says as he turns the key in the ignition. "He denied it. He said she's only a friend."

"Friend? Did he tell you I caught him proposing to that stupid, slutty bitch today?"

"Why didn't you call me? What the hell were you thinking?"

"I don't know. I was mad and hurt."

"But Blaze?" I hear the overt disgust in his voice. "Give yourself some credit. You could do so much better than that piece of shit."

I scrunch my face up as I let my emotions have their way with me. They're so all over the place. One minute I want Jordan, the next I never want to see him again. It doesn't matter anyway. Jordan and I are done. There's no coming back from this. Even if I did misunderstand, which I'm certain I didn't, I can't imagine what's running through his mind after finding me with Blaze. I hit my head against the window. Not hard enough to break it, just hard enough to feel it.

"You're mad at yourself right now, so I'd appreciate if you don't take it out on my car."

I close my eyes. I don't want to talk anymore, and since Jonah's acting like Captain Ass Face right now, I don't want to hear anything else that he has to say.

*

"How is she?" I hear Jordan's voice. I don't open my eyes, or move. I'm not ready to face him. Plus, I'm afraid if I move I'm going to throw up all over my bed.

"I don't know. I practically had to carry her up here," Jonah answers. "I think she's just wasted."

"Did he hurt her?" I feel the mattress shift, and I know Jordan is sitting near me.

"Damn if I know. She didn't say anything like that. I think Blaze was telling the truth. I think she sought him out. Looks like whatever happened was consensual."

Consensual? That usually refers to sex acts. I didn't have sex with Blaze, did I? Why is my mind so foggy? I try letting their voices lull me back to sleep, but it's not working.

"The right side of your face is swelling up. Looks like you've got a shiner there."

"He got a few lucky shots in. You should see his face."

"I'll go get some ice."

I hear the door to my room close, and I know I'm alone with Jordan. For years I would've given my left eye to be alone with him behind a closed door. Now all I can do is pretend I'm asleep and hope to avoid him. How did this all go so wrong so fast?

Jordan must be experiencing similar feelings because he doesn't try to talk to me, or wake me. He sits in silence, not moving. In fact, I wonder why he's even here. Is it guilt? Is that why he was with me to begin with? Because he felt guilty about promising me a future together and then snatching it away before it ever began? I'm glad he's leaving me alone. I feel so betrayed I'm not sure I ever want to talk to him or feel his touch. Ever again.

The door creaks open. There's movement in my room, and Jonah's voice is close.

"I guess I'll leave you alone. If you need anything, come get me."

"Thanks. For being there for her." There's a long pause before either of them speak again. "Do me a favor?" I can't imagine what more Jordan could possibly want from Jonah. "Check in on her tomorrow. Make sure she's okay."

I hear the door to my room close again. I don't know if Jonah responded at all, or if he was the one that left. All I know is that if I cry from this moment until the second my heart stops beating, it won't be long enough to empty my heart of the sadness I feel.

He's leaving me, and while it's killing me slowly inside, the worst part is I'm relieved. Angry. Hurt. But relieved nonetheless.

Chapter 24

My head hurts. It's pounding and throbbing. I don't want to open my eyes. I had the craziest dreams. Memories flood into my conscious: Jordan proposing to the blonde, kissing Blaze, Jonah driving me back to school and carrying me up the steps. Fuck. It all happened. It's the last memory of last night that nearly causes me to lose it.

Jordan sitting at the foot of my bed. "I'm so sorry, Stephanie. I'm so fucking sorry."

The bed shook. I knew he was crying, but stubborn as I am, I wouldn't console him. He didn't deserve me telling him it's okay and I forgive him, because it's not and I don't. Still, I know I have to face him sooner or later. I can't pretend to sleep for the rest of my life. Even though he's not touching me, I open my eyes expecting to find him sleeping at the other end of the bed. He's not. And the blanket is folded over me, suggesting no one slept on that side of the bed. Where the hell is he? Why isn't he here waiting for me to wake up? Seething inside, I reach for my phone and send him a text.

Where are you?

Home

So this is how it ends.

No. I need to cool off for a day or two before we talk.

I shake my head. Stupid, self-centered jerk.

I wasn't asking you. I was telling you. It's over. Anything and everything between us.

You don't mean that.

Yes. I do. We're done.

*

Thirty minutes later I'm showered, in sweats, and waiting for the ibuprofen to kick in and stop the jack-hammer in my head from trying to break its way through my skull. The knock on my door doesn't surprise me. I expect Jonah to check up on me sooner or later. I don't bother looking through the peephole, and just swing it open. I'm paralyzed a moment. I don't expect Jordan to be standing on the other side. Once I regain my bearings, I push the door closed, but not before his foot is lodged between the door and the jamb.

"Let me in."

"No. Leave. It's what you're good at."

"Not until we talk."

"I said all I have to in my last text."

"Well I didn't." His fingers crawl around the edge of the door, and I wish I had the strength to slam it hard and crush them.

"Then you should've been here when I woke up."

"Open the door! I don't want to hurt you."

Angry, and frustrated, I throw the door open. "You don't want to hurt me? You don't want to hurt me? That's all you've ever done, Jordan. Hurt me." I pound my fist into my chest, accentuating my words. "Only this time it's special. This time you perfected it. You hurt me so much you brought me to the point of no return."

"And you're innocent in all this?" His eyes look me up and down, with a look of distain, making me feel lower than dog shit. "You think I'm not hurt?" I close the door hoping it will muffle his raised voice for anyone that might be passing in the hall. I'm floored that he has the nerve to yell at me. "Seeing you with Blaze last night ripped my heart out."

I glare at him. My eyes are little more than narrow slits sizing him up. He thought his last little comment would stun me, shut me up. Not today.

"Yeah, well, I'm sure Missy will make it all better." I spit out.

Something changes in his eyes. Is he surprised I called her by name?

"And that's why you were fucking Blaze? Because of Missy?"

Before I have a chance to think about what I'm doing, my hand slaps his face. I can't believe what he just said to me. Worse, if he didn't come and interrupt us, I might have done exactly what he just accused me of. I'm angry with him, but I'm angrier with myself.

"I hate you!" I shove his chest letting the overwhelming anger inside me take control.

My jaw is tense as Jordan grabs my wrists and holds them tight. I want to pummel his chest, punch him in the face and give him another black eye to match the one he already has, but I can't. He's too strong. "Are you done?"

"Not even close."

"Fine. I'm not letting go until you calm down."

"Go to hell."

"Where do you think I am right now?"

I bring my leg back to kick him in the shin, but before I can, Jordan steps his front leg behind me and uses his hip to knock me off balance as he gently guides me down to the floor. He pins me down so that my hands are on either side of my head, and he's straddling me. I try to thrash and break free of his hold, but I can't. He's too strong.

"Just because you're mad doesn't give you the right to hit me, or kick me."

"No, but you're attitude does." I don't know what's come over me. I can't seem to control myself.

"Let's not go there, Stephanie. Because if that were the case, there's no telling what I'd do to you right now."

Resigned, I stop fighting. "Why didn't you tell me the truth about her?"

He looks at me for a long moment before he answers. "I didn't want to hurt you."

There's no denial.

He no longer claims that she doesn't mean anything to him.

There's not one thing he bothers to say in his defense.

I feel bile rise in the back of my throat, mixed in with the fragmented pieces of my heart. "So you lied to me. Betrayed my trust. And hurt me all the same."

"I didn't mean to. I tried to keep her away when you were there. I'm sorry."

"That's all you have to say for yourself? That's it?" I manage to work one hand free, I pull it down to floor so I can gain momentum when I swing and clock him in the jaw, but he regains his hold before I make contact.

"Can you stop fighting!"

"Fine." I give up. "I'm done fighting. Some things just aren't worth it."

"I'm not going to read into that comment and play these fucking games with you. Not yet. First, I want you to calm down. I love you, but you're not the only one hurting. I'm trying to figure out if I could ever forgive you."

"You bastard!"

He sighs. "This is why I thought we should wait to talk. But as always, you had to have your way."

"My way was to never speak to you again in case you don't understand what the word done means."

"I know you don't mean that. You said that because you wanted a reaction. Deep down you wanted me to come, to show you I give a shit and hash this out."

"Of course." I answer back snidely. "Because I'm selfish. And I don't really give a shit about anyone else when I'm hurt. Isn't that right?"

"Stop."

"No. That's what you said over the summer. And that's what you mean now."

"Okay fine, you want to play this game? You win. Then what the hell do you call hooking up with Blaze last night?"

"Retribution." He looks stunned, like I just slapped him in the face. It motivates me to keep going, to keep twisting that knife in his heart. "You should've been honest with me. You should've told me about her sooner."

"I know. I said I'm sorry damn it."

"Sorry?" He doesn't answer, but I feel slack in his hold. "The day you brought me to school, is she the friend you stopped off to see?

"Yes."

I nod.

"The second you said goodbye to me, you were on your way to see her."

"Stephanie . . ."

"No. I've heard enough of your lies and excuses. I'm done."

"You're not hearing me out."

"Because I don't care what you have to say. Don't you get it? I. Don't. Care."

He moves off me, and I raise myself up to a sitting position. The more I talk, the more I see my words getting to him. I keep at it. Keep using them to pound away at him.

"I was young and naive when we met. Completely infatuated with you. And yes, I was weak. I thought you made me better. Stronger. All this time, I had this illusion of you, that you were better than everyone else. And you know what I realize now? You don't make me better, or stronger. You make me weak. You break me. Over and over again.

And I'm done, Jordan. I'm. So. Done. With. This. Done with you."

Everything I'm saying is true, but what frightens me most is how much I mean it. We argued over the summer and I kicked him out of my life, but this is nothing like that. My voice is strong, clear. It doesn't crack at all. No tears stream from eyes down my face. Aside from the snowballing anger that's swimming through my veins, I'm completely composed.

"You're upset. I shouldn't have come. I'll leave and give you some time. Give us both some time to think."

"I don't need to think. I thought for years, and where did it get me? It convinced me to wait for you. It convinced me you loved me. And I was wrong. What you really love is the control you have over me. That's what you lost last night. Control."

"I never tried to control you."

"Sure you did. You controlled everything in my life including who I dated. Hell, my freshman year you threatened a locker room of guys to stay away from me because while you didn't want me, you didn't want anyone else to have me."

He shakes his head as he backs up to the door.

"You're wrong."

"You've controlled what happens between us and when. You even admitted as much, remember? You had your mind set you weren't going to kiss me at prom. No matter what."

"You're twisting things. Damn it, Stephanie. Stop."

"Oh, no." I continued ticking things off on my fingers as I go. "You controlled when we would see each other and for how long. It didn't matter that I wanted to work through whatever issues you had spending the night with me that auto-magically disappeared when you found out I hung out with Jonah and Logan. You even controlled when we had sex for the first time: where, when, what I wore. I get it now. I never had a say in anything. What I wanted didn't matter as much as what you wanted. What I wanted never mattered at all."

"You've got it wrong. All of it. Whatever I did was because I love you. Yes, I've always loved you, even when you were a shy little girl, I just didn't realize it. And the things that were being said in that locker room . . . I tried to protect you."

"You protected me alright. From everyone but the one person I most needed protection from. You."

I look at my desk, and pick up the first thing I see, the bottle of ibuprofen, and fling it at him. Jordan swats it down with his hand. I continue picking up the contents of my desk, my books, my stapler, the remote control. I don't care how much noise they make as they hit the floor, or the door behind him. I continue to launch whatever I can get my hands on at Jordan, one at a time. I just want to get one good hit in before he leaves.

"Get out!" I scream.

"Stop!"

"Get out and don't come back!"

The knock on the door startles us, and stops us both for the moment.

"Go away!" I shout.

"Stephanie, I need you to open the door right now," Trina warns, "Or I'm keying myself in."

Jordan opens the door. I think he's relieved that I stopped chucking things at him.

Trina and Jonah are standing side by side, but Trina appears to be the one in charge.

"Are you okay, Stephanie?"

"Depends on what you mean by okay."

"Has he done anything to hurt you?" she continues.

I nod.

I catch the uncertain look between Jordan and Jonah.

"Do I need to call security?" Trina asks.

My heart pounds furiously as I look hard at all three of them before answering. Again I think I've arrived at the point of no return, and just to solidify my spot here I answer. "Yes. Call security. I asked him to leave and he won't go. I want him taken off campus. Now."

"Wait!" Jonah intercedes as Trina lifts her phone from her side. "We don't need to do that just yet. He'll leave on his own." Jonah puts his hand on Jordan's good shoulder and tries to usher him into stepping out of my room, but Jordan slaps him away.

"Don't make us do this," he says to Jordan. "If we have to call security, it's going to create a scene. You don't want her to have everyone staring and talking about her, do you?"

Jordan stares Jonah down. No one moves. I notice the lump in Jonah's throat bob as he swallows and tries once again to talk some sense into Jordan.

"It's best if you just turn around and leave."

Jordan sneers at Jonah. "You'd like that wouldn't you? You've been trying to get me out of the picture since she got here."

"I'm calling security."

Before Trina could press the button on her phone, Jonah stops her once again.

"Last chance, Jordan." Jonah explains in a calm, cool manner. "Leave now on your own, or we call security and have you physically removed."

Jordan looks into my eyes one last time. "This is what you want?"

I have difficulty saying it. My eyes don't leave his as I gather my strength. I nod, and force myself to say the one word that will put an end to everything. "Yes."

Jordan backs out. He continues moving backwards, his eyes never leaving me, until he's no longer in my line of sight. I don't hear what Jonah and Trina say as I back up to my bed and sit, unable to believe the greatest love story ever ended this way.

Before they leave, Jonah apologizes for failing in his attempt to talk Trina out of writing up a report about what happened. Fantastic. Way to keep a low profile and not have my freak status follow me into college.

Chapter 25

I don't know what to do with myself. I don't want to see anyone, especially not Jonah. The sun is setting and I'm seconds away from losing my mind. Maria is driving me crazy with texts. I can ignore her only so long before she sends Jonah over to check up on me. That's the last thing I need. All I want to do is forget everything that happened this morning. And last night. And over the last two weeks. I throw on a pair of yoga pants and a tee shirt. I decide to try something I've never done before. I shut my phone off and decide to run.

Tired, sweaty, and still unable to quiet my body, I drag myself back up the hall steps to my room. I'm not sure what the distance is between the dorm and the football field, but that's how far I ran. There and back. I'm sure my muscles will be sore tomorrow, but right now, I'm inviting physical pain to help ease my emotional torment. I don't bother to check my messages. I don't care if he's been trying to call me. I need a clean break.

I gather everything I need to take a shower. It's an awkward time; everyone's either out, or already cleaned up. I don't have to wait for anyone to finish like I do in the mornings. I'm right in assuming I'll have the bathroom to myself. I close the curtain behind me and turn the water up as hot as it can go.

I step under the stream of scorching water. Each drop pelts against my skin, like hundreds of tiny knives threatening to cut and slice me open. It hurts, but I don't move. This is what I've been looking for, something strong enough to bring the pain bubbling up to the surface. It works. As the drops run down my body, the tears stream down my face. I don't want to move. I want to stay here and cry. Cry until my eyes are swollen shut. Cry until the tears steal the salt and water from my body and leave me a shriveled lump on the floor.

I barely notice the change in temperature at first, but the water is now cold. I turn the knob and shut it off. Cold water doesn't have the same effect on me that the hot water does. I continue to stand there, tears still dripping from my eyes. I think I'm ready to move on, literally, figuratively. Before I take a step, loud, agonizing sobs escape me once again. I hate this; feeling weak, and broken.

"I. Hate. You." I remind myself over and over, uncertain if I'm referring to Jordan or myself. I wrap the towel around my body and tuck the edge in so it won't fall as I walk. Instead of leaving this closet like space, I drop onto the bench holding my dirty clothes and toiletries. I pull my knees up and hug them tight. The sobbing begins all over again.

I'm startled by a voice. A deep voice.

"Are you alright?" The voice is familiar, and he's standing on the other side of the shower curtain. I don't answer. I don't know who it is, or who he's talking to.

"Hello?"

I want to yell at him, tell whoever it is to go away and forget I'm here. Instead of getting the words out, a loud sound escapes my mouth, like a seal barking. The harder I try to find a way to speak, the louder, the worse the strider sounds.

"Are you all right? Do you need help?"

"Go away!" I manage to articulate.

"Stephanie? Is that you?" The curtain is pulled open. I feel so beaten down, so defeated I don't even flinch.

"Did someone hurt you?"

Not unless you count ripping my heart right out of my chest and putting it through a meat grinder. I shake my head, and find myself staring right into Logan's beady eyes. He's bent down so we're face to face. Instead of doing something obnoxious like looking me up and down, and undressing me with his eyes, he smoothes my wet hair, pulls my robe off the hook, and drapes if over my shoulders.

"Do you want me to call your boyfriend?"

I shake my head, "I don't have a boyfriend."

"Trouble in paradise. Okay, I'll go find Jonah." He stands, but before he can turn and leave, I reach out for him.

"No. I don't want to see him."

"You sure about that?"

"Yes. No Jonah."

"Well then, you're stuck with me. Let's get you back to your room."

"I'm fine. I can do it myself" I answer, no longer crying, suddenly feeling self-conscious and aware of how little I have on.

"It's my good deed for the day."

"Like you'd know what a good deed is."

"Come on, now. That hurts." Logan takes a seat on the bench, crowding me in the small space. "Here I am trying to be a gentleman and you're insulting me."

I smile. It's fake and forced, but I feel a smidgeon better than I did a minute ago.

"And if I don't agree are you going to sit in here all night with me hogging the bench?"

"Pretty much."

"Fine. I'll go back to my room, and you'll go to . . ."

"Careful now. I'm looking out for you remember?"

"I was just going to say your room."

"Okay." He stands and reaches for the basket with my toiletries. "I'll walk you there. Once I know your inside safe and sound, with the door locked behind you, I'll leave."

I shake my head. "I don't get it, you're not going to gloat, to rub the fact that he cheated in my face?"

He stares at me for a long moment. "I'm a little behind in my good deeds. Seems like I've been giving this girl on the floor a hard time for so long she truly believes I'm a dick. Tonight, I'm trying to catch up on my good deeds so I could even out karma's score. Never want to miss with a bitch that vengeful."

"Okay. Fine. But turn around so I can adjust my towel."

Logan does as I ask. I keep my eyes on him the whole time, making sure he's not looking for a cheap thrill. Surprisingly, he's on his best behavior. Once I'm satisfied my towel won't fall, I put my robe on, and clutch my dirty clothes close to my body for the short walk back to my room.

"Thank you," I say once I'm inside.

"I won't even pretend I'm offended you didn't invite me in."

"And I won't pretend I'm sort of grateful you showed up out of the blue."

"It's my phantom power." There's an awkward silence for a beat. "Seriously though, you sure you don't want me to call anyone? Even if I was mad at Avery, or if she was mad at me, if she was as upset as you are I'd want to know about it. I'm sure you're boyfriend . . ."

I look down at the floor and shake my head. "No. God, Logan, you were so right about him."

His shoulders slump a little. "I doubt that. The guy seems pretty crazy about you."

"Please. I can't do this."

"You got it. Now go inside before I lose my reputation and people start thinking I'm a nice guy. Then I'll have all sorts of girls hanging all over me."

I smile, but this time it's real. "Thanks."

"Goodnight."

*

"Stephanie."

Someone's shaking me. I force my eyes open as I struggle to come to my senses.

"Hey you," the voice coos. "Wake up."

Someone's in my room. He's not just in my room, he's on my bed. With my heart pounding, I shoot up from the prone position, and wipe the drool from my mouth.

My eyes open wide as I see Jonah sitting next to me.

"What are you doing here?"

"You didn't answer your door. I wanted to make sure you were all right. I know it's been a rough twenty-four hours for you."

"But why are you in my room? You could've called me. Did you key yourself in?"

He drops his eyes to the floor. "I wanted to see you."

"You can't do that!" I raise my voice, annoyed at his brazenness. "You can't just let yourself in my room whenever you feel like it. What if I was naked? Or if I wasn't alone?"

He reaches over and cups the side of my face. "I knocked first. I knew you weren't with Jordan. I just needed to see that you're okay." He pauses. "And I hoped we could celebrate." He holds up a bottle of champagne in his free hand. "I never had a chance to tell you, I sold two paintings last night."

"That's wonderful." I smile, and forgetting how annoyed I am at him for a moment, I throw my arms around Jonah's neck, happy for his success. "I'm sorry, I didn't even ask. I guess it went well then?" I ask as I pull back, only he doesn't let me. With his hand wrapped around my lower back, he moves it up and holds me close.

"It would've been better if you were there."

His eyes, glued on mine, are full of emotion and more intense than I've ever seen them. I feel like they're trying to peel through my skin and reach inside me. I have to break eye contact. Looking at him is too uncomfortable. I turn my head toward the door, searching for an excuse to create distance between us. Before I come up with one, I push away from Jonah, and stand. That's as far as I get before he's on his feet, pulling me into him. "I'm sorry you're hurting, Stephanie. But now you can forget him. You can finally move on."

I smell the alcohol on his breath, and I'm immediately brought back to Blaze and the bar, and every stupid thing I've done since Jordan came into my life. I just want to get Jonah out of my room and away from me.

"It's been a long day for both of us. We can talk about this tomorrow."

"Now's as good a time as any."

"You've been drinking, Jonah. I'd rather talk when you're sober."

"I am sober. I only had some champagne. I haven't drunk enough to make this any easier." His blue eyes look frightened, as he swallows hard. "Stephanie, I have a confession."

"Don't."

"Why not? I've been waiting. I waited so long, and he always got in the way. I thought it might never happen. But here we are."

Already I feel weighed down with guilt. Jordan warned me. Instead of listening, I wanted to deny it. I looked the other way, like I always do. Jonah's been so nice since I moved in, always there when I need him, always looking out for me. I didn't want to believe there was more to it. Things never should've gotten this far.

"Finally you're free. This is the right time. We can finally be together."

I shake my head. I don't want him to say any more. If he goes any further, we'll never have that easy, carefree give and take again.

"It's not that easy."

"Of course it is. The thing is, Stephanie. I'm in love with you." He moves in slow motion, inching forward in tiny increments until his lips are pressed against mine.

I don't push him away. I let him have this moment hoping he'll realize it, that he'll feel how wrong it is. Knowing how bad it feels to be the one putting your heart out on the line and not having those feelings reciprocated I try to shield the blow even if just a bit.

Jonah's mouth opens, and his tongue pushes between my lips. There's nothing about this kiss that excites me, nothing that sends the blood shooting through my veins at hyper-speed. All it does is make me feel bad. Awful. Riddled with guilt.

"Sorry," he says after a moment, "I haven't had a lot of practice."

At least my plan worked, he realized it was off, that the kiss lacked something elemental and essential. It lacked the chemistry needed to make us yearn and ache for more. I take a deep breath before breaking out of his embrace and sitting on my bed.

Jonah follows my lead and sits next to me. I don't miss how his eyes avoid mine. "You don't feel the same do you?"

I shake my head. "I'm sorry."

"I understand. You thought you were getting back together and instead he broke your heart. I should've given you more time."

I hate being the one to say no, to hurt him. It wouldn't bother me half as much if I didn't know exactly how he feels.

"I love him, Jonah. I've always loved him, and no matter how hurt I am right now, it's only proof of how much I still love him. If after all this time and all my tears the love is still there, I don't see that changing anytime soon." Or ever. "I wish to God my answer was different, but it's not, and letting you think it can be wouldn't be fair to you. Because if I could still love him after what's he's done, after today, I don't think I'll ever stop loving him. You deserve someone who's going to put you first and cherish you. You deserve more than I can give."

"But I'm willing to . . ."

"Don't be. Look at you." I reach for his hand. "You're smart and cute, and extremely talented. Any girl would be lucky to be with you."

"Any girl, but you. You'd rather be with an asshole like Blaze . . ."

I cut him off. "Blaze was a mistake. I regret every second with him." I offer a sad smile, "But I know at least two great girls that would love for you to pay some attention to them. Maria made sure she made it to your show last night."

He shakes his head. "I can't be with her. She's too concerned about her image and what people think of her. I can't be with anyone that shallow. Besides, she didn't even know I existed in high school."

"She's changed a lot since then. And she knows you exist now. Besides, if you'd prefer the quiet, shy type, there's Carla down the hall. She's crazy about you."

"Stephanie, the problem is, I want you. Not Maria. Not Carla."

Jordan always warned me Jonah had a thing for me. I took it as a joke. I never believed there was anything serious to his claim, but now I realize as usual, Jordan was right. He's always right, and it drives me insane. Especially since with us together, I had no one to interpret him. I had nothing to go on but what he told me.

"I'm sorry, Jonah, but I'm exhausted."

He nods. "If you change your mind . . ."

"If I can't sleep I'll call you."

Once I close the door behind Jonah, I lean my back against it and let out a long breath. Jordan was right. He's always right, and I never listen. Why don't I? And why the hell didn't I hear him out earlier? I still mean something to him if he's trying to get me to listen. Why have I allowed idiots like Logan and Blaze to get in my head and plant tiny seeds of doubt about him? I knew Jordan cared about me long before he ever admitted it, even when my mother and Maria tried to convince me he didn't.

I hope it's not too late, that I didn't push him so far that he'll never speak to me. I need to talk to him, at least give him the opportunity to tell me what happened, and figure out where it all went wrong. Before I make a move to grab my phone, I hear voices outside my door. I look out the peephole. Logan is there talking to Jonah, but neither of them look happy. It's weird that they should be talking right outside my door when they could be talking in either of their rooms. I press my ear against the doorjamb, hoping I'll hear more through the tiny crack than I will through the door.

"You had your chance. She shot you down. It's over."

"It's not over. I just need more time."

"You had time. She's miserable."

"I can make her happy."

"She didn't want you. It's not going to happen. Do what you have to. I'm out."

I know they're talking about me, but again, it doesn't make any sense. Did Jonah really expect that I'd go from Jordan's arms into his? And what the hell does Logan have to do with any of this? I'm feeling played by Jonah again, just like I did the day I overheard him talking about Jordan on the bus.

It's becoming clear in my mind that the pain, the break-up, it hasn't been all Jordan's fault. I've been accusatory and mistrusting from the beginning because I didn't think it possible that he could really love me. Deep down I didn't believe we deserved to be happy together. But I do deserve him. And he does love me. I know he does. I've always known that. Why am I willing to let him go without a fight? I was willing to put up a fight when he was with Madison. Isn't he still worth fighting for?

Of course he is. Even more so now that I know what it feels like to be fully enveloped in his love. When we were just friends, Jordan never divulged his secrets when he was upset. That was my MO. He always shared things in bits and pieces, and always on his own terms, in his own time, never when I pushed him to. So he didn't tell me about the disgusting notes left on his windshield. Maybe if I acted like a loving girlfriend rather than a jealous shrew he would've. He didn't change. I did. And worst of all I just gave up. Why? What the hell is wrong with me?

I climb back into my bed and reach for my phone. Shit it's after one in the morning. I want to call Jordan to just hear his voice, but it's too late. I check my text messages. There's one from Maria.

Call me ASAP I need to talk to you!

I know I'm acting like an awful friend, but I can't handle more drama now. That call can wait till the morning. My heart beats faster when I read Jordan's name.

I'll keep coming back.

I scroll down to read the next message he sent.

Something to think about until I can tell you myself.

I press on the link he sent me, and it's a recording of Shred Em's song Until the End of Forever.

I hug my phone and smile. I didn't fuck up that bad. He still loves me. We have a boat-load of shit to muddle through, but I'm willing to do it if he is.

Chapter 26

I'm up early. I can't sleep. Not because I'm upset or crying. I can't sleep because I'm excited. My chest is tight and heavy with every breath. I'm nervous. I'm going to call him, I only hope he answers. The realization that I have no way of getting to him if he doesn't pick up is starting to sink in.

I shower and dress. I even put on makeup before calling him just in case he might want to switch over to video. I stare at the clock, and take the plunge at ten-thirty. I squeeze the phone tight in my hand as I wait for him to answer. After the fifth ring it goes to voicemail. I don't leave a message. I don't know what to say. Instead I end the call.

I find myself sitting at my desk with my hands clenched tight. I have a massive ball in the pit of my stomach. He didn't answer. I'll never be able to live with myself if I lost him for good. Not if it ends this way, because I gave up. I stare at the clock, hoping I called while he slept or I caught him in the shower. I try again at eleven. Still no answer. I have no doubt he's awake and avoiding my call.

I want to fall apart, but I know I can't. I need to keep my wits about me. I never responded to his messages last night. I nibble on my lip while deciding my next move.

I decide to send a message of my own. He can choose to ignore it, but at least he'll know I'm ready to meet him half way.

Sorry about yesterday. I'm ready to talk.

There's nothing left to do but sit and wait.

And wait.

And wait.

I keep checking my phone to make sure I didn't somehow go deaf and not hear the alert for a new message, but there's not one. No return call. Nothing.

The knock on my door sends my heart sputtering. I jump to my feet and trip over myself trying to get there. I pull the door open fully expecting to see Jordan on the other side. My smile vanishes, my excitement fizzles. Jordan isn't on the other side, Logan is.

"Don't look so happy to see me," he smiles.

"Go away."

"Can we talk a minute?"

"Why am I thinking I don't really have a choice?"

"Because you don't." He steps into my room and shuts the door behind him.

"I don't recall inviting you in."

He shrugs. "Fine. I'll leave, but only if you agree to come with me."

"No."

"Okay." He plops on my bed and stretches out with his arms folded behind his head. "Then I guess I'll just have to make myself comfortable here."

"Get off of my bed. Now."

He sits up, his eyes are serious as they meet mine. I wait for him to speak, but he stares at me in silence. "You don't trust me."

"Wow, it took you a whole semester plus to realize that."

"I understand. But what if I give you ammunition to use against me?"

"What the hell are you talking about?"

He gets out of bed, walks over to my desk and picks up my phone.

"Give me that." I attempt to snatch it out of his hand, but he pulls it away, out of my reach.

"I love Avery. I mean I know she's a bitch and all, but God there's not much I wouldn't do for her."

"What does that have to do with me?"

Logan's messing around with my phone as he approaches me. "As much as she likes me, she doesn't like you."

"And?"

"If I were going to fool around with anyone she'd be pissed, but you, she'd dump me in a heartbeat."

"That's good and all, but I'm not about to . . ."

Logan bends forward and snaps a picture as he presses his lips against mine. I shove his chest hard pushing him away and stare at him, dumbfounded.

"What the hell?"

"Now you have something to use against me." He hands my phone back to me. "I need you to come with me so I can explain everything. You deserve to know the truth. And it's time you hear it."

"About what exactly?"

"Me, Jonah, everything."

"Why can't you tell me here?"

"Listen, I know I've given you absolutely no reason to trust me, but right now, you need to take a leap of faith. Please. Come with me."

There's something about his choice of words, 'leap of faith' that has me willing to take the risk of trusting him. I know it's crazy, but Jordan used those exact words, and I feel like they are some sort of sign that I should go with him.

"Okay. But I'm pre-dialing nine, one, one. You do anything, and I mean anything inappropriate and I'm calling the police."

"Okay."

I follow Logan out of my room. As I lock the door, he's looking down the boy's hall.

"Let's go down this stairwell."

"You don't want any witnesses?"

"So suspicious." He takes my hand. "I don't care who sees us, as long as it's not Jonah."

"Why? Because he'll kick your ass for bothering me?"

Logan shakes his head. "No, I don't want to risk him stopping me from telling you."

I'll admit, he piqued my interest. "What if someone sees us and they tell Avery?"

"She'll be fine. She'll be happy it's finally over."

I stop in my tracks and eye him with caution. "At least tell me where we're going."

"For a walk. That's all"

"Fine. But you need to start talking now."

He nods. "It started at orientation. I thought being at college meant partying, even just for that one night. It was all about meeting people and having a good time. A few guys I met said they arranged a get together by the fountain that night."

I looked around. "Is that where we're going?"

"Yes. But for different reasons."

I give him a sly look, not trying to hide my skepticism. I can only imagine he has Avery there waiting to pounce on me.

Sensing my unease he assures me, "I'm looking to clear my conscious, not add more shit to it."

"Fine." I answer so he'll continue and get to his point.

"When I got there, I recognized Ian, we were in the same group that morning. Then I saw Avery. We hit it off and sort of moved off to the side, away from the group. I heard one of the guys bragging that he had a case of beer in the trunk of his car. A few people disappeared and then came back with cans in their pockets."

Logan stops talking until we reach the exit at the bottom of the landing. Again he looks around, and I can't help but think he's checking to make sure the coast is clear. I'm not even exactly sure where we are in relation to anything else since I don't use this exit to leave the building.

"Avery wanted to drink, so we rejoined the group. I was too focused on her and the possibility of getting laid. I didn't realize that it thinned out. I should've walked away as soon as I smelt it, but I didn't want her to think I was a pussy. Some guy handed me a joint. Again, I was thinking with the wrong head, so I smoked."

"Why do you think I care? And what does this have to do with me, or Jonah?"

"I'm getting to that. I don't know if it was someone who left that narked or what the deal was, but security came. Do you know some of those guys are real cops?"

I don't answer I just stare at him.

"Anyway, I didn't want to get caught. If I did, I wouldn't be able to come here, and my parents would've locked me in the basement for the rest of my life. Before the rent-a-cops were close enough, Avery, Ian and I ran. We used the trees to hide as we made our way back to the main building."

"Great you didn't get caught. Yippee. Can I go back to my room? I'm expecting an important call." I turn and try to take step away, but not before Logan jumps in front of me.

"You promised. Besides, I needed to set it up so you'd understand. I thought I got away with it, but I didn't." He looks away. "I panicked. But I didn't know what to do. The next morning Jonah pulled me aside. He had pictures of us. He zoomed in, and there I was with a beer can in one hand, a joint in the other."

"You could've always said it was a cigarette."

"Except the picture is clear enough, and the bastard zoomed in. It's obvious what it was."

"Okay, big deal. Jonah watched you and took pictures."

"I know this is all sounds crazy. But I swear it's true. I never bothered to ask if he was the one that called security, because it didn't matter. The only thing that mattered is that he knew I was there and had evidence of what I did."

"So Jonah's a little creepy. Maybe he has a thing for you."

Logan shakes his head. "That's my point. He has a thing alright, but not for me. For you."

The hair on my arms stands. Logan has my complete attention.

"I don't know if he arranged it or if was just my dumb luck, but when I got here, he happened to be my RA. I knew I had to play nice, just in case he still had the picture."

"Does he?"

Logan nods. "Yeah. He does. I've been under his thumb the whole time. But I can't do it anymore."

I look around as we approach the fountain. The bright sun in the blue sky looks as if it would tame the cool, brisk temperature, but it's not. I'm a little nervous because other than the beautiful landscaping, there's no one, nothing around.

"Look, I'm sorry Jonah's been a dick to you . . ."

"Come sit."

Logan heads toward a bench in the alcove obscured by the surrounding trees. I know there's more to the story, and remembering part of the conversation they had the previous night outside my door, I follow, because I'm curious to know how I'm involved in all this.

"According to Jonah the others weren't allowed to come after they got caught. They lost the privilege of living on campus. I can't confirm or deny it. All I know is since I didn't get caught and I did come to this school, I'm the only one he could screw with."

"How?"

"Do you remember we all had dinner together the day we moved in?"

"Trust me I'd love to forget."

"Jonah came back to my room and reminded me that I owed him for not ratting me out, and said it was time to pay up."

"This is where I come in?"

His eyes meet mine, and for the first time since I met him, I actually have an ounce of compassion for Logan.

"Jonah liked you. A lot. He saw how much it bothered you when I said stuff about your boyfriend. I don't even remember what it was. He thought if I made you uncomfortable you'd turn to him. You know, go to him for help. And this way you'd get close."

With my elbows on my knees, I lean forward, and rest my head in my hands, my eyes squeezed shut.

"He wanted to break me and Jordan up."

Logan shrugs. "Eventually I guess. He just wanted to give you a reason to go to him, to trust him. He said you'd been with this guy for a long time but he treated you like shit. What did I care? I just met you, and if all I had to do to stay out of trouble was act like an obnoxious dick, I could do that. Besides, Avery and I were already together so it's not like I was trying to impress anyone."

"She knows doesn't she? She's known all along. That's why she's hated me from the beginning. That's why she acted like I couldn't be trusted. She thought I'd go run to Jonah because that was the plan."

"Yes. Look, I know she's been a bitch to you, but she's really not that bad. She resents you because as gorgeous as she is, she's jealous of you."

"Because Jonah likes me?"

He gives me a mocking smile. "Because she's worried I do. I know you have no use for me, but under normal circumstances, the chicks love me."

I laugh. I'm not sure if I'm laughing at him or with him.

Logan leans forward and rubs my back. "I'm sorry, Stephanie. Do you think we can put this behind us?"

"Why tell me? I mean why now? You know my boyfriend and I broke up. Jonah's in the clear. You're in the clear. So what's in it for you?"

"There always has to be something in it for me?"

I take a good long look at him before answering. "Yes."

"I didn't like what I saw last night. You were so upset your guard was down completely, and with me of all people. I wouldn't hurt you, but you didn't know that. You think all I care about is getting into your pants. And I feel a little guilty. I can't help but feel I might have played some small part in your break-up."

I shake my head. "You weren't the reason I wasn't enough for him."

"Are you sure that's the case? 'Cause I'm not."

"Look, Logan. I appreciate you coming clean. I'm glad to know maybe you're not as much of a jerk as I think you are. But you don't even know Jordan."

"That's where you're wrong. I've gotten to know Jordan very well over the last couple of weeks. He convinced me it was in my best interest to lay off you."

A warm feeling spreads inside knowing even now he's still looking out for me. "He spoke to you?"

"Crazy son-of-a-bitch stalked me and threatened to put my head through the wall if I went near you," Logan smirks.

I look down. "I fucked up. He fucked up. I don't know where we can go from here. That's the important phone call I'm waiting for. I'm hoping he'll call me back."

"Why settle for a phone call when you can have me in the flesh?"

I can't believe my ears. I'm afraid to. He can't be here.

My heart soars up to the sky like a rocket. It's thumping hard and fast. I just don't know if it's going to keep climbing or explode.

I lift my head, my gaze with it. I'm unable to shift my eyes once they lock with his. I'm once again mesmerized by Jordan Brewer.

My heart stops. It, like the rest of me is stunned.

Afraid.

Exhilarated.

Jordan is standing only feet away from me, his hands tucked into the front pocket of a hoodie. I soak in his disheveled hair, the stubble covering his face, and the greenish coloring around his eye. He's perfect. Just like this.

"I got her here." Logan gets to his feet. "Good luck." He pats Jordan on the back as he walks away.

"Sorry," Jordan says taking a step forward. "But you can be so stubborn. I needed to get you out in the open where we could talk without anyone interrupting us or threatening to have me physically removed."

I nod. "I'm ready to listen."

"Good." He sits next to me, not touching me, his hands still tucked away. "Stephanie, I love you. Only you. There's nothing going on with Missy. Nothing. When you said you knew about her I thought you understood who she was."

"You're going to sit there and tell me she's the sister you never knew you had?"

"No. She's not my sister."

"Oh, I get it," I say sarcastically. "She's my long lost sister and you're going to help reunite us."

He closes his eyes. "Didn't you talk to Maria? Isn't that why you called me?"

"No. I called you because I . . ."

I turn and look at the dead, dried grass on the ground. I called because I love him, and I'm not willing to just walk away. I know I'm in his heart, and if she wants him, she's going to have to fight for him. But now it sounds ridiculous and I'm too ashamed to say any of this to Jordan face to face.

He doesn't wait for me to finish explaining. He reaches his hand over and cups my face. His hand is warm and gentle. I miss his touch, and I want to melt into him. "She's Madison's sister."

"Madison?" I meet his stare, The intensity of his eyes squeezes my heart.

"It sounds so stupid now, but I didn't want to introduce you to her because I thought if you knew who she was you might feel like you were in Madison's shadow, and I never wanted that." His hand drops and covers mine. I don't move. I'm afraid if I so much as breathe he'll pull away. "She knows all about you, how much you mean to me. She wanted to meet you, but I kept putting it off. I didn't think it was a good idea."

"If she knows about me, and there's nothing going on with her, why were you both so pissed when Blaze dedicated the song to me?"

Jordan hesitates a moment. "It was Madison's birthday. Missy was on the warpath. She was unbearably bitchy. So much so, Pete broke up with her earlier that night. She came crying to me before the show about how she lost everything important in her life and it was all because of the stupid accident. I knew once she heard that she'd accuse me of cheating on Madison and flip out."

"Is that what happened?"

He nods. "And I guess while nothing happened between us physically, I realized emotionally I cheated on Madison all along. I mean even before your prom. The night I found you at the cemetery I told her you come first, that if you ever need me I'll be there in a heartbeat. That's why she never liked you."

"I didn't know that."

"Maybe that was another reason I kept you and Missy away from each other. I was afraid it would come out and you'd both realize what an ass I am."

"You are an ass, but that's not why. How could you leave me at the bar like that? All you had to do was come to me and tell me to wait, that you'd be back. I still would've been pissed, but I wouldn't have felt like you didn't care, like you chose her over me."

"You're right. I panicked and I fucked up. I let my guilt over what happened to Madison cloud my judgement."

"You have to forgive yourself, or this is going to destroy you."

He nods. "I know. But right now, I need to own up to what I did and hope that you can forgive me. Even as I did it, I knew it was wrong. I wish I could go back and change that one thing, because that seems to be the breaking point. The point where everything went to shit."

"Why do you still talk to her?"

He runs his free hand through his hair then scrubs it over his face. "You know what a mess I've been since the accident. Missy and I leaned on each other when it first happened. We got close because it affected us both so much. She kept telling me she didn't blame me, and that's what I needed to hear. Especially from Madison's family."

"Did you buy that ring for Madison? Is that why Missy was so emotional?"

A sad smirk covers Jordan's face, and it makes me realize I'd do anything to put a smile back on it, one with the teasing light shining in his eyes.

He lets out a long sigh before he speaks. "I made a lot of mistakes, Stephanie. But the biggest mistake was buying you an engagement ring when you didn't even trust me."

I must have heard wrong.

"Me? The engagement ring is for me?"

"It was."

Was. As in, it's not anymore. He wanted to marry me, and I ran off to hurt him with Blaze. The most amazing guy in the world was offering me not just his heart, but the promise of the rest of our lives, and I threw it all out like a smelly, old fish. I bury my head in my hands.

"I'm such a fucking idiot." I chance a look at him. I don't know if he lost all feeling for me, or if I'm so overwhelmed with sadness and regret that I can't read him.

"Jordan, there are no words. None at all that can express how sorry I am, or how bad I feel. I don't even know where to begin."

He nods. "That makes two of us. But maybe . . . There's someplace I'd like to take you."

I'd still go to hell and back with him. "Anywhere."

"Come on."

I stand and walk with him. My hands are down at my sides. I want to reach out for him, but I can't. He must hate me. I hate me. I don't think there's a way I can ever make this up to him. I'm silently berating myself when I feel his hand slip into mine. At a loss for words I squeeze and look up to meet the warmth of his stare.

He hesitates, then pulls our joined hands up and speaks. "Is this okay?"

"Always."

Chapter 27

There's still so much to say. As I sit in the car with him, I can't believe he's even talking to me.

"Why'd you turn to Blaze?"

I knew he'd ask sooner or later, I just wish he'd ask much later, like when I'm on my death bed.

"I didn't really think of why. I acted on impulse, like I always do. When you chased after Missy, I confronted him and asked questions. I thought he was telling me the truth. He did. I mean he never actually said there was anything going on with you and Missy. He led me to believe it though."

"Yeah. He's good at that."

Silence. Thick, heavy silence. As uncomfortable as the silence is, I'm welcoming it, because I know it's worlds better than what will follow when the words come again.

"Did you go there to fuck him?"

I squeeze my eyes shut. I can't believe I'm having this conversation with Jordan. That the love of my life is really asking if my intent was to have sex with another guy.

"Of course not. I don't even know what I was thinking. I just . . . I just wanted you to hurt the way I was hurting. I didn't really think any further than that."

"Steph, I want the truth. I need to know . . . Before I got there, did you have sex with him?"

"No."

"You're sure?"

"Jordan, I wouldn't have let it go that far."

"It looked pretty far if you ask me."

"I know. I'm so sorry. I just wanted to go flirt, maybe kiss a little, and have you find out about it so I could rub it in your face. Once he brought me into the bathroom I realized I was in over my head. I said 'no,' I swear I did. I wanted him to stop, to go back out in the bar. Just before you got there I called out for you."

"Did he force himself on you?"

I shake my head. "Not really. I can't imagine how it looked, but it was really just some hot and heavy kissing."

"Fucking great."

"He wanted more, he kept trying, but nothing else happened." I sigh. "I drank." I look away because I know on top of everything else I've done, drinking was a betrayal. If drinking with Jonah and Logan was bad, I'm afraid drinking with Blaze is unforgivable. "I wanted to numb the pain, and I didn't care how I did it. I drank and he gave me a brownie. I'm thinking it was laced with marijuana."

He doesn't say anything. He pulls into the parking lot of an apartment complex, and shuts the engine off. He sits without making a move, and I'm worried that's it, after my confession he's done talking.

"You knew about the letters." He says matter-of-fact, tracing his finger over the bottom of the steering wheel.

"I found one under my seat in your car, and then on Halloween I found one on your windshield when I got there. I read it, and my heart broke for you. I ripped it up and threw it away because I couldn't let something like that hurt you if I could help it."

"I should've told you. I didn't want anything to change your opinion of me."

I place my hand on his thigh, hoping he'll look at me. "Nothing can change my opinion of you. You've always been my knight in shining armor. You're always there when I need you, even when I don't deserve for you to be, like the other night when you shouldn't have given a shit what happened to me."

His hand presses down on my hand. "No matter what happens between us, I'll always care what happens to you." He opens his door, and looks back at me. "Come on, let's go."

I have no idea what we're doing here or where we're going. I walk around to his side and match Jordan's strides. With my eyes fixed on him I reach down and take his hand. He stops and looks at me. I don't know if I crossed a line, I thought it was okay since he took my hand a little while ago.

"Is this okay?" I ask, nervous to hear his answer.

He shakes his head. "No."

My heart, my stomach, everything inside me that up until this minute had hope, sinks.

"I want more." His hand wraps around my shoulder and he pulls me in close to his body. I let out a long relieved breath.

"You really don't hate me?"

"I'm still mad as hell at you. But I don't hate you."

I wrap my arms around his waist and squeeze him tight, listening once again to the thump, thump, thump of his heart.

Chapter 28

"What are we doing here?" I ask as we walk up to an apartment door.

Jordan doesn't answer. Instead he pulls his keys from the front pocket of his hoodie. My mouth opens as realization dawns on me. He moved. He moved here, closer to me.

"This is your apartment?" I ask as he opens the door and leads me into the living room area.

"It was supposed to be a surprise. I told you I hated being so far from you."

I cover my mouth, afraid to speak. If I knew, if I understood . . .

"It came furnished. The lease is only for three months with an option to renew."

I look around the living room. There's nothing fancy. A simple couch, with a painting behind it, a coffee table in front of it, one on either side, with matching lamps, and an entertainment center holding a television.

I follow him into the kitchen area. It's small with only a few cabinets. The utility portion of it narrow, with what looks like miniature appliances. A wood table for two sits in the larger area that spills into the living room. For a minute, I allow an image to form in my head. I'm at the stove cooking breakfast, and Jordan comes up behind me, slips his arms around me and kisses the back of my neck.

He takes my hand bringing me back to the moment, reminding me that's what I could've had if I wasn't such an imbecile. "I know it's small, but I figured it's just me," he shrugs and looks into my eyes. "I don't need a lot."

After showing me the bathroom he leads me to the single bedroom. I walk over and sit on his side of the bed for a moment. I know it's his side because the picture of us from prom is on the night table, along with some spare change. I pick up the picture, look at it, and then back at him before placing it back down.

Without saying anything I follow Jordan back to the living room. He sits on the couch, and I sit next to him. There's been so much communicated between us. So much that I understand without speaking. We never needed words for me to know what's in his heart. But right now, I need it to be said, because I don't have a clue where we stand. He leans his head back and closes his eyes. I can't help myself. I reach out and brush my fingertips over the yellowish skin around his eye.

Jordan opens his eyes and turns toward me.

"I'm sorry." I want to say I never meant for him to get hurt, but I don't bother because we both know it would be a lie. I meant for him to hurt, and hurt a lot.

He reaches for my face, a hand on either side of my head. I feel the pull toward him. The draw of my body to his that I spent so much energy fighting over the years. I can't control it now. Instead I allow the lure of touching him, of feeling his body against mine to lead me, to control me. I scoot over and turn toward him. Once I see that he's not pushing me away, I move onto his lap and straddle him.

My body tingles and twitches in places I didn't know could feel such things without being touched and caressed there. He doesn't make a move. Instead his eyes fall to my mouth and soaks it in. I don't know if we're making up or breaking up. Right now I don't care. I'm yearning for him to kiss me.

To love me.

I need to feel his mouth against mine. I need to taste him. I need him to hold me, to touch me, because the sensation of his fingers on my skin is food for my soul. Most of all I need him to fill every bit of me, to consume my body because he is my oxygen, he is everything vital I need to live.

Moving with caution I bring my lips down to his. His lips part, as he begins to take control. I'm dizzy, lost in the exhilaration of the moment. It's been so long since we've been together, I don't realize my body's responding to him on its own, without any conscious thought from me. My hips move, back and forth, rubbing against him, feeding his need and desire.

My pulse quickens. I feel it everywhere. I'm not nervous or afraid. I'm here in the moment, longing to feel every emotion, every sensation that being with him brings to the surface. My head falls back and I moan his name as his tongue circles and swirls against my skin, his lips roam over my neck and shoulders. My fingers are lost in his hair, entwined, pulling, keeping his head close to my body as his hands press me tight against him.

I don't wait for him to make the next move because I'm afraid he won't. Over the years he's proven he has more restraint than me. I'm done holding back. I pull away just enough to lift my shirt up, bring it over my head, and toss it on the floor. His eyes smolder as they drop to my breasts, his hands along with them.

I reach down to the button on his pants. He doesn't say anything, doesn't do anything to try to stop me. I see his chest heaving. I feel his need in the way his eyes hold mine.

"Are you sure this is what you want? That I'm what you want?" he asks before making another move.

"You're all I've ever wanted. Now, and forever."

He guides me down on the couch. Before either of us speaks another word, his hands are fast to undress me. When he finishes, he turns his attention to his own clothes. I watch him closely, enjoying the way his muscles ripple beneath his skin, how beautiful and perfect his body is.

He climbs on top of me, his eyes locked with mine. "I love you, Stephanie."

In a flash, he's once again in control of the situation, allowing me to feel his hunger as he places demands on my body I'm all too happy to meet.

Chapter 29

We're lying together side by side, as Jordan kisses me again and strokes the side of my face, pushing back my damp hair. The air around us is thick with tension. Neither one of us has spoken in over half an hour. We're just holding each other, not wanting to move from the comfort of the other's arms. I know I should quit while I'm ahead, be happy that we're speaking at all, but as usual, I can't. I have to press my luck.

"Where are we?"

The eyebrow lifts, "We're in my apartment."

I kiss his sternum. "You know what I mean. With each other, where are we? Where do we stand?"

He sighs and lets go of me while he pushes himself up.

"I don't know," he says while reaching for his pants and pulling them on.

I nod and begin the process of dressing myself not trying to hide my disappointment. I thought for sure what just happened was a reconciliation. I shouldn't have assumed. I don't regret having sex with him; I just wish it could fix some of what I broke.

"The thing is how do we move forward in a relationship if we don't trust each other?"

Way to go me. I proclaim myself the gold medal winner for the mother of all fuck-ups.

"I trust you."

He snickers and looks away. "You trust me so much you accused me of cheating or wanting to cheat every time another girl was near. Which makes me wonder," his dark stare reaches out and holds me prisoner, as he looks serious once again. "Was it just Blaze, or were there others?"

I shake my head. I want to yell and argue that I never cheated, that Blaze wasn't cheating at all, but I know in my heart he was. I know that no matter what I thought, I owed it to Jordan to hear him out before I considered being with another guy.

"No. No-one else. I don't understand. Why you didn't tell me there was nothing going on with Missy? I swear, if I knew the truth, I never would've turned to Blaze."

"You mean tell you again? I did tell you. Over and over. I can't count how many times I told you. It didn't make a difference. You never believed me."

I lean forward, my elbows on my knees, and dig the heels of my palms into my eyes. He's right. He did, but I wouldn't listen.

"I knew you were pissed when I went after her, but then you said you knew about her. I figured Blaze told you."

"He did. He told me that she's more to you than just Pete's girlfriend, that she's the reason you played with the band to begin with, and that Pete broke up with her."

"You put that together with the fact that I didn't even acknowledge you before I went after her and assumed the worse."

I nod.

"I'm sorry. That should've been the first thing I said to you. Followed up by she's just a friend."

"It doesn't matter. By then I was too hurt to listen. I knew you were hiding something about your relationship with her. I wouldn't have believed you."

"It didn't occur to me that you still thought I was cheating until you poured the water over my head, and even then I wasn't sure. I saw the hurt, the betrayal in your eyes and I couldn't move. I knew how bad I fucked up and that I lost any shot of you talking to me. I just didn't think you'd run straight to another guy, let alone to Blaze."

"Jonah kissed me," I blurt out. I didn't want to tell him like this, but the thought popped into my head, and I'm afraid I'll forget to tell him if I don't do it right now, this instant, because it meant absolutely nothing to me, and I refuse to give Jordan another reason to doubt me ever again.

"That's fucking great. Why not just open a kissing booth and charge while you're at it?"

"He kissed me, I didn't kiss him. It happened last night. And I made it clear I'm not interested. I told him that even as hurt and upset as I was, I still love you. And you're the only one I want to be with."

"Yeah, just me and Blaze."

He's so hung up on Blaze, I don't think he heard what I just said.

"She cheated on you didn't she?" I know this is risky. I've never been able to say anything negative about Madison since the accident. He barely tolerates me mentioning her name. If I push too far on this path, he may shut me out completely and walk away.

He's quiet again, but I have his complete attention.

"She wanted to get engaged or see other people, but she was already seeing other people, or at least one other person. She was cheating on you with Blaze. That's why the fact I went to him bothers you so much."

"It doesn't matter who you decided to go fool around with, it would bother me."

"But it bothers you more because of Madison. That's the bad blood between you. That's why Chaz said I shouldn't be involved in it. It's because of her."

"I couldn't prove anything." He looks away, "But I suspected. I mean I know they hooked up and were sort of together when she and I started dating, but you see how he is. Blaze and I never liked each other, but it got so much worse after she died."

"Was he the friend she was going away with?"

"No. But I thought it was him she was going to see. They still spoke and hung out sometimes. He left Shred Em and sang with another band for a while. They had a few shows up in Connecticut. I think she followed him."

I bite on my bottom lip. He said something, that I wasn't the only girl . . ." I shake my head. I don't need to hurt Jordan any more than I already did. "Never-mind."

"Do you know what it did to me when he sent me this?"

He plays with his phone and opens his messages. I stare at the picture of me along with the message Blaze typed with it.

Look at the QT I'm going to fuck 2nite.

I cover my mouth as I read the rest of the conversation.

Touch her and I'll kill you.

Go for it. We're at the Tortoise Shell. Can't wait 2 c u.

"I fucking lost it. I called Maria and begged her to go get you. I thought she could get there before I could. Instead she sent Jonah."

"How did you team up with Logan?"

"I told you I only needed a few minutes to straighten his ass out. I knew what he looked like. I waited outside your building for him to come out. I thought he was going to shit his pants when I confronted him, and then he confessed. I made him a deal. He looked out for you, and I'll straighten Jonah out when the time comes. All he had to do was call if you needed me."

"Did he call you this morning or last night?"

"Last night." He pauses. "I waited till about three in the morning for you to call, but you never did. I'm sure you think this is part of me trying to control you . . ."

"No. I shouldn't have said that. I was hurt and mad."

"Do you know why I wanted to wait until Halloween?"

"So you could buy me something sexy and I wouldn't be insulted?"

"No." He sniggers, "You always look sexy. Four years ago I came home from school and found these freshman girls outside my house, all slimy and full of shaving cream and eggs."

"You remember?"

"Of course I do. And I remember staring at you, wishing you were wearing a bikini and wrestling in a pool full of gelatin instead." He smiles. "The dreams I had that night." He gives me a sideward grin. "It's the first time I remember wanting you, I mean really wanting you."

"I didn't realize. I can't believe you even remember that. The day you jumped off the bus, when we were standing by your locker, I swore you wanted to kiss me, I thought that was the first time."

"I did want to kiss you then, but that wasn't the first time. It was Halloween."

I don't know what to say after this. There's only one thing left to say, to clarify, but I'm afraid to broach the subject. I wait for him, but he doesn't say anything more. The silence becomes deafening once again. We're sitting, staring at each other. Each second we don't speak each beat of my heart becomes more painful.

"Jordan, is this goodbye?"

He stares at me long and hard, and I have no idea what his answer will be.

"Do you want it to be?"

I shake my head, and my eyes fill with tears. "No."

"I'm asking you again, now that you know I'm far from perfect, that each day is a struggle, a fight I'm trying to win. Are you sure this is what you want? That you want to be in a relationship with me?"

I stare at him, wondering how to find words to express all the things I want to say. I know and love every side of him. I've seen his beautiful as well as his ugly. I've been on the receiving side of his gentle kindness and the target of his deep, slicing comments. He's made me feel beautiful and broken in one fell swoop. He's shown me his strength along with his vulnerability, and I love each and every facet that makes him who his is.

"I do. I want you. Only you. I swear. And if you can forgive me, I'll never do anything stupid like this ever again."

"Maybe this will help you trust me," he pulls a single key from the front pocket of his sweatshirt. "This is for you."

I stare at it unable to believe what I'm seeing.

"You're giving me the key to your apartment?"

"That's the plan. You can come and go as you please. At least for the next three months. We can decide together if I should stay longer. You don't have to call first. It doesn't matter if I'm here or not, because you'll never interrupt anything that's more important than you. Just show up. Whenever. Stay as long as you want."

"Anytime I want?"

"Anytime you want. You can visit me, spend the night. Hell, you can live here if you want."

"You planned to forgive me all along?"

"I told you, Steph. You're my life, plain and simple. We both messed up. I'm hoping you could find it in you to forgive me, too."

"Of course I can. I already do."

"But if you ever do anything like this ever again I swear . . ."

I lunge at him and cut him off with a kiss. There's no need for him finish that sentence because I'll never risk losing him again. I waited long enough for Jordan, I'm not going to let anyone or anything come between us ever again. Not even me.

Chapter 30

A comfortable quiet nestles between us as Jordan drives me back to school. I still feel awful about what I did, but we both made mistakes and we agreed to give each other a second chance. I remind myself that nothing good ever comes easy.

I don't know if he plans on staying the night or not, but it doesn't matter. His apartment is only a few minutes away, so even if he's tired, he shouldn't be in a rush to leave. We hold hands as we walk up the dormitory steps. Guilt washes over me and I stop dead in my tracks.

"What's wrong?" Jordan asks.

"I'm so embarrassed. With everything going on I didn't even ask how depositions went."

"It would've gone better if you were there." He looks at the ground as he starts walking again. "At first the other lawyer acted like a dick. Kept asking what I ate and drank during the day and leading up to the accident, asking me if I was sure I didn't have a beer at lunch or before I got in the car. Then he focused on drugs, even over the counter ones that might make me drowsy. But it's total bullshit. They have the toxicology report from the hospital. There wasn't anything in my system."

I'm angry that he had to go through this, that anyone would insinuate he had any fault in what happened.

"I thought the other driver admitted to falling asleep."

Jordan shrugs. "He did. They were looking for a way to justify offering less money. My mother's right. They want to settle out of court. They already made their first offer."

I nod. I don't ask about the money because I know for Jordan it's not about that. He'd trade every penny and then some if it meant bringing Madison back.

"So then that's it? It's over?"

He shakes his head. "No. Not exactly. We didn't take the offer. And there's more that's going to come. Her parents are suing both the company and me, well my insurance anyway, not me personally."

"That's not fair."

"That's just the way it is. She was in my car; it has to happen like that."

"I'll be by your side through it all." I pause as his eyes find mine. "If you want me there. If you don't, I understand and I'll keep my distance . . ." I don't want to force myself on him.

He pulls me against his side and slings his arm over my shoulder. "I'd love having you by my side. Knowing you're there will help a lot."

"And you have Missy's support." I want to sound encouraging. I still don't like her, but I understand why he feels he needs to stay connected to her.

He shakes his head. "Not so much anymore. I told her that it's best if we don't spend so much time together."

"Oh." I don't try to hide the surprise in my voice. "And you're okay with it?"

He gives me his sideward smirk, "It was my idea, wasn't it?"

"You know what I mean." I can't help the feeling of guilt spreading through me. If he needs her, or thinks he needs her, I don't want him to feel forced into giving her up.

Jordan stops and turns me toward him. His hands reach around to the back of my neck and his fingers thread into my hair. "I'd give my right arm up for you, so Missy's a no brainer. Besides, I think it will be better for me to see less of her. I'll never forget Madison, but maybe I don't need to be reminded of her every second of the day either."

*

We turn onto my hall and Jordan's body goes rigid. He sees Jonah before I do, turning the key in my lock. The fact he's still keying himself into my room tells me Jonah has no clue we're here. My knee-jerk reaction is to grab Jordan's forearm. I want to hold him back. The last thing I need is for him to confront Jonah in the hall.

"Bastard!" Jordan's jaw is tense as he shrugs me off and goes after Jonah.

"Stephanie?" Jonah calls out standing just inside my door, looking in the room for me.

"Jordan!" I shriek as he shoves Jonah to the ground from behind. "Don't!"

"What are you doing here?" Jonah says scrambling to his feet, his eyes darting from Jordan, to me, and back to Jordan. "I'll call security. You're not supposed to be here."

"Did you really think you'd just swoop in and take my place?"

"I never said one word against you. I helped you. When she wanted nothing to do with you, I made her listen."

I'm holding Jordan's forearm to keep him from taking a shot at Jonah. It's not that I think Jonah doesn't deserve it, he deserves a good, swift kick in the balls which I'd be happy to deliver, but there's a part of me that knows letting Jordan go after Jonah is wrong.

I hear the anger in Jordan's breathing. Jonah is a good excuse, the perfect target for it. I know the rage I see shading his eyes has been building for months. It's like a house that's been built brick by brick, ready to implode. He's ready to take it all out on Jonah, the letters, Blaze, Missy, even me.

Jonah's his target because Jordan is too much of a gentleman to take it out on me. He'd never do it. Never, ever. But if he goes after Jonah, if he lets it all out on him, I don't know what he's capable of. I move my body in front of Jordan. His eyes are locked on Jonah in a death glare.

"I got this," I say placing my hand on his cheek, trying to break through to him. "Jordan, look at me." I wait for his eyes to leave Jonah and land on me. I don't make a move until they do, until I know he's going to allow me to handle this.

"Jonah," I turn back to the nervous boy standing near my bed. The boy that posed as my friend in the hopes that other feelings would surface and take over. "Give me your phone."

"No." he says, his eyes still locked on Jordan.

"Give me your phone and I won't let him hurt you. If you don't give me your phone, all bets are off." I hold my hand out. None of us move. We all stare at each other. I stare at Jonah, he stares at Jordan, and Jordan's stares back at him. Time drags.

In a slow, laborious movement, Jonah reaches into his pocket and pulls his phone from it. "You touch me again, and I'll call security. She doesn't have to press charges, but I can."

I feel the anger, the tension oozing out of Jordan and filling the room. "You touch her again and you won't be able to call anyone."

"You fucked up, Brewer. You let her down. Stephanie and I have more in common, and I was here when she needed someone. I put her first, when you wouldn't. Even when it meant taking her to see you."

He extends his hand and offers me the phone. "Unlock it." I order before Jordan has a chance to respond.

"I don't understand what you need my phone for?" He's shifting his weight uncomfortably from one foot to the other.

I don't answer. Instead I search through his pictures. He has a lot. Mostly landscapes, things I've seen him bring to life in his paintings. I scroll up further, and find what I'm looking for. Logan. There are a series of shots of him and Avery. A few of them are duplicates that were zoomed in and enlarged. I delete the pictures and hand Jonah back his phone.

"Logan told me everything."

Jonah's eyes close and his head tilts to the side.

"What hurts the most is that I thought we were friends. It felt good to know I had someone here I could turn to, someone I could trust."

"Nothing's changed, Stephanie." Jonah takes a step toward me. "We are friends. Best friends."

I feel Jordan's body twitch. I didn't even realize he was right behind me. Again I reach out to calm him, to assure him I've got this.

"No, Jonah. Jordan's my best friend. Always was, always will be. And I love him. That's forever. So even if he tells me to jump and I ask how high, it's really not any of your business. So do me a favor, steer clear of him. And most of all steer clear of me. And if you think you're going to somehow pay Logan back for this, or if you have copies of that picture that happen to resurface, Jordan's coming after you."

I turn away from Jonah. I don't want to look at him. I'm angry, and I want to let myself be angry. I don't want him to twist things around or see the hurt that was in his eyes a moment ago, because even though I'm angry, I understand where he was coming from. I see myself in him. He's me on prom night. He's me not giving up on Jordan. Ever.

I don't move after Jonah leaves. I'm a jumble of mixed up confused feelings. Not all of it is Jonah's fault, or even Jordan's. A lot of it is my own fault. I messed up because I'm impulsive and reckless. Because I turned to the wrong person. Because I allowed the wrong people to insert slivers of doubt into my mind. Jordan's hands rest on my shoulders, pulling me from my thoughts.

"You are stronger than I think," he whispers. "You're incredibly strong and did a great job handling that." I turn and face him. "I would've just punched him."

"Maybe you should've." I shrug.

"He's right about something though. I didn't put you first. I tried to, or at least I thought I tried to, but I failed."

"I thought we spoke about all of this already."

"We focused a lot on the things you did wrong. They're still there, believe me, every time I close my eyes I deal with it."

"I'm sorry."

"It's okay." He cups my face and brushes his thumb back and forth over the skin on my cheeks. "It's my turn to own up for my mistakes. I'm sorry for lying, for hiding things from you and not telling you the whole truth. You knew there was more going on. I don't just mean with Missy. I mean with everything, with Blaze, the letters. I should've leaned on you. I should've known that you're strong enough to hold us both up. And if the time ever comes where you're not, then I'll just have to man up and carry you."

Epilogue

Jordan and I celebrated my birthday at home with my mother, Eddie, Maria and her parents Monday night. Jordan and Eddie prepared dinner for us. Their idea of preparing dinner was using paper goods and their fingers to punch in the number for Chinese takeout. I didn't mind at all. I loved that they joined forces to treat us like queens. Unlike last year, this birthday celebration was quiet, peaceful and held no drama.

I haven't seen Jordan since. I miss him like crazy. Since I came home for the summer, he usually spends one or two nights a week at his mother's, and I spend a few nights over at his apartment. My mother wasn't happy about it at first, but it's worked well, and gives her and Eddie some privacy, too. This week Jordan's been keeping his distance.

"Are you sure everything's okay?" I asked when he called to say goodnight. He's quiet and distant.

"Not just okay. Perfect."

He brushes it off just like he has all week when I've asked. I know he's lying, but I don't call him on it. I won't push the issue. He'll tell me when he's ready. I promised I'd trust him, that I'd believe what he tells me, and I have no plans on going back on that promise.

"I can't wait to see you tomorrow. I'm not used to these long weeks without you anymore."

I smile. "I miss you, too."

There are some days I still can't believe he forgave me. He's never once brought Blaze up, or my boneheaded behavior. He never questions me about where I'm going or who I'm going with, even though Jonah and I are on speaking terms again. Not one time since we got back together do I recall him acting like he doesn't trust me, when he has every right to. I wonder how I got so unbelievably lucky. Not just that he fell in love with me, but that his love is so all encompassing and forgiving.

"I owed you." He explained as we lie in bed the night we made up. "You stuck by me, never gave up on me when I needed you. Even when I said cruel things to you. I know I fucked up. I fucked up big time. The morning I almost hit you, I deserved for you to tell me to go to hell, and I'm lucky you ever spoke to me again. It's only right that I forgive you one HUGE fuck up as well. But that's all you get. Just one."

"That's all I need."

I'm a little nervous. He said he has a gift waiting for me at his apartment. I won't lie. When I opened the little, black velvet box he gave me Monday night I was disappointed to find earrings. I hoped. And he saw it.

"Sorry. I didn't mean to make you think . . ."

"It's fine. I didn't." I try to convince him and myself as well. "I didn't expect anything. They're beautiful. I love them."

"I returned it, Stephanie. It already had too many bad memories associated with it."

It's okay that he didn't give me a ring. I'm only nineteen. No one gets married this young today unless there's a baby on the way, and even then most don't bother with the lifelong commitment. But he followed up by not seeing me for the rest of the week, and now he's acting strange. I hope he doesn't feel pressured. That's the last thing I want to do. If it ever happens, I want it to be right for both of us.

The ring is the one thing we didn't hash out when we made up. We never spoke about it at all. Neither of us mentioned it, until my birthday.

I'm still throwing clothes in a bag when he comes. I have stuff at the apartment. Jordan insisted I keep clothes and toiletries there so that I could just show up and feel like I belong there instead of feeling like a visitor. Still I pack things away, hoping to rotate some of my stuff because I have a lot of nervous energy that I'm looking to do something with.

I run down the stairs when I hear the doorbell ring, pull open the door, and catch my breath as I stare into the eyes of the man I love. Jordan's hand is on his head mid-way running it through his hair.

He's nervous.

"Are you ready?" He asks.

"Give me a minute. I run inside and say goodbye to my mother while I grab my bag.

"Have fun," she calls.

"I hope you don't mind," he says as I close the door behind me. "But I was so excited, I brought your gift with me. It's waiting in the car."

My eyes are automatically drawn to the parked automobile. I see something moving around. No, not something, a ball of fur, and it's jumping from the front seat to the back.

My mouth opens wide. "A puppy?"

He smiles that mischievous smile, and I can't help myself. I throw my arms around his neck and plant no less than twenty kisses on his face.

"Come meet her."

I sit in the car and he hands me the energetic ball of fur. She's beige and shaggy, and I'm absolutely in love with her.

"I was nervous. She's a big commitment, and I worried you might not like her."

"Are you kidding? She's so precious!"

"She'll stay with me at the apartment. I thought we could raise her together."

"Does she have a name?"

"Not officially, but I do have something in mind."

"What is it?"

"Angel. Because she reminds me of you."

"Hey, Angel. Do you like your name?" I ask in baby talk. The wiggling bundle of energy licks my nose. I laugh and giggle and try to keep Angel from climbing into my mouth the entire ride back to the apartment.

"I'm glad you like her. I wasn't sure how you'd feel about sharing my attention with another woman," he teases as we walk from the car to his apartment, Angel stops to relieve herself along the way. "Shit," he says as he looks at his apartment. "I forgot to leave the light on."

Jordan unlocks the door and steps aside, motioning for me to go before him. "Ladies first."

I turn back and make a face at him. Good thing I know exactly where the light switch is. Once I'm in the hall I flip it on.

"Surprise!"

I jump, startled not just by the loud shouts, but by the amount of people that are crammed in the small area waiting for us. I look around the room at our friends, and I realize Angel was the deterrent. This is the real surprise.

"Go on in," Jordan nudges me.

I don't make it more than a foot further into the room before Maria is hugging me.

"You have no idea how hard it's been not to slip up."

"Hi," I give Ross a quick hug. He's Maria's latest beaux. They've been together since I came home from school. While they were both interested, they needed a little encouragement. That's where Jordan and I came in.

"Chaz! Wendy!" I'm surprised to see them. I haven't seen Chaz since the last night Jordan played with the band. He's the only one out of that group Jordan still talks to, but I didn't realize they were this close.

"I always knew you were a keeper," he says with a wink.

"Jonah." I hesitate, surprised to see him here. Yes, we started talking again, but neither I, nor Jordan trusts him, although things are a little easier between us now that he has a girlfriend. "It's nice to see you. You, too, Carla." I give them each a quick embrace.

It's the last couple in the room that has me totally confused. I'm not really sure why they're here, but I walk over and say hello anyway.

"Logan, Avery. Thanks for coming." I don't mean for my voice to go up at the end as if I'm asking them a question, but it does.

"Who loves you, baby?" Logan asks before throwing his arms around me, and giving me a great big bear hug. Maybe he doesn't look so much like a rat, maybe more like a ferret.

Avery doesn't quite answer. Something close to a grunt comes out of her mouth. We still don't like each other, but right now I'm so over the moon, her presence doesn't bother me in the least.

After I'm done greeting everyone, I notice the plates of chips and dips, and the cooler of beer in the corner. I don't know if Jordan had help or not, but it looks like he thought of everything.

"You're amazing," I say cornering him in the kitchen and holding him tight.

"You're just buttering me up for later tonight. You want to make sure I cuddle up in bed with you and not Angel."

"You've got me."

"Hey, Chaz. You ready?" Jordan calls from behind me.

"Whenever you are," his friend answers.

"Every one, if I could have your attention." Jordan pulls a kitchen chair into the living room and faces it toward the couch. Chaz sits in it holding his guitar. Where did that come from?

"Chaz would like to perform the acoustic version of a song for Stephanie, so please, have a seat."

Jordan places me on the couch. He's on one side, Wendy's on the other. I know the song before Chaz plays a chord.

The music starts, and everyone quiets down and listens as Chaz sings. His voice is beautiful. I don't know if it's his voice, or the words, but I'm struck with so much more emotion than when I heard Blaze sing it.

"He's really good," I lean over and whisper to Wendy.

She nods. "But when he sings in front of a large group he gets so nervous, he literally croaks it out. Besides, I don't want the girls hanging all over him the way they do with Blaze."

I don't bother answering. I don't know how much if anything Wendy knows about what happened with Blaze and me. But I'm happy, and I don't want to talk about him or think about him ever again.

"It doesn't matter. I'm sure Chaz would be polite with girls while keeping them at a distance. It's clear he only has eyes for you."

"Like Jordan and you." She nudges her head in Jordan's direction, and her eyes fall to his hand, resting on my knee. When the song is over everyone in the room claps.

"Are you happy?"

"Are you kidding? The puppy, the surprise party. This is the best birthday ever!"

He nods, the playful light shining in his eyes, the flirtatious smile crosses his lips as he gives me a quick kiss and gets up.

Jordan clears his throat, and the room quiets once again. He's standing in front of me, his hand holding mine. All eyes are on us and my heart races as I wonder what's coming next. Is he going to pull me up to my feet and hold me close as he kisses me in front of everyone? Corny, but I won't mind at all.

"I'd like to thank all of you for coming and celebrating Stephanie's birthday with us. You've all meant something in this incredible journey we've had. Some of you have been around since we first met," he looks at Maria. "Some of you we've met only recently." He directs that comment toward Logan. He stops and pauses a moment. "Stephanie?" There's something strange in the way he just said my name.

"Yes?" I answer waiting for my cue.

The unthinkable happens. Jordan reaches into his pocket while dropping down to one knee. My eyes open wide and fill with tears. My mouth drops to the floor, and it's all I could do to cover it with my other hand.

"Stephanie Barrano." He opens the little black box, but I can't look down at it. I can't peel my eyes away from his. "You're the girl that haunted my past. No matter where I went, or what I did, you were there. I watched in the background and waited for you to grow up. You're my best friend, and the love of my life. I don't see a future without you in it. So I'm asking, in front of our friends, if you will share your life with me and be mine until forever ends."

"Yes! A thousand times, yes!" I shriek as I fly off the couch and into his arms.

Jordan pulls the ring out and slips it on my finger.

"You have to graduate first. That's what I promised your mother. But from here on out, all you need to do is look at your finger to know what my intentions are. Look at this ring and know I'm committed to the promise of a life and future together."

I don't care that every set of eyes in the room is on me. I hold him tight, allowing the tears to fall. These are the happiest tears I've ever cried in my life. I kiss him. I kiss him to say 'yes.' I kiss him to say 'I love you.' And I kiss him because there is nothing in the world that can ever compare to the feeling I get when we are connected in this way.

After I catch my breath, I pull back and meet the eyes of my future husband, of my always and forever, and I know after everything we've gone through to get here, we will live happily ever after.

Thank you for reading And Forever. If you enjoyed it, please leave a review on the site where you purchased it, and recommend it to a friend!

Continue reading for an excerpt of ***Regret Me Not***

Other books by Danielle Sibarium

For Always (Eternity 1)

And Forever (Eternity 2)

The Heart Waves Series

Heart Waves (1)

Breaking Waves (2)

Waves of Love (3)

Stand Alones

To My Hero: A Blog of Our Journey Together

Into You

Regret Me Not

Chapter 1

Brayden looks at me with the same intense longing I've seen in his eyes all night. Every touch lasts a moment too long, making me want to taste the sweet warmth of his delicious lips. Every look smolders, bringing color to my cheeks, as he pairs a look with a stroke of my exposed skin. His hand moves from the top of my back, slowly, straight down to the bottom, pressing me against him, making my body tingle, my insides quiver. He knows what he's doing, that he's creating a fierce desire inside me; that's what he's counting on.

He inches in a bit closer as we move in perfect precision to the music, slow music that seems to want to keep us on the dance floor, locked in each other's arms. Holding me close, he brushes up against me. In an attempt to escape the look in his soft brown eyes I lean into his chest, and rest my head there, bringing me right up against the warmth of his body. The familiar smell of his cologne comforts me, but only for a moment before it feeds the growing fire burning deep inside.

I want him.

Each beat of my heart, every breath, brings me closer to succumbing to this unyielding desire. Every sweet caress only serves to convince me we belong together. No matter how I try to convince myself its wrong, that we'll only end up hurting each other in the long run, I keep getting lost in the pleasure the present promises. A soft moan passes his lips, and I hold him tighter, my fingers dig into the hard muscles beneath his clothes. I know I don't have the strength to fight the cataclysmic pull that keeps me drawn to him, that keeps me unable to move out of his arms.

I look around the large, dimly lit room, but only for a few seconds. I don't care about anything else in here, not the decorations hung on the walls, or the bubble machine chugging away somewhere on the side. I don't care to see what the other girls are wearing, or even if they're pretty. Not tonight. The only thing I want, the only thing my brain could wrap itself around is Brayden; Brayden's brown eyes and award winning smile. The feel of his arms holding me against him. The fresh clean smell that hangs on him no matter the time of day or night.

All I know is Brayden.

"I miss you," he whispers, his breath tickling my ear. "I'm so glad you're here."

I give myself the benefit of the doubt, thinking I could chance a look in his eyes and not be captivated by their intensity.

I'm wrong. There's heat in his eyes. They're smoldering.

Unconsciously I lick my lip before answering. "I miss you, too."

He takes a chance. I knew he would eventually. He leans in, and presses his lips against mine. They're soft and warm, as always. I don't pull away, I want more. My mouth opens, inviting him in as my hips press against his. I want this kiss. I've wanted it since Brayden picked me up. I didn't initiate it because I wasn't sure one kiss would satiate me. I'm not sure one night will either.

His eyes trail from my head, down, all the way down. I don't miss how they hesitate at the neckline of my dress. I know he wants to bring his hands there; they always seemed to gravitate to that area. But Brayden, being the perfect gentleman, resists the urge. It's a battle apparent in his eyes. He waits and feels me out. He can read my reactions. He knows my body, just as well as he knows my heart.

"Do you feel that?" He brings his mouth beside my ear and speaks in a soft, velvety tone. "Your pulse racing, the swirling of your stomach? Do you feel the heat between us? It's a wild fire burning out of control. It's getting bigger and hotter by the minute." He kisses me again. This time there's hunger and need in his kiss. One hand gets lost in my hair, the fingers on the other hand press into my flesh. He wants more. He wants all of me, and I want to give it, give in. I swallow hard, still delusional that I have an ounce of control over what I'm doing or where things are leading.

"Kenzie, I love you. And I want you back."

That's the final straw. It's the reason I came. I want to make sure it's still there. Not just the attraction, that never left, but the love, the desire, the all-out need for each other. I felt it all night. I see it every time he looks at me. But hearing his declaration, I'm lost, prisoner to his every whim.

About The Author

Danielle grew up as an only child of divorced parents in Brooklyn, New York. Her imagination was developed at an early age. Surrounded by stuffed animals and imaginary friends, she transported herself into a fantasy world full of magic and wonder. Books were the gateway between her play world and reality.

In October 2011 Danielle's debut novel *For Always* was released. She has since released *The Heart Waves Series*, *To My Hero: A Blog of Our Journey Together, Into You* and *Regret Me Not*.

Danielle graduated from Farleigh Dickinson University with honors, and currently lives in New Jersey with her husband and three children.

You can visit her website at: http://www.daniellesibarium.com/

Find her on Facebook:
https://www.facebook.com/#!/DanielleSibarium?ref_type=bookmark

Or Twitter @sibarium

Newsletter sign up
http://www.daniellesibarium.com/contact

Made in the USA
San Bernardino, CA
07 July 2016